I0554374

Titles by Patricia Sheehy

Fiction
Veil of Illusion

Field of Destiny

A Thousand Whispers

Non-Fiction
Dancing Under the Full Moon:
101 Ways to Attract Money into Your Life

Giving with Meaning:
*turn ordinary items into meaningful gifts
using legends, folklore and traditions*

Praise for Field of Destiny

"Sheehy is a masterful storyteller whose style is poignant, evocative and powerful."
— Inner Tapestry Journal

"Field of Destiny transports its heroine [who has died tragically] to a world beyond this one, where after a time of reflection, she gets another chance at life . . . a great read, the plot is a page-turner."
— Wethersfield Life

Get ready to lose sleep . . . guaranteed to keep you up at night; a compelling must-read."
— Prill Boyle, author, Defying Gravity

"Sheehy has the ability to tell a story that keeps the pages turning. I, for one, read the entire book in a two-day period and admit to thoroughly enjoying the more romantic aspects of this tale, especially the very credible relationship between soul mates Nunki and Jabbah, incarnated as Natalie and Johnny. Their reunion elicited a few well deserved tears, so intense is Sheehy's skill in recreating that feeling one gets from a gift of mutually shared love."
— Diana F. VonBehren, top Amazon reviewer

"Field of Destiny piques your interest and keeps it with twists, turns and delightful surprises. Great book club item, as it sparks a curiosity of life's purpose. Loved it!"
— Windmill Book Club

"I can't remember when I have read a more engrossing book. The author brings her fascinating characters to life in such a way that one cannot help but connect with them from the very first page, rooting for them as they travel on their life's path, anxious when they turn an unknown corner, sympathetic when they stumble, sad when they fall, and happy and excited when you pick themselves up again. Ah, was it my destiny to discover Patricia Sheehy and Field of Destiny or was it a happy accident? Whatever it was, I am the richer for it."

— Jan Mann, author, Cruising Connecticut with a Picnic Basket

"Sheehy has created characters that stay with you and a plot that keeps you turning pages. Even as we get entangled in the protagonist's earthly struggle with her destiny, we are forced to think about the big questions. Are we destined for our future? Do we make our own choices? Is our path the one we are meant to take in this life? The beauty of this work is that while it poses these universal quandaries, it immerses you in a fictional world that you are hesitant to leave. A great read!"

— Judy Mandel, author, Replacement Child

"A thought provoking tale of loyalty, betrayal and personal growth with a touch of suspense."

— Ann Tupper, Amazon reviewer

FIELD OF DESTINY

— a novel —

Patricia Sheehy

Field of Destiny: copyright © by Patricia Sheehy

For information, contact:
Arcadia House: ArcadiaHousePublishing@gmail.com
Patricia Sheehy: patriciasheehy@aol.com • www.patsheehy.com

Cover Art:
Designed using an original pastel painting entitled "Infinity" by James Sheehy

Interior Design:
created by Jeffrey W. Duckworth: www.duckofalltrades.com

Printed in the United States of America:
Second edition: September 2010
ISBN: 978-0-9825234-2-1

1. Women-Fiction   2. Title.   3. metaphysical/new age

for Natalie Grace Millerick,
whose smile lights up a room,
and for my husband, Jim,
who fills my life
with love, friendship, and surprises.

The tissue of the Life to be
We weave with colors all our own,
And in the Field of Destiny
We reap as we have sown.

— John Greenleaf Whittier (1807-1892)

Field of Destiny — **Major** Characters

Look to the heavens — in awe and in memory — for the stars
in the night sky carry the eternal names of souls we've
known from the very beginning of time

Eternal Soul Names

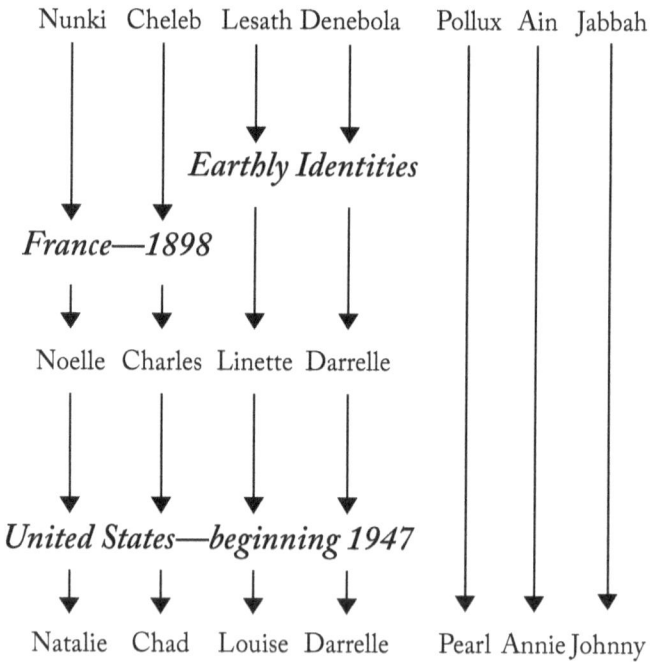

Nunki Cheleb Lesath Denebola   Pollux Ain Jabbah

Earthly Identities

France—1898

Noelle Charles Linette Darrelle

United States—beginning 1947

Natalie Chad Louise Darrelle   Pearl Annie Johnny

ONE

France – December 3, 1898

"Noelle . . . Noelle!" Charles Robidoux stood in the doorway of his home, shouting into the icy night. Rain slashed across his face; gusts of wind whipped around his large frame, sending bursts of chill into the room. Just behind him, his three young daughters sat in front of the fireplace, gripping one another's hands, forming a small tight circle.

Charles could barely see the outline of his wife now, hunched and staggering, as she moved through the darkness along the stone path that led away from their village of Montmarte toward the nearby boulevards of Paris. Once she passed the church, she would be lost to him. There were too many alleys. She could disappear into any one of them.

"Noelle," he cried out again, buttoning his sweater, preparing to run after her. A backward glance at the girls and he changed his mind. He couldn't — no, he wouldn't — leave them. "Noelle, come home at once," Charles commanded one last time, scanning the darkness before slamming the door shut.

She would be back.

Charles walked to the long, wooden table, which had been set for dinner earlier in the afternoon. The children would be hungry soon. He studied the room. Yes, everything was as it should be: bowls...spoons...breadboard...*no, something was wrong, something out of place.* His gaze darted across the table. *What? What was it?* The carving knife. The carving knife was missing. *There it was. On the floor.* He should pick it up, scrub it clean. It was important to have clean utensils. Noelle was always so neglectful. Yes, he would take care of that. Charles ran his fingers over the near empty bottle of Absinthe. First, another drink.

He didn't bother with a glass this time. He had no desire for the seductive, time-consuming ritual of dripping ice water over a sugar cube into the toxic liquor. Shoving aside the stemmed glass and slotted spoon, Charles put the bottle to his lips and drank until it was empty and the taste of anise and sweet licorice filled his mouth with bile. He threw the bottle against the wall and watched as drops of green liquid washed across the white surface. A harsh bitter-sweet smell wafted across the room just above the lingering notes of Jicky, the perfume his wife had worn every day for as long as he could remember. Even now, with everything that had just happened, the heady combination of lavender and herbs filled him with desire, made him think of oriental spices and the scent of her skin when it was warmed by the sun. Struck by how quickly the smell of Absinthe was beginning to dominate the room, Charles inhaled deeply, deeply and frantically, desperate to capture Noelle's scent before it was erased. Before it was gone forever.

No, not forever.

She would be back. He would wait with the children until she returned. Raking his fingers through his hair, Charles pursed his lips and nodded: yes, Noelle would be back. She would beg for forgiveness. He would grant it. He would hold her and say what she needed to hear. And then he would punish her. In a thousand small ways, across all the years of their life together, he would exact his revenge.

"Mère," three-year-old Darrelle cried out, breaking into his thoughts.

She was sobbing, unable to stop no matter how hard her sisters squeezed her hands in silent warning. *Shush*, they kept telling her, *shush*, whispering the word as softly as they could.

Charles walked over to his children and crouched on the floor beside them, warming his hands in front of the fire. Simone and Brigitte stiffened at his approach. It was Darrelle who broke their circle of solidarity. It was Darrelle who came to him.

"Papa, papa," she cried, throwing herself at Charles.

Without hesitation, Charles took Darrelle in his arms, stroking her black curls, rocking back and forth on the floor in front of the fire. "Shh. Shh. She will return," he told her. "Mère will return."

Charles remained on the floor, clutching Darrelle, rocking and stroking, trying to sort through the last hours, while trying even harder to empty his mind of everything that mattered. It was all lost now. Hopeless and lost. He stared at the fire, at his other two daughters, just five and six, forming a silent circle of two. What would become of them, of all of them?

Still crying, Darrelle tucked deeper into her father's arms, pressing into the dampness of his familiar sweater. Charles placed his hand on the back of her head, pushing gently, burying her face deep into the folds of wool. *Not his.* The words echoed inside his head. Sweet, pretty Darrelle. *Not his. Not his.* He continued pushing against her black curls. . . harder. . . still harder. "Shh, little one. Shh," he crooned, all the while pushing, feeling her chest heave. . .pushing, resisting her need for air.

A log snapped in the fireplace. Charles jumped as though a gun had been fired into his temple. Releasing his grip on

Darrelle, he lifted her face away from him, kissing her scratched and reddened cheeks. "Breathe deeply," he ordered. "Stop crying. Breathe."

She was the one who was so much like Noelle. Much more than the other two. She would have to go away. Perhaps to the convent.

"Shh," he said softly. "Mère will return. Tomorrow. She will return tomorrow."

Throughout the night Charles held Darrelle, his blood-covered hands staining the back of her white dress.

———◆———

Crouched in the doorway of a small alley, Noelle pressed her hands against her stomach. The blood kept coming, seeping through her dress, oozing through her fingers. One minute warm and liquid. The next, cold, congealed, filling the damp air with its thick, sour smell. Pain seared through her body. Charles had stabbed her twice, maybe three times. It was hard to know.

The rain had stopped, leaving behind an icy mist that hung in the air, coating the alley in a blanket of wet. Despite the cold, Noelle's face was flushed, filled with heat.

"Simone. Brigitte. Darrelle." She called out the names of her daughters. "Charles," she whispered. "Charles." He was a good man. He would come for her. He would forgive her spiteful confession. He would forgive that Darrelle was not his, that she'd had a brief affair with an artist she barely knew, an artist who promised her the world and gave her nothing expect despair. Despair and Darrelle. And now everything was lost.

Noelle heard laughter and drunken conversation coming from the direction of the boulevard Rochechouart. The cabarets must be closing. *How much time had passed? Why hadn't Charles found her?* She needed to go home, make everything right.

Noelle's breathing became shallow and uneven. Her throat burned with unshed tears. There were more voices, people walking by, off in the distance. Noelle tried calling out, but she was too weak, and the boulevard was too far away. She would save her strength. Someone would come and find her.

Although it had only been a few minutes, it seemed like hours had passed when Noelle heard the voices of men cutting through the alley. The night was too dark and her vision too blurred for her to actually see them, but she could tell from their steps and the increasing sound of laughter that they were getting closer. She called out to them, but above their own drunken ruckus, the two men could not hear her raspy cry for help. *Something to throw.* She needed something to throw and get their attention.

Noelle bent forward, wincing as she unlaced her right shoe. Her fingers fumbled and failed. Please, God, please. She had to do this before they passed, before they left and never knew she was there. *Stop, stop*, she hollered in a voice loud and commanding. But the voice was only inside her head. Finally, the lace was loosened. With what seemed her final ounce of strength, Noelle removed the shoe and threw it in the path of the men. But it was too late. They had walked by just seconds before. The shoe hit the ground with a thud. The two men stopped to listen. "Alley cats," they hissed as they continued on. "Damn alley cats."

The click, click of high heels alerted Noelle to a woman's approach. She was walking in an unsteady pattern, singing softly and mumbling to herself.

"What the —?" The woman stumbled over something in her path, then bent down to retrieve what she had kicked. "What's this? A shoe?" She pulled a bottle of gin from her purse and took a short swig. Holding the shoe close to her face, she examined its smooth leather. "A damn good one at that. Wonder where the mate is."

"Help. Please. Help."

"What's that? Who's there?" The woman shouted, the clicking of her heels making a loud, erratic noise as she turned in circles, looking to see who stalked her. She spotted Noelle hunched in the doorway and approached cautiously.

"Well, now, what's this?"

Noelle clutched the woman's ankle. "Please. Help me."

"I'll help you chère. But first I'll help myself." She shook Noelle's fingers off her ankle and took another swig of gin. "Here." She put the bottle to Noelle's mouth and tipped it until her lips were covered with liquid. "A little hair of the dog." She held the shoe to Noelle's face. "This your shoe, chère? Sure is a nice one. Don't mind if I take the mate now, do you? Call it the price of a drink." She bent down and removed Noelle's other shoe.

Noelle grabbed at the woman's hair. "Please. . .help. Hurt."

"We all hurt. Now let go." The woman was actually gentle as she unlaced Noelle's fingers from around strands of her long brown hair. "That's it, let go. Got anything else, chère?" She looked around for a purse, slipped her hands into the pockets of Noelle's dress and then fingered the length of her garment hoping to find something of value pinned to the waist or hem.

"Nothing? Nothing? Poor soul. You're worse off than me." She poured more gin into Noelle's mouth, tucked the shoes under her arms and left, singing softly into the empty alley.

Noelle listened as the clicking of the woman's heels faded into the distance. There was nothing now but the silence, thick and palatable, like unrelenting fog. She didn't care about the shoes, but it suddenly felt as if her necklace was missing. Where was it? Where? She couldn't feel it; she should be able to feel it against her skin. Had the women found it and taken it? She tore at the high collar of her dress. *Where was it? Where?* She grabbed at the fabric, sticky blood-covered fingers searching frantically. There. There it was, lying against her skin, but not where it should be.

It had fallen off. The clasp must have broken, but it was safe; it was still hers.

Noelle wrapped her fingers around the necklace, a slender chain holding a gold charm, the interior of the charm's circle fashioned in white and green enamel to represent a lily-of-the-valley. Her sister, Linette, had given it to her on the day they buried their mother. "The flower, it's a symbol of grieving, and remembrance," Linette told her. "Wear it and you'll remember our mère always; she'll be with you forever. So will I."

Noelle pulled her knees up and cradled her body against the brick wall of the alley, clutching the necklace in the palm of one hand as she pressed hard against the knife wounds. Fading in and out of consciousness, she had the sensation of floating away from her body. First, deep, throbbing pain and then the lightness of leaving it behind. It was nearly dawn when she called out to Linette, seeing her as she had been years before, lying in bed, sick with pneumonia. She could smell lavender, her sister's favorite scent.

"Forgive me," Noelle whispered. "I was not a good sister. I should have stayed. I should have nursed you."

As the sun rose in the morning sky, Noelle found herself surrounded by radiant light, warm and healing, filled with promise. With the light came Enif, her long-time friend and guardian. She recognized him immediately. He would save her.

"Come with me now. Leave the pain behind," Enif told her. "As we move upward, do not look down. Look up. Only up."

Noelle tried. But she couldn't make herself obey. As they traveled into the light, she turned to view her body as it no longer struggled to stay alive. She saw her crumpled form and blood- stained hands, taking in details, like her dress — torn at the neck — and a thin chain of gold cascading across the hand that had tightened into a fist and hardened around the charm that stood for grief and remembrance.

"Darrelle," she cried out, seeing the image of her youngest daughter kneeling on the ground next to her.

In that one downward look, Noelle was pulled back to the earth plane. Enif waited a moment before joining her. "It's time to go," he told her. "That was only Darrelle's spirit saying goodbye. She is at home, in Charles' arms, sound asleep. Let go, Noelle, let go."

She followed Enif's voice back into the light, floating upward, upward.

Back in the alley, Noelle's body gasped one final time and then fell forward, snapping the silver cord that connects soul and earthly form, sending her spirit spiraling toward the heavens, through all the stages of the Bardo, until she found herself in a place of light and love and hope.

"Welcome back, Nunki," Enif said. "Welcome to the Bardo of Becoming."

Two

Nunki. **What a** comfort it was to hear her true name. No longer encased in an earthly body, Noelle assumed the ethereal light form of the Bardo and immediately recognized her soul name. All those years on earth, such a chaotic life. Noelle had never once looked up at the stars with that sense of remembering, of knowing, that some people experienced. Now, here in the Bardo — a word that means transition and is every soul's home between lives — it was easy to remember how she had been created from a burst of light and then given her eternal name. No matter what she was called on earth, her true name was Nunki. And there was a star twinkling away in the heavens, named in her honor.

"Nunki," Enif interrupted her thoughts, "your death was very difficult. Nunki? Are you listening?"

"I was thinking about the stars, remembering how on earth the very first humans wanted to name everything they saw, and the only names they knew were one another's soul names —"

"And so," Enif finished the memory, "when it came to the night sky, they gave it an identity that actually mirrored their own. They named each star after a soul they'd met at the moment of creation, or later, here in the Bardo. Very good. You're remembering already. I'm proud of you."

She glowed with the memory, and with the praise.

"Now, as I was saying, your death was very difficult. You'll need a long rest."

"There's no time. I must rescue Darrelle. There's no telling what Charles will do. I must go back. I'll save Darrelle, have my revenge and then —" She stopped, recoiling at the sudden pain, as though her energy was being seared with hot currents. "You lied! You said there would be no pain."

"Nunki! You know I would never lie. Never." His tone made her recall another lifetime on earth, when Enif was her father, and a very strict one.

"But you said there would be no pain if I followed you."

"There never is. Not when you follow with wholeness and intention. But you have chosen to leaves pieces of your energy back on earth, hovering over your body, wanting revenge on Charles. You must let go and become whole in order for the pain to leave."

"Oh, Enif. Why weren't you with me this time? I've made such a mess of things, haven't I?"

"You left for earth very abruptly last time. You chose to live without me. As your soul memory returns, you will remember everything."

"I want to see Charles again. Enif, you must let me go back. I don't care about my pain. I want to hurt him like he hurt me."

"Nunki. Nunki. Your light. It's becoming much too erratic. Please calm yourself. Yes, that's better. Doesn't it feel better?" Enif didn't wait for her to respond. "Revenge, you know, has never motivated you. Stubbornness, yes. But not revenge."

She didn't want to hear what Enif had to say, even if it was true. Especially if it was true. Every lifetime, it had been the same. Her stubbornness. The lessons she needed to learn. Nunki cast her light in the direction of friends from previous lifetimes, off in the distance, each silhouette like her own, a fluid light-filled form. "I'd like to go say hello."

"You'll notice that many of your friends have made great progress. A few have not."

"How do I look?"

"You look just fine."

"You know what I mean."

Of course Enif knew what she meant. In the Bardo, each soul's progress is measured by the depth and purity of its light, as earthly failures are atoned for across lifetimes, and rings of darkness are transformed into rings of light. With enough growth, the entire being is filled with translucent light. From his "just fine" answer, Nunki understood that only her first few layers had been transformed.

"Have I advanced at all?" Nunki pressed the issue.

"You're the same," Enif told her. "It was not a time of growth. Hopefully, you will learn that — and learn from that — in your life review."

Enif left then, allowing Nunki the privacy she needed to acclimate, to visit with friends and finally, to accept her transitional stage of a soul between lives. Soon, she would settle into a deep healing sleep. When she woke, she would spend decades in the Chambers of Learning, preparing for her next life.

THREE

When Nunki woke from her long sleep, she resolved to master the lessons needed for a more enlightened life. In the Chambers of Learning, she studied God's teachings of love, compassion and forgiveness while attempting to understand the tug-of-war that exists between destiny and free will. She also had to relearn the concept of karma, the idea that whatever we put out into the world will return to us, sometimes two-fold, whether in the same lifetime or in another; we are forever accountable for our actions.

In earth years, it was 1945. As Nunki left the Chambers of Learning for the day, she found Jabbah waiting for her. He twinkled and she could imagine a handsome earthly figure winking at her.

"I'm glad I caught up with you," Jabbah said. "I'm going back to earth any moment now."

"It's not fair," Nunki said. "We've barely seen each other since my arrival. And now you're leaving."

"Of course it's fair. It's just not to your liking."

"I'll hurry and join you. I'm tired of the Chambers anyway."

"My Nunki, always so impetuous."

"Don't say that! I'm ready. I know I am."

"Do you like impulsive better?" Jabbah's light shook with laughter as he extended a beam toward her. "It's a soul trait. You can work on it, but I'm not sure it'll ever completely go away. It must drive the Masters crazy. But I've always found it endearing."

"A lot of good that does. I'll never finish my earth cycles if I don't mend my ways."

"Is earth so bad?"

"It's hard. You know that. The hardest of all levels. But it's always been easier when I've shared them with you. When are you leaving?"

"Any minute. I'll be their first child. I just came to say good-bye."

"Have you asked about us?" Nunki had been avoiding plans for her next lifetime, but suddenly she was eager to know what she would face. "I really want us to be together again. It's our destiny. I was always better, or capable of being better, when you were in my life."

"Me, too," Jabbah admitted. "Which was your favorite?"

"I liked 1655. Remember, we were brother and sister then? We were so close; we had so much love. I hated the woman you married, though. She wasn't nearly good enough for you, and she was always starting fights between us. But the next lifetime — that was definitely one of my favorites. I knew we were soul mates the moment I looked into your eyes. 1809. That was the year we married. You were known as Jacob and I was Nellie."

"It was a wonderful lifetime," Jabbah agreed, "but much too short. I watched you die in that fire. I died the next year. I just didn't have the will to go on. It's one of the lessons I'm still struggling with, learning to go on in the face of adversity. I must deal with disappointment, even death, and not destroy myself in the process."

"We'll help each other this time. If you've asked. Have you?"

21

"I have." Jabbah was teasing her, withholding the answer, knowing how impatient Nunki had always been.

"And? What? What was the answer?"

"The answer is *yes*, as long as you also ask, and providing you give yourself some true challenges this next time. The Masters worry that you have gone back too many times without a plan and frittered away the opportunity for growth."

"I will. I promise. I'll meet with the Council of Masters as soon as possible. That means I'll have to read the Akashic records. I've been avoiding that step. The review, it's so hard."

"I know," Jabbah said.

"But now I have a reason to move things along. I'll be back there before you can wink your earth eye three times."

They fell silent, listening to the melodic ringing of bells that filtered through the Bardo, wending its way through the light like the tinkling of wind chimes on a summer afternoon. The ringing came in a specific succession of long and short sounds.

"They're calling for me. I took a great chance leaving the Waiting Area to come find you. If I don't go now, the baby could be stillborn."

"Jabbah, wait." Nunki was desperate to know which one genetic feature from past lifetimes he had chosen to keep. In all the times she had known him, his eyes had been the most remarkable combination of bronze and deep olive, laced with gold flecks. "How will I know you?"

"The same way you always have," Jabbah answered as he turned to leave. "The Masters also said something about a coin, but I'm not quite sure how it will work. You keep that dimpled smile of yours, and we'll know each other anywhere."

FOUR

"It's time, Nunki," Enif said.

"Do I have to?" She knew the answer, but apprehension made her ask anyway.

"You do, if you still want to go back during this reincarnation period. There's going to be a large influx of souls in the next ten years. After that, you may have to wait quite a while."

"I know. Besides, I promised Jabbah." In earth time, it had already been over a year since Jabbah left the Bardo.

"Then it's time to go."

"Will you stay with me?"

"Every step of the way. Oh, and I have good news. I have been assigned to you, as Major Guardian, for your entire next lifetime."

"And you're just telling me, with a by-the-way? Honestly, Enif, sometimes you are so absent-minded."

"Yes, I suppose I am," Enif laughed. "I will try to improve on that."

Together they moved through the light and seemingly infinite space of the Bardo until they came to the Akashic Record Room, a circular space of finite proportions. Here, the light appeared filtered, as though streaming through a soft lens.

"I'd forgotten how beautiful it is," Nunki said as they entered. "I can feel the memories already. Nothing specific, just this flood of feeling."

"Nunki, you must reduce your vibrations. There is nothing to fear."

"Except myself. I don't know if I'm ready to face the truth about myself."

"It's the only way," Enif said. "From these truths you go on, to create new truths. The spirit is always growing. The challenge is to learn from each step, to go forward."

Enif moved closer to Nunki, mingling his light with hers to help soothe her. "That's it, Nunki, reduce your vibrations. Move to the meditative state, as they taught you in the Chambers of Learning. That's it . . . that's it. . . slow right down. Release the fear."

As Nunki responded to Enif's encouragement, her light waves calmed to a steady, serene glow. Nothing would hurt her, not here. Not even the truth. She was ready.

"I have already read your records," Enif told her, "so I am with you now solely for support and guidance. As you know, the Akashic Records are the eternal source for the deeds and thoughts of every human being in every incarnation. Nothing goes unnoticed, or unrecorded, and sometimes it is the smallest deed or thought that reveals the soul's true intention. In reviewing your life, Nunki, look for patterns of thought and behavior. Determine if they measure up to your own challenges for growth and renewal. Begin to determine what debts you would like to repay in the coming lifetime."

As Enif talked, a beacon of translucent gold light bathed the area directly in front of them, creating a Circle of Illumination, a circle they would soon enter. Volumes of bound records were revealed, each suspended within the spherical space of the record room, just outside the Circle of Illumination. Each volume was engraved with the name of a soul.

"Nunki, you know the next step. You must find your volume and remove it from the stacks. I cannot do it for you."

She was not allowed to read any records but her own, yet there were so many she longed to open, so many souls she had known from the very beginning. Lovers, friends, even enemies. How often their lives had touched: sometimes only in passing; other times, deeply and at great cost. After locating her volume, Nunki increased her vibrations and directed a ray of silver light onto its spine. As soon as it struck, she entered the Circle of Illumination. Enif remained outside; this was Nunki's moment. Once she opened the book, he would join her.

Nunki watched in awe as her volume traveled along the wave of silver light and returned to its energy source — to her — to the very soul it had recorded. As her book entered the Circle, Nunki's ray of light transformed itself into a pedestal upon which the volume rested. The opening ritual was complete.

With Enif by her side now, she studied the index of names scripted in gold, each one representing one of her lifetimes on earth. There were thirty-two in all. Nunki was drawn to a few in particular: Neola, Naomi, Norbetta, and she immediately wanted to review those lifetimes. They seemed safe to her, even happy. But Enif stopped her from digressing, directing a single, forceful beam to the name Noelle. That was the lifetime she was here to review first. Then, perhaps, the others, to look for patterns, for karma that could be balanced.

Nunki would have preferred to view her past life randomly, moving at will from one interesting event to another. Enif, however, strongly suggested that the review be done chronologically. "It's the only way you'll gain insight. If you choose random observation, you'll be forever flickering your light, moving on to the next moment, never stopping long enough to understand or contemplate. The goal here is insight, not entertainment."

"You're right. You're always right."

"Before you begin, you must heed this warning: when you choose a page from your book, that particular life event will manifest itself just outside the Circle; it will seem as though it is really happening. The Circle is your only protection. It allows you to view the past event objectively. But the beams do not filter out everything. If the accompanying emotions are particularly strong, they can break through. You may actually feel them, even though they are in the past and no longer real. You will be tempted to step outside the Circle and interact with that particular experience."

"I know, I remember," Nunki responded impatiently.

"Nunki, do not disregard this. I am very serious. Do not step out of the Circle for any reason or your soul will be etched with the experience of that moment and you will carry it into your next lifetime."

"I will be very careful. I promise."

One by one, Nunki turned back the gilded pages of the volume until she came to the chapter marked Noelle Robidoux: 1871 – 1898. She was only twenty-seven years old when she died.

———◆———

Just beyond the Circle's protective beams, Nunki's lifetime as Noelle was played out for her. Almost immediately, she was embarrassed by her apparent lack of commitment to anyone's needs but her own. It seemed that caring about herself was all that mattered.

But it hadn't started out that way.

Noelle's mother had been a guiding force in her life, setting an example of caring by helping those less fortunate and insisting that Noelle participate in volunteer work. It all ended a week before Noelle's fourteenth birthday.

Nunki viewed the scene now, the coffin with her mother's body as they lowered her into the ground. She saw herself, a young, heartbroken girl, shrugging off concerned touches, pushing away her father and her sister, Linette. There — Nunki froze the scene for closer examination — the decision not to care anymore — it was made right there, staring at her mother's coffin. It was too hard, Noelle had decided. Caring. Worrying. Being obligated to others. It all took too much energy, too much thinking.

Nunki moved on, stopping at a scene two years later. Her father was reaching out to hug her. She pulled back, flinging her hair so that the mass of black locks struck his cheek. She giggled at his stricken look.

"It's better this way," he was telling her. "I cannot help you. I love you, Noelle, but I cannot help you."

Noelle did not believe his declaration of love. She only knew that her father was sending her away.

"Linette, is warm and kind, so much like your mère. She understands you. With her, you can learn about things. Woman things. I cannot give you what you need."

Linette, pregnant with her third child, welcomed Noelle into her home. But Noelle pulled away from her embrace, much as she had from her father's.

In quick succession, Nunki saw all the ways she ran away in her life as Noelle: when her father broke his hip, she returned to his home begrudgingly, only to run off to Paris a week later; when Linette was bed-ridden with pneumonia, Noelle ran away to marry Petrus. Only they never married. Two years later, when Linette's husband died, Noelle was too busy going after Charles to notice her sister's sorrow. When she finally married Charles, eleven years her senior, she began running away from him in hundreds of ways, the most devastating was her affair with Emile.

Enif intercepted Nunki's beam, directing her toward the last set of scenes waiting to be reviewed.

They were all in the house — Charles, Noelle, and their three daughters, the fireplace crackling, rain slashing against the windows. Charles had been drinking Absinthe all afternoon; the room was filled with its sickeningly sweet odor. Noelle wanted to go out dancing, to have some fun. The girls would be fine alone. Charles was refusing her, shaking his head no. She was pacing, color creeping up her neck, her hair wild about her head.

"You are so boring. Old and boring," Noelle shouted, deliberately trying to make him angry. He was always withholding feelings. Always too controlled. And controlling.

The children, accustomed to her outbursts, barely looked up from their game. Only Darrelle, three-year-old Darrelle, threw her an accusing glance. As though she knew. As though she could read her future.

"Then don't take me," Noelle shouted when Charles didn't respond. "Old boring man. I will go without you. You are old and boring. Do you hear me? Old and boring. Do you honestly think you could father a child as special as Darrelle?" Noelle glanced toward her daughters, saw the blood drain from their faces. She saw their fear, felt it fill the room, but she could not stop. "You are not man enough. You think she's yours? Think again, old man. She belongs to Emile Armat."

Noelle never saw Charles pick up the carving knife from the table. She only felt the sharp, serrated blade as it sliced through her stomach.

As Nunki watched from within the Circle of Illumination, it seemed to be happening all over again. Or, for the first time. It was suddenly impossible for Nunki to sort out the past from the present. At the very moment when Charles slashed the knife through Noelle's stomach, she broke through the Circle, trying desperately and unreasonably to save Noelle from her fate.

As the knife turned in Noelle's body, it pierced Nunki's being, imprinting her with the searing pain.

FIVE

"You stepped outside the Circle, Nunki." It was a simple statement. There was no recrimination. No judgment. Just the simple fact of it.

Nunki faced the Council of Masters. Each of the three Masters had earned this place of high regard through soul growth, first on earth and, later, in the Bardo, serving as guide and then Major Guardian.

"I couldn't help it. I just —" she stopped, unable to explain further, knowing they required no explanation.

"Do you understand that you have been imprinted, that you will carry the experience into your next lifetime?" Regulus asked. Of the three Masters, he was the oldest soul, the one who emitted the most radiant and pure light.

What had she done to herself?

"Don't be afraid," Regulus said, as through reading her thoughts. "This is not a punishment. We do not punish souls. We help them to learn. Stepping out of the light at that moment means that the experience called to you, for whatever reason. You have not yet been able to achieve distance."

"I will do my best to accept whatever comes from this. I want to learn and do better."

"Excellent," Altair said. It was easy to recognize her as the newest member by the vibrancy of her light; it had not yet mellowed to the same depth and maturity of the two elder Masters. "We are pleased with your determination. Would you like us to sanction your return to the Akashic Record Room to review some of your other lifetimes, to see how often you have connected with certain souls and reflect more on the lessons you need to learn?"

"No. Yes." Nunki was so nervous that her light began to flicker in a random pattern of light and dark. "I mean, yes I would, because it would be informative. But I've seen enough. I believe I know what I need to know. I am ready for the opportunity."

"And what opportunity is that?" Regulus asked.

"To be with Lesath. She was my sister, Linette, in France this past life. She was like a mother to me after our own mother died. But I was nothing like a daughter. I would like to correct that. Also," Nunki continued, wanting to convince the Council of the rightness of her decision, "I understand from Enif that after I died . . ." Nunki was hesitant; it was still difficult to speak of her death in that lifetime. She paused, started again. "After I died, Linette watched over my children. She protected Darrelle from Charles. I want to pay back my debt to her. I want to thank her."

"You are correct in your assessment of how you treated Lesath," Merak said. "She has been back on earth for twenty-five years. She spent very little time here after her death as the woman Linette. Her name, now, is Louise Hamilton. You should be aware that there are certain circumstances —"

"Before we continue in that direction," Regulus interrupted, "we must hear Nunki's requests. Then we can determine if she is up to the challenge of this, shall we say, *particular* circumstance. Nunki, you understand that there are consequences for every action — *as you sow you shall reap, as you reap you shall sow* — and that these consequences present themselves as challenges, even across lifetimes. It is the law of karma. Do you fully understand?

"Yes. I do."

"Then precisely what are your Resolves, and which specific karmic challenges do you wish to face?"

"I have given this considerable thought. One of the greatest lessons I have learned is the folly of an unplanned life. That will not happen to me again. On earth, as soon as I'm old enough, I'll determine my life's goals and then make a plan to achieve them."

"Plan from here, Nunki," Altair cautioned. "That is wise and necessary, and you failed to do that last time. But do not over-plan when you are actually living the life. That can be as disastrous as no planning at all. It can lead to a heartless existence. You have too much passion for that. Leave room for your heart."

"I think planning is essential. It was my biggest failure last time. Going back without a plan, living without a plan, always headstrong, always following a whim. That will not happen this time." As far as Nunki was concerned this point was not negotiable. "Test me often. I will come through."

"You will be tested, Nunki, do not worry. And what is your second Primary Karmic Goal?" Regulus asked. "You must have two in order to go back with our sanction."

"There are so many I could choose from. I have not grown much across lifetimes. I would like the Council to test my ability to be loyal, as you have in the past. Except this time I will not fail."

"How will you do this?" Merak asked.

"Through strong resolve. This time, I will stand by the people in my life, no matter what, for as long as they need. The whims that led me astray in the past will no longer exist, because of deliberate planning. I will remain loyal to my plans and to the people I choose to spend my life with." Nunki had planned and memorized this part and now delivered it with what she hoped was the appropriate balance of enthusiasm and respect.

"We agree," Regulus responded, scanning the other two Council members for their agreement, "that both of these challenges — planning and loyalty — are necessary for your spiritual growth. But, perhaps, they should be undertaken separately, in different lifetimes."

"Yes," Altair said. "I can see this presenting all varieties of conflicts. To what, or whom, will she be loyal: the plan she is intent on creating, other people, herself and her own values? I am afraid that planning and loyalty will conflict to such a degree that there will be no growth."

Nunki remained motionless as they discussed her fate, knowing she could choose whatever she wanted, but that going back once again without sanction would be karmic suicide. If the Council accepted both of her Primary Karmic Challenges, they would move ahead to specific planning. The three Council Masters conferred, sending private light messages from one to the other.

Finally, Regulus addressed Nunki. "We are delighted with your resolve and determination to have a new life filled with growth and spiritual development. We accept both of your Primary Karmic Challenges — that of Planning your Life and that of Learning the Lessons of Loyalty. We do this, not so much with reservation, as with a cautionary note. Remember, Nunki, to live a heart-centered life. It is much more fulfilling than one directed solely by the head. Keep this thought deep in your soul: True loyalty is not simply blind allegiance. Be faithful, always, to what you know to be right and good."

While Nunki didn't completely understand the Council's warning, she chose not to question it. They might reverse their decision if, after all this, they thought she was unprepared for her challenges. "I understand. Thank you."

"Let us move to specifics," Regulus said. "The Council will determine the tests necessary to challenge your goals. You will not pass every test. But that does not mean you have failed. You will judge for yourself, when you return to the Bardo at the end of your lifetime, that you have failed a test only when you neglected to learn from it. Now, what specific opportunities would you like to have?"

"My requests are few, but very important to me. I would like to be Lesath's daughter. And I would like to share a life with Jabbah. And I need to keep my smile."

"Ahh. Your smile. A good choice," Merak said. "It has always defined the authentic you — warm, fun, intelligent. I'm assuming you want the single dimple as well?"

"Oh, yes. It has to be."

Merak glanced at the other Masters. "Request granted."

"Jabbah has also requested to share this lifetime with you," Altair said. "We agree that the opportunity for a life together will present itself. You will recognize him by the color of his eyes. Once again, they will be a rich, earthy color of bronze and olive —"

"With gold flecks?" Nunki interrupted.

"Yes, Nunki, with gold flecks. You will hand him a found coin when the time is right. His heart will be waiting for that coin. We also agree to your desire to repay karmic debt to Lesath. We will present you with the opportunity to be her daughter —"

"Thank you," Nunki interrupted once again. "Thank you."

"We are simply presenting opportunities," Altair cautioned. "Free will can impact your chosen destiny at any time."

"I know. Truly, I do. But I have a strong feeling that this life will be as exactly as I desire it to be. I'm very determined this time."

"Then you completely understand," Altair said, "that, aside from retaining your smile as a physical trait, the only *absolutes* you are returning with are, in essence, opportunities: the *opportunity* to be Lesath's daughter, the *opportunity* to spend a lifetime with Jabbah, and the opportunities — or challenges — we will provide for spiritual growth. How it all turns out is dependent upon free will, upon human choices."

"Cause and effect," Merak added.

"Let us talk about Lesath," Regulus said. "She is an old soul, very enlightened. She spent very little time here between her last earth life and the present one. She is already an adult, living an interesting life. There are special circumstances surrounding your desire to be her daughter. Perhaps you will change your mind once you hear them. But you must decide now so that we can find another soul for the unborn child."

"Nothing can make me change my mind. I know that she already has one child and it seems that she cannot have any more. And Enif told me that the baby just conceived by a young girl name Marilyn Davenport is going to be adopted by Lesath — I mean Louise — and her husband. As soon as I heard this, I knew how to realize my goal. I could be born to Marilyn and raised by Louise. It's a perfect plan."

Altair left her place at the Council table and moved next to Enif. "You did not tell her the rest?"

"It was not his place to tell her," Regulus boomed. "It is ours."

"Tell me what?" Nunki's light flickered with fear. "What is there to tell me?"

"Cheleb — your husband, Charles, in your recent past life — is on earth right now, also repaying karmic debt to Lesath," Regulus explained. "The son she gave birth to. . . it is Cheleb."

"But how? How could that be?" Of all things, Nunki had not expected this.

"Similar to how you left last time. Impulsively," Merak answered. "He died in prison in 1923, came home to the Bardo, and returned to earth in 1944. He went back too quickly, we believe, without enough introspection."

Altair added, "And without our complete sanction, a situation that could result in repeated patterns. If you are Lesath's adopted daughter, you will also be Cheleb's adopted sister."

Nunki became erratic; her outermost core, the one with the strongest emissions of light, began to fold inward. How could she spend a childhood, an entire lifetime, connected to a man who had murdered her, the very man responsible for the imprinting of her soul? But then she remembered her determination for spiritual growth and her promise to Jabbah.

"If I am truly determined," she said, "I could also resolve karmic debt to Cheleb this next lifetime." Her light dimmed momentarily, but then came back strong, filled with resolve. "I had not planned on such a challenge, but, perhaps it could work. At the very least, I might learn to forgive him and we could have an amiable life."

"And he you. You must forgive each other. He has not set forth that challenge, nor did he express any desire to balance negative karma accrued with you," Merak said. "How do you feel about this Regulus? Altair?"

"I feel it is too much," Altair said.

"As I do," Regulus answered. "But the decision is Nunki's. She has shown considerable maturity in her approach to rebirth. I believe we should sanction this, if she so desires."

"I do. I really do! I want this opportunity with my entire being. I could grow tremendously with such challenges, which is the whole purpose of going back. Am I right?"

"She is right," Merak said.

"Yes, you are right," Regulus agreed. "The Council, then, is in accord. Nunki, you will return to earth to be born to a young, unwed woman named Marilyn Davenport. You will be challenged with karmic debts to Lesath and Cheleb, known this lifetime as Louise and Chad. Your Primary Karmic Challenges will be to plan out your life in order to avoid living by whim and to both learn and employ the lessons of loyalty."

"I will not fail you," Nunki said.

"It is yourself you must not fail," Regulus said. "We will not meet again until your new existence is complete and you return here to the Bardo. You will be taking on another earthly form, but you are still Nunki. Everything you need to know — every truth you search for — you already have, deep inside of you, in the essence of who you are. As you face the challenges ahead, we pray that you discover your inner knowledge and have a truly enlightened life. Farewell, Nunki. God speed."

"Thank you," Nunki said.

"Come," Enif said, escorting her away. "Now comes the hard part."

She looked at him, puzzled. What could be harder than this?

"Waiting," Enif said. "Don't you remember? It's the hardest time of all."

Six

Now that the major decisions for her next life had been approved, Nunki was impatient to begin her earthly existence. But already she was being tested. Marilyn Davenport was two weeks overdue. And because the Bardo rules of infinity and timelessness do not apply to the Waiting Area, Nunki experienced those two weeks in earth time. While the young Marilyn went to the movies, slept late and didn't care if the baby ever came, Nunki paced and worried as she waited for the melodic chiming of bells, a chiming that would be specific to her vibration, signifying the start of her rebirth.

Enif moved closer to Nunki, aligning their edges perfectly, giving her a hearty ethereal hug. "You'll do wonderfully," he said. "You have planned well."

"I'm worried about being with Cheleb. Maybe it was a mistake. What if I can't live up to my own expectations? What if I can't resolve our negative karma and we fall into the same patterns?"

"What if? What if? It's futile trying to imagine what might happen. You simply have to try. Perhaps you start with forgiveness."

"Forgiveness? You want me to forgive him for stabbing me? For killing me? I know that's what I said to the Council, but honestly Enif, do you really believe it's possible? I'll be nice to him, I promise you that, but I'll never forgive him. I'll —"

"Do not do this to yourself." Enif stopped her from continuing. He began to lecture her about forgiveness, about cause and effect and free will, but Nunki waved him off with a beam of light, having spotted her old friends Pollux and Ain on the other side of the Waiting Area. She hurried off to join them.

"You're going back, too?" Nunki asked. "Maybe we'll meet. I hope so. I think I have some hard times ahead."

Pollux smiled. "We'll meet. Don't worry. I made a last minute visit to the Council. They've agreed to let me test your resolve around the lesson of loyalty. You've helped me so many times before. Now it's my turn."

"I hope I don't make a mess of things."

"You won't," Pollux said. "At least I hope you won't. Besides, you know what the Council says —"

"We all get precisely what we need, even if it's not what we want," the three friends recited in unison, children mimicking a parent's mantra.

"What about you?" Nunki asked Ain.

"We'll see each other. I'm about ready. My bells have been ringing for a while. Apparently a long labor. I have a lot of things to work out, but if I get on the right path, the Council said I could repay some debt to you by serving as a voice for the other side, whatever that means."

"The other side? A voice for her, the Bardo? I don't understand," Nunki said.

"Maybe Ain will offer point-counter-point to your ideas," Pollux suggested. "A different point of view?"

"That's as good a guess as any," Nunki said. "It'll be interesting."

"To say the least," Pollux said. "I've been conceived by a Negro couple." She stopped and listened. "There they are. My first bells; she's in labor."

"You're going to be colored?" Nunki asked, ignoring the specific rhythm of bells that signaled Pollux's impending birth.

"Apparently. That's how DNA usually works," Pollux joked and then turned serious. "Why are you so shocked? You've been a lot of things over lifetimes, but prejudiced has never been one of them."

"It's just that, well, the times. They're not the best for Negroes right now."

"When has it ever been? But you're right, and it will probably get worse," Pollux said. "My goal is to handle this choice so well that I'm given the opportunity to work with an important world leader. He's already been born. As it stands now, he's destined to make an enormous difference. I've asked for a chance to help."

"Was it granted?"

"As much as it can be. It's the only thing I really want. I'll be on my requested path from the moment of rebirth, but you know how it is. There are challenges all along the way. And our destiny is always affected by free will." Pollux twinkled, rubbing her light against Nunki's in fun. "You'd better be good to me. Your free will could make a difference to my future."

"No pressure, hey Pollux? You've always been demanding!"

They joked a while longer, but then it was time to part and join their guardians, each listening for the bells that would beckon them to earth.

Finally, Nunki's first bells chimed. Marilyn's labor had begun.

"Just do your best," Enif said. "Remain committed to your goals. And, remember, I am not allowed to interfere with your life no matter what choices you make. But I will be there to help guide you. To stir your awareness."

They waited silently until Nunki's bells rang once again. Things were moving quickly now.

"I'm so nervous," Nunki said. "I can't remember anything I've learned. You promise you'll be there?"

"I promise. In the beginning, I'll be by your side every minute. Then, later, as you need me. You'll feel my presence. There will be times when you experience an unrelenting nagging in your brain or a deep discomfort in your soul. Other times, you'll feel a stirring in the wind. That, my dear Nunki, will be me trying to get your attention. You won't have conscious memories of the Bardo or your past lives, but, if you listen deeply, with an open heart, you'll know exactly what you need to do this time around, and you'll have a good life."

"Open mind. Open heart. Courage. Forgiveness. Loyalty. Patience. I don't know, Enif, it's a lot for one lifetime. Maybe I'm not ready."

"You're ready."

Once more, bells wafted through the Bardo.

One by one, the three friends were reborn, whisked into the universe below, through the sky with all of its suns and stars, through all the layers of creation until, finally, reaching the level of earth, they exchanged ethereal form for the human body.

First Pollux. Then Ain. And, finally, Nunki.

SEVEN

July 17, 1947

Textile production was running at an all-time high in the small mill town of Fall River, Massachusetts due, in no small part, to the fact that long skirts were no longer illegal, as they had been during wartime. Day and night, factories cranked out their goods, belching up steady streams of thick, gray smoke into the summer sky. It seemed as though every pore of the town was filled with the noise and pollution of renewed prosperity. And Marilyn Davenport hated every sound and every smell.

Lying in her hospital bed, she cringed at the blast of noon-time whistles, never having allowed herself to become accustomed to their abrasive onslaught. To accept them was to accept being the daughter of a mill worker. And, deep down, she knew she was better than that. She held her breath until each one stopped and the world was once again quiet. Oppressively quiet. The mid-day sun poured into the hospital room, a small fan and half-drawn shades having little impact on the sweltering air. Marilyn pressed an ice cube to her forehead and then popped it into her mouth, curling her tongue around it as icy droplets trickled down her throat. Just three days ago she'd given birth to a baby girl.

Propped up against the bed's bar-like headboard, Marilyn balanced the child in one arm, while extending her free hand outward, examining her looks in a small plastic mirror. Thank goodness for big favors, she thought. This whole birthing process had not destroyed her looks after all. She placed the mirror down on the bedside stand and began patting her face, reassuring herself that her flawless skin was still smooth and firm. Opening up bobby pins with her front teeth, she managed to pin her thick auburn hair away from her face. Only when she had finished primping did Marilyn's attention return to the baby in her arms.

"You look just like an Indian," Marilyn laughed, "but I bet you're going to be a beauty, once you get rid of that red face and this thing here." She flicked her finger across the tuft of sable hair growing upward from the center of her daughter's head. "Yep, a real beauty, for sure," she repeated, "and you be sure to use those looks to catch yourself a good man. Just like I'm gonna do." She wrinkled her nose at the mass of offensive odors permeating the room, especially since the fan had been turned on high. It was a God-awful combination of body sweat, spit up, disinfectant, and rubbing alcohol. "This is no place for either of us, baby girl."

There were four beds in the room, each one occupied by a girl from the Convent of St. Agnes, otherwise known as the Catholic Charities Home for Unwed Mothers. Over each bed was a crucifix, and over the small porcelain sink was a picture of Jesus surrounded by adoring children. The girl directly across from Marilyn was reading a romance magazine and, although the other one appeared to be sleeping, Marilyn noticed fresh tears on her cheeks. In the bed next to her was Joyce Fischer, lying completely still, staring up at the ceiling.

"You okay?" Marilyn asked.

"I guess."

"How does it feel?"

"Sad. Empty, kind of."

"Do you wish you'd kept him?"

"How could I? I'd already promised."

"Promises can be broken," Marilyn said. "My motto is they're made to be broken."

"How could I?" Joyce asked again. "My parents would never let me. I'm only seventeen. I have to go home, finish high school."

"Me, too. I'm seventeen. Would have graduated in June, though, 'cuz I'm an October baby. Started school at four. But they sent me here. Wouldn't let me finish up. I say, forget it. Who needs a diploma? All we need is the right guy." She thought for a minute and then announced, "I'm not going home. Not ever." Marilyn snuggled the infant tightly against her chest. "My father hates me. My mother's dead."

"How could you not go home? What will you do?" Joyce turned toward Marilyn, her brown eyes wide with disbelief.

"Get a job. And I still have my looks." Marilyn pointed toward the small mirror. "I just checked," she laughed. "Look for a man. A real man this time, instead of some stupid boy. Someone who won't check out when things don't go his way."

"They'll be coming for her soon," Joyce offered. "I snuck a look at the list. Me. Then someone down the hall. Then you."

Marilyn shivered, pulling the thin hospital blanket up over her arms. For a fleeting moment, even the intense July heat could not stave off the wave of cold passing through her body. "I've named her," she whispered to Joyce.

Naming a baby about to be adopted was tantamount to committing a mortal sin. For the last six months the nuns had doled out that message to their resident wayward girls before each meal, along with a hearty helping of prayers for the redemption of their souls.

"You can't name her," Joyce objected. "It's against the rules."

43

"How did you ever get pregnant? You follow every rule that's ever been invented. I know: he must have told you that doing it was a rule! That's just about what Eddie did. I can here his voice now: *the most important thing about loving someone, Marilyn, is proving your love!* Can you believe I fell for that shit? Anyway, I did name her. She's Natalie. Natalie Marie Davenport."

Joyce blushed at Marilyn's outburst. It was one thing to get pregnant; it was another to discuss it openly. "It's a nice name," she said. "But they'll never let her keep it. The new parents, I mean. Especially the mother. She'll never let her keep the name Natalie if she knows you picked it."

"You could be wrong. After all, it's a beautiful name and it's in honor of Natalie Wood who, everyone knows, is the best child actress since Shirley Temple. Some of us girls went to see Natalie in *Tomorrow is Forever*. My water broke right at the end. I think it was some kind of sign. It's a swell movie. Did you see it?"

"No. I don't like movies much."

"Oh, I do. They're filled with exactly the kind of life I want. Anyway, Natalie Wood plays this orphan girl. She's so sad and so brave, all at once. As soon as I gave birth and found out it was a girl, I knew the movie was a sign. My baby has to be called Natalie. I told Sister Mary Anthony. She just gave me one of her deadly dirty looks. Like this. . ."

Marilyn was contorting her mouth into a deadly dirty look when Sister Mary Anthony walked in, smelling like old skin and antiseptic, her starched white habit crinkling with every movement.

"Stop doing that with your face," the Sister scolded and then waited for Marilyn to compose herself. "It's time," she said, extending her arms toward Marilyn. "You must give the child to me. The new parents are waiting."

Sister Mary Anthony stood close enough to the bed so that the infant would not be dropped while being transferred from mother to nun, but far enough away to maintain the distance traditional between those in religious life and everyone else. It was a distance seldom, if ever, crossed.

Marilyn had anticipated this moment, knowing it relieved her of further responsibility. She could move ahead with her life, unencumbered and forgiven of all sins. Yet, under the weight of Sister Mary Anthony's orders, Marilyn froze. Something was wrong. But what?

Then it struck her.

"She has a name," Marilyn said, edging away from the nun's outstretched arms. "I told you before, her name is Natalie. Natalie Marie Davenport. She is not *the child*. How do I know you've picked a good home for her when you don't even care that she has a name."

"We have a very good home, my dear. You can be sure of that."

"How can I be sure. How?" Marilyn was nearly hysterical and not quite sure why.

"You must have faith my dear," Sister Mary Anthony said with exaggerated patience. "The baby's new parents are generous, God-fearing Catholics. The Hamiltons live in a very substantial home just outside of Boston, with enough money for anything this child might want." She inhaled deeply, exhaled just as deeply, and then waited, snapping the clicker that lay inside the folds of her pocket. It was the only sound in the stifling room. Click. Click. Click. It was a sound that signaled the expectation of total obedience. It was also a sound that made Marilyn clench her teeth in defiance.

"Marilyn, I'm being very tolerant," Sister Mary Anthony said, finally breaking the silence. "It's time to end this little rebellion. You made me say their name and that's strictly forbidden. I've entrusted you with information. Now you must trust me." She moved closer to the bed, her arms once again outstretched.

Marilyn smirked in response, remembering all the times Sister said she had 'little tolerance for wayward girls with fickle minds and loose morals.' Giving up their babies was God's will, a true test of faith, she told them. She never spoke of the real reason, but the girls all knew: adoptive parents were always extremely grateful, and their gratefulness led to the kind of generosity that would help build a new hospital wing. Tolerant? When had Sister Many Anthony ever been tolerant?

"Wipe that smile off your face, young lady," Sister Mary Anthony hissed, "and stop being obstinate. Hand me that child. Now!"

"I told you," Marilyn said, "she has a name! And, anyway, I've decided to keep her, so put that in your pipe and smoke it." Marilyn jutted out her chin and pulled herself to the far corner of the bed. "Natalie is mine," she said, tucking the infant tightly against her chest.

All eyes in the room rested on the teenager laying claim to her baby. There had been an audible intake of breath and then nothing. Nobody dared breathe. Not even Marilyn, who suddenly felt dizzy, unable to exhale. Maybe giving birth made people insane, she thought. Only a crazy person would dare talk to a nun like that, and it would take a really insane teenager to change her mind about adoption. Marilyn only wanted to name the baby; keeping it had never been in her plan. After all, how would she ever find a husband with a child in tow? But once the words were spoken, she would have rather died than take them back. It had to be a sign. First the movie, now saying such a crazy, unplanned thing — well, it just had to be a sign. And, if nothing else, Marilyn believed in signs and personal mottos. The child was hers, and hers to keep.

Sister Mary Anthony rearranged her posture so that she was standing even straighter than before, if that was at all possible, shoulders square, head high, assuming ultimate authority as she tucked her hands into the sleeves of her habit and then folded them across her waist. "Marilyn," she said, her voice taking on the stern, sing-song quality of a parent trying to subdue a toddler's temper tantrum, "you know you can't raise a child. You have no means. And just think how society will look down on you, what people will call you, and, worse, what they'll call the child. And the Lord, Marilyn, think about the Lord. Give up the child now and the Lord will forgive you for your sins."

"I don't care. I don't care about the Lord or other people. I just want my baby." Inside she was trembling. Did she really want her daughter or was she simply enjoying a delicious moment of defiance? Maybe, she'd gone too far.

"But you must care, and you must give her to me," Sister Mary Anthony commanded, losing control of her carefully controlled voice. "No more nonsense, Marilyn. Now!"

Breaking the unwritten code of distance, Sister Mary Anthony lunged at Marilyn, her wrinkled hands attempting to seize the infant from its mother. She pulled and tugged at Marilyn's nightgown while Marilyn pulled just as hard in the opposite direction. It was a spot of water on the floor that caused the good Sister to lose her footing and fall backward. She landed on top of Joyce, who cried out in shock while the other two girls giggled behind sheets pulled up to their eyes. Marilyn bit her tongue to keep from laughing out loud.

"This is unforgivable. You will pay in hell for this." Sister Mary Anthony struggled off Joyce's bed, readjusted her habit and stormed out of the room, shouting a final warning to Marilyn. "This is not over young lady. Not by a long shot. The new parents will go away today, but they'll be back tomorrow, and by then you'd better be ready to part with that child, a child who has no name because you have no right to name it."

Late in the day, Marilyn finally relinquished Natalie, allowing her to be returned to the nursery. Her diaper needed changing;

she needed to be fed, and she kept fussing so much Marilyn couldn't think straight. By law, they couldn't take her baby until she agreed and signed all the papers. Still, Marilyn walked down to the nursery often, making sure Natalie was still there, all the while asking herself: now what? She had a baby with a name, but no money, no husband, and no plan. She lay awake all night trying to figure things out. It came to her just before dawn.

While everyone else was sleeping, Marilyn filled her suitcase with every baby item she could get her hands on, as well as whatever clothes she and the other girls had in the hospital room. She took twenty dollars from Joyce's wallet, leaving her, not an IOU, but a quickly scrawled note that simply said "I'm sorry. Good Luck." She then tiptoed into the nursery when no one was looking, grabbed Natalie from her bassinet, and ran out into the muggy July morning, just as the sun was beginning to rise, half-dragging, half-carrying the heavy suitcase.

The taxi driver didn't ask any questions as he drove Marilyn and her newborn to the bus station. But if he had, she would have told him that she was on her way to a new life, to Aunt Willie's house in Hartford, Connecticut where all of her dreams would come true.

EIGHT

Three hours of sitting in a stifling bus on a hard, narrow seat so shortly after giving birth was bad enough. Add to that a fidgety, unhappy newborn, her own hunger pains, and the smell of sweating strangers, and the experience was more grueling than anything Marilyn could have anticipated. By the time the bus pulled into the Hartford terminal, tears were spilling across her cheeks, glistening against black flecks of dust and grime.

Cradling Natalie against her chest, Marilyn once again struggled with the heavy suitcase, stopping every few steps to readjust her grip, shifting her baby from one side to the other and back again before continuing her journey across the terminal. And all the while, Natalie kept crying. Why wouldn't this baby stop wailing? Why? Why? Why?

Finally, Marilyn simply stopped walking. She looked around the bus station wondering whether anyone would notice if she placed her baby down on one of those long wooden benches and then just walked away, slowly so as not to call attention to herself. Maybe leave the suitcase as well. A clean break.

She saw just the right bench, far off across the large room; she moved toward it, this time keeping her suitcase in front of her, sliding it forward with her feet, slowly, stealthily, all the while eyeing the spot that would release her from bondage. But the closer Marilyn got to it, the louder and more fretful Natalie became. It was all too much. She gave up and slumped down on the bench closest to her. Only hours into this thing called motherhood and Marilyn knew it wasn't for her; she was tired of being tired and disgusted with smelling like spit-up. What she wouldn't give for a long, cool bath and a splash of Evening in Paris cologne.

Marilyn sat there, jiggling Natalie, swiping at her own brow with her forearm. How was this ever going to work out?

She hadn't been to Aunt Willie's since she was nine. When her mother was alive, they would make the trip to Hartford several times a year. But her father never liked Miss Wilhelmina Perkins, as he called her. She was too much the maiden school teacher, a sister-in-law too outspoken for his taste, always trying to turn his dear Ellie against him whenever he lost a job or drank a bit too much. When his wife died, so did Marilyn's visits to Hartford.

Willie, however, put great stock in the promises she made to her dying sister, always prepared to step in if and when the situation called for it. She insisted on monthly hand-written reports from Marilyn and every October, armed with gifts of flannel pajamas and second-hand books, she made the bus trip to Fall River, to make sure her niece's reports were, indeed, accurate and she was being properly cared for. That one weekend each year, father and daughter pulled together, operating out of the unspoken fear that Aunt Willie would try to pull them apart. Now, there was no putting them back together.

Marilyn discovered she was pregnant right after Willie's visit last October. She never told her aunt, not after her father's reaction: he would never forgive her for the shame and she would never forgive his drunken, abusive outrage. He sent her to St. Agnes and she continued faking her monthly reports. What else could she do? But now she was counting on Aunt Willie's promise to look after her always. That's all she had. That, and her good looks, of course, good enough, she hoped, to land her a rich husband. Marilyn's thoughts trailed off into the world of possibilities and for a moment she actually forgot she was in an airless bus station with a wailing infant and no future. But her reprieve was short lived.

Standing in front of her, as though manifested by some magic trick, was a very tall, very beige woman, looking down at Marilyn, commanding answers to her questions.

"Young lady? Excuse me, young lady, I don't mean to interfere, but is your baby ill?"

The woman was all light tan — not in a striking, summery way, but in a bland, oatmeal sort of way. Her small light brown eyes were barely distinguishable against her freckled skin and once-blonde hair, all of which seemed to blend into her long-skirted tan dress. But there was nothing placid about the woman herself.

"I don't know what's wrong with her," Marilyn said. "She just keeps crying and crying and nothing I do works."

"Is she hungry? Have you fed her?"

"I tried. On the bus. Twice." Marilyn pointed to the half-empty bottle of formula she'd taken from the nursery, haphazardly tucked into the side pocket of her purse. "She just keeps crying. I'm about ready to die from all her fussing."

"It's so hard, I know. Your first, no doubt. Here, let me have her." The woman held out her arms and Marilyn happily surrendered Natalie. "Oh, she's so new. Can't be more than a few days old." She flushed in obvious delight.

A few coos and strokes and Natalie started to settle right down. Here was a woman born to motherhood, Marilyn thought, born to raise my baby. Smiling up at the stranger, telling her how wonderful she was, Marilyn used the toe of her sneaker to edge

51

the heavy suitcase away from her and, then, slowly, very slowly, holding her purse against her body, she began inching across the bench. If she did it just right, small silent slides, while the woman focused on Natalie, she'd be across the bench and out of the bus station before anyone knew what happened.

"Oh, I can see you're in a hurry to leave," the woman said. "Don't forget this little one," she laughed, cooing against Natalie's cheek, "as though anyone could forget you. Give me another minute and I'll have her nice and quiet. Stomach problems, sure as can be. Rub her tummy in circles, like this." She demonstrated the movement for Marilyn. "She's going to be a colicky one. I can spot them a mile away."

Marilyn slumped against the bench, ashamed at being caught in the act of trying to escape. "It's so hot."

"What can you expect? It's July in the city! And, you've just given birth. No wonder you're hot. Probably tired senseless too. Where's your husband hiding himself? He should be right by your side helping every step of the way. My Sam was like that. Such a help. But not too many men are. Most disappear in search of a cold beer the minute they think you can't go after them. Well, I'll just wait with you. Might even give him a piece of my mind when he returns."

"Well, thanks. But, you see, well, he's not exactly here."

The woman continued rubbing Natalie's stomach. "Not here? Well, goodness, where is he then?" She looked hard at Marilyn, insisting that she answer.

"He's umm, well, he's umm, dead." Marilyn didn't have to fake the tears welling in her eyes.

"Oh, you poor thing. Couldn't have been the war. Timing's not right. No, it must have been something else. What was it dear?"

"A train wreck." Marilyn jutted out her chin. "It was a train wreck. A small freight train in Fall River where I come from.

He died almost instantly." Marilyn brushed at her eyes. "Two months ago."

"A train wreck? Don't hear about too many people dying from something like that. How awful for you." She held Marilyn's gaze as she handed Natalie back. "There, she's all quiet. About ready to sleep, I'd say. You poor thing. No husband and a new baby." She clucked her tongue and waved to a car parked outside the terminal's glass doors.

"That's Sam. He's always tooting that silly horn. We're here to pick up his sister but it seems her bus got delayed. I know," the woman said, suddenly inspired, "we'll take you where you're going, as long as it's not too far. That'll keep Sam occupied. He loves helping out."

Marilyn wiped her forehead with the back of her hand. She knew the sight she must look, but in this case it was probably a blessing. If she'd looked all put together, this woman might not have taken pity on her. "I'd kill for a ride. I can't bear the thought of another bus. I'm going to my Aunt Willie's on Palm Street. It's somewhere off this real long street called Blue Hills Avenue."

"If it's anywhere in Hartford, my Sam will know where it is. He's a salesman. Fuller Brush. Ever hear of it? He sells every kind of household brush you could imagine, and some you couldn't." She chuckled at her own joke. "He knows every inch of every street in this city."

"How can I ever repay you?" Marilyn asked as she climbed into the back seat, knowing there was no way in the world she could repay anybody for anything. But asking was the only polite thing to do.

"Just be the best mother you can be," the woman answered cheerfully. "Take good care of your little one. I raised five myself. Nothing easy about it. But you're young. It's easier when you're young, believe me."

Marilyn didn't believe her. And she wasn't interested in any words of wisdom as they made their way through the streets of Hartford.

"I'll be good to her," Marilyn finally promised, figuring that if all this woman wanted for her kindness was a promise, the least she could do was comply. "But she'd better be good right back."

NINE

Marilyn let out a sigh of relief when they arrived at Aunt Willie's house. Finally, the trip, and her troubles, were over. She stood on the sidewalk waving good-bye to Helen and Sam Long, promising to visit someday, knowing she'd never see them again. Nice enough people, Marilyn decided, but much too ordinary for her new life, which was to have no resemblance whatsoever to the mill town existence she'd left behind. Marilyn watched Sam's black Ford drive out of sight before she turned to appreciate her new home.

"Ohmygod," she cried out, frantically searching the block to see if the Longs were coming back for her, realizing they'd dropped her off on the wrong street. She stared hard at the number on the house: 256. It was the right number. So it had to be the wrong street. It just had to be. But she'd watched very carefully as they'd turned off Blue Hills Avenue and followed the next long street all the way down to Palm. No, it was the right street. And, apparently, the right house, just not the one she remembered.

The house she'd visited with her mother was a grand, gingerbread palace, perfect for a princess-in-waiting. This one was sturdy and practical, made of ugly brownstone and small windows without shutters. The wooden porch needed painting, as did the two rocking chairs off to one side. Although decently groomed, with beds of geraniums and impatience along the front, the yard was small, patches of once-green lawn burned yellow by the summer sun. The street was lined with trees, just as she remembered, but they were no longer young, elegant trees; they were old and knotted, dwarfing every house in sight. It was a neat, tidy neighborhood, far away from city traffic or the sound of factory horns, but it was neither the house nor the neighborhood of her childhood memory.

"Shhh, Natalie, quiet now. Please, please be quiet," Marilyn said as Natalie began to cry. "Aunt Willie doesn't even know we're coming, so let's be very good when we surprise her. And don't worry, kiddo, we won't be here forever. This is a sign, I'm absolutely sure of it. It means we're not meant to stay here long. It means we're going to find us a man real soon."

<hr />

Willie welcomed them both, tsking and clucking about the goings on of young folks, and what the world was coming to, but in the same breath, declaring she was pleased that Marilyn had left her weak-willed father and come for a dose of real mothering. Since she'd taken early retirement from teaching, days had loomed too long for Willie. Now she could keep her promise to Ellie. It had always bothered her, not doing more to help raise Marilyn; she could see now what her neglect had come to.

Once Marilyn became accustomed to Aunt Willie's ways and figured out how to get around some of her more unreasonable rules about men and curfews and helping with chores, she actually found it easy to settle in and be cared for. More than being mothered herself, Marilyn liked the way Aunt Willie fussed over Natalie, as though she were her very own child.

Even though she was eager to start a life of her own with a rich attentive husband she had yet to find, Marilyn discovered that the living arrangements suited her nicely. She was able to claim and care for Natalie whenever it suited her; otherwise, she could count on Aunt Willie to take over the daily, thankless job of looking after her fretful, strong-willed daughter.

As she grew older, Natalie turned from a colicky infant to an out-of-sorts child with anxiety and stomach aches. Even as a youngster, Natalie was aware of an empty space inside of her that never seemed to fill up — like always being hungry — as though she knew that Marilyn's capricious use of free will had altered her life's course. When the feeling was really bad, she'd ask her mother for her favorite bedtime story; it was the story of Natalie's birth and how much she was loved because she'd been kept at all odds.

Natalie particularly liked the part about how Marilyn stood up to Sister Mary Anthony, telling her that *the child* had a name and that name was Natalie Marie Davenport. She would wriggle contentedly beneath the bed covers, feeling that all the misplaced pieces of her life had been found and put together. It was a delicious feeling. It was something to hold on to. But then her mother always spoiled it.

At the end of the story, Marilyn would kiss her daughter on the cheek and then whisper in her ear. "And now, Natalie, you must be a very good little girl, and you must always listen to Mama." Winding her index finger around a strand of Natalie's hair, she would look deep into her daughter's eyes, studying her face, admiring her looks. Natalie's sable hair had softened into a rich chestnut color that seemed to capture and then reflect even the smallest amount of light. Her creamy skin tanned golden in the summer; her hazel eyes were neither blue nor green, but a combination of both, the color of sea and sky. But it was her smile, and the small, single dimple, that promised to captivate hearts. "You have the looks to get anything you want," Marilyn would say, "so don't go settling for small potatoes. You must make a plan to have a very good life."

Long after every light in the house had been turned off, Natalie would lie awake wondering just what kind of a plan would be good enough to satisfy her mother who had sacrificed everything for her.

———◆———

The first time Natalie was consciously aware of Enif's presence, she was six years old, lying in bed, unable to sleep, her head filled with worries over her mother's bedtime mandate. She was certain she'd be punished if she didn't find a way to be good, although she thought she was quite good already. Somehow she had to find a way to be even better. She had to make a plan, and she wasn't at all sure what that meant. Natalie pressed on her stomach with both hands wishing she could make the pain go away. It was then that Enif arrived.

There was only the slightest flutter of air and light, but Natalie noticed it immediately. "Who are you?" she asked into the darkened room, curious but unafraid. When there was no response, she asked again. "Who are you?" Still, there was no answer, but Natalie began to feel soothed, as though a warm blanket had been thrown over her, an enchanted blanket woven with fairy dust and rainbows and enough magic to take away all of a little girl's worries and stomach aches. Natalie slept peacefully the entire night, Enif's presence comforting her in the way that being rocked to sleep in her mother's arms might have done.

The next time she was aware of Enif was on her seventh birthday, a sweltering July afternoon in 1954. "We're having peanut butter and jelly. And tea," she told him. She was eating lunch alone in the back yard, picnicking on a plaid cotton blanket, a new Toni doll by her side. The doll, hastily wrapped in leftover wedding paper, without a bow or card, had been given to her that morning just as her mother left for work. Aunt Willie's present — cheeseburgers and ice cream sundaes at Jensen's Soda Shop — would come that evening.

"Here, have some." Natalie broke off a corner of her sandwich and placed it on the blue and white plate that belonged to her tea set. She then poured lemonade into the small cup. "It's not really tea," she confessed. "I'm not allowed. But it's very, very good. Aunt Willie made it." Taking a sip from her cup, she insisted that her friend do the same. "Let me help you," she suggested, and took a sip from Enif's cup as well. Soon, both lunches were gone and Natalie laid back on the blanket feeling very satisfied.

"See my new doll." She held her Toni doll up to the sky. "She's my best friend. Except for you. I like you best." It was a perfect afternoon, now that her friend had come to wish her a happy birthday. She laughed out loud, a light, lilting sound that lingered in the air.

"Let's play house. I'll be the mother." Natalie began skipping across the yard to the play house she built from old blankets and boxes she'd discovered in Willie's attic. Feeling a sudden stirring of breeze, she halted and looked up, digging her toes into an area of the yard that was more dirt than grass.

"Don't go. Let's play." Dropping her doll to the ground, Natalie put her hands on her hips, insisting that her friend stay. "Don't go, don't go," she cried, as Enif moved father and farther away. Then she became silent. As though the wind could speak, she tilted her head to one side and listened. "Yes. Yes. Okay," she answered. "But come back. Please come back."

Enif was almost out of the earth plane when Natalie hollered upward, "My name's Natalie. What's yours?"

Enif glowed with delight and sent his name down to her, tumbling along the air currents, rustling through the leaves of fully-bloomed trees. Natalie listened until she had her answer and then called back to the largest tree she could see, certain that's where her friend lived. "Edith. That's a nice name."

Natalie sat down on the ground, hugging her new doll tightly to her chest. "Edith is such a nice name. I'll call you Edith, too."

TEN

It was October 1958 and they were still living with Aunt Willie. Eleven-year-old Natalie was sitting at the kitchen table, toying with the hot oatmeal she hated, waiting for Willie to make her favorite breakfast food — warm cinnamon toast. She took small spoonfuls of the dreaded cereal, knowing she wouldn't be allowed the toast without some sign of having eaten "what's good for her." In about ten minutes it would be time to leave for school.

Marilyn breezed into the kitchen. She poured herself a cup of coffee, fixed the bow on her black and gold waitress uniform, and then began an assortment of bodily contortions in an attempt to straighten the seams of her stockings.

"Damn things," she muttered redoing the back garter. "Too tight, too loose, never straight enough. I should just wear bobby sox like the other girls and forget all this human torture. But then that's no way to catch a man, is it?" She winked at her daughter. "Wear sexy stockings and heels high enough to make 'em drool. Now there's a motto to live and die by. And it'll prove me right, just wait and see." She patted her newly permed hair, readjusting the wave over her left eye, and then sat down at the kitchen table.

Leaning on her elbows, Marilyn edged herself toward Natalie, flashing her brightest smile and using her best voice. "Listen, sweetie, don't take this wrong or nothin, but I don't want that colored girl here when I get home tonight. I finally landed a date with Ralph Swit...Swit-something-or-other. He's Polish, I think. But don't hold that against him," she laughed. "He's rich, I just know he is, which means he could be my meal ticket out of here. No offense Aunt Willie, but, honestly, we can't stay here forever."

Willie shrugged her shoulders and grunted in response, her back turned as she continued fixing her own breakfast. For eleven years now, she'd been listening to how Marilyn couldn't stay with them forever, while turning down every proposal from every man eager to marry her. None of them quite good enough. None of them rich enough.

Natalie wasn't the least bit interested in Ralph whoever-he-was. Pearl was her only concern. "But it's all planned," she argued. "Pearl's coming right after school and staying until Ozzie and Harriet is over." How could her mother say Pearl couldn't come over when it had all been arranged? Pearl Blackwell was her best friend. Her only friend.

"The answer is no, plain and simple," Marilyn said.

"But mama, please. It's for school. We're working on a project for extra credit, a mobile made out of coat hangers and construction paper. Mrs. Blackwell even bought us three kinds of glitter and Aunt Willie promised us TV dinners."

Marilyn scowled, casting a deadly look in Willie's direction. "Aunt Willie, springing for TV dinners? My, my, what's the occasion? I'm sure she means well, Natalie. After all, isn't Aunt Willie always trying to do right by us? But tonight that wouldn't be the case. Having that Negro girl here all the time is simply not good for my image. I don't want Ralph getting the wrong impression by thinking we have colored friends."

"Mama," Natalie said, taking a breath deep enough to steady her voice. This had been burning in her a long time; she had to say it even if it made her mother angry. "You know how you tell me the story of when I was born and how you hated it when Sister Mary Anthony wouldn't call me by my name? Well you do that with Pearl all the time. You never call her by her name."

"Why you ungrateful —!" Marilyn took Natalie's chin in her hand and squeezed hard. "That's an awful big mouth you have young lady. Taking sides with a colored girl against your own mother. Apologize right now."

Natalie swallowed hard and lowered her eyes. She wouldn't let her mother see tears. And neither would she apologize.

Marilyn squeezed her daughter's chin even harder. "Did you hear me? Say you're sorry."

"Marilyn, that's enough. Stop right now and let go of that child!" In one quick movement, Willie had turned from the stove, slammed a spatula on the counter and straightened her large frame to its full height, placing both hands squarely on her hips.

"Not until she apologizes. Now apologize," Marilyn yelled, never once loosening her grip on Natalie's face. "I don't know where you get your attitude from, but I won't have it. It's high time you learned to listen when I speak."

"I'm sorry," Natalie said, her voice catching in her throat, her eyes never once leaving the checkered vinyl tablecloth. But, she wasn't sorry at all. Pearl deserved to be called by her name, and, even more, she deserved to have Natalie defend her. She was her one true friend. Pretty much everyone else at school either ignored or made fun of Natalie. They never invited her to parties and only a few were allowed to come to her house to play. She heard them whispering and giggling in gym one day, and it all came down to one indisputable fact: Natalie was illegitimate. Nobody believed Marilyn's story about her husband dying in a train wreck. But Pearl didn't care about that. Pearl was a true friend, and it was very important to Natalie to be a true friend back.

"That's better," Marilyn said. "Look what you made me do." The imprint of her fingers had stained Natalie's face like crimson

63

birthmarks. "Here, look at me. You have splotches all over your chin." She rubbed Natalie's skin, trying to even up her skin tone. "We can't have that beautiful face marred, now can we? Such a beauty. You really are such a beauty. But your behavior, Natalie, it's just not good enough. You're always going to have to obey someone. If not me, your husband, so you might as well start right now, young lady, or you're going to have a mighty miserable life. Now eat."

Natalie wanted to ask who her mother obeyed, but instead she began spooning nearly-cold oatmeal into her mouth, holding her breath and swallowing in huge gulps so that the gooey mush went directly from her lips to her stomach with no time to rest in between. Only when she had finished, would she be allowed to have a slice of Aunt Willie's hot cinnamon toast.

Natalie's eyes darted around the room looking for something to distract her as she continued shoveling cereal into her mouth. This was her favorite place — Aunt Willie's blue and white kitchen where sunshine poured in every morning and afternoon, and every nook and cranny was filled with the aroma of warm cinnamon and freshly brewed coffee. It was the largest room in the house and sadly in need of repair. In front of the sink, the blue linoleum floor was worn so thin it was actually black. There was a smaller worn spot in front of the stove. The white porcelain sink was chipped and stained despite bleach and cleanser and hours of elbow grease, and most of the woodwork needed repainting. Natalie's eyes rested on the pots of red geraniums lined up on the far window sill; maybe if she stared long and hard enough, she could actually see one grow.

"Are you listening to me?" Marilyn asked, interrupting her daughter's geranium watch. "Stop gagging on that cereal. Honestly, you put on such a show. Just forget it." Marilyn pushed the bowl aside. "Here, eat your toast and listen good: I don't want any funny stuff tonight. I let you and this Pearl —

see smart aleck I used her name, just for you — I let you and her stay friends because Aunt Willie keeps telling me it's a good thing, that maybe you'll finally get rid of this imaginary friend you call Edith. If you ask me, imaginary is better than colored. But you do anything — and I mean anything at all — to hurt my chances with Ralph and it's all over. Are we clear?"

"Okay, mama, okay. Really, I understand." Natalie just wanted this conversation to be over and done with. If it kept up much longer, Pearl would leave for school without her and she'd be so late she'd have to run all the way. "I know, I have an idea." Natalie brightened. It really was a good idea. "What if I go to Pearl's house instead?"

"You just don't give up, do you? I don't ever want you inside there. When you call for her, you'd better be waiting outside on the porch like I told you a thousand times. Never inside, do you hear? Never. Who knows what you'll catch. All those colored houses are the same, filled with the stink of ammonia. Makes you wonder just what they're trying to scrub away — oh, goodness, look at this —" Marilyn checked her watch — "I'm going to miss my bus, and you're going to be late for school."

With arms spread wide, Marilyn bent down next to her daughter. "Here, give your mama a big hug and kiss." Natalie did as she was told, careful not to muss her mother's hair. With index finger pressed to her daughter's nose, Marilyn recited her daily parting line, "I'm the queen and you're the princess and if we plan real hard we can get ourselves a prince charming and a huge, wonderful castle." She then stood up and put on her coat, taking great pains not to crush the perfectly tied bow at the back of her uniform.

Halfway out the front door, Marilyn called back into the kitchen, her voice once again sugary. "Oh, by the way, Nat, don't slip up and call me mama in front of Ralph tonight. Your little mistake frightened the pants off Woody. Once he learned I had a kid, it was good-bye Charlie. You know the drill. You're my little sister until I say otherwise."

ELEVEN

When the Blackwell family moved into 272 Palm Street during the summer of 1958, they became the first colored family on a street comprised mainly of white Protestants. Until then, nearly all the Negroes lived north of Palm Street, and most of the Catholics, south and west. The Blackwells were colored and Catholic. Marilyn, who had herself faced the sting of neighborhood censure, was pleased to join forces in a common ground of disapproval, gossiping with others about what those kind of people would do to property values. She was mortified that her own daughter had befriended the youngest of the Blackwell brood.

Both eleven years old, Natalie and Pearl became inseparable from the moment they laid eyes on one another, as though they'd known each other forever, or as Aunt Willie observed, "as though they'd been born side-by-side in the same hospital and raised as best friends ever since."

From across the street, Natalie had watched white-gloved movers remove furniture from the van, carrying each piece into the Blackwell house as though handling priceless treasures. Peering from behind a massive maple tree, Natalie counted six mattresses. Six! Was her mother right about all colored folks breeding themselves onto welfare? She tried to remember precisely what her mother had said about Negro houses and how they were different from everyone else's. As far as Natalie could tell, everything they had looked the same as theirs, only newer and a lot prettier.

Deep in thought, Natalie didn't see Pearl come out of the house until she caught sight of a chubby, mahogany-colored arm waving madly in the air. Pearl was smiling, all white teeth and bright eyes, in a round, dark face encircled by braids that bobbed with her every movement.

"Want some?" Pearl called across the street, holding up a fistful of strawberry Twizzlers.

Natalie came out from behind the tree, figuring it mustn't have been such a terrific hiding place if she was spotted so quickly. She took a few hesitant steps in Pearl's direction, glancing over her shoulder to see if Marilyn was watching. Convinced that she wasn't, Natalie bolted across the street,

"They're my favorite," Natalie said. "Thanks." She took one and dangled it in her mouth like a long cigarette. "I've got some pennies. Wanna' go to the little store?"

"What's that?"

"It's a little store," Natalie giggled, jingling the coins in her pocket. "It's this real tiny store, down the street and up the block. It has the best penny candy in the whole wide world. Come on, let's run."

Halfway down the street, their hands brushed against one another as their bodies collided, each attempting to stay on the narrow sidewalk, running and laughing all the way. By the time they reached their destination, breathless, beads of sweat dripping off their foreheads, Natalie's small white hand was firmly grasping the larger dark hand of her new friend.

———◆———

It was in the summer of 1960, shortly after their thirteenth birthdays, that the two girls took the serious step of becoming blood sisters. They'd packed a lunch of peanut butter sandwiches, potato chips and Cokes with the idea of going off and exploring on their bikes for the day. Taking roads they'd never been on, they found themselves at the entrance to an ancient cemetery. The small brass sign read Old City Burying Ground.

"Let's ride through," Pearl said, straddling her bike.

"No way. It's creepy. Let's just stay on this road." Natalie started walking her bike forward, past the entrance.

"Oh, come on."

"No." Natalie continued walking.

Chicken!" Pearl called after her.

Natalie kept walking slowly, steering her bike around ruts on the side of the road, her chin jutted high in the air.

"Chickeeeen!" Pearl taunted, tucking her hands under her arm pits and flapping her elbows wildly. "Chicken, chicken, Natalie's a chicken,"

"For Pete's sake, you're a pain in the you-know-what." Natalie picked up the front of her bike, slamming the tire down as she turned it around. "You always have to have your own way." Natalie readjusted her headband to push stray hairs away from her face. She hated giving in, but even more, she hated being made fun of. She jumped on her bike and pushed past Pearl, peddling down the cemetery's snake-like road.

Pearl caught up with her and together they rode so slowly that the wheels of their bikes wiggled and teetered, making them barely able to maintain balance. "Don't be mad, Nat, I was just kidding."

"You know I hate that."

"I know. I'm sorry." Pearl grinned at her until Natalie had no choice but to smile back. "But isn't this neat?"

"You find the strangest things neat. It's just a bunch of old markers sitting on top of a bunch of old dead people."

"But who are they? And do their ghosts still lurk..." Pearl reached over and tickled the back of Natalie's neck.

"Stop that!"

"Stop what?"

"You know what. Grabbing my neck and trying to make me think it's a ghost."

"Grabbing your neck? I didn't grab your neck." Pearl raised both hands innocently above her handlebars, palms up. "I'm right here. How could I grab your neck?"

"All right, you *touched* it. Admit that you touched it, or I'm not moving from this spot." Natalie stopped and straddled her bike, waiting for Pearl's admission.

Pearl, now in front of Natalie, stopped and looked back at her friend, grinning widely. "Maybe it was old man Ackers reaching his bony hand out from the grave, trying to get you to stop right in front of him so he could gobble you up. And look, you played right into it." She pointed to an ancient marker beside Natalie. "You stopped right in front of his stone."

"Stop it, or I'm going back right now."

"Did you hear that?" Pearl asked hopping on her bike and riding out ahead. "Hurry, Nat, get on your bike now!"

"What?" Natalie looked around. She hadn't heard a thing. Everything was perfectly quiet. Maybe too quiet. "What did you hear?" she called out to Pearl, now a considerable distance ahead of her.

"Hurry, Nat. Get over here now, before it's too late."

Not taking any chances, Natalie peddled fast, away from the grave of Thomas Ackers. Pearl had stopped so Natalie could catch up, waiting at the last headstone in the cemetery, where the narrow road split in two. As soon as Natalie was close enough to hear, Pearl emitted low, groaning ghostly sounds.

"You're a jerk," Natalie said. "There are no ghosts, only human jerks, like you."

"So why were you afraid?"

"I wasn't. I was just pretending to be. But I'm tired of this place. I'm hot. And hungry. Let's get out of here."

"And crabby," Pearl observed. She pointed to a paved road on the left that lead up and away from the cemetery. "Let's see where that goes."

They rode until they came to a fence and huge iron gate. The sign on it read Central Quarry and Paving. No Trespassing.

"Great. Now what? This isn't fun anymore." Natalie turned her bike around, ready to head back through the cemetery.

"Hang on," Pearl said. "Look, the fence ends down by that big tree. It doesn't connect all the way around the woods. We can leave our bikes here and walk to the other side."

"It says NO TRESPASSING. Can't you read?"

"It'll be fun, Nat. We said we wanted to explore. Don't forget your lunch." Pearl ran out ahead, swinging her own lunch bag, giving Natalie little choice but to follow. But she wasn't happy, kicking the ground as she slowly caught up to Pearl.

Together, they crunched through leaves that had died seasons ago, skirting around trees and ducking low-growing branches. Eventually, they came out on a gravel service road high above the city. They walked to its far edge and plopped down on a bank of dirt, dry and dusty, glittering with stone fragments; they were perched along the cliff of the city's largest quarry. They looked down on walls of blasted rock — sheer, sharp walls that dropped hundreds of feet to a pit of solid ledge where most of the quarry's work took place. The trucks on that ledge looked like miniature toys and, although the noise of their labor filtered upward, it was nearly impossible to tell that they were actually moving and working. Shading their eyes with their hands, Natalie and Pearl looked out across the horizon, a panoramic view of the world beyond.

Pearl extended her arm, taking in the scene. "Wasn't this worth it?"

"I guess," Natalie said, blowing a bug from her forehead with an upward sweep of breath.

"Nat. Just look. It's like being on top of a huge mountain."

"Yeah, with the center of it carved out waiting for us to fall in." Natalie peeked over the edge and her stomach lurched. "It's scary, if you ask me."

"See those little trees, and those violets growing in the rock. I mean, isn't that cool, how things survive no matter what?" Pearl leaned over and pointed to the small saplings and clusters of wild violets growing out and upward from the mined walls. "I think it's more nice than scary."

"You would," Natalie said, sliding back a few feet.

They ate their lunch in silence, pressing their bodies into the layers of dirt and crushed stone, the quarry below parched under the intense summer sun. But a mountain-like breeze, blowing in from the horizon, swept over their bodies, keeping them cool and comfortable. Off to the left, in the far distance, a solitary hawk circled the sky.

There on that lazy afternoon in a place totally removed from their real world, Natalie and Pearl took the solemn oath of blood sisters, an oath that would bind them forever. They searched the gravel, each looking for a perfect sliver of stone. The tip of it had to be sharp, but not too thin or it would break with the first attempt, and yet not so thick that it wouldn't penetrate skin with a few tries.

"I've got mine," Pearl announced first, holding up an arrow-shaped stone of silver and dark gray.

"Me, too," Natalie called, running back to join Pearl.

71

On the count of three, they each poised an angular piece of rock over their index finger and began jabbing away. One jab after another. With each unsuccessful stab, they winced and screamed. Pearl was the first to draw blood.

"Hurry," Pearl shouted. "It's just a tiny blob. It won't last forever." She squeezed her finger, trying to keep the blood flowing. "Hurry. I'm not doing this again."

"For Pete's sake, I'm trying. You've got more blood. Your fingers are fatter than mine. "

"They are not!"

"Are so." Natalie took a deep breath and held it. Instead of jabbing at the tip of her finger, she turned the thin slab of stone into a knife, slicing sideways into the skin. "Oh, God, oh, God," she cried, exhaling so violently she nearly vomited.

"Nat, what's wrong, what's the matter?" Pearl had been lying on her back, giving great attention to keeping her finger squeezed and the small droplets of blood flowing. She jumped up on both knees and bent over Natalie.

"I don't know." The pain left as quickly as it had appeared. Natalie wiped her cheeks with the back of her soiled hands, taking long, steadying breaths. "Right when I sliced my finger, right then and there, it felt like the stone went through my stomach instead of my finger. It was almost like a knife."

"You okay now?" Pearl asked, sitting back down on the ground, brushing dirt and stones from her knees. "Did you draw blood?"

"You jerk." Natalie laughed through her tears, squeezing her index finger real hard. "Yes I drew blood."

They sat cross-legged facing one another. Pearl placed her finger on top of Natalie's. Together they rubbed and pressed until all signs of red had disappeared and all that was left was a sticky, smeary mess, convinced that each would now have a drop of the other's blood forever flowing in her veins.

"Friends forever," they chanted. "Loyal to the death. No parent or teacher; no friend or foe; no boy or girl shall ever break the bond we have set in blood."

Feeling content, almost giddy, with the rush of intimacy, the girls sat hugging their knees, looking out at the horizon.

"What do you believe?" Pearl asked.

"About what?"

"I don't know. God. Life." Pearl picked up a handful of stone fragments and began flipping them like jacks, from her palm to the back of her hand and back again, seeing how many she could catch. Only three.

"I can do better than that!" Natalie said, counting out ten stones.

"So, what do you believe?" Pearl asked.

"You always get too serious, Pearl. I don't know. We don't talk about stuff like that at home. Marilyn's not into it. But if you want to know about signs and horoscopes —"

"Come on, Nat. Seriously." Pearl fixed her gaze on a small plane off in the horizon. "I'm afraid of going to hell."

"Why?"

"Because sometimes I have really bad thoughts, and even when I confess them, I'm not really sorry."

"Like what?

"Sometimes, late at night when I can't sleep I actually dream up ways to kill Alberta Lindstrom."

"Well, she is mean. More to you, than me. I wouldn't mind killing her. Maybe we should come up with a plot," Natalie giggled.

"Promise not to tell?

"What?" Natalie leaned in toward Pearl, eager for her secret.

"Promise?"

"I promise, already, I promise." Natalie formed an exaggerated cross over her heart.

"I spit in Alberta's Coke."

"You what?"

"I spit in her Coke." Pearl started to laugh.

"Gross!" Natalie stuck out her tongue. "When? How?"

"At Maxwell Drug one day after school, right before the end of last year. Everybody was at the counter having Coke and fries. You were with me, but you were over looking at magazines. Anyway, remember how I was so upset because they were hassling me about sitting at the counter with them and I sat down, anyway, right next to Alberta? She made me feel like a piece of shit."

Natalie nodded, vaguely remembering the incident.

"Anyway, I never told you, but when Alberta turned her back to me, I leaned over real cool like and spit in her Coke. I was half wishing I had some kind of disease that would kill her."

"Yeah, but then you'd die too."

"Right. Instead we both lived. But I spit in her Coke!" Pearl said the words with exaggerated evilness, her large brown eyes nearly popping out of their sockets. "You have to promise, never ever to tell," she reminded her blood sister with extreme seriousness.

"I already promised. I'd never break a promise to you. We're blood sisters. Even if we weren't, I wouldn't."

"I know. Anyway, it's those kinds of things that make me afraid of going to hell," Pearl said. "I keep saying how I want to help my people when I grow up and then I have all these impure thoughts and do these crummy things."

"I thought impure thoughts were about sex." Natalie lowered her voice. "I heard some high school boys talking about French kissing yesterday. They were hanging around outside Jensen's when I went with Aunt Willie for an ice cream. It sounded disgusting! She almost died of embarrassment. Told the boys to clean up their act. I was mortified."

"Oh man. It is disgusting, though," Pearl said. "Nathan described it to me in total detail last year. Gross!"

"And you never told me? I hate you! I wish I had an older brother, then I'd get the real scoop. You have to promise to tell me everything, always."

"Yes ma'am," Pearl saluted.

Natalie sat up straight and threw a handful of stones down over the edge. They sat and listened for the sound of stone hitting stone, but it never came. Natalie stood and looked down. "Cripes, that's far," she said, rotating her feet into the gravel to keep from losing her balance.

"Watch out," Pearl warned, "or you'll end up dead meat."

"Then we'd know about hell for sure. As far as Marilyn's concerned I'll never be good enough for heaven."

"My Uncle Bobby says we never really die. That we keep coming back as different people until we get it right, or something like that. He almost died when he was in the war. He says he saw things that changed his whole way of thinking about life and death. He says he even knows some of his other lives."

"That's a good one," Natalie said. "Next life I want to be rich and have a mother who wants me." She started toward the path they'd followed into the quarry. "It's getting late; we better go."

"This will be our secret place," Pearl said, catching up to Natalie. "For ever and ever."

———◆———

Natalie and Pearl took their blood-sister status seriously, determined to see each other through all their troubles, at home and at school. Pearl helped Natalie keep Marilyn's demands in perspective, trying to make her see that, while she couldn't change her mother, Natalie could try to develop a better attitude about things. After all, Pearl was quick to point out, at least she had a nice home and an aunt who was pretty okay. In return,

75

Natalie listened to her friend's dreams about changing the world, all the while trying to keep her from saying and doing things that would further alienate people who seemed to dislike her solely on the basis of her skin color.

It was nearly winter and the brisk, late-day air stung the girls' legs as they walked home from school, their thighs chafing with every step. It was time to switch from bobby socks to tights.

"I know how you feel," Natalie said. "But you can't go getting into fights all the time."

"Why not? I could have decked her." Pearl jabbed her fists into the air.

"Think of what my mother would have said! Just think of that. If you think she's against us being friends now —"

Pearl arched her head toward the curb and spit out a lump of saliva and tears. "Stupid Alberta Lindstrom. We should have made a plan to kill her! She's got everybody in school against me. Stupid pastie-faced Howie actually blocked my way to the lunch table and told me to sit at the back of the room."

"I know. It's all over school," Natalie said.

"We moved here to get away from all that."

"Was it as bad as here?"

"Worse," Pearl said haltingly. "You can't even imagine. Separate schools, separate busses, separate everything. Once..." she shook her head, as though she still couldn't believe what she was remembering.

"Once what?"

"Nothing, forget it."

"No secrets. We promised. Once what"

Pearl used the back of her hand to swipe away remaining bits of saliva; she swallowed hard before continuing. "I was walking home from school, it was nearly a five mile walk and every day the bus with white kids would pass right by me and drive only blocks away from my house. It never stopped to pick me up, even though there was always room. One day, this older white boy came up behind me, out of nowhere it seemed. He must have been hiding in the bushes, just waiting. He started calling me all kinds of names, really ugly names. I just kept walking, trying to ignore him. Then, he started beating up on me. He slapped my face so hard, my nose started to bleed, and I fell to the ground. Just then the bus came around the bend. It stopped and for one stupid minute, I actually though the bus driver was going to get out and help me. Instead he hollers for the boy to hurry and get on, and then he slams the door shut leaving me bent over on that dirt road. All the dust from the tires kicked up in my face and when I finally looked up, I saw all those laughing white faces pressed to the back window."

"Oh, Pearl —" Natalie started, then stopped, not knowing what to say.

"That's when we decided to move up north. My father promised things would be different here. In a way it is, but only on the outside. Inside, most people feel the same as the whites down south, they're just not honest about it."

Natalie reached up to put an arm around her friend's shoulder. Pearl had suddenly grown tall, and they no longer walked eye to eye or waist to waist, as they had just a short time ago. "I'm sorry," she whispered.

"Why did they have to tear his picture?" Pearl took the torn magazine picture from her notebook, holding the ragged halves together as they walked. "I bet they don't even know who he is."

"It's a colored guy," Natalie shrugged. "That's all they need to know, you know that. I don't get why you carry it around. You're just asking for trouble."

"You sound like your mother. Next you'll be telling me it doesn't matter what I think or feel, just *package* myself for everyone else!"

"Maybe that's not so bad," Natalie said defensively, jutting out her chin. "I mean, look, you know how everyone feels about negroes. Couldn't you just leave the picture home and not always say everything you're thinking?"

"Some friend you are." Pearl stomped out ahead of Natalie until the tears came so hard she collapsed on the curb a few blocks from her house, crying and hiccupping at the same time. Natalie sat down next to her, both of them shaking and chilled in the dampening dusk.

"I can't go home like this," Pearl said, taking deep breaths and wiping tears from her face. "My mother gets so upset. She's ready to move again."

"Pearl, I'm sorry. I didn't mean it, about the picture and all. You have every right to be just who you are and to bring it to school if you want." The torn picture was on top of Pearl's notebook. Natalie ran her fingers across the jagged edges, sliding the two halves together as close as possible. "Martin Luther King," she whispered into her friend's ear. "We'll tape it. He'll be good as new, and still handsome, even with this ugly scar." Both girls started to laugh, tears streaming down their faces, arms around one another, rocking back and forth on the cold asphalt curbing.

Pearl took both pieces of the photo and tucked them back into her notebook. "I like having his picture. It helps get me through, you know, when the kids are being mean, and it reminds me of what I want to do."

"I know, I know!" Natalie puffed out her chest "work side-by-side with Martin Luther King and save the world from suffering and bigotry." She'd heard it often enough that she was able to recite verbatim her friend's statement of destiny. Natalie admired Pearl's determination, wishing she could be equally dedicated to something, often wondering if that was the missing piece in her ability to please Marilyn, who showed just as much dedication to her cause of finding a rich husband.

They walked silently the rest of the way to Pearl's house.

"I wish you could come in," Pearl said.

"You know I can't. Besides, I have an assignment."

"You mother wouldn't know. We can study together."

"Not that kind of assignment. Marilyn," Natalie said, exaggerating the name, purposely not calling her mother, "bought me a present yesterday and I have to read five pages every day before she gets home from work."

"What is it?" Pearl asked.

"You're gonna die."

"So kill me. What is it?"

"How to Win Friends and Influence People."

"What do you mean?"

"I mean, she bought me the book, *How to Win Friends and Influence People*, and I have to read five pages a day. She says it will help me make more friends."

Pearl wrinkled her nose. "You mean friends other than me? That's her real reason. We both know it."

Natalie shrugged in response. "You've got your problems and I definitely have mine, but, at least we have each other," Natalie said as they pressed their index fingers together.

"No matter what," Natalie mumbled under her breath as she walked away, feeling a stab of loneliness at the sound of Pearl's front door slamming shut, "we'll always have each other."

TWELVE

All of the dogwood trees along Palm Street had burst into bloom, transforming the neighborhood into a fairyland of pink and white. The sky, a delicate, nearly translucent blue, was dotted with wisps of white clouds. A soft summer-like breeze tickled the unseasonably warm air. Marilyn was sure it was all a sign. Finally, she had done things right, and the absolute perfection of this day was proof that her dreams were about to come true.

It was April 25, 1961. For Marilyn Davenport, this was the single most important day of her life. For her fourteen-year-old daughter, however, it was one of the most devastating.

It wasn't Ralph who finally married Marilyn on that warm April afternoon, but a skinny, plaid-trousered man with a broad smile and thinning hair. His name was Harry Golden, and he had the Midas touch. Everything seemed to come his way. Every scheme he invested in, every product he sold on the road from Florida to Maine, turned into cold, hard cash, and it was cash he was not afraid to lavish on the pretty Marilyn Davenport. Aside from his looks, which Marilyn was certain she could improve with a good sprucing up and less flashy clothes, nearly everything about Harry set well with Marilyn, including her new name —

Marilyn Golden — Mrs. Marilyn Golden. Finally, life had sent something good her way.

Having promoted herself to Harry as a God-fearing Catholic woman who could never go all the way without a wedding ring on her finger, Marilyn had no choice but to insist on a large church wedding. She knew it was the only way any self-respecting virgin of thirty-one would ever agree to marriage. After all, she argued, if a person waited that long for everything, it should be absolutely, positively, just right.

Harry's mother, however, had a showy display of chest pains whenever the happy coupled mentioned their plans. How could she invite all her friends to witness her Harry's denouncement of his Jewish heritage? She knew all about those Catholic weddings where the priest made the couple promise to have children and bring them up Catholic so they, in turn, could produce children who would be brought up Catholic. How could she invite her friends to that? Her poor Harry. Marrying a shiksa. For sure, God would strike her dead, and maybe that wouldn't be so bad.

In the end, Marilyn managed the politics of her marriage, by agreeing to a chapel wedding with only Willie, Natalie, and a best man in attendance. His mother would stay home and pretend the whole event never happened, shocking her friends later with tales of elopement. The reception at Willie's house would be small and, in payment for Marilyn's understanding, Harry promised to spend lots of money on a lavish honeymoon and a fabulous new home.

As much as Marilyn was on the lookout for signs of fatal doom, the wedding went off quietly and without a hitch. Natalie was pleased for her mother. Maybe now Marilyn would stop concentrating on what she needed to make her happy and just be happy.

While Natalie didn't really know Harry, mostly because Marilyn whisked him in and out of the house and never planned any time together for all three of them, she sensed he would make a good husband, maybe even a good father. It was exciting to think about starting over in a grand house where all the furniture would be new and she could decorate her room any way she wanted. Even though she worried about missing Aunt Willie and Pearl, Natalie was certain that Harry and her mother would buy a house close by, maybe even in the same school district. Everything would be the same, only better. In the end they would be one happy, dream-filled family.

Natalie had to agree with Marilyn: the day really did seem to hold the promise of a fabulous future. She enjoyed the quiet, simple wedding ceremony almost as much as she hated the noisy, liquor-filled reception back at Aunt Willie's.

All afternoon, Natalie tried to hide the way her nipples bulged against her pink chiffon dress by folding her arms across her chest and slouching ever so slightly. She stood in corners and against walls, wondering when the party would end so their new life could begin. Every so often, Natalie would catch Marilyn's disapproving look, combined with an array of hand signals that meant mingle, uncross your arms, stand up straight. Finally, late in the day, when Marilyn was able to break away from Harry and a small group of men chewing on their cigars, she walked straight over to Natalie, firmly uncrossing her arms and placing them down by her side.

"Natalie, sweetie, for goodness sakes, don't be ashamed of your body. How many times do I have to tell you, it's God's special gift to good women." Marilyn put her hands on her waist, jutted one hip out coquettishly and lowered her voice. "It's how we catch men," she confided with an exaggerated wink. Natalie wrinkled her nose in distaste, but obediently kept her arms by her side while Marilyn grabbed hold of her daughter's chin and tilted her face toward the light.

"I think you might be getting a zit. Right here." She picked at Natalie's skin with a long red fingernail. "Yep. Just starting. Use some Clearasil on that tonight." She patted Natalie on the head and then glided away to join her friends, mostly waitresses and some women who worked at the cosmetic counters of various department stores in downtown Hartford.

Floating from one group to another, Marilyn recounted the story of her luck. "I just knew it was a sign," she reminded them. "Here I had just bought this new lipstick, Rendezvous Red. I'll never forget that name," she giggled and winked, "and there I am, wearing it at work for the absolute, very first time. I mean the first time ever to touch my lips, and in walks Harry, this stranger who sits down right at my station, flashing me a smile that wouldn't quit. I mean, how can you ignore a sign like that? It was meant to be." In response, a bevy of shrilled voices attested to Marilyn's good fortune, reminding her not to forget the little people now that she was wedded and rich.

It seemed to Natalie that their small living room had shrunk over the past few hours, as guests sprawled across chairs and pushed at one another in a vague attempt at dancing in any spot where two people could stand together. A cast of cigarette smoke had settled over the room, punctuated by the smell of whiskey and perfume. Natalie tried drawing in full breaths as she pushed her way through the crowd, but only when she finally reached the kitchen was she able to take a long breath of air that pushed the heaviness from her lungs.

"That room is no place for a fourteen-year-old," Natalie giggled.

"Or for a sixty-nine year old," Aunt Willie answered.

Willie had spent most of the afternoon in the kitchen keeping busy with things Harry had hired others to do. "Aunt Willie, leave the dishes," Natalie said. "The caterers will do them before they leave." She walked over to the sink and touched Willie's

83

shoulder. "Besides, you'll spoil your new dress, and you look so pretty today."

Willie turned the water off slowly. First the hot faucet, then the cold. She took a blue and white checked dish towel and carefully dried her hands, all the time, keeping her back to Natalie. When she finally turned around, remnants of tears glistened in the corners of her eyes. Barely noticeable. But Natalie noticed.

"Aunt Willie?"

"Oh, don't mind me." Willie swiped at both eyes with the knuckle of her index finger. "An old woman indulging in sentiments." She sat down at the kitchen table, twisting the cotton dishtowel around her left hand and then unwrapping it, only to repeat the process over and over again.

"You're not old, Aunt Willie. Not even close to old." Natalie leaned over and touched a tendril of gray hair that had escaped from Willie's meticulously knotted French twist. Natalie pulled out a wooden chair from underneath the square kitchen table and sat down, scraping the legs of the chair on the floor as she edged closer to Willie.

"Do you think she'll be happy now?" Natalie asked.

"Who knows? She has what she's always wanted. But there's that old saying, be careful what you ask for, you might get it. So, who knows." Willie shrugged her broad shoulders. "You can't just decide what's going to make you happy and then go out and try to get it, like buying a loaf of bread or a pair of new shoes. You have to be open to things and then happiness will come. Naturally. Not artificially."

Natalie studied Willie's face. Her skin was creamy and smooth, almost flawless, the lines around her eyes adding a sense of character rather than age. It was easy to imagine how she must have looked as a young woman, with thick hair almost as deep and richly colored as Natalie's, and brown eyes that never seemed to hide from the truth. Yet, it seemed to Natalie in a sudden flash of perception that perhaps Willie had been hiding all of her life.

"Aunt Willie?" Natalie hesitated, then plunged ahead. "How come you never married? How come you never moved from this house?"

Brown eyes met hazel. Willie's voice was low and sad. "Afraid, I guess."

"Afraid? You?"

Willie didn't answer.

"Of what?" Natalie asked.

Still no answer. And then, slowly, she began to talk. "I don't know. Not measuring up, maybe. Not meeting expectations. I was very bright and really quite pretty. Not petite. But handsome looking. I think I was always afraid if I made a decision, it would be the wrong one and then the truly right choice would come along, and it would be too late."

Willie sat up straight and looked across the room as though seeing the distant lands she never visited. "My fatal flaw," she continued. "I wanted things to be perfect. And they never are you know. I wanted people to point and stare and even be a little envious. Look at her, they'd say, doing such wonderful things, making all the right choices. I became so paralyzed by that need to be perfect in everyone else's eyes that I just saved all my money waiting for that one opportunity. I never went anywhere, except for small trips here and there, but they didn't really count. I was really always waiting for that one perfect adventure to present itself. Or one perfect man. Who knows? Then, all of a sudden, it was too late."

Natalie sat quietly and waited for her aunt to continue. The sun streamed in from the window over the sink, causing her to squint against its intensity, but she didn't reposition her chair or get up for the glass of water she desperately wanted, afraid any word or movement might break the spell of this moment between her and Willie, between two women trying to sort out their place in the world. After a while, Willie continued, talking more to herself than to Natalie.

"I was like the man who won't spend his money on vacations for the family. He's going to save it all for one grand, glorious trip when the kids are all grown, and then his wife dies two days before the last child graduates from high school. That was me. Saving my life for something that never came along — saving and not doing — not letting myself settle. Then my parents got sick, one after the other, and everyone expected I would stay home and take care of them. So I did." She looked hard at Natalie, willing her niece to understand what she was saying about lost opportunities.

"And then we came," Natalie said. "Then you lived your life for us."

"My destiny was set long before that. I could have made other choices. You, my dear, were a blessing."

"Wasn't there ever anyone, you know, anyone you loved?"

"Once. When I was twenty-four. It was the best year of my life."

"What happened, did he die or something?" That's the only reason Natalie could imagine for not marrying your one true love.

"No." Willie hesitated before going on. The schoolhouse clock on the wall ticked loudly as it moved to the next minute. "He wasn't good enough."

"What do you mean? Was he awful to you or something?"

"No, he was wonderful. The kindest, sweetest man I've ever known."

"Aunt Willie?"

"He delivered milk."

"What do you mean?"

"I mean, he delivered milk and I thought people would laugh at me, would think I married down. I was educated for a woman of my time. I taught English. Andrew only delivered milk, and he could barely read. He wanted to settle down right away and have a passel of kids." She looked down at her hands, twisting and re-twisting the dish towel that had been on her lap.

"I thought people would laugh," Willie repeated. She looked over at Natalie, locking eyes with the young woman. "Live life for yourself, Natalie. I don't mean to the exclusion of others and I certainly don't mean that you should be selfish, like your mother can be. But, learn to make choices for the right reasons. There are so many wrong reasons for the choices we make. Be loyal to what's deep inside of you, forget about up here." Willie tapped her left temple with her fingers. "Nine times out of ten, it's the head that gets people into trouble, makes them unhappy, not the heart. I wish I'd known that when I was your age."

Natalie wanted to ask more, but Aunt Willie looked so. . .so what? Natalie squinted her eyes and peered hard at Willie, not knowing how to describe the look on her face. It wasn't exactly sad, and she didn't seem to be mad or hurt. It was as though she was just there, without any particular emotion. *Empty.* That was the word. Willie looked so empty. Natalie wanted to reach over and rearrange Willie's face into some kind of recognizable expression. Instead, she grasped for something to say, something that might make a difference.

"Listen, Aunt Willie, in a couple of weeks, when Mom and Harry get back from their honeymoon, we'll be leaving here. Not too far away, don't worry. Harry promised Mom a brand new home anywhere in Connecticut, she told me, and I just know we'll live real close by. Anyway, once we're out of your way, you can start all over again. You won't have me to look after all the time, or Mom to holler at." Natalie tried to laugh, knowing how sad leaving would really be. "Anyway," she brightened her voice, "you can start over again. Travel to all those places you always wanted to go. You can do anything you want. Anything at all."

"Maybe," Willie answered, taking Natalie's hands in hers. "We'll see." It had worked and Natalie breathed a small sigh of relief. Willie's face had turned soft again. Stern, but soft, just like she always looked.

"Hey, hey, what's this? Somber faces on my wedding day. Not allowed. Not even one little bit." Marilyn breezed into the kitchen, tripping slightly at the doorway and almost falling inward. "Come on guys, it's time for me to throw the bouquet." She put an arm around Natalie's waist and drew her up, out of the chair, leading her back into the living room. "You, too, Aunt Willie. I want my two best girls right there when I throw this thing and I want both of you to try and catch it. That way you can save it for me. It's the prize possession of the day. Aside from my Harry, of course."

"Ma, can I ask you something?" Natalie's voice came out louder than she expected, as she tried to be heard over the din of music and celebration.

Marilyn pulled Natalie to one side of the room, moving her hand from Natalie's waist to her bare upper arm, applying pressure with every word. "The name is Marilyn," she said through clenched teeth, all the while smiling and nodding her head so that everyone would think they were having a warm sisterly moment. "Are you deliberately trying to ruin my day, my one and only wedding day, here in front of all my friends? You're a spoiled, no-account little girl who's going to amount to nothing unless you learn the rules of life. Do you hear me?"

"Yes, Ma. . .Marilyn."

"That's better." Marilyn removed her hand from Natalie's arm and began fluffing her daughter's dress. "Now, what do you want? Make it fast, I have to throw this bouquet and hightail it out of here or we'll miss our train."

"I was just wondering about, you know. . ."

"About what? Hurry up."

"Nothing." She'd been about to ask Marilyn about their future, where they were going to live and all the things her fourteen-year-old mind suddenly needed to know, but the look of impatience on her mother's face made her change her mind. "Never mind, throw your flowers, then I'll walk you out to the car."

"Oh that'll be real sweet, honey. Real loving, just like a good girl."

Marilyn patted her hair, feeling to make sure the spit curls on either side of her forehead were still in place, and then called for everyone's attention. "This is it, girls. Gather around. Whoever catches this is the second luckiest girl in the room today." She turned her back to the crowd, took a deep breath and flung the bouquet over her head.

It was caught by a cocktail waitress named Crystal Glasse who had pushed herself to the front of the room and then waved her arms wide and long as soon as the flowers left Marilyn's grasp. Crystal, of course, feigned both delight and surprise at her unexpected turn of luck and immediately went in search of her date. "George, George," she called out, "you can stop hiding. I caught it, and you know what that means, you lucky man you." Everyone laughed and applauded and then turned their attention back to Marilyn who was clinking a spoon against the rim of her wine glass.

"Attention! Everyone, attention, for one more minute and then you can all party until you drop. Or until Aunt Willie kicks you out! Harry, come up here, please."

The group parted, both men and women slapping Harry on the back as he made his way forward. By the time he reached Marilyn, he was grinning broadly. He whacked his new bride on the fanny. "Hi, doll."

"Hi, yourself," Marilyn smiled back, planting a kiss on Harry's cheek and leaving behind a smear of Rendezvous Red lipstick. "Tell them. Tell everybody what you just told me."

Natalie had worked her way to the other side of the room, close to the front door, so she would be prepared to walk Marilyn and Harry out when they left. She was only half listening as Harry began to speak.

"Well, it's like this," Harry told the group, "you all know my Marilyn here has been more than understanding, compromising her idea of what a wedding should be, not that this here one wasn't terrific. But what do I know from weddings? Any who," he grinned up at his bride, "I promised her a great big fancy house, the best that money could buy once we tied the knot. She said she wanted to live in Greenwich and I said okay."

Marilyn giggled and patted her hair. "What could be more fitting than the Goldens living on the Gold Coast?"

"You got me up here, doll," Harry said, waving a skinny hand, "now don't interrupt."

Natalie's attention was now riveted to her mother and Harry. Greenwich? Where was that? It didn't sound like any town close by. She listened as Harry continued talking.

"Any who. I got this great idea just last week. I would surprise my bride with the mansion of her dreams. And I mean mansion! He pulled his left hand from behind his back and began waving a photograph for everyone to see. "Two car garage, two full baths, and a complete finished rec room, bar and all. Bought and paid for!"

"Bought and mortgaged you mean," shouted Harry's best man.

Harry laughed. "So true. But it's my Marilyn's house just the same. And she's worth every damn penny."

Aunt Willie had been standing close to Marilyn. Natalie watched as the color drained from her face. Why did Aunt Willie look so upset? *Where was Greenwich anyway?*

The answer came from Crystal, perched on her boyfriend's lap. "Greenwich? Lord, Marilyn, you might as well be movin' to the moon. That's practically in New York!"

"Don't worry. You'll get sick of seeing me. I mean us. We'll be here visiting more than we'll be there."

"You taking the kid with you?" It was one of Harry's friends shouting from the other side of the room.

Natalie pressed up against the door, waiting for Marilyn's response. It felt like she was at one of those press conferences she'd seen on television, with reporters firing questions and flashbulbs going off, everyone eager for comments from the luckiest woman in the world.

"Of course not," Marilyn answered. "I mean, I love Natalie and all, but Aunt Willie's been like a mother to her — to both of us — how could I possibly take my little sister away. It wouldn't be fair."

Natalie couldn't breathe. She heard murmurs of agreement and words of congratulations, all muffled, as though miles and miles away, as she felt the rug of her life being ripped from under her feet. She ran out the front door and down the darkened sidewalk. In the last few minutes, evening had set in; suddenly it was cold, more like fall than spring, and her teeth began to chatter. Sitting in the glow of the street light was Harry's black Cadillac, all done up with streamers and tin cans. Natalie tore at the decorations, throwing the old soup cans as far as she could, taking small pleasure in the hollow rattling as they hit the street and then continued to roll. She didn't know Marilyn had come outside until she felt her mother's arms around her.

"Natalie, don't. Stop, just stop. Be a good girl and stop." Marilyn tightened her grip on Natalie until they were standing on the sidewalk wrapped in one another's arms, perfectly silent and absolutely still.

"You know," Marilyn began softly, "I remember the first day I stood here, on this very sidewalk, just like this with you in my arms, looking up at Aunt Willie's house. I was scared to death and I made us a promise that very moment. I promised I would find us a rich man and live happily ever after." She shook Natalie ever so slightly. "And it's come true, Nat, my promise and my dream, all at once, out of the blue. It's come true."

"For you, maybe. But not me. You're leaving," Natalie accused.

"I have to. I'm married now, but I'm going to send you and Willie money, lots and lots of money. Maybe help get you an education so you can find yourself a rich man. See it all runs together. One thing leads to another. But you have to play it right."

"Why can't I go with you? I thought we were going to be a family, a real family. And what about Aunt Willie? I heard what Crystal said. You're moving far, aren't you?"

"Listen and listen good," Marilyn said, her voice changing from soft and slightly desperate, even sad, to stern and impatient. She removed her arms from around Natalie, only to grip her daughter's shoulders tightly, turning her so that they faced each other squarely. The street light threw an ugly yellow cast across Marilyn, leaving one cheek and half an arm in a disfiguring pocket of dark. For a fleeting moment, Natalie imagined she was being held captive by some monster from Mars and when she was saved she would be in the hands of her real mother, a warm, kind, caring person who would never leave her. She blinked hard and discovered she was still in Marilyn's grip.

"Harry thinks I'm pure," Marilyn said. "At your age, I'm sure you know what that means. He doesn't know I have a kid and, until the time is right, he can't know. Do you understand?"

"I guess." Natalie swallowed hard, trying to dislodge the growing lump of tears from her throat. "But why can't I come anyway? As your sister. You know I'd never tell."

"Maybe not on purpose. But you'd slip up, I know you would." Marilyn patted the tears on Natalie's cheek with her fingers. "Stop crying. It's not that awful. Besides, you can't leave Willie. Imagine what it would do to her if the both of us left all at once. Just think of me as one of those explorers you're studying in school, forging out to make a new life for us. When it's all safe and set, I'll come back to get you." Marilyn smiled at the comparison. "That's well put, don't you think? I never quite though of it that way, but now you understand, don't you?"

Before Natalie could answer, Harry came bounding out the front door, followed by the entire reception crowd. "Come on, doll. If we don't hurry, we'll miss our train. And if we miss our train, we miss our plane to the West Coast. Move it." He belted her on the behind and Marilyn jumped.

"What a man." She turned to her friends and smiled brightly. "Living with him is going to be verrry interesting." With no more than an air kiss for her daughter, Marilyn hopped into the passenger seat, locked the door, and rolled down the window. "Whatever my man says is —"

"Mama, mama," Natalie grabbed at locked door handle.

"Mama?" Harry asked, stopping to glance over at Marilyn, ignition key poised in one hand.

"She calls me that sometimes," Marilyn blanched and then quickly recovered. "She was so young when our parents died, makes her feel good calling me mama sometimes." Harry nodded as though that make perfect sense, as he put the key in the ignition and started up the car. Marilyn leaned out the window, a celebrity smiling and waving to all of her fans, all the while whispering to Natalie through clenched teeth, "See, I told

93

you you'd slip up. Now be a good girl, a real good girl, and when the time is right I'll send for you."

That night Natalie clung to her worn Toni doll, willing the pain inside her heart to disappear. Burying her face in Edith's coarse brown hair, Natalie rocked from side to side in the bed, whispering the same words over and over again. "She's gone, Edith. She left us. But we'll make her want us again. All we have to do is figure out a plan for a very good life, and mama will want us back. I know I can come up with something. Just wait and see."

Thirteen

From the moment Marilyn rode off with her new husband, Natalie was determined to reason matters out. If her mother wanted her to make a plan for her life — a plan that would ensure she married well and made Marilyn proud — then that's exactly what she would do.

But how?

"Just be yourself and forget all this nonsense." That was Aunt Willie's standard advice whenever Natalie broached the subject. "Surround yourself with people who love you, rich or poor, and forget about the rest. Don't try to be what you're not and don't go running after false dreams."

Pearl's answers were no more helpful than Willie's. "What do you care about finding some rich guy?" she would say. "Find someone who's committed to something and you'll have someone real. Besides, what do you care about boys anyway? All they are is a pain in the you-know-what. For my money, I'm going to study hard, get all A's and get into a top college. I'm going to make a difference in the world. The heck with boys."

Meanwhile, on the last Saturday of every month, when Marilyn came to visit, flashing another piece of jewelry Harry had bought her and lavishing Natalie with new clothes, she would get an altogether different story. "Always be a good girl and learn how to please the boys. I don't mean by givin' it away," her mother would wink, "and you know just what I mean by that. Figure out which boys come from money and then edge your way into their hearts. Men are basically stupid, Natalie baby, and they'll fall hard for you — that's at least a million dollar smile you got there — you just gotta know how to work it. Now, I know you're smart, and you know you're smart, but nothing ever got gained by letting boys know you're smart. Keep that little piece of info to yourself and then use it to your advantage."

While Natalie understood the gist of Marilyn's advice, she couldn't quite figure out how to make it happen. Then one afternoon, walking home alone from school it struck her. THE PLAN. It was so perfect, she couldn't imagine why she hadn't come up with it sooner. It was the perfect strategy for ensuring a perfect life.

Natalie knew she could never pretend to be dumber than anybody, no matter what her mother said. But she could learn to temper her opinions and how to present herself so that she was considered an asset to the richest families in town. She started by subscribing to an assortment of magazines, reading *Time* and *Life* for a distilled version of current events, and then studying others like *Modern Bride*, *Seventeen* and *Cosmopolitan*, so she would know how to be the ideal girlfriend and, eventually, the ideal wife. She cut out pictures and articles and cataloged them in notebooks, everything from choosing silver and china patterns, to designer clothes, and rules of etiquette. Every night before going to bed, Natalie studied a section of her notebook, refining her understanding of how to act, what to wear, and even how choosing certain colors might reveal an aspect of her personality.

By the summer of 1963, when Natalie turned sixteen, her personal transformation seemed to be paying off. Not only did she have the right look, with her tall, slender figure and long legs, she had developed the "right" personality, a combination of warmth, innocence and mystery, tinged with an irresistible touch of sadness. The new Natalie had attracted the attention of Arthur Barnett, the richest boy in the junior class. Suddenly she was part of the cool kids, taking trips to the beach in Artie's red convertible and going to parties she'd only once dreamed of. Or, more to the point, parties Marilyn only once dreamed of. And while it'd started as a way to please her mother, there was no denying that Natalie thrived on the acceptance and approval. Boys liked her. Marilyn was proud and affirming. What more could she want? But, beneath it all, there was sadness. Natalie's nearly perfect summer was bittersweet, peppered with feelings of guilt and betrayal and a problem she couldn't seem to reconcile.

That problem was Pearl.

There was no denying the bonds that ran deep between them. Pearl was the one person who truly appreciated the bright, witty Natalie and yet understood the frightened, little-girl Natalie who courted her mother's love and still woke in the middle of the night hugging her doll, Edith. Pearl could be counted on to cajole or tease her out of a bad mood and to love her unconditionally when things got really bad. Pearl was her truest and best friend. That was a simple, undisputed fact. But Pearl was colored. Another undisputable fact and one that was suddenly presenting insurmountable problems.

White girls with aspirations for the good life didn't have colored friends. That was the unspoken law of Weaver High. Often, it was not quite so unspoken. Natalie found herself dancing between two worlds, unwilling to abandon the one real friend she'd ever had and, yet, equally unwilling to risk the ridicule and abandonment of her new friends by openly including Pearl in any social activities. In an effort to keep all the pieces of her life in tact, Natalie learned the art of subterfuge, seeking out Pearl's company only when it was safe, still talking with her on the phone every night, maintaining the illusion of an unchanged relationship. If Pearl noticed, she said nothing, allowing Natalie the comfort of her makeshift reality.

It was August 1963, when her separate worlds collided. Natalie was sitting on the front porch late in the afternoon, fanning herself with a magazine, picking off the small black gnats that stuck to her skin as soon as they landed. The air was thick and humid, heavy with the threat of rain. She reached into the pocket of her shorts and pulled out a small book tied with a red satin ribbon. Carefully untying the bow, Natalie flipped through the pages until she came to the one she had inscribed, the one about friendship. The book was a miniature hardbound copy of *The Prophet*, something for Pearl to read on the bus, but, more than that, it was a way for Natalie to show Pearl she really did care, no matter how it might sometimes seem.

Natalie swallowed hard as she re-read what Kahil Gibran had to say: *When you part from your friend, you grieve not; For that which you love most in him may be clearer in his absence, as the mountain to the climber is clearer from the plain. And let there be no purpose in friendship save the deepening of the spirit. For love that seeks aught but the disclosure of its own mystery is not love but a net cast forth: and only the unprofitable is caught. . .*

Natalie let the book lay open on her lap as she thought about those words. Her friendship with Pearl was only for the deepening of spirit. They were friends for all the right reasons. But everyone else was simply caught in her net. Would they prove unprofitable in the end?

"That's it," Natalie said out loud, nodding her head, deciding that from now on she would not be ashamed of Pearl; their friendship would be out in the open and honest. No more tucking Pearl into a corner, using her only when it was convenient. "That's it," she repeated, feeling very good with herself.

"What's it? And what's that?"

Natalie jumped at the unexpected voice, the book falling from her lap. "Cripes, Pearl, you scared the S.H. out of me. Where'd you come from?"

Pearl smiled her broad, white-toothed smile. "I live on this street too," she laughed, straddling her bike. "I was on my way to the little store and saw you sitting here. Wanna' come? Get some Twizzlers?"

"It's too hot. All I want to do is sit here and wish I was at the beach. You're going to be on that bus all night, how come you're not taking a nap or something? Tomorrow morning, instead of marching and listening to your hero, you'll be asleep on some park bench."

"Are you kidding? I'm so excited, I don't think I'll ever sleep again. I still have to pinch myself. Me. Pearl Blackwell actually going all the way to Washington, D.C. to hear Doctor Martin Luther King. This is history in the making, Nat — what's that?" Pearl interrupted herself, pointing to the book Natalie had picked up and tucked behind her back.

"What?"

"That!"

"Nothing."

"Come on. Tell me. No secrets. Remember? What is it?" Pearl begged, never able to stand a secret or a surprise.

"You're such a pain. Here. And here's the ribbon that's supposed to be around it." Natalie thrust the book at Pearl. "Satisfied? It was supposed to be a surprise, for your party tonight. To read on the bus."

Pearl let her bike fall to the ground as she moved to hug Natalie. "Thanks, Nat. You're the best. You're still coming tonight?"

"Of course. I wouldn't miss your mother's cooking for anything!"

"Oh you!" Pearl punched her friend in the arm.

Natalie punched her back. "Just think. By this time tomorrow, you'll have already heard him speak. Your hero. Your idol." Natalie put her hand to her forehead and pretended to swoon. "He'll see your face through the crowd. He'll point and shout, there she is. There's the woman of my dreams. Pearl Blackwell run away with me. Be mine forever!"

"You jerk," Pearl said, picking up her bike. "Be over between 5 and 5:30. And, thanks." She patted the book, safely tucking into the waist of her Bermudas. About to ride off, Pearl stopped to ease a stone out of her sneaker. At that precise moment, Artie pulled up in front of Natalie's house, blasting the horn on his convertible, which was packed with "the group," all squeezed in tightly, sitting on one another's laps.

Natalie jumped up from the porch, nearly tripping as she ran to the car, praying Pearl would just ride off. But she didn't. Instead she fiddled with her sneaker and watched. The winds of destiny were stirring and only later would Natalie begin to understand how every moment touches the next, how even one minute — sixty brief seconds — can alter the course of everything.

If only Pearl had simply rode away, ignoring the pebble in her sneaker, if only Arthur had hit one more red light on his way over, or stopped to get the soda Maxine had been begging for. *If only.* A second here, a half-second there. If only Natalie had acted differently when their lives did intersect, everything might have turned out differently.

"Artie, stop leaning on the horn," Natalie ordered as she ran to the car and pulled his hand away from the steering wheel. "You know Aunt Willie hates that."

"Right, the cool Aunt Willie." Arthur brushed back his raven hair with his free hand, the other still in Natalie's grip. "Hop in, babe. We're heading up to Skeeter's lake house. His folks are in Europe."

"What for? Look at that sky, it's going to pour any minute."

"What for, she asks." Arthur looked around at his entourage and they all laughed. "What for?" he stroked her cheek. "There's a fireplace and a great big bear rug! That's what for." As though on cue, everyone in the car let out a low moan.

"I can't," Natalie said, wishing Pearl would leave so at least she could lie about the reason she couldn't go with them. She would never let Pearl down. Tonight was too important, but she didn't want to tell them what she was doing. So much for *The Prophet*. So much for the promise she'd just made to herself.

"Come on, Natalie, I said hop in. Maxine you get in back." Arthur ordered. "Skeeter, move over and make room for her."

"Artie, look I can't. I promised. . ." her voiced trailed off, wrestling with whether or not to tell him the truth about her plans. She shook her head and quickly kissed him on the cheek. "I just can't."

"Well, unbreak the promise. Unless, of course, you're cheating on me."

Natalie's face flushed with the accusation. In some strange way, she felt as though she was cheating on him. All the while, Pearl continued to watch the exchange. Nobody had said hello to her and she hadn't said a word to any one of them. "How can you say that? You know I'm not cheating on you."

"Maybe she's taking the bus to Washington. Maybe she's going to march with all the other coloreds." Maxine taunted, jumping out of the car and walking over so that she stood between Natalie and Pearl, putting one hand on her hip. "Is that it, Natalie? You going to Washington with your colored friend here?"

"Crawl back into your hole, Maxine," Natalie said. "You're just pissed 'cause I'm with Artie now and you're in the back seat."

"Talking about back seats," Maxine said, ignoring Natalie. "Hey, Pearl — that is your name? Right? Strange name. Aren't

101

pearls usually white? Maybe your mother thought you'd turn out to be one of those rare black pearls. But instead you're just an ordinary colored girl with delusions of grandeur, going off to march for nigger rights. As though they had any rights to begin with." Maxine threw her head back and laughed, her straight blonde hair cascading below her waist.

"Leave her alone," Natalie said, glancing from Artie, to his friends, and back to Pearl. She wished desperately at least one other person would stand up for Pearl, or at least against Maxine's meanness, but they all laughed right along with Maxine.

"Come on, babe, let's go. Maxie, in the car, pronto." Arthur leaned on the horn, his signal that he was ready to roll. "Natalie?"

"I can't. Please understand, don't hate me." Natalie was close to tears as she stroked her boyfriend's hair. She wanted so much to go with them, mostly because she feared if they were all together without her, they'd discover she didn't really matter, and maybe they, especially Maxine, could talk Arthur into dropping her. But she couldn't let Pearl down. She'd promised to come to dinner and tonight was special for the entire Blackwell family: Pearl would be marching in Washington with Dr. Martin Luther King, standing up to be counted with activists from across the country. It was the beginning of seeing her dreams realized. The dinner party was their way of celebrating before Pearl left on the bus later that night.

"Please understand, Art," Natalie whispered in his ear. "I just can't come tonight. I want to, but I can't."

"You're going to be with her, aren't you?" Maxine demanded, still standing between them.

"So what if she is?" Pearl shouted. "At least I'm not a phony jerk like you."

Maxine sucked in her breath; her body stiffened and her eyes popped wide, a well-known signal that she was about to retaliate. Everyone went still, waiting for Maxine to strike. Everyone, that is, except Pearl. She swung one leg over her bike, about to ride away, when Maxine took a giant step in Pearl's direction and grabbed the handlebars.

"Running away? Why don't you take your friend with you? Miss Illegitimate, here. We're throwing her back. We don't want her. But, Natalie, dear," Maxine's voice turned syrupy, "be careful what you drink when you're with this one. I understand she spits in white folk's Cokes. That *is* what you told Joanie, isn't it?"

Everybody maintained their frozen-in-time-and-space position as Artie blasted his horn. Maxine gave the bike a shove, throwing Pearl off balance, before running back and jumping into the convertible, casting a smug, satisfied look in Natalie's direction.

"Are you with us or not?" Art demanded of Natalie.

She brushed him aside with the wave of a hand, barely hearing the screeching of tires as he peeled away. She walked over to Pearl, placed her hand on top of her friend's trembling one.

"You told?" Pearl asked so softly the words were nearly lost in the thickness of the afternoon air.

"I didn't mean anything by it. Honest. It was a dare. They were just beginning to accept me. I had to tell Joanie one secret about somebody else, and she was never, ever supposed to tell. Kind of like a secret club."

"So you told *my* secret? Mine? You made a fool of me."

"I'm sorry, Pearl. Really I am. I just didn't think."

"Yes you did. Trouble is, you thought too much. And you figured they were better for you than me."

"It's not like that."

"Yes it is. It's *exactly* like that. All because your mother wants you to climb the social ladder. Guess you figured you had to trash me to do it."

"You've got it all wrong." Natalie kicked at the sidewalk with her sneaker, unable to look Pearl in the eyes.

103

"I don't think so. You're the one who's got it wrong. You don't know anything about friendship. You broke your promise to never tell, and you made a fool of me." Pearl leaned over and spit a mouthful of saliva onto the ground.

"I know. I'm sorry. Really I am." Natalie reached over to wipe away her friend's tears, but Pearl grabbed at Natalie's hand, not allowing it to touch her face. For a brief moment, a small white hand rested in the grip of a larger colored one. It reminded Natalie of the first day they met.

"Remember that first day when we ran all the way to the little store..."

"I remember," Pearl said, walking her bike away from Natalie. "But you're not that person anymore. That person was a friend. You're a rat fink." She jumped on her bike and rode away, calling back over her shoulder. "You're a rat fink and I'll never forgive you."

FOURTEEN

Natalie jumped when the phone rang, even though she'd been sitting beside it, watching television, waiting for the call. Outside, rain pelted against the windows in hail-size drops, as downspouts gushed with an overflow of water. Whenever a bolt of lightening slashed through the room, turning the television picture to snow and momentarily halting the turning of the small table fan, Natalie would pick up the phone to make sure it was still working.

Now that it was finally ringing and she was about to be vindicated, Natalie gave in to her irritation over how long it had taken Pearl to come to her senses; she let the phone ring five times and might have let it go longer, but Aunt Willie came into the room, not at all pleased with Natalie.

"Are you going to get that, or should I?" Aunt Willie asked, a book in one hand, her reading glasses in the other. She'd seen the angry exchange between Natalie and Pearl from her bedroom window that afternoon and wouldn't rest until Natalie confessed everything. She'd insisted that Natalie go to the Blackwell's for dinner as planned and not play the silly game of "who's right and who's not." But Natalie had refused.

"It's cool, Aunt Willie, I'll get it," Natalie answered, waving her away, while her hand moved in slow motion toward the ringing phone.

In analyzing what had happened that afternoon, Natalie decided it was Pearl's obligation to see things from her point of view. After all, she hadn't intentionally hurt Pearl. She just did what she had to do to stay in the group. Besides, it was an old stupid secret, so what was the real harm? No way was she going to show up for dinner and be snubbed; neither was she going to beg for forgiveness. She had apologized once. Now it was up to Pearl. As she answered the phone, Natalie was feeling smug, certain her plan had worked. Pearl was calling to make things right.

The voice on the other end barely waited for Natalie to say hello.

"Natalie, it's Mrs. Blackwell. Is Pearl there with you?" Her voice was unusually sharp.

"No. I thought you were her. Isn't she there?"

"Why would I be calling you if she was here? We've been holding dinner for over an hour. Why aren't you here?"

"I wasn't sure she wanted me."

"Oh, for Pete's sake. She always wants you. What's going on?"

"Nothing, not really. We just had kind of a misunderstanding, that's all. Nothing much."

"When? Where?"

"It was nothing, Mrs. Blackwell. We just disagreed on something this afternoon and she rode off to the little store by herself."

"What time was that?"

"I don't know. Probably around 4:30 when she left."

"Natalie, It's seven now. The bus leaves for Washington from downtown Hartford at ten sharp," Mrs. Blackwell said, and Natalie had the impression that if they were in the same room, Mrs. Blackwell's firm hands would be on her shoulders, shaking her. "Pearl wouldn't miss this for anything in the world, so something must be wrong. Very wrong. Now think. Where was she going when she left you? Do you have any idea where she could be?"

"Mrs. Blackwell, I don't know. Honest, I don't know anything. All I know is that she rode off calling me a rat fink. She went right past your house as though she was going to the store. That's all I know."

"All right. Listen." Natalie could hear Pearl's mother take a deep wheezing breath as though she was starting one of her asthma attacks. "The men are going out to look for her. They'll start at the little store and go from there. I'm really worried now. It raining so hard. Thank God, at least it's still light out. You stay by your phone and think hard Natalie. Think of anything that might help us find Pearl."

FIFTEEN

Pearl peddled away from Natalie and past her own house, pressing on through the heavy, humid air with no direction in mind, no thought except to get as far away as possible. With every rotation of the pedals, she relived the sting of Natalie's betrayal: *She sold out our friendship. For what? For a ride in a convertible? For some hot and heavy petting sessions down at Skeeter's? How could she? Rat Fink. Rat fink. Rat fink.* The accusing phrases looped through Pearl's mind as she rode harder and harder, across streets and through neighborhoods, until she found herself at the Old City Burying Ground, the cemetery that led to the quarry where she and Natalie had become blood sisters.

Slamming back the brakes, she stood looking past the entrance of overgrown shrubs and cement pillars toward the uneven rows of ancient markers, wiping grime and tears from her face. Although Pearl had been to the quarry several times on her own, finding it one of the best places she knew to just sit and think, she and Natalie hadn't been there together in nearly two years. In the beginning, after they'd first discovered it, they'd brought picnic lunches, winter and summer, never telling anybody where they were going, or where they'd been, using the quarry as their special place, where they could divulge secrets and dreams, and tell their deepest, darkest fears, knowing every confidence would be upheld. But once Natalie had developed her "Plan for Success" everything changed.

"I should be getting home," Pearl said out loud, even as she began riding along the narrow path of the cemetery. "I'll only be a few minutes," she promised herself, not certain what force was propelling her to touch base with the past, only knowing she was compelled to continue on.

Pearl traveled the familiar path toward the quarry entrance, past Thomas Ackers' headstone, the memory of that first time flashing in her mind. She'd scared the daylight of Natalie. Pearl had laughed, but Natalie had been really mad. Later, it was hysterically funny to both of them. *Natalie the traitor. Pearl the fool. Rat fink. Rat fink. Rat fink.*

As usual, the iron gate leading to the quarry was locked. Pearl dropped her bike to the ground and followed the fence to where it ended by the large oak tree, making her way through the woods until she came out on the service road high above the quarry. No matter how many times she'd been there, Pearl still marveled at how the same panoramic view was never quite the same, how it was constantly, subtly changed by the slightest whim of nature — the distant trees in varying stages of blooming or dying; the sky always a different color, the horizon itself altered ever so slightly with the slant of the sun or the configuration of clouds. Only the jagged walls of excavated rock were the same.

Standing near the edge of the steep bank, looking down at the hallowed-out mountain, Pearl actually smiled, remembering how Natalie once said it felt like being on the rim of a huge empty ice cream cone, looking down into its point. Although she never admitted it, standing close to the edge gave her the same woozy feeling she got climbing the ropes in gym class. The climb up was fine, even being up there, touching the ceiling was fine; but when she looked straight down, past her feet, at all the kids waiting for their turn, that's when the gymnasium seemed to grow small, its polished floor careening upward, closing in on her. That's when her stomach swirled, filling her throat with bile. Like now. Pearl backed away from the edge of the cliff.

As the sky began to darken, it took on a haunting quality, the dense, charcoal clouds casting a deep purple twilight. The air itself was charged with the electricity of an impending storm, yet there wasn't any wind, nothing to help catch a cool breath of air. Pearl tilted her head to one side, listening for sounds. Never before had she experienced such silence. Even in the quietest of moments, there was always some noise: the ticking of a clock, the settling of windows, the chirping of a bird. But, here, this evening, there was nothing. The workers in the pit below had gone home, their bright yellow trucks lined up in neat rows like miniature toys put away for the day. And, without any breeze, there was nothing to rustle through the trees, no moving air to toss the dry, fallen leaves. In this place, in this moment, the world was hushed and heavy and perfectly still.

Pearl sat on the ground and took out the book Natalie had given her, still tucked into the waist of her Bermudas. *The Prophet.* "She does have good taste," Pearl mumbled to herself, and then added cattily, "too bad she doesn't come by it naturally. This must have been on one of her lists of Perfect Gifts to Give." Flipping through the palm-sized pages, reading selections at random, Pearl nearly forgot her anger. Until she came to the selection on friendship.

Natalie had underlined the last two stanzas and then written a note in blue fountain pen. Pearl read the underlined words: *And in the sweetness of friendship let there be laughter and sharing of pleasures. For in the dew of little things the heart finds its morning and is refreshed.* Underneath, Natalie's handwriting was small and precise: "To Pearl, my blood sister and best friend always.

We've shared so much. I'll always be there for you, like you are for me. Love, Natalie."

"In a pig's eye," Pearl shouted. "You were never there for me. You're a liar and a cheat, Natalie Marie Davenport and I never want to see you again. And I don't want this stinking book either!"

Pearl hurled the book into the air, intending for it to plummet over the edge of the cliff, wanting it to tumble down the embankment of gravel and across the sheer wall of rock until it landed in the pit at the bottom of the quarry. Tomorrow when the workers came, their trucks would roll over it, over and over again, until it was mangled and out of sight forever. When the miniature book fell short of the edge by several inches, she ran over and began grinding it into the ground, her back to the quarry, feeling immense satisfaction as it vanished under her foot, disappearing into the layers of dirt and crushed stone.

For some reason, probably to see just how far the book should have fallen, Pearl glanced over her right shoulder as she continued grinding away at the gravel. In that moment, it was as though she was back in gym class, clinging to the top of the rope, terrified of looking down, yet too frightened to move her eyes anywhere else; only this time it was the quarry pit, and not the gymnasium floor, that was turning and twisting and traveling upward.

"Oh God! Oh my God!" Pearl cried out. A scream caught in her throat, dry and filled with dust. The movement she felt was not the bottom of the pit careening upward; it was the edge of the bank caving in under her foot.

Losing her balance against the momentum of streaming dirt and gravel, Pearl threw herself to the ground, her face pressed into shards of stone, her left leg dangling over the ledge, searching for a foothold. The sound of stone spilling over stone echoed in the silent, shadowy twilight. Extending her arms as far as they would stretch, Pearl struggled to pull herself forward. But her leg was like an anchor, weighing her down, pulling her over the cliff.

Burrowing her fingers deeper into the gravel, Pearl searched for something to hold on to, some buried root or rock, anything that would keep her from slipping backward. Razor-like stones dug in under her nails and scraped long thin cuts onto her hands until it felt as though the first protective layer of skin had been sliced away. She began offering up silent prayers for mercy.

"Please God. I'll do whatever you want. I'll forgive Natalie. I'll be her best friend forever, no matter what. I'll do whatever you want."

The ground beneath Pearl continued slipping away.

"Please, God," she whispered.

For a long moment, Pearl didn't move. It was as though the world itself had stopped. She willed herself not to scream or cry or move any muscle that might tempt the unstable earth. With her body flattened against stone and dirt, she tried to visualize her way up, imagining what it would take to save herself. She then slowly, deliberately, began her ascent. It was such a short distance, yet it might as well have been the ends of the earth. Arms fully extended and face down, Pearl wriggled forward, a soldier crawling through a mine field, inching her way to safety. As soon as she was certain both legs were positioned on solid ground, she scrambled to a standing position.

She was safe.

Now, she had to get out of here. And pronto.

Although Pearl had no idea what time it was, she knew she had to get home quickly if she was going to make the bus to Washington. Pearl's body, however, would not obey her commands. The muscles in her arms and legs trembled; her feet remained rooted to the ground. No matter how hard she tried, Pearl was unable to walk.

"Move! Move, you stupid thing," Pearl shouted, lifting and dragging her right leg forward, pulling up on the thigh and then dropping it, allowing her foot to hit the ground. In response, her knees buckled, and all of Pearl's efforts went into the simple act of remaining upright. And then the sounds came. Odd rustling sounds that seemed to come from one side of her and then the other. She stiffened and listened.

"Who's there? Is someone there?" she called out.

The noises stopped.

In the distance, house lights and street lamps flickered on, as the world beyond the quarry responded to the evening's impending darkness, and for one long moment the earth once again become silent. But the sounds returned. Louder this time. Closer. Random. Noise, then silence, then noise again. Pearl was certain they were footsteps, scurrying through the brush, crunching through old, dry leaves. Still unable to move, she strained her neck in every direction, looking over her shoulder toward the cliff and then bending forward, peering into the woods. Her heart pounded against her chest. She tilted her head to one side, listening. There. There it was again. Somebody running through the woods. Somebody big.

"Move! Move or I'll cut you off," Pearl commanded of her legs, slapping them hard, "we have to get out of here."

Rain began striking the ground in large drops. "Shit," she cried out. "Shit. Daddy, please help me. Somebody. Please." Tears and rain streamed across her face as she tried frantically to unweight her body, lifting one leg and then the other.

The footsteps were coming closer.

The more Pearl pounded at her paralyzed muscles. . .the more the rain pelted against the ground . . . the more aware she became of a single rumbling sound stomping through gravel and stone. Any minute there would be hands around her neck, squeezing until she could no longer breathe."

"Help!" Pearl cried out. "Please, somebody, help me!"

She was being swallowed up by the sounds, her heart hammering against her chest, her body drenched and heavy with rain. A slash of light exploded in the sky, turning the ground an ugly, garish yellow. It vanished as abruptly as it had come, like a flashlight turned on and off quickly, its disappearance creating a darkness that didn't exist before, enveloping Pearl in a thick shadow that smelled of rain and wet dirt.

Pearl screamed and couldn't stop.

The thunderous roar that followed, reverberating off the walls of the hallowed-out mountain, sounded like a herd of men she'd once seen, men wearing hoods and carrying torches, slashes of light in the night. She was only five then, hiding in the woods, watching as they burned down her cousin's house. Men carrying torches; lightening and thunder. It was hate, rather than fear, that raced through her body now, forcing her knees to bend and her legs to move up and down. She had to get to Washington; she had to march with Martin Luther King.

Another flash of light torched the sky and, in that one moment of illumination, Pearl was quick to see there was nobody around. There was nobody stalking her. No stranger with outstretched arms. No men in white hoods.

Mounds of tiny stones began rolling out from beneath Pearl's feet. A low rumble of thunder beneath the ground pounded its way upward. With the next flash of light, the earth beneath Pearl collapsed, plunging her across the steep embankment of gravel and down the sheer vertical wall of blasted rock.

SIXTEEN

Marilyn **rushed to** her daughter's side the moment Willie called with the news of Pearl's death. "It's all my fault," Natalie sobbed, rushing into her mother's arms the minute she came through the door. "I might as well have taken a gun and shot her or pushed her over the cliff with my own two hands. I killed Pearl and I'll never forgive myself."

"Now, now," Marilyn said, stroking Natalie's long chestnut hair. "You did no such thing. The police ruled it an accident, the edge of that quarry just gave way for no good reason, except it was its time and Pearl happened to be there. Beating yourself over the head isn't going to change a thing, not one iota. What is, is, no matter how sad you might feel. Right, Aunt Willie?" Marilyn hollered into the kitchen. "Aren't I right? Certain things you just can't go changing, so you might as well accept them and get on with life. My horoscope said something just like that only yesterday."

"Marilyn! I didn't expect you so quickly." Willie said, coming into the living room, holding a long-handled spoon in one hand, wiping the other across her apron, leaving behind a streak of grease. "Would you like some chicken soup? Freshly made, to help soothe Natalie's nerves."

"Are you crazy?" Marilyn grabbed Natalie's hand and patted it. "She's crazy. It's a hundred and five degrees if it's a Fahrenheit, and she's servin' up chicken soup."

Taking a monogrammed hankie from her purse, Marilyn carefully lifted the cluster of curls that rested on her forehead and patted at the beads of sweat that threatened to drip and muss her makeup. "Nothing for me except a huge glass of iced coffee, light and extra sweet, just like I always like it. First, though, go ahead, tell her, Aunt Willie. Tell Natalie, I'm right about getting on with life."

"Perhaps," Willie said, her voice cracked with weariness. "But sometimes we need to take time and look at what it all means. To grieve. To see if there's some lesson to be learned. Pearl was so young."

"There you go," Marilyn said, flinging her arms in protest. "There you go again. No wonder Natalie has so many problems trying to sort out her values. You're always confusin' her with talk like that."

"Me? Between the two of us, you can bet which one doesn't have many values, unless they're wrapped in twenty-dollar bills. You're forever encouraging this poor child to plan out every inch of her life around getting a man, even at the expense of her own ideals."

"For instance? Just give me one for-instance when I did that?" Marilyn put her hands on her hips and stood there challenging Willie to come up with an answer.

"When haven't you done that?" Willie shook the long wooden spoon at her niece. "You want an example?" She straightened her tall frame to its full height and assumed her lecture position, head high, eyes glaring and direct. "How about Natalie wanting to become a nurse, and you refusing to sign her freshman course schedule until she changed her mind and took business courses instead of science and Latin. How about that for an example?"

116

"And I was dead right. Nursing is scut work. Besides, there are too many nurses looking to snatch up a few available doctors. Pretty as she is, the odds just aren't there. She'd end up marrying some orderly, or something! But in business, even if she's a secretary, why in a good firm, she could have her choice of up and coming young men. Why — "

"That's exactly what I mean," Willie interrupted. "You don't give two cents about her wanting to work in a helping profession."

"That's you talking. Not my Natalie. I'm surprised you don't have her becoming a teacher. With the right husband, she can help by writing checks. Believe you me, checks work, and they make people respect you."

"Stop it! Both of you, just stop it." Natalie used the back of her hand to wipe her nose and swipe at the tears she couldn't seem to control. "You're hollering and talking about me like I'm not even here. I don't want to be a nurse. I don't want to be a teacher. Or a business person. I don't want a rich husband and I don't want any stupid chicken soup. I just want Pearl. Pearl's dead and it's all my fault and you don't care." She ran upstairs to her bedroom and threw herself across the bed, burying her face in the pillow.

A few minutes later, Marilyn walked in and sat on the bed beside her daughter, rubbing her back in a soft, circular motion. "We're sorry, Nat. Willie and me both. We're real sorry."

Natalie turned over, her hazel eyes challenging her mother. "About what?"

"Your friend, of course. It's a horrible thing, what happened. And about how we acted, so insensitive like. We really are sorry." Marilyn reached over and wiped black mascara smudges from her daughter's cheeks. "Just look at you. A sight to behold." She tried smoothing down strands of Natalie's hair, but they continued to stick out in every direction. "Too much static in the air. Now watch, Mama has just the trick for that naughty hair."

Marilyn got up, spritzed hair spray on a comb and returned to sit by Natalie, gently combing her daughter's hair. "I loved to comb your hair when you were little. And ribbons. Do you remember how I always put lots and lots of ribbons in your hair?"

"I remember. Sometimes you'd put in so many, I could barely see my hair. I'd sit in front of the mirror and laugh and laugh. I looked like a ribbon doll at the carnival."

"You have such a pretty laugh. It's more like a giggle, really. And that smile of yours. If I've told you once, I've told you twice, it's a million-dollar smile. But you don't use it enough. You're much too serious, Natalie. You need to have more fun." Marilyn continued combing her daughter's hair in long gentle strokes.

"Where's Arthur?" Marilyn asked.

"I don't know."

"Did you call and tell him about your friend?"

Pushing Marilyn's hand away from her hair, Natalie bolted up onto her knees. Tall and straight and immovable, she looked down at her stunned mother. "Pearl. Not, *your friend*. Not, *that girl*. Pearl. Her name is Pearl! For once, mother, just say her name."

"Pearl," Marilyn said softly. "Did you call Arthur and tell him about Pearl?"

"Why should I? Everybody'll know soon enough. As if he would even care."

"He'll care, because you care. And it's his place to be here with you in your time of need."

"I don't want him here. I don't ever want to see him or his stupid friends again. Pearl never liked them and she was right."

"See that? Do you just see that? She's dead and she's still running your life! What am I going to do with you? You're still choosin' between your mama and that colored girl. A dead colored girl to boot!"

Marilyn threw the comb she was still holding across the room, watching as it bounded off the closet door. She got up and paced the length of the room several times, the expression on her face changing as she seemed to be thinking through the situation. Finally, she sat back down on the bed and pulled her daughter to her; cradling Natalie's head in her lap, Marilyn gently fingered her daughter's hair, winding it around her index finger, and pushing it back behind her ears. It was a sweet, gentle touch, and when Marilyn finally spoke it was just as soft and sweet, almost sing-song, as through she were crooning a young child to sleep.

"Sweetie, I'm really very sorry about Pearl. She was your friend and losing her hurts. I know about loss. I lost my own mother when I was even younger than you are now, and you know how I almost lost you. Without courage I would have. It takes courage to do the right thing and to seek out your true destiny. Pearl would admit to that now, wouldn't she?"

Natalie nodded, too weary to argue and enjoying the closeness that agreeing with her mother brought. Besides, there was no arguing with that statement. Pearl would definitely agree. She always had the courage to seek out her own destiny. Going to Washington was proof of that. Natalie took in a series of small steadying breaths, afraid to take in the deep one that would really help, afraid to move or do anything that might make her mother pull away.

"Well, I truly believe, way deep down, here in my heart," Marilyn continued, touching her heart with the palm of her hand, "that Arthur and his type of friends, rich and classy like they are, well, honey they're your true destiny. You're classy, Nat, right down to your toes and that's what you deserve in return. It's like you were born to the manor, but this manor isn't what it should be, so you gotta' go out and get it. Why, when you introduced me to Arthur that first time, well I tell you it was a moment to make a mother proud. A snapshot moment, as they say."

Natalie lifted her head from her mother's lap and looked up into her eyes. "But he didn't accept Pearl. None of them did, and she was such a good person. I feel like if I stay friends with them now, after all this, I'll be turning my back on Pearl forever."

"Nonsense. Pure nonsense. Natalie, sweetie, everybody is not made for everybody. Just because they didn't cotton to Pearl doesn't mean they're not good people. Don't go throwin' your life away for some silly, misplaced reason. Now, come on, make me proud. Go wash your face and I'll find you something perfect to wear. And then you'll go call Arthur."

Without another word, Natalie steeled herself against the inevitable. Marilyn would have her way eventually, so why fight it? Natalie clenched her teeth for the briefest of moments, closed her eyes tightly and then opened them unnaturally wide, as a smile, vacant and pleasing, filled her face. In one quick motion, she was off the bed and across the hallway, slamming the bathroom door shut.

"That's my good girl," Marilyn called out loudly. "After all, who's going to take care of you if you don't first take care of yourself. Except, maybe your mama." She laughed one of her gay cocktail party laughs, "and that's only if you make me proud." She continued shouting to Natalie through the closed bathroom door. "I promise you, we'll do something wonderful to remember your friend. We'll send money for the headstone, how's that? A nice big, fat check."

Natalie could hear Marilyn rummaging through her closet, scrutinizing her clothes. "Okay, this pretty short outfit for tonight, if Arthur comes over. Then, for the service, something navy," she called out, "or maybe white. White's an accepted color for mourning these days. That's it, this white sundress is perfect and we'll pull your hair back, very simple and sophisticated like. You'll be the belle of the funeral."

Natalie ran the cold water — a normal, steady stream at first, but then harder and harder, trying to create a gush of sound that would drown out Marilyn's voice. She flushed the toilet, let the tank refill and then flushed again. Still, Marilyn's high-pitched voice penetrated the small, private space. Natalie covered her ears with both hands, watching in the mirror as the water on her face dried quickly in the August heat. Too quickly. She was hot again. So hot. She twisted the cold water handle, but it was already on full force.

Natalie splashed her face over and over and over again. Wouldn't Marilyn ever shut up? Her mother was shouting something about a white sundress. *She's your mother, your only mother.* Natalie kept splashing her face. *Be a good girl and make her happy.* Splash. *You just lost your best friend, you don't want to make your mother mad.* Splash. *She'll leave and then where will you be? Make her proud, and everything will be okay.* Natalie studied her reflection in the mirror of the medicine cabinet, water dripping from her chin. *I can do that. I can make her proud.* Natalie patted her face dry, pinched her cheeks and opened the bathroom door.

Marilyn was standing in the hallway, holding up the outfit for tonight. "When you call Arthur and ask him to come over, tell him you need him. Men always like to be needed. And smile, just a little, at the corners. Men don't like women who are too sad."

"Okay, Mama, whatever you say." Natalie said, chewing on the inside of her bottom lip.

That evening, they all sat in the living room, eating popcorn and watching television, she and Arthur on the sofa holding hands, Aunt Willie in her rocker, and Marilyn on an old stuffed chair. At eight thirty, Dr. Kildare was interrupted for special coverage of the march on Washington that had taken place earlier that day. Natalie wrenched her hand from Arthur's and sat on the floor, inches away from the screen.

"You're not going to see any better down there," Marilyn reprimanded, "and, besides, they say those radio waves, or whatever they are, are bad for your skin. Might even cause cancer."

"For goodness sake, Marilyn, leave the child alone," Willie ordered.

The living room, and everyone in it, disappeared as Natalie studied the images on the small black and white television set. She held her breath as Martin Luther King began to speak.

"I have a dream," he told a crowd of over 200,000, mostly colored people, all listening expectantly as he promised to show them a new world in which violence and skin color would play no part. But Natalie wasn't listening to the speech that would make history; nor was she paying attention to the man who would change the course of civil rights. As the camera began scanning the crowd, she leaned in closer toward the television, her eyes riveted to the screen; she was afraid to blink, afraid she'd miss what she was looking for.

Natalie spotted the braids first. Those silly child-like braids she always loved to wear, bobbing up and down in her enthusiasm, just like that first day when they met and shared strawberry Twizzlers. She was standing in the front row, exactly as she'd planned, carrying the long-stemmed white rose she would throw at King's feet. The camera moved in closer, stopping for an instant to capture the dark, beaming face of an anonymous crusader, a teenage girl, smiling broadly, a single tear sliding across her cheek, as King repeated, "I have a dream."

"Pearl," Natalie whispered. "Pearl," she cried out loud. "Aunt Willie, look it's Pearl."

"Oh, Natalie, honey. . ." Aunt Willie started and then stopped.

"That's just a whole bunch of coloreds and you know how they all look alike," Marilyn said and then softened her voice. "Natalie, sweetie, you know Pearl is dead. She can't possibly be there."

Still, Natalie saw Pearl's face and she was certain her best friend was there, exactly where she was supposed to be. Maybe no one else could see her; maybe it was her spirit or whatever it was called, but Natalie was certain Pearl was there. She leaned forward, to stroke the face of her best friend and, as she did, a sharp stabbing pain seared through her stomach stirring a memory deep within, a haunting, elusive memory of spiteful words and discarded trust.

SEVENTEEN

August 1969

Twenty-two year old Natalie Davenport couldn't stop smiling as she walked down Clarendon to Newberry Street in Boston. Life was good. She was finally putting her plan into motion. Marilyn would be proud once it all worked out.

Several blocks ago, she'd slipped off her suit jacket, holding it loosely over her right arm, inside out, to avoid wrinkles. It was the kind of airless day everyone complained about: oppressive, hot, sticky, with no breeze finding its way from the sea, no cool, clean air wending its way between buildings. But Natalie didn't mind. For the first time in her life, it felt like everything was falling into place, that she was finally taking the right step toward her future. Granted, it was just a feeling, nothing concrete, nothing she could touch, but it was there, and it was enough to make her happier than she'd been in a long time.

Once Aunt Willie had decided it was now or never and she was going to take that trip to Europe she always wanted with a group of "aging but active adults," Natalie decided it was time to leave Hartford. She should have never gone back there after graduating from Katie Gibbs in Boston, but, as usual, it was easier to obey Marilyn than fight her. In the end, it always came down to Marilyn.

While Marilyn had encouraged Natalie's attendance at Katherine Gibbs because it was the best secretarial school around and, ultimately, it would help her daughter find a rich husband, she insisted that Natalie could achieve that dream in Hartford as much as anywhere. She could never approve of a permanent move to Boston. Whenever they'd argued about it over the past two years — and, lately, they'd argued a lot — Natalie wondered if, maybe, the issue was not Boston itself, but its proximity to Fall River and her mother's unresolved past. But Natalie wasn't interested in the past. It was the future that held her interest. For once, she refused to listen to her mother; moving to Boston was a small rebellion and they both knew it.

Natalie was convinced that pleasing herself and making her mother proud were not mutually exclusive goals. All she had to do was find a job that suited her, rather than the boring, subservient secretarial work Katie Gibbs had prepared her for, and then land a rich, doting and very generous husband. Josef's would be the answer they both sought. Natalie was certain of it.

Early for her appointment, Natalie walked slowly, half-browsing in the shop windows, praying the heat wouldn't melt her carefully constructed appearance. She took a deep breath, but the air was too close, too stifling to satisfy her lungs. She inhaled several more times, closing her eyes as she did.

"I can't believe I'm so nervous," she muttered aloud, annoyed with herself as she carefully wiped her hands on the sides of her skirt. A few doors down from her destination, Natalie stopped to put on her jacket. Checking her reflection in the window of a boutique, she looked wistfully at the European fashions in the window. That's how she really wanted to dress — hot pants and bright colors, long silver earrings and loose, wild hair.

Somewhere, deep inside, there was a gypsy longing to be set free. But that would just be asking for trouble. She chuckled at the very thought of it. Someday, maybe, but not now.

Today she was dressed for a job at Josef's, one of Boston's best jewelry stores. Her hair was pulled back, slick and smooth, and wrapped in a French knot. She wore a cream-colored linen skirt hemmed to the safe length of precisely mid-knee and a brown and cream double-breasted blazer. Lengths of vintage chains adorned her collarless blouse. Natalie couldn't afford good jewelry, and she would never allow herself to be draped in cheap, off-the-assembly-line pieces, so she became an expert at exploring flea markets for interesting, expensive-looking items that might suggest they were family heirlooms. She carried a small purse and a leather portfolio, both good luck gifts from Aunt Willie. Yes, Natalie thought as she examined her reflection critically, she looked absolutely perfect for the position at Josef's.

"Lookin' good, m'am, looking good."

Natalie turned to see a thin, shabbily dressed man grinning at her, sweat pooling on his tanned face and arms, as he shifted systematically from one foot to the other behind a worn cardboard box. Slightly stooped, with graying stubble on his chin, he reminded Natalie of the men Aunt Willie's friends would talk about in hushed tones, the ones who'd been in the second world war and never quite recovered. Shell-shocked was the term they used.

"Thanks." Natalie smiled, wishing she had a cold soda to offer him. He made her hot and nervous the way he kept shifting from one foot to another. "It's awfully hot to be out here, don't you think?"

"Sure is hot, m'am, sure is hot." He bent down and reached into a crumbled paper bag. "Can I offer you a Coke, m'am? Sure is hot. Have a Coke." He held out a bottle filled with dark liquid.

Warm dark liquid, she was sure. She cringed involuntarily at the thought of drinking it.

"No. Thanks. I have an appointment. I have to go." Natalie walked by the man, peering into the cardboard box as she passed. It held a few dollar bills and some change. She stopped and turned around. "What's your name?" she asked the man.

"Henry, m'am. My name's Henry." He smiled at her as he continued his rhythmic shifting from side to side. "Most people don't ask," he offered. "Henry. My name's Henry."

"Well, Henry. My name's Natalie." She reached into her wallet and took out three singles. There goes dinner, she thought and almost put two back. But then she glanced up and saw the anticipation of her small donation in the set of Henry's mouth and quickly dropped all three dollars into his box. She'd have a peanut butter sandwich tonight. No problem.

"Are you here every day?" she asked.

"Yes m'am. Every day. Nearly every day. Sometimes there." He nodded as though pointing to a specific place across the street. "Sometimes there." He titled his head, indicating some spot further down Newberry. "Mostly here."

"Well, if I get the job I'm hoping for, I'll see you then. Nearly every day."

"Thank you. Thank you. Sure hope you get that job." He called after her as she continued on.

She'd never thought about helping out in such a small way, never imagined it even mattered, until she studied at Katie Gibbs and spent her free time exploring Boston, observing how others lived — the rich and the poor; the housed and the homeless. Natalie discovered she had a compassionate, altruistic side that didn't require planning or scheming; it just required being and feeling, and it gave her deep pleasure. Reaching out to others somehow calmed the restlessness inside of her, making her feel connected to something more than the here and now. And more than anything, she longed to feel connected. To belong. That's why Natalie still burned with the need to please her mother. And that's why this job was so important, even if it was just for a sales clerk.

She stopped at an oversized, intricately carved door inscribed with the store's name: Josef's. Taking a long, deep breath, she tucked her leather portfolio tightly under her arm and pulled open the heavy door. As Natalie entered, the coolness of the air startled her momentarily, but she quickly noticed that nothing in this magnificent space was overdone, neither lighting, nor air conditioning, nor decor. And in that understatement existed the most delicious and decedent environment she could have ever imagined.

Gold necklaces and bracelets shone like Christmas tinsel in the soft lighting; emeralds and sapphires, nestled in white silk, glistened under glass cases; diamonds of all sizes and shapes sparkled, shooting out thin, prism-like bands of color. Placed artfully throughout the store were exquisite pieces of Waterford, Limoges, Llardo, and Lalique — beautiful, wonderfully expensive items that Natalie longed to own. She reached out and ran her index finger across the base of a Waterford Crystal lamp.

"I'm here to see Mr. Richards," Natalie told the blue-haired woman who walked over to help her. "I have a two o'clock appointment."

"He's back there," the woman nodded and smiled. "The one with the carnation."

Natalie walked toward the rear of the store, her eyes taking in every case, every display. "Mr. Richards?" she inquired of the man in the navy suit, a white carnation in his lapel. He was about fifty, yet he had an eccentricity that made him appear older. He was rearranging a display table, touching every piece of china gently, almost lovingly, as though they were his own possessions rather than stock belonging to the store, absently running his right index finger across his pencil-thin mustache as he adjusted and readjusted items. "I'm Natalie Davenport. I called this morning. About the position for a sales clerk."

"Oh, my. Is it that time already? I get so caught up in things, you know, that I tend to lose track of all else." He carefully placed down a Limoges pen tray. Natalie recognized it from one of the bridal magazines she'd been studying.

"It's beautiful," she said.

"Yes, it is. Do you enjoy fine things, Miss Davenport?" He extended his hand. "I'm Avery Richards, manager of Josef's."

"I believe that fine things mean the difference between living and simply existing," Natalie told him as they shook hands.

"Indeed." Avery Richards nodded as he motioned for Natalie to follow him. He led her to the section where brides registered, where hopes and dreams were put down on paper for friends and relatives to fulfill. Richards sat behind the Queen Anne desk, while Natalie sat in the tapestry chair set off to one side. "Now then," he said, folding his hands in from of him, "tell me about yourself."

"Well, I'm twenty-four years old, from Hartford, Connecticut. I just moved here a few days ago. I have a degree in retailing from the University of Hartford, and I've worked in two of Hartford's best department stores since graduation. It's all here, along with letters of reference."

Natalie opened her leather portfolio and pulled our her resume and two letters of reference. Did she look twenty-four and well-schooled and not the inexperienced twenty-two year-old secretary she really was? She'd never lied quite so blatantly before. But this was the only way she knew, the only way that wouldn't take a thousand years to achieve her goals. Besides, who did it hurt? It wasn't really lying; it was just adjusting the truth for a job. Adrenaline surged through Natalie's body. She wondered if the lies would be evident when presented in black and white, if the words, liar, liar would bleed out in red across the documents she now slid across the gleaming cherry wood.

Avery Richards studied the resume, professionally typeset and printed on crisp white water-marked stock, every now and then his eyes leaving the paper to study her face, examine her demeanor. Natalie longed to twist in her seat and readjust herself; her fingertips twitched with the need to flick and flail, to rid themselves of lingering tension, but, instead, she tightened all of her muscles and remained still, cool and unflappable. She watched as Avery Richards moved his attention from the resume to the two letters of reference, typed on stationary stolen by friends who worked as clerks in two of Hartford's best department stores, signed with their actual names, but with highly inflated titles. If Mr. Richards called the stores, he could actually talk to these people — these executive references of hers — one a clerk in the shoe department and the other a secretary in billing. If he called. Natalie was willing to chance it. She smiled at him, a warm, secure smile that suggested she was perfect for the job.

"Very impressive," Mr. Richards said, placing the papers down on the desk. He was a slight man with graying hair, a thin, gray mustache and the palest of blue eyes. He gave his full attention to Natalie. "Now tell me, Miss Davenport, what brings you to Boston?"

Natalie lowered her voice and spoke slowly, as though taking Mr. Richards into her confidence. "Well, Hartford, as you may well know, is a wonderful little city and Connecticut is certainly an ideal place to raise a family, but it's not exactly a mecca for culture. Not like Boston."

"Are you thinking of starting a family?" He looked sharply at her left hand. No rings. "Are you engaged, or married? We lost our last girl because of..." he looked around as though afraid of being overhead, and then nearly whispered the delicate word, "pregnancy."

"Oh, no, nothing like that." Natalie displayed just the right amount of surprise at the very idea, and then giggled. "I didn't mean that at all. As a matter of fact, that's exactly why I decided to leave Hartford. All my friends were getting married and starting to raise a family. I've made a decision, instead, for a career in retailing and I'd like to specialize in jewelry and fine china. So, you see, Mr. Richards, it seemed like the right time to move away, go out on my own, to establish myself in the world as a serious career woman. I thought of going to New York, but the city is awfully frightening, don't you think?" Natalie had never been to New York City, but she'd read about it and she could imagine. "San Francisco and Chicago are so far away but, somehow, Boston seemed just perfect. It offers everything. Including this wonderful store." Natalie let her eyes sweep the expanse of the large room, before resting them directly on Avery Richards. "This position is just what I'm looking for."

"I see," Richards said, tapping his fingers on her resume, flushing under the directness of her look. He pulled index cards from the inside pocket of his jacket and shuffled though them, studying his notes. He seemed to be deciding whether to ask more questions or simply hire her on the spot. He put the cards back into his pocket. Natalie leaned forward in anticipation. It had worked. The job was hers.

"Well, looking at these, you certainly appear to be well-qualified, well suited, shall we say, to the position at hand." He slid her resume and letters of reference back across the smooth desk. "But to be honest, we do prefer someone who knows Boston, perhaps already familiar with the clientele. As you may well imagine, our clientele is everything to us, and your being from out of state —" he left the sentence unfinished.

Natalie felt as though she was being pulled underwater; there was no air to breathe and soon she would drown. She'd been so certain. Just seconds ago the job had been hers. What had she done wrong that he suddenly changed his mind? Natalie smoothed her skirt, trying to buy time, trying to regain her composure. She kept her eyes cast downward. Instinctively, she did next what any drowning person would do: she tried to save herself in the way she'd been taught, in the way her mother had trained her to do.

Natalie flashed Avery Richards a brilliant smile, at the same time slowly crossing her legs, placing one long, shapely leg over the other as the hem of her skirt slid upwards along her thigh. She leaned in toward Avery, laying one hand on the desk, nearly touching his. "Mr. Richards, I know I would mix well with your clientele. All I need is the opportunity to prove myself. Call my references. I'm sure you'll find them impeccable." Rather than pick up the precious papers and return them their portfolio, Natalie slid them back toward Avery Richards, daring him to call, daring him to hire her.

"Excuse me. Avery, I'm so sorry to interrupt." Natalie hadn't seen the woman approach, but suddenly there she was, her perfectly manicured hand resting on Avery Richard's shoulder. Natalie flushed and quickly slid her skirt back down toward her knees, mortified at being caught in such an obvious ploy. She looked up, the heat in her face now replaced by beads of sweat, to find the woman smiling pleasantly, without judgment or rancor. Maybe she missed the whole thing, Natalie thought. With any luck, maybe he did, too.

"Can you help me?" the woman asked. "Nobody can find the ring I ordered for my niece. And the party is this evening."

"It's no bother at all," Avery said, and Natalie could tell immediately that he meant it. Mr. Richards seemed genuinely pleased at the interruption, almost smitten, as his eyes tried to meet the woman's and failed, as though her porcelain blonde looks were too much for his mere mortal eyes. Natalie guessed she was in her early fifties. And definitely moneyed. It was such a subtle thing, but obvious at the same time — the precision cut bob that came just below her chin, the beautifully applied makeup, luminous and not a bit overdone, and her clothes, tailored, simple yet elegant. Was this a look you could acquire, or were you born to it, Natalie wondered?

"It came in just this morning." Avery Richards' voice interrupted Natalie's thoughts. "I took great care to put it safely aside for you," he said, flashing the woman a tentative schoolboy smile as he smoothed his mustache. He pushed back his chair and stood up. "Excuse me one moment ladies."

"Linette?" Natalie asked of the woman, blurting out the name without thought or reason.

The woman tilted her blonde head to one side just slightly as though struck by something familiar. "No," she said thoughtfully, "I'm Louise Hamilton." She extended her hand to Natalie. "And you're —?"

"Natalie. Natalie Davenport. I'm sorry, I don't even know a Linette. I have no idea where that came from."

"Well, it's certainly a beautiful name. Someone else called me that, a long time ago, the first time I visited France. Interesting. Well, at least you have the initial right!" Louise joked. "I'm sorry to have interrupted. Hopefully, it will only be a minute. Are you registering?"

"Registering?" Natalie remembered then that she was sitting at the bridal registry desk. "Oh no. No such luck. I'm applying for the job as sales clerk." She looked over her shoulder to see Richards coming back toward them. "But it's not going well," she whispered to Louise. "He seems to want a Bostonian, born and bred. I'm so disappointed. I really wanted this job."

Avery returned, extending his hands toward Louise, clasping hers in something between a handshake and a squeeze. He had recovered his composure and was, once again, the consummate host and manager of Josef's. "I've put the item in Claudette's capable hands. She'll take care of you now, while I finish up here. As always, it's a pleasure seeing you." He watched a moment as Louise Hamilton walked away and then returned his attention back to Natalie. He remained standing and Natalie knew it was her signal to do the same.

Avery placed a hand on Natalie's shoulder, steering her toward the front of the store. "Perhaps in a year or two, once you've come to know Boston and the kind of people we serve here at Josef's. In all other ways, you do seem perfectly qualified, Miss Davenport, so don't take this personally."

As each step brought them closer to the front door. . .the door she had opened so expectantly. . .the door that would now place her back into the heat of Newberry Street, still unemployed, Natalie tried to think of something to say, something that would change his mind. But she couldn't. She'd lost her chance.

"I'm sure you can find your way from here," Richards said suddenly. "It appears that Mrs. Hamilton needs me. I hope nothing is wrong with the ring. "Good luck, young lady."

Instead of leaving, Natalie found herself captivated by Louise Hamilton. She watched as the woman held the ring at arm's length, examining its sparkle. Once Avery approached, she urged him away from the counter, apparently wanting to speak with him privately. They talked briefly, each breaking into a smile of mutual understanding. Louise returned her attention to Claudette, nodding her approval of the ring, but not before acknowledging Natalie's gaze with a whisper of a smile. *Who is she?* The question tugged at Natalie's brain. Intellectually, she knew they'd never met before that afternoon, and yet it seemed they had: it was as though a memory lay locked behind a closed door, walled off in some portion of her mind, inaccessible during waking hours. She shivered, wrapping her arms across her chest, as an unexpected coolness traversed her body.

"Is the air conditioning too cool, Miss Davenport?"

Natalie jumped as the voice warmed her ear. She had seen him walk across the room back towards her, but her mind had not registered his presence, had not placed him so close to her.

"Just a chill," Natalie said, pulling her attention away from Louise and the odd mixture of familiar and strange. "Thank you for your time, Mr. Richards." She extended her right hand. Suddenly she was eager to be done with this, to be back in real air and real light, to try and regain her balance.

"Not so fast," Richards said sternly, then breaking into a grin as though ready to share a private joke he'd been harboring. "If you'd still like the position, we'd be honored to have you on our staff."

EIGHTEEN

Natalie loved working at Josef's. Whenever possible, her routine included a quick visit with Henry, who spent his nights in city shelters and his days on Newberry Street, making the expanse of sidewalk his home, often moving from corner to corner, as though each corner was a different room in his house, providing a unique view, used for a particular reason. Sometimes Natalie would surprise him with coffee and a muffin; other times, when she was in a rush, she'd say a quick hello and put a dollar in his cup. All in all, she enjoyed the rhythm of her days and the scent of possibility that lingered just below the surface.

She'd only seen Louise Hamilton a couple of times since she'd been hired, but there were regulars who challenged her skill and tried her patience. Irene Brainbridge was one of them.

"Jewelry should be given or, better yet, received," Irene lectured Natalie the very first time they met, "but never bought for one's self. It's unseemly. Girls today make such a fuss about having careers instead of jobs and they go ahead and take away all kinds of pleasure from a man by going out and buying their own jewelry. Personally, I'm outraged at the very notion." She patted her lacquered white hair and nodded curtly. "I'm from the old school. I'll go home and drop hints and then somebody will be in to buy precisely what I want and surprise me with it. Now, pay attention, Miss Davenport, my son can be a real nimble-brain and my husband is forgetful, although my niece is usually quite good at this. I'll count on you to remember everything I've chosen. I detest owning things I detest, but I don't make returns. It's rude and ungrateful. Claudette is always so good at remembering, I don't understand why Avery has asked me to work with you. But I suppose a young girl has to start somewhere. Just don't let me down."

That warning came during her second week of employment, and Natalie never let Irene Bainbridge down, not even for a moment. In fact, it was her demands that gave Natalie the idea for a service she began offering to all of her customers.

It was now mid-October and Natalie was showing Irene several new items. "Why don't I add both of these bracelets to your list?" she asked. "That way your family will have several things to choose from when they come in looking for the perfect Christmas gift."

Natalie removed a small stack of index cards from her blazer pocket, shuffling through them for the one marked Irene Bainbridge. She wrote down the style and price of both pieces and slipped the cards back into her pocket. "Make sure Mr. Bainbridge remembers to ask for me when he comes in." Natalie smiled and shook the old lady's wrinkled hand, all the while feeling Claudette's unfriendly stare from across the room.

Shortly after Irene Bainbridge left the store, Natalie realized she was temporarily and unexpectedly alone on the first floor. She glanced around quickly and then walked over to the bridal section. Pulling open the bottom draw of the desk, she withdrew the bridal registry, a leather-bound book considered to be the sacred responsibility and privileged information of one Miss Barbara Griswold, a sixty-five year old unmarried woman who took her charge with extreme seriousness. As she had been able to do only once before, Natalie thumbed through the pages looking ahead to the next couple of months, noting the times and places of wedding receptions and jotting down the information on a small piece of paper. She worked quickly, looking up every few seconds to see that nobody was coming, and returning to her counter just as Miss Griswold returned from the ladies room.

It was closing time when Avery Richards approached Natalie. "May I see you Miss Davenport?"

"Certainly," Natalie answered, locking her cases in preparation to leave. She looked up at her manager, who stood with his arms folded across his chest. Lately, he'd begun using her first name when there were no customers around, familiar but still professional, and Natalie liked that. The *Miss Davenport* suddenly seemed so formal and distant. And troublesome. Something was up. She could feel it in her bones. She tried to keep her voice from trembling as she responded.

"What can I do for you, Mr. Richards?" Natalie asked.

"Not here. Upstairs, in my office. Immediately, if you don't mind. Mr. Donovan will Windex your counters." He raised his hand to catch the attention of the middle-aged man across the room. "Take care of these counters as soon as you've finished yours," he ordered and then turned back to Natalie. "Come with me."

Natalie stuffed her hands into the pockets of her full skirt as she followed Avery Richards up the stairs and into his office, fingering the scrap of paper she'd placed in her left pocket earlier that day, the paper that held the information she needed to find a husband. *He knows.* That's what this is all about. He knows I've invaded the sanctity of the Registry and he's going to fire me.

As she followed her manager's rigid frame, Natalie tried to dream up a plausible explanation for her behavior. Her throat felt thick and constricted and, with her heart pounding against the wall of her chest, Natalie was unable to think clearly enough to come up with any reasonable excuse. Insanity, that's my only defense. That, or the truth: I'm desperate to find a rich husband so my mother, who pretends I'm her sister, will accept and love me. Somehow, insanity seemed the better explanation.

"Well?" Richards demanded of Natalie as soon as they were in his office. He stood behind his desk, running his fingers along his mustache, first one side and then the other. "Close the door," he ordered. As she turned to obey, Natalie spotted Claudette tucked into a far corner of the room, her thin lips pulled into a tight, satisfied smile.

"Well?" Richards repeated, his voice an octave higher and louder than just a moment ago.

"Well, what?" Natalie shrugged, knitting her eyebrows into what she hoped was an innocent, puzzled look. When in doubt, play dumb. This was always Marilyn's advice.

"Don't assume that dense attitude with me, Miss Davenport. You know perfectly well, what." He sat down and then stood up again. "Deceit. I cannot, and will not, tolerate deceit. You deceive me. You lie to me. You're out. There is no difference in my book between a big lie or a little lie. A lie is a lie and a deceit is a deceit. Do you understand what I am saying, Miss Davenport?"

"Absolutely," she answered. The resume. And references. He called and learned they were phony. Her knees began to buckle. If only she could sit down. There was a chair, right there, two chairs in fact, but she hadn't been invited to sit. And she wouldn't do it, anyway, not while Claudette stood. She needed an equal sense of power. "But, Mr. Richards, I haven't lied to you. And I certainly haven't deceived you in any way I know of. I really don't understand what this is all about." Natalie forced herself to look back at Claudette and include her in the confrontation.

"You know exactly what you're doing," Claudette said from her corner, the words hitting Natalie's back. She moved toward the center of the small office, apparently determined to accuse Natalie directly, her face turning whiter and sterner and meaner with every word. "Spying on our clientele, keeping notes on them, using them to your own evil advantage to take customers away from the rest of us. I've been watching you. You take those notes home and do God-knows-what with them, when absolutely nothing about Josef's is ever supposed to leave the store."

Natalie nearly laughed in relief as she backed away from Claudette, raising her eyebrows in an effort to catch Mr. Richard's attention and have him see exactly how preposterous this entire incident really was. Claudette pointed at Natalie's blazer. "They're right there, in her pocket. Let her deny it now!"

"These?" Natalie pulled out the stack of index cards, secured by an elastic band, and reached across Avery's desk, handing the evidence directly to him. "Is this what all this is about?"

"I'm waiting for an explanation," Avery said, thumbing through the cards, each one bearing the name of a customer, along with the descriptions of various jewelry selections. Seeing Claudette's histrionics had served to calm his own rage and he now invited both women to sit. "Let's see if we can get to the bottom of this in a calm and civilized manner. Miss Davenport?"

Natalie kept her left hand in her skirt pocket, even as she sat, her fingers wrapped tightly around the incriminating piece of paper. If it fell to the floor now, all would be lost.

"Mr. Richards," Natalie leaned toward him in a friendly gesture, "this is all a huge misunderstanding." Claudette pressed her folded arms tightly to her breast as Natalie spoke. "Seriously," Natalie said, looking at Claudette, "just hear me out."

"Go on." Avery waved one hand at her. "But be precise and truthful, and quick about it." He glanced at his watch.

"Well, it was Irene Bainbridge who first gave me the idea."

"That's a lie, right there," Claudette interrupted. "Irene Bainbridge doesn't give anybody ideas. And if she did, she'd give them to me."

"Well it was Irene," Natalie continued calmly, "although she doesn't realize it. As well as some of the books I've been studying on sales techniques and new ways to meet customer needs without changing your product base."

"Go on," Avery urged, his body relaxing slightly as he leaned in toward Natalie.

"Well, you know how whenever a customer comes in, we don't push them to buy? In fact, we encourage them to think about their purchase, because usually it's an expensive item. Sometimes we write down what they've looked at on one of our business cards and give the card to them so they will remember exactly what the piece was; often they give the information to their husband or whoever." She stopped, waiting for him to agree to the current process.

"Yes, yes, I know exactly how we work. Why must you do all this dramatic pausing. Just get to the point," Avery said, while Claudette shifted impatiently in her chair.

"I'm just not a fast talker," Natalie said, annoyed with his attitude. In this case, she really was innocent of anything except trying to improve business.

"You talked fast enough to get the job," Claudette muttered. "Just get on with it," she said louder.

"More often than not, our customers rely on us to remember what they looked at," Natalie continued. "Some of us are getting older and our memories are failing and that challenge may become too difficult." She tossed Claudette a thin smile. Slam Dunk. "Besides, even at its best, that method is unreliable. So I decided to try something new. I was planning to try it out through Christmas and if it worked well with my few customers,

I was going to bring it to you and suggest working an advertising campaign around our new store-wide service for Mother's Day."

"You say that now that you've been caught," Claudette accused. I wonder —"

"Wonder what? You're just jealous because you probably haven't had a new idea or read a new book since you've been here," Natalie countered.

"Girls, girls, stop this bickering," Avery interrupted. "If I wanted to be in a hen-house, I would have married and had five daughters. Continue Miss Davenport, but do get to the point."

"It's really quite simple," Natalie continued. "We start a gift registry, in many ways similar to the bridal registry. Whenever a customer comes in and finds something she likes, or he, for that matter, we enter it in the registry, along with our own initials as original sales clerk. That way several things happen" — she held up her right hand and ticked off the points — "one, we don't have to commit everything to memory; two, we don't have to rely on the customer to keep our card with the description and pass the information on to family members; and, three, it won't matter who actually sells the piece, because both the originating sales person and the final sales person, if they're different, get a percentage of the commission. I think it will increase sales because we don't have to rely on the customer to relay information and there's the whole element of surprise, because if there's an ongoing registry, gifts can be purchased without the recipient ever actually knowing. And, if the original sales clerk is out sick or on vacation or even at lunch, we don't miss out on a sale. Anyone can help. It's all in the registry!" Natalie sat back and took a satisfied breath.

"Brilliant. Absolutely inspired. Brilliant." Avery stood and began pacing behind his desk. "I have noticed your sales have been steadily increasing. Claudette, I told you there had to be a reasonable explanation to all this." He stopped pacing and looked at Natalie. "But, Miss Davenport, secrets are absolutely forbidden here at Josef's. They are the same as lies and deceits. You should be fired for such an indiscretion. But, perhaps I didn't make it clear upon hiring you. You're young. And new. I'll allow this single indiscretion, but consider this a severe reprimand. I will welcome your ideas, but you must bring them to me first, not after a trial period. Is that understood?"

"Yes, Mr. Richards. Perfectly. I'm sorry." But she wasn't. Her sales had definitely increased, but it was only partially due to her new system. She wasn't about to tell him she'd also been researching folklore and superstitions and the meanings behind gems and decorative items. That was her real secret.

Whenever Natalie showed an item to a customer, she tried to imbue it with meaning by telling the story or folklore attached to the piece. She discovered that creating a connection between the item and its deeper meaning often made the difference between a sale or an I'll think about it. Just the other day, Mrs. Sherman bought an outrageously expensive cloisonné turtle simply because Natalie explained that, according to folklore, it would help her daughter-in-law have an easier pregnancy and labor. Lately, Natalie had begun dreaming about writing a book, where she'd list all kinds of traditions, superstitions, and folklore and give her readers different ways to interpret them for modern gift giving ideas. In her ideal world, after finding the perfect rich husband, she'd write that book and then open up a shop with the same name. She'd call it *Giving with Meaning*. That was her real secret. And she wasn't about to share it.

"I'm sorry," Natalie repeated when Avery Richards didn't respond to her first apology.

"Yes, well, a gift registry. It's a fresh idea, Miss Davenport, but you should have come to me with it." He smoothed out his mustache and tugged at his sleeves, rhythmically over and over again, first the mustache, then the sleeves, while he processed

Natalie's idea. "All right, that's it," he boomed uncharacteristically, as though exploding with the idea, "we're going to move forward with this. Claudette and Natalie, put aside whatever happened in this room. I want you to work together on developing this concept. I want nothing left to chance. By this time next week, we will hold a staff meeting to explain the process to everyone. We'll take out ads in all the papers." Avery looked at his watch. "Now go home, both of you. We've done all we can for today."

———◆———

Annie Roth sat cross-legged on Natalie's bed, bare feet tucked under a long flowered skirt, her straight brown hair skimming the bedspread each time she tilted her head backward to blow rings of cigarette smoke toward the ceiling. She wore long silver earrings, several strands of beaded necklaces, and two bracelets, each engraved with the name of a Vietnam prisoner of war.

Natalie and Annie met in August as each moved into the Berkley Residence Club on the corner of Berkley and Appleton and ended up with rooms on the same floor. A YWCA facility, it was close to everything and nicer than the typical Y, with its library, garden room, and cafeteria. Given another set of circumstances, she and Annie might never have chosen each other for friends, but, here, both newcomers, they became immediate and best friends. Annie flicked her cigarette ashes into an old paper cup "Boy are you a lucky shit," she told Natalie after hearing about her close call with Avery and Claudette.

"No kidding," Natalie mumbled, a Twizzler dangling from her mouth. She was on her knees, pinning the thin tissue of a Vogue dress pattern to the sapphire-colored satin fabric she'd picked up on the way home. She sighed impatiently, wishing she'd been able to check the bridal registry sooner. It would have given her more time. Now, the dress had to be finished in less than two weeks and she was a slow sewer. If done right, Natalie would have a sheath dress that looked totally haute couture; if not, it was all a waste and she would never wear the garment, no matter how much the fabric had cost or how much time she'd put into making it.

Once she was completely satisfied with her work, the finishing touches would be expensive buttons and a designer label on the matching jacket. She planned on going to one of the better departments stores, probably Bonwitt Teller, on a Saturday when it would be busy; she'd try on expensive dresses and then carefully remove the label from one of them with a small pair of scissors she'd tuck into her purse. The final touch of authenticity. Fake authenticity. The idea of hiding in a dressing room and cutting out a label, made her stomach swirl with guilt, yet not doing it seemed even worse. She needed all the confidence she could find to crash this particular wedding, which was being held at the Ritz-Carlton, the grande dame of Boston hotels.

"I don't know why you work so hard at all this," Annie said.

"Yes you do." Natalie took a bite of the Twizzler and pulled the rest out of her mouth, waving it at Annie. "I've told you a million times."

"I know, I know. But, man, what a waste of energy." Annie blew a series of smoke rings, watching as they grew larger and larger, until finally they lost their shape and were absorbed into the air. "That's us," she mused out loud, "big and large and important for a while and then pouf, we lose our shape and get sucked into the universe. You're way too obsessed about this whole richness thing, Natie. I mean, there are definitely more essential things to think about. It's not like your actual life depends on it. Not like with the war —"

"You're right. I admit it. I'm obsessed. Maybe your life doesn't depend on finding a rich husband, but mine does. It's the only thing that will please Marilyn. We've been around this corner a thousand times. Just drop it."

"Yeah, but so many brains and such misdirected values." Annie couldn't let it go. "You could be helping to stop the war or save the Earth, or something. I mean, like, I'm glad this Avery cat didn't catch onto your real scam, lifting names from the bridal registry, and put you in the soup-kitchen lines or anything, but who cares about money and all that shit. Not me."

"Right," Natalie looked up at Annie, "as long as your father keeps sending checks to support your idealism, you can scoff at capitalism. But the rest of us have to take care of ourselves, and I intend to do it in style."

"I only take enough to live on. No extras. Cigarettes and a few dumpy clothes. And living here at the Y here isn't exactly the Ritz."

"Your choice. Mine too, I guess. But it won't be forever."

"Come to a sit-in with me on Saturday. Protest the war." Annie pointed to the button on her blouse. It read: *Draft Beer, Not Boys*.

"It's not a war, it's a conflict. Haven't you heard?" Natalie grimaced and threw Annie an I-don't-buy-it-any-more-than-you-do look. She didn't believe in sending boys off to someone else's war any more than Annie did. But she wasn't about to chain herself to a fence or risk getting arrested for a protest that wouldn't do any good anyway. Besides, she had other things to do on Saturday.

"I can't," she told Annie. "I have to finish this dress and then I need to go label shopping."

"Oh, come on," Annie begged. "Who needs a ripped off designer label to pretend your dress is something it's not, when the world is coming to an end?"

At Natalie's frosty silence, Annie tried again. "Okay. I know it's important to you. How about working the soup kitchen then, the following Saturday?"

Natalie shook her head as she continued smoothing out the thin tissue and sliding dressmaker pins through the pattern and the slippery fabric. "Can't. It's the wedding."

"What wedding?" Annie asked, lighting another cigarette.

"THE wedding? The reason I'm slaving over this stupid dress."

"Oh, right. The wedding. I have to admit, you're an amazing study in contrasts: one minute you're giving money to Henry the Homeless Guy, bringing him coffee and clothes from Goodwill and the next you're working on satin dresses and rich husbands. Priorities, Natie, what exactly are your priorities?"

Natalie stood up, stretched out her back and then sat back down on the floor. "Damn you, Annie, you always do this to me. Try and make me feel guilty. Well I do feel guilty. And bad, like there's a hole in me. I'm chasing some kind of empty, stupid dream that's not even mine. But it's the only thing I can think, to feel like I belong. You don't get it, 'cause you have your family, unconditionally, no matter what. But I don't." Natalie's voice got louder and angrier as tears threatened to run down her face. She put the backs of her hands to her eyes as though to pat them dry. "You don't know enough about me to challenge what I do and don't do, or how I think, so back off."

"Whoa. Sorry," Annie held up her hand. "You know me, always pushing like it's my job to challenge everyone's status quo. I'm sorry. Really. Don't be mad. Please say we're cool. Are we cool?"

"Yeah, okay," Natalie turned back to her dress, bending her head over the fabric so Annie couldn't see that she was still upset. "You know," she finally said, "money can fund an awful lot of good things. Marrying rich isn't the sell-out you pretend to think it is."

"Okay. But just think of this. Maybe it is cool to be rich and write checks. And, granted, every charity needs its dough. But it's much more rewarding to give when the giving is hard. Like you're doing now, with Henry, giving him cash and stuff when you can barely afford this dump. That's cool. It says a lot about you. But —"

"But what? Giving when you're comfortable doesn't count? Give me a break."

"It's just that when you're rich you're giving from your excess, instead of from your substance."

"Oh, please," Natalie scoffed. "That's an Ashburyism if I ever heard one. Were you wearing a long robe and sucking on a joint when you learned that one?"

Annie took a long drag of her cigarette. They both let the room go silent. It a minute they would go too far, and each girl knew it. Natalie continued pinning, nearly ready to cut. Annie moved around the room in her bare feet, absently looking at pictures on the wall and touching different things on Natalie's dresser. Finally she broke the thickening silence.

Okay," Annie said jamming her left hand deep into the pocket of her full skirt. "Forget about sit-ins and soup kitchens and consider this." She pulled out two airline tickets from her pocket. "Two weeks in Saint Martin. Courtesy of my Uncle Jacob. He manages some joint there." She waved the tickets in the air, as she jumped up and down, a wide smile filling her thin freckled face.

"Lucky you," Natalie said, pushing her sewing to the side. She would work on it later, after Annie left. "When do you go?"

"Me? You mean us. First two weeks in January. Two weeks and prime-time, no less. Uncle Jay sent them, telling me to invite a friend. I think, maybe, he's hoping I have somebody special in my life. But you're the friend I want to invite."

"Me? Isn't this just a little too decadent, too capitalistic, for someone who doesn't believe in money? Aren't you afraid your uncle and I will corrupt your delicate values?"

"So corrupt me. Everyone needs corruption now and then. Even me. When we get back, I'll realign with the stars and get back to real things." Annie walked over to Natalie and squeezed her hand, raising her voice to a high-pitched pleading. "Please, please, come with me. I don't want to bring some stoned-up hippie, which constitutes the majority of my friends. In a lot of ways, you're the best friend I have and I really want you to come."

I don't know," Natalie answered. "I'm not even sure I could get the time off."

"We're talking January, here. You've got time to plan, Nat. There's more to life than work. Besides, isn't that a slow time in the jewelry biz?"

"I'd have to take it off without pay."

"So, do it," Annie begged. "Loose the f'n job if you have to. The trip won't cost you anything. Probably not even food, 'cause we'll be staying right at Uncle Jay's place, some resort, I forget the name right now, but classy, I promise. Common' Natie. Live a little. Just think, two weeks in the sun and you'll look just like a rich bitch and you'll be able to catch any man you want."

"It's tempting...I don't know." Natalie pulled another Twizzler from its cellophane pack and took a bite, watching Annie pace the room again, picking things up, examining them, putting them back down.

"You're too f'n neat," Annie said, wandering around Natalie's room. "Not a speck of dust anywhere. It's not normal." She ran her fingers across the ceramic face of Edith, Natalie's old Toni doll, and then picked up the note card lying next to it.

"What's this?" Annie asked, reading the single-letter signature written in bold script. "M? For marvelous?"

"Try Mother or Marilyn. Convenient, isn't it? She always signs everything with a great big M, to be interpreted any way

149

you like. But she also encloses cash. That's how I bought this fabric."

"She'd approve, I'm sure. But really, Nat, just gag me with a spoon. She's so over the top." Annie locked one hand around her neck making loud gagging sounds and then read the note aloud in her most dramatic voice, "Remember, Natalie, it's time for my girl to become a princess. I gave up my youth so you would have a happy life. Use the enclosed money wisely. Don't let me down." Annie looked across at Natalie, "Holy f'n shit! She's worse than a Jewish mother."

"Yeah," Natalie agreed, "when it comes to Marilyn, my bags are always packed."

"Your bags? I don't get it. Packed for what?"

"The Guilt Trip!" Natalie laughed. It was something she and Pearl used to say all the time. Natalie hadn't used that line in years, not since Pearl died. God, how she still missed her.

"Please come to Saint Martin," Annie begged again, crouching down on the floor beside Natalie, placing the tickets in her hand.

"Okay," Natalie relented, fanning herself with the tickets. "Here's the deal: you let me go to this wedding, no more shit about selling out, and I'll go to St. Maarten without any comments about your selling out."

"It's a plan." Annie grinned, picking up her sandals and walking barefoot down the hall, leaving Natalie to work on her designer dress.

NINETEEN

The grand ballroom of the Ritz-Carlton shimmered in the glow of candlelight, crystal chandeliers and an autumn color scheme of bronze, crimson and gold. Natalie had attended — more correctly crashed — only one other wedding since she'd started working at Josef's, a simple day wedding that couldn't compare to this lavish evening event. This was done on a scale so grand it was impossible to wrap her mind around the time or money that must have gone into it. Who could even dream up something like this, never mind turn it into reality? In her mind, she was already naming it The Wedding of the Century.

In the center of each round dinner table was a gold urn spilling over with terracotta roses, a color so unlikely, she at first thought they were artificial. But their scent told her otherwise. These exotic roses were arranged so that they cascaded down a center trellis and over the sides of the urn; ivory candles — tall and tapered — were placed at descending levels among the greens and roses to create a waterfall effect. Around each urn, the florist had scattered terracotta petals, along with lemon leaves that had been sprayed shades of bronze and gold.

The grand entrance, as well as the length of the head table, was draped in a garland of green roping, woven with sheer bronze ribbon and vines of autumn-colored roses. Lemon leaf, cinnamon sticks, and sprigs of rosemary were tucked into the greens, their scents filling the room with a quiet blend of flowers and herbs. At each window, ivory candles were nestled in freshly cut greens, gold netting and tiny white lights, their flames flickering seductively against the twilight sky that blanketed the world beyond.

Beyond all this, what amazed Natalie the most, was the portrait behind the head table, a nearly life-size oil painting capturing the moment the groom had proposed. He was holding out a diamond ring so large it sparkled even in the painting, to the apparent surprise of a demur, happy and very blonde young woman. The proposal had taken place in Boston's Public Garden just as the foliage had turned, burnishing the sky with their brilliant colors. The famous swan boats had been filled with crimson and bronze flowers, creating the stage for what Natalie decided must have been The Proposal of the Century. Hence, the autumn wedding, Natalie nodded in understanding. Nothing like maintaining a theme!

I'm in big trouble. Way over my head. Those words looped through Natalie's head even as she forced herself to walk deeper into the room. Overwhelmed by such an obvious display of wealth, she was certain she'd be discovered as the "country mouse who came to the big wedding" long before the cocktail hour was over; without a doubt, she'd be escorted out by one of the burly men, standing off to the side, singled out as the imposter she was, and then fired from Josef's for using information from the bridal registry.

She ran her hands across her plain satin sheath, smoothing out imagined wrinkles. Annie was right: this was just plain stupid. She studied the other guests — the *real* guests — and realized just how much her dress paled in comparison to the velvets, chiffons and silks, all adorned with what Natalie called serious jewelry. These women had spa bodies and the newest precision haircuts and not one of them wore the frosted eye shadow she'd considered chic until this very moment. Natalie longed to go back to her small rented room and start over again. Or hide, and not start over at all. But that would defeat her plan.

Taking a breath deep enough to access her courage, Natalie began strolling among the guests, socializing with the few people who hadn't yet formed into groups, agreeing with them about the loveliness of the bride and what a wonderful twosome the new couple made. When questioned about her relationship to the newlyweds, Natalie confessed to being the friend of a friend, if she was talking to relatives of the newly-married couple; if talking with close friends of the bride and groom, she admitted to being a third cousin once removed and thrilled at having been included in this lavish affair. So far, her identify had not presented any problem. Nearly everyone was more interested in talking about themselves, about their recent trips abroad or some new acquisition, be it a car, boat, or summer home, and Natalie was a good listener.

During dinner, which seemed to last forever, Natalie walked around the hotel, sat in the lobby for a while, and then, finally, made herself comfortable in the lounge of the ladies room, pretending she'd just come in to powder her nose. She chatted with whoever came in: "yes, isn't the food wonderful? What a terrific wedding, don't you agree? One of the best this season." She knew it was safe to re-join the reception once the beat of the music intensified and a steady stream of women began filing in to freshen up.

Standing on the fringes of the dance floor, watching as couples paired up, her stomach swirled with renewed fear . . . the fear of being caught. . .the deeper fear of never fitting in, of never finding her place in the world, of never finding someone who would love her unconditionally. Of disappointing her mother. She stood very still, watching, waiting, shifting her small sequined purse from one hand to another.

"You look nervous," a voice whispered against her ear. "Or bored. Do you hate these things as much as I do?"

"Excuse me?" Natalie looked up at the man who'd moved in beside her. His hair was dark, nearly blue-black; he had a rakish smile, the kind that made him look secretly amused, and the darkest, most intense eyes she'd ever seen.

"Drink or dance?" he asked. "Both guaranteed to help relieve the pain of tedium."

Her response was a bold, hearty laugh. She couldn't help it.

"The pain of tedium? Do you always talk like that?"

"Only when I'm trying to impress."

"Not working," she laughed again. "You need another approach."

"A spitfire. I like that. Most of the girls here are too polite to say what they really think."

"What I think is that most of us passed *girl* a long time ago."

"You're a libber to boot. Forget the politics and let's skip the dance. What do you drink?"

"Scotch and soda, heavy on the soda," Natalie said. "I'll wait here."

"Oh, no you don't. Too many people. Not enough beautiful *women*. See, I'm a fast learner." He put a hand under her elbow and directed her toward the bar. "Haven't you noticed the average woman here is over sixty and wearing chiffon? God, I hate chiffon!"

Natalie giggled and again felt self-conscious, wondering if this man who hated chiffon could tell her dress was homemade. She ran her hands along the straight skirt of her sheath, comforting herself with its rich smoothness and the designer label carefully sewn inside her jacket. Even if no one saw it, she knew it was there.

"They're not all chiffon," she said, eyeing an elegant gown of cream-colored silk that just passed by, "or over sixty."

"But sometimes simple blue satin is refreshing," he said as he continued steering Natalie toward the bar.

"Glad you approve. Otherwise, I guess I'd have to run home and change."

"Scotch and Soda, heavy on the soda," he told the bartender. "And another Absinthe Cocktail for me."

"What's Absinthe?" she asked.

"Long story. Filled with mayhem and murder." His dark eyes flashed with mischief. "We'll save it for another time. Unfortunately, this is an Absinthe Cocktail, without the Absinthe. Or the ritual. The best they can do here is Anisette, a little sugar and some orange bitters."

"Mayhem and murder? Sounds fascinating." Natalie accepted her drink and watched as the bartender made his. "Here's to Absinthe and another time." She held up her drink in a mock toast.

"Here's to it," Chad agreed, taking a short sip of his drink. As they walked back toward the dance floor, Chad looked at Natalie long and thoughtfully. "Do I know you?"

"I don't know. Do you?" Natalie was trying for an air of mystery even as the swirl of fear continued building in her stomach. Should he know her? Did he know she didn't belong; was he just playing her? Hopefully, being a spitfire would save her. "You really do need some new material."

"It's not a line," he laughed. "You seem so familiar — "

"Oh, well, no, I don't think so. I'm Natalie."

"And I'm Chad. Nice to meet you Natalie-with-the-beautiful-smile."

"You, too. Nice to meet you, I mean," Natalie said. So, maybe everything was okay; maybe she could actually relax and enjoy this moment with this man.

They stood off to one side of the dance floor, sipping their drinks, watching the dancers, all the while commenting on the other guests. Chad had started a game of what Natalie privately called *observe and comment*, calling her attention to the run in one woman's stocking or the fringe of slip hanging below an older guest's dress whenever she lifted her heavy arm. Natalie was amazed, not only at his apparent eye for detail, but at his sharp, unrelenting judgment of others. She found herself matching him, observation for observation, running on a surge of adrenaline, powered by the pleasure she felt at being Chad's confidant and co-conspirator.

Chad leaned in toward her with another comment and Natalie's stomach lurched at the smell of the sweet licorice liquor on his breath. It was almost like a memory. It made her want to touch him, to feel the charge of electricity she was certain lay between them, to quell the uneasiness that rested at the tips of her nerve endings and the warning that seemed to lay in the sudden, slight breeze that ruffled her hair. And then it passed. She shuddered, nearly dropping her empty glass.

"Cold?"

"What?" she asked, feeling slightly out of her body, as though waking from a drug-induced sleep. "I'm sorry, what did you say?"

"You seemed cold all of a sudden. Are you?"

"A little. Must be the air conditioning." She looked up but couldn't see any ducts that could be responsible for the sudden sweep of air across her body.

"Another drink? That'll warm you. Or I can do it." He winked at her.

"No. To both." She looked up at him. "But thanks."

"You sure?"

"I am."

Chad took the glass from Natalie and placed it on the table closest to them. With a linen napkin he dabbed at the condensation on her hands. "A tee-totaler," he said.

"Or a cheap date." Natalie pulled her hands away from him and clasped them behind her back, as though attempting to ground her growing discomfort; coursing through her body was the oddest mixture of fear and longing.

"A cheap date," he laughed. "That'd be a change. My women are generally very high maintenance. So, Natalie, exactly who are you and why haven't I seen you at one of these soirees before?"

She shrugged, smiled, and tossed her hair back. "I guess you haven't been looking."

He moved in closer and the swirling sensation in her stomach transformed itself into a faint stabbing pain. She backed away slightly, hoping he wouldn't notice, not wanting to put off this handsome, rich man who could make all of her problems disappear. And all of her mother's dreams come true.

"Leaving room for the Holy Ghost?" He laughed out loud.

Natalie blushed, feeling like a schoolgirl, but didn't reply.

"You're different," Chad said, stroking her cheek. Let's get out of — " Before he could finish his thought, a tall, too-thin blonde woman intruded herself between Natalie and Chad, linking her arm through his.

"Here you are," she said. "Shame on you for leaving me alone for so long. I've missed you."

"I've missed you too," Chad said, looking around her at Natalie and rolling his eyes. "But it looks like you found the bar without my help." He nodded toward the empty champagne glass, putting an arm around Regan to help steady her.

"And I need another. But it's too far to walk on these damn high heels. Be a doll —" Regan stopped mid-sentence suddenly aware that Chad's attention was elsewhere. She turned toward

Natalie, backing up a couple of inches so that she could get a good look at her.

"Hi, I'm Regan, and you're? New around here." She laughed at her own humor.

"Natalie Davenport." Natalie extended her hand. "Nice to meet you, Regan."

"Which side?"

"Excuse me?" Natalie said.

"Bride or groom? Which side? We're on both, but that can't be your case or I'd know you for sure. Right, Chad?" Regan kissed Chad on the cheek and then rubbed off the smear of pink left behind.

"So, bride or groom?" Regan repeated. She leaned over and fingered the pendant resting on Natalie's dress. "Cute." She smiled and let the thin chain drop back against Natalie's chest. "Darling, I really could use another champagne cocktail." She looked up at Chad.

"You'll have to wait a few minutes, Regan. I just got word they had to send out for more. You and the girls have apparently drained the barrel."

"Oh YOU," she giggled and turned back to Natalie. "So tell me —"

"That amethyst is beautiful," Natalie said, indicating the large stone around Regan's neck, hoping to turn the conversation away from the bride and groom. "It certainly puts my cute necklace to shame. Did you know that amethysts protect against overindulgence? In fact, if you wanted to take it off and hold it under your tongue, you could drink champagne all night without getting drunk."

"Are you implying — "

Chad laughed so loud that it was more like a roar. "She should have tried that an hour ago. Too late now! But I can just picture that massive stone under her tongue and that heavy gold chain dangling across her chin. Sorry Regan, dear, but it is funny." He stroked her blonde hair as though to tame her rising temper. "Did you just make that up?" he asked Natalie.

"No. I don't have that much of an imagination. I read a lot about folklore and superstitions. That really is what they say about amethysts."

"Interesting. Isn't that interesting, Regan?" Chad asked.

"Very." Regan pressed in closer to Chad. "I'm sure she could entertain us with all kinds of stories. But I'm really interested in knowing which side she's on. So tell us —"

"We'll have to save that story for another time," Natalie said quickly, feeling the flush of lies and embarrassment rush to her face. "That and Absinthe." She looked at Chad seeking a private understanding. "I see somebody I really must say hello to." She pointed toward the door with an urgency that suggested the person she needed to see was about to leave. "Really nice meeting you." She held Chad's eyes for a full moment and then included Regan in her gaze. "Both of you," she added as she hurried away from them and toward the exit.

Tears collected in Natalie's eyes as she stood outside waiting for the doorman to hail a taxi. The November night had turned raw, the threat of an early winter hanging in the air. Regan had spoiled everything, reminding her just how much she didn't belong, and how ordinary she really was.

Natalie finally understood: you were born into a life; you couldn't just barge into one. The joke was on her; there was no missing glass slipper and no prince ready to turn her into a princess. Sorry Marilyn. Annie's right. It's time to get my priorities in order.

TWENTY

As hard as she tried, Natalie couldn't get Chad off her mind. Intellectually, she understood that her obsession was just that, a foolish go-nowhere fixation that could only derail her goal of finding Mr. Right-and-Rich. Unless fate intervened — and she didn't believe in fate — she'd never see him again. She didn't know his last name and without that, there was no way to execute a plan, no way to find out who he was, no way to accidentally-on-purpose bump into him. Still, he invaded her dreams. And her day dreams. It was more than a crush on a dark, handsome stranger. There was something about him that haunted her, something compelling and unfinished.

"Face it, Natie," Annie cautioned one night as they lounged in Natalie's room. "He didn't even try to chase after you. There's no Cinderella ending here. Forget about him. Get through the holidays and focus on Saint Martin."

"I know."

"You say that. But I see the look on your face."

"It'll pass. What choice do I have? Still, can you just imagine how happy Marilyn would be if I landed a Chad?"

"Or a cad." Annie laughed. "You don't know anything about this guy. Let it go."

"Yeah, yeah, yeah," Natalie, said throwing a pillow at Annie.

"Yeah, yeah, yeah," Annie echoed in the tune and cadence of the Beatles song as they both sang "She loves you, yeah, yeah, yeah" throwing the pillow back and forth like third graders at a sleepover.

"I'll let it go, I promise," Natalie told Annie. And she nearly did. There were entire days when she was no longer on alert, no longer watching, looking, thinking maybe he'd come into this or that restaurant or bookstore, just when she was there, or that he'd miraculously be crossing the same street she was crossing at the very same time. For a person who didn't believe in fate, she was looking for destiny to intervene at any given moment. And then it happened. Just after Thanksgiving, there he was, walking through the door of Josef's, heading right toward Claudette. Natalie panicked at the realization that he might see her there, working as a clerk. She kept her head down, finished up with her customer and asked Mr. Richards if she could take an early lunch. It was only 11:30 and normally she didn't go until close to one o'clock.

"We're busy, Miss Davenport. You can't just run out on me."

"I'm not feeling well. I couldn't eat breakfast. And now I feel faint. I think I need to eat something. Please Mr. Richards."

He sighed, fingering his white carnation. "All right. Go. I don't want you getting sick in front of the customers. But don't make a habit of this, Miss Davenport. I'm concerned that you're beginning to take advantage, taking off two weeks in January before you've even earned your full vacation, and now changing lunch hours around —"

"Thank you, Mr. Richards. Thank you." Natalie glanced over and saw that Chad seemed to be finishing up his transaction. She went into the back, grabbed her coat and purse and, leaving by the delivery entrance, raced up a side street and across Newbury, so that she could watch the store from across the street. As soon as she saw Chad open the front door, she began dodging traffic, moving diagonally across the street, so that she literally bumped into him as he was about to cross the street in her direction.

"Sorry," she said. "Too much of a rush. Did I hurt you?" She smoothed out her coat, careful not to make direct eye contact.

"You're too small to hurt anyone," Chad laughed. "Where's the fire?"

Natalie looked up at him and smiled, a wide, radiant, dimpled smile that she hoped would strike his heart, if not his memory.

"It's you. You're Natalie." Chad said, putting his hand around her waist, guiding her away from the curb and back toward the shops. They stood in the doorway of a store only a couple of doors down from Josef's.

"You're right. I'm Natalie. At least I was the last time I checked. And you're —?" She frowned slightly, as though puzzled.

"I'm Chad. Chad Hamilton. We met at the Butler wedding. You left so quickly."

"Oh, right. How are you?"

"I'm fine. I tried to find you, but you left and nobody knew who you were."

"Apparently you didn't ask the right people." She smiled what she hoped was a mysterious and mischievous smile. "I caught up with some old friends and we left, went out for drinks where we could talk. It was too noisy in there."

"Hmmm. Well it's too noisy out here with all the traffic. And cold. Let's go have lunch. I know a great place just outside the city. My car's right over there."

"I can't. You were right about my being in a rush." She waited only a second or two before making her suggestion. "How about a compromise? A tuna sandwich at that corner restaurant? It's the best I can do today."

"Sold. As long as I can get roast beef. I hate tuna."

"Hate's such a strong word," Natalie countered as they walked toward the deli.

"But it gets the point across. Sometimes it's the only word that works."

———◆———

Over lunch, Natalie soon discovered that there were lots of things this engaging, flirtatious man hated in addition to tuna fish: liver, cottage cheese, cheating wives and laziness.

"Cheating wives?" Natalie asked, "That's an odd thing to sandwich in between food and personality preferences. Are you talking from experience?" At twenty-eight, he seemed jaded beyond his years.

"Just what I observe. I have a couple of buddies, burned badly. The wives cheat and then try and take 'em for everything they've got." He took a bite of his sandwich. "I say kill 'em."

"Excuse me?" She put down her sandwich and studied Chad. "What did you just say?"

"I said kill the cheating wives. That would simplify things, don't you think?" He took another bite, never looking away, never changing his expression. "This isn't half bad," he said, holding up the remainder of his sandwich.

Natalie couldn't let it go. She knew he was baiting her, but she persisted anyway. A hundred needles, it seemed, were prickling the back of her neck.

"You're joking, aren't you?"

"Maybe," he winked.

"Well, it's a bad joke."

"Lighten up."

"All right," she challenged, "so what about the cheating husband?"

"Not his fault," Chad said, "Most likely he cheats because she's not a good enough wife."

"Talk about chauvinistic. Do you really mean that, or are you just trying to get a rise out of me?"

"A little of both," Chad admitted. He reached over and touched her face, a single gentle stroke along the side of her cheek with the back of his thumb. The warmth of his skin against hers felt like an intimate gesture, unsettling in its directness and simplicity. "Let's agree to disagree." His voice was soft, seductive. "You don't cheat and we don't have a problem. That is, if you agree to see me again."

If she agreed? Of course she agreed. A corporate attorney. Apparently monied. How could she not agree, even when something deep inside warned otherwise? It was just her own guilt, she decided, over lying, presenting herself as something she wasn't.

They dated right through Christmas, seeing each other at least twice a week, generally on Monday and Thursday nights. Who he saw the other times, Natalie could only guess. Probably Regan. But there was an energy between them that neither of them could ignore. A spark. An attraction that seemed both familiar and risky.

When Chad asked for her phone number, she gave him the one to the pay phone just outside her room at the Y, cautioning him that she rented an apartment with a couple of other girls and the phone could be busy lots of the time. She insisted on meeting him for their dates, claiming it was just easier that way; when he drove her home, it was to a five-story brownstone on Commonwealth Avenue. She never invited him in and he never pushed. As soon as he drove away, she'd ride the "T" as far as Clarendon, and then walked the remaining few blocks to her small room at the Y where she would lay in bed, planning out her future.

———◆———

By their sixth date, Chad had pretty much revealed everything there was to know about his life. He was a corporate attorney who enjoyed turning deals and, as he put it, "swimming with the sharks." It was all about the challenge, the game. And the winning. He loved winning. He grew up in Dover, part of Brookline, just outside of Boston proper, in a fifteen room mini-mansion with separate quarters for the maid and cook. His mother still lived there. His father, Everett Jonathan Hamilton, died of a heart attack when Chad was twelve and his adopted brother, Clayton, was nine. Chad followed in his father's footsteps, going to Harvard and then joining a prestigious law firm. He now lived in the family's second home, a redbrick townhouse in Louisburg Square, part of Beacon Hill, and Boston's most elite neighborhood.

Tonight they were enjoying veal picata and Chianti in a small Italian restaurant where empty wine bottles were transformed into candleholders and strolling musicians played old world love songs. Natalie had perfected the art of asking questions, following Marilyn's advice about keeping it light and acting interested in every detail of a potential husband's life. In this case it was more than just acting interested: if she could keep Chad telling stories, he might forget that he actually knew very little about her, beyond her favorite foods and how easily she cried at sad movies.

"There's not much else to tell," Chad said when Natalie prodded for more. He stabbed a piece of veal and chewed heartily.

"Tell me about your mother," Natalie insisted. "Or your brother."

"You already know the big picture," Chad said. "Aside from my father dying, probably the worst day of our life was when I was six and Mom and Dad were supposed to adopt a baby girl. Whatever happened, things turned sour. I still remember that day, her coming home empty-handed. I didn't care about not having a sister, just about how sad she looked. She still talks about it, like the kid was really hers or something. Eventually they tried again. Adopted Clayton." Chad shook his head in a combination of disapproval and amazement. "He's a good guy. But what a jerk, throwing away a brilliant future as an art historian to join the Peace Corps and dig wells in some God-forsaken country. I'll never understand him."

"But you love him," Natalie said.

"Yeah, I do." He took a drink of Chianti and then looked straight into Natalie's eyes. "Okay, that's it. That's all she wrote. Now it's your turn. Tell all, Natalie Davenport. Who are you? And why do you fascinate me so much?"

"Maybe because I'm the woman you've been looking for all your life?" she smiled, hoping a little flirting would stall the conversation.

"You may well be right." Chad stroked her hand. "Go on."

"Okay. But it's really boring. Not much to say."

Chad reached over and covered her hand with his. "Let me be the judge."

Or jury, she thought.

"Okay, here it is: I come from Hartford, you already know that. My parents died when I was three and I was raised by my sister Marilyn and my Aunt Willie. That makes me an orphan, sort of, and I find it embarrassing. I don't like to talk about it. Like you, we have money. My parents had lots of insurance. But, unlike you, we don't spend it easily. There are moths growing between our bills —"

"I'm not looking for a dowry, Natalie," Chad interrupted.

"Just a blood line?"

He removed his hand from hers. "Is that what you think? Do I come off that badly?"

"I'm sorry." She studied his eyes, the set of his mouth, sensing a vulnerability she'd never noticed before. Should she take a chance and tell the whole, unvarnished truth of Natalie Marie Davenport? It would feel good to get it all out. Start fresh.

"Okay, look," she started again. "I'm a working girl. The truth is —" She stopped, seeing how the phrase *working girl* had shifted his facial lines, settling into his jaw with a tension he probably wasn't even aware of, an unspoken response that settled things for Natalie.

"Go on," Chad urged, breaking the silence building between them.

No way was she about to confess family truths. Not after that look.

"Gotcha." Natalie laughed as though she'd told a joke but hadn't yet delivered the punch line. "I do work. At Josef's. But only because it's my uncle's place. My mother's brother. I'm being groomed to it take over."

"That odd guy Richards? He's your uncle?"

"No, no." Natalie blushed with all these new lies. She put her hands to her face. "Whew. Chianti always does this to me. No, Richards is just the manager. My uncle is too old now to run the daily operations. It'll be mine one day, provided I learn it from the ground up. That's the condition he set. I'm doing the equivalent of starting in the mail room. Learning all about jewelry. Learning how to please the customers. Later, I'll get involved in the business end of it. That's why I enjoy studying folklore and superstitions. Add a little bit of meaning to anything and you can sell it." She took a long drink of water before continuing. "The plan is that in two years or so, Uncle Joe will turn Josef's over to me."

Once she started down the path of The Lie, Natalie couldn't seem to stop herself. What did it matter? Small lie. Big lie. It was all the same at this point and at least she didn't have to make up stories about where she went every day or how she earned a so-called living.

"That's quite a plan for a nice girl from Hartford. Here's to owning the sweetest jewelry store in Boston." Chad lifted his wine glass in a toast. She clinked his glass and took a steadying drink, all the while wondering just how long she had before getting caught.

———◆———

Natalie went home to Aunt Willie's for Christmas. Marilyn had invited her to Greenwich, but the stress of pretending to be her sister was more than she could bear right now. There was enough subterfuge going on in her life, enough lies to keep straight. Besides, she was in no mood to fend questions about her life in Boston or, more specifically, about Chad, the catch-of-the-day, as Marilyn was already calling him. If Chad had invited her to spend Christmas with him, she would have jumped at the chance, even at the risk of disappointing Willie. But that didn't happen. Neither did a date for New Year's Eve, although he did invite her to brunch for New Year's Day.

"Sloppy seconds," Annie observed. "That's how he's treating you, Natie. He doesn't ever give you prime dating time. Mondays and Thursdays, occasionally a Friday, but never a Saturday. And no holidays. What does that say? And then what? A dinky bottle of perfume for Christmas?"

"We've only been dating a short time. Besides, I think it's pretty expensive perfume. He said I should make it my signature scent. Then I'll have everything going for me. That's pretty much a direct quote."

"Oh, pleezze. A signature scent? What are you, fifty? I think you have everything going for you, without it. And whoever heard of this perfume anyway? Jicky? What kind of a name is that? Here Jicky Jicky; here Jicky, Jicky. . ." Annie kept repeating the phrase, imitating a farmer's wife calling to the chickens.

Suddenly they were both on the floor doubled over, holding their stomachs, and hitting each other, laughing so hard that tears streamed down Natalie's face and Annie started to hiccup.

"You're crazy," Natalie said, finally catching her breath. "Funny, but crazy." She took a bite of her Twizzler and pushed aside the travel book on Saint Martin they'd been looking at. "Maybe he suspects. Maybe he knows everything and he's just playing with me. That's why he only gave me perfume when he could afford anything."

She opened up the bottle and dabbed a touch of the yellow liquid on her wrist. "It's nice, don't you think?" She held out her arm for Annie to smell. "Kind of heady, seductive. Sort of oriental. It reminds me of something. I can't quite figure it out."

"Suspects what?" Annie said, wrinkling her nose at the scent, or more likely at the idea that any man would be presumptuous enough to give a woman a signature scent. "That you're a poor girl from Hartford who lied about her age and experience to get a job and then lied about owning or — *excuse me* — almost owning the place? Oh, and then there's the lie about dead parents and lots of insurance money. Ya think?"

"I don't know. I don't want to think about it." Natalie took another whiff of her wrist and closed her eyes trying to imagine why it seemed so familiar. "Anyway," she said looking over at Annie, "it's the thought and not the gift. Besides — chew on this — I didn't tell you before 'cause I figured you'd freak out — I'm going to New Orleans with him."

"You're what?"

"Going to New Orleans. In February. How's that for not being a sloppy second?" Natalie smiled smugly.

"Oh Man. Tell all."

"Well on New Years I told him I'd be gone for two weeks in January. He actually seemed upset. Jealous, maybe?" Natalie punched Annie in the arm. "Before I know it, he's telling me about a convention he's attending, just for three days, in New Orleans the second weekend in February. And he wants me to go with him. We'd leave early Friday morning. He must have seen the look on my face because he promised separate rooms and that nothing would happen that I didn't want or wasn't ready for."

"And you said?"

"What do you think I said? I couldn't wait to call Marilyn. This is a huge break-through."

"She must have wet her pants. Her baby got herself a rich corporate lawyer. She's finally becoming a princess."

"I'm going to have a horrible time getting the days off. I hope I don't lose my job over this. Maybe I'll call in sick."

"What, you think your *uncle* is going to fire you?

"No, but Richards might. You're such a smart ass."

"No more than you, Nat. You'll figure it out. For now," Annie said blowing smoke rings and fingering the guide book, "let's forget everything, except our trip. This time both our bags are packed!"

TWENTY-ONE

Natalie and Annie lazed on the beach unable to fully believe their good fortune. While all of Boston was locked down in January ice and snow, here they were, swimming in turquoise waters and soaking up the Caribbean sun.

Divi Little Bay, the resort managed by Annie's Uncle Jake, was once the only beach-front resort on Saint Martin. In 1955 it had only two rooms. Now, with a hundred and twenty rooms, a restaurant and a casino, it was still one of the smaller hotels on the island. And that was just fine with the snow birds who returned every year drawn to the resort's old-world charm and personal service. Jake Roth knew the name of every returning guest, what they liked, and how they could best be served.

"I could get used to this," Natalie said, sitting up and scanning the horizon, watching the water roll toward shore in long, lapping waves. She bent her head forward, letting the light breeze cool her back and neck, noticing how the palm trees had done the same thing, and now their trunks were deeply curved, shaped by years of bending to the kind, but consistent, trade winds.

Annie sat up beside Natalie. "We've been here for three days, and for three days all you've done is talk about Chad," Annie complained. "This is your life, right here, right now. Sunshine and hibiscus. Gorgeous water. Great food. Just be in the moment, Natie, please. Enjoy this with me. I feel like you don't even want to be here."

"I know. I'm sorry. Honest. I wouldn't trade this for anything." Impulsively, she threw a handful of hot white sand across Annie's feet. "But Chad really is cute. No, take that back. Handsome. He's handsome. And rich."

"Rich is relative. He's got money. But I bet he's not rich by rich standards." Annie dusted the sand off her feet and looked out over the water. "Uncle Jay says I can stay. Work for him, if I want."

"You're not going to, are you?" Natalie laid back down on her stomach, burying her head in her arms. She was starting to burn. They would have to head for shade soon. It was almost one, and they'd been out on the beach since breakfast. The light winds tickled and cooled her skin, creating a false sense of safety against the tropical sun.

"I'm sure you'll meet a real dreamboat if you do stay," Natalie giggled, "squatty and old and verrry married. Have you noticed, there's nobody here under retirement age?"

"No kidding. Uncle Jay says it's the time of year. Apparently prime season in the islands attracts the long-lived and well-heeled. Should be right up your alley!"

Ignoring Annie's jibe, Natalie turned her head and asked, "So?"

"So what?"

"Are you staying or going?"

Annie stood and threw her towel over one shoulder. "Going. The sun's brutal. Let's find some shade."

"Not that, you dummy!" Natalie followed Annie off the beach and up the stairs onto the cool, tiled patio toward their third-floor room. "Are you really going to do it? Stay here? Leave me?" *Would Annie really do that?*

"It'd be such a sell-out, don't you think, coping to the establishment when I'm always bitchin' and moanin' about it."

"I don't know. It has its appeal. Although not much excitement. Once you've mastered the art of collecting sea shells and identifying lizards, what would be left? Dealing Blackjack?"

"Marry a native and have lots of babies?" Annie eyed one of the porters in tight pants. "Nice buns," she whispered and the two girls broke into gales of laughter.

"What about me? Could you really just up and leave Boston. And me?"

"Before you know it, you'll be married and having rich babies. We both know that. You can't even forget Chad for two weeks; sooner or later, I'm going to be on the outside looking in. Might as well stay here and start now."

"Don't say that. We're best buds forever," Natalie said. "Let's make a pact: for the rest of the vacation, it's just you and me. After that, you decide where to live — and I'll support your decision — and I'll figure out how to snag Chad — and you'll support me. Until then, he doesn't exist." Natalie raised the three middle fingers on her right hand. "Scouts honor."

"Right." Annie laughed as they let themselves into their room. She threw her wet towel at Natalie. "You don't have that much control over that anal-retentive, over-active, over-organized mass of cells you call your brain."

"Translation?"

"You think too much and plan too hard. Loosen up."

"You got it," Natalie said.

"I do?"

"Absolutely," Natalie said, pushing wire hangers along the closet's wooden rod, pulling out and putting back her silk dresses and linen skirts. "Starting right now." She walked over to the dresser and pulled out a pair of shorts and sleeveless blouse.

"Just look at those clothes," Natalie said, pointing to the closet. "They're so...so..."

"Beautiful? You made most of them. They really are beautiful."

Natalie scrunched her face. "Yeah, they are. But they're so Boston."

Annie hit her forehead with the palm of her hand in feigned awareness. "No shit!" She lit up a cigarette and sat cross-legged on the bed in her almost-dry bathing suit. "Any solutions to the Bostonian f'n safe wardrobe problem?"

"Shopping. Let's go into Phillipsburg. I want to buy something incredibly tropical, maybe a long gauzy skirt and one of those off-the-shoulder blouses."

"You mean, you want to dress like me?" Annie said.

"God forbid! I draw the line at Granny dresses. We'll take the shuttle in, maybe walk back if we have the energy."

"You're on." Annie jumped up off the bed, crushing out her cigarette in a water glass as she stripped off her bathing suit and grabbed a pair of cut-off jeans and tank top from underneath the bed. As Annie struggled into the tight clothes, Natalie pulled her hair back into a low ponytail, using a ribbon to conceal the rubber band, and then carefully applied lipstick and mascara. Annie impatiently pushed her long hair behind her ears, using her fingers as a comb. She watched Natalie primp. "There's no hope for you, you know. But let's try anyway."

The narrow streets of Phillipsburg were lined with gift shops and restaurants and, every now and then, a casino. It was a cacophony of bright colors and sounds and the aroma of spicy food being cooked just behind open doorways.

"Okay, here's what I want," Natalie said as they sauntered in and out of shops. "I want that kind of outfit —" she pointed to a tiered print skirt and eyelet peasant blouse — "but in a beautiful fabric. And well made."

"Natie, Natie, you're in the islands. That is their beautiful fabric. And it's most likely their best made. Flow, go with the flow." Annie waved her arm in a long, sweeping motion.

"No," Natalie said, grabbing her friend's hand and literally pulling her out of the touristy souvenir shop. "This place is strictly for people off the cruise ships with no time to spend looking. Let's hit some of the side streets. We're on a mission here, and when we're done I'll treat you to fries and a Coke."

"Wow. How can I resist such a deal?" Annie skipped out ahead of Natalie. "Well, come on, what are you waiting for? The mission awaits."

They spent the rest of the afternoon searching shops for Natalie's one perfect outfit and ended up with two skirts, three blouses, silver hoop earrings and a lapis necklace. The gypsy in her had been satisfied. Annie bought a pair of feather earrings, so long they dusted her shoulders, and T-shirts for three of her friends back home.

"Well, you did it." Annie picked up a fry with her fingers and rolled it in ketchup. They were sitting on the small patio of a local restaurant. "You don't give up easily, but I guess it pays off. You got some great stuff." She popped the French fry into her mouth.

"Hmmmm....right," Natalie replied. She spoke absently, her attention captured by three men, in their mid to late twenties. One had dark hair and deeply-tanned skin, probably Italian or Greek, Natalie thought. The other had dark brown skin and close-cropped wiry black hair. And the third, the one facing her, had thick, light brown hair, cut short, and cheeks a little too pink from the sun. He was slightly rumpled, boyish and immensely attractive. Natalie watched as he attacked a hamburger and fries as though they were the first he'd had in a very long time. He took a huge bite of his burger and opened his eyes wide with delight.

His eyes. Even from several tables away, she could see they were the most remarkable combination of bronze and deep olive. Earthy. Ancient. He caught her stare and held it, as though sending some long-held secret message. Natalie broke the trance first, flashing him a wide, dimpled smile before looking away. "Let's go," she told Annie. Standing abruptly, she drained her glass of Coke and headed toward the cashier.

"Why, what's wrong?" Annie asked, grabbing a handful of fries, scanning the restaurant to see what could have set Natalie off so suddenly.

"Nothing. Nothing's wrong," Natalie said once they were back out on the street. "I just felt dizzy all of sudden. Too much sun and shopping I guess. I need a nap if we're going to hit the casino tonight. Let's head back." She glanced over her shoulder toward the restaurant as they walked away, but she couldn't see him, and she felt a deep sinking sensation, as though she'd just lost something of extreme value.

———◆———

Behind doors of thick beveled glass, just to the rear of Little Bay's lobby, was one of the island's few casinos, an enormous rose-colored room thick with smoke and gaming tables, with slot machines and casually dressed, over-tanned people hoping to make the night as scintillating as the day had been tranquil. The place was charged with the sounds of gambling — electronic bells clanging to announce slot winners as coins fell to a metal trough, clicking against one another in their descent. . .the spinning and whirling of roulette wheels. . .the roll of dice followed by bellows of enthusiasm or disappointment.

While Annie tried her hand at blackjack, Natalie had settled in at a roulette table, each time playing the same six numbers, each time holding her breath as the small white ball bounced in and out of slots until finally resting on one lucky number.

"Number nine," the dealer announced. "Lucky number nine." He placed a marker on the spot and smiled over at Natalie. "That's twice in a row, folks. Lucky number nine."

Natalie chatted with the woman next to her, running her fingers along mounds of green chips as a new stack was pushed toward her. Someone had moved in behind Natalie, probably waiting for a seat, but he was standing too close and it annoyed her. She arched her back and shoulders hoping he'd get the message: move back, stop breathing down my neck.

"Place your bets," the dealer announced, spinning the wheel.

She began placing chips on her favorite six numbers when a voice whispered in her ear: "Don't play nine again. It'll never happen, not three times in a row." She jumped at the warmth of his breath.

"It's just me, name's Johnny," he told Natalie when she turned and looked up at him "From the restaurant, this afternoon?"

"I remember." How could she *not* remember? His affect on her, even across the patio, had been unsettling to say the least. "I have to play it. It's one of my numbers." She turned away from Johnny and continued placing her bets, the same six she'd been playing all night.

"Play seventeen. It works for James Bond," he said. "Live on the wild side. Bet seven numbers this time."

Natalie shrugged without looking back at him. "Can't. I'm superstitious. Like my mother. It's a fatal family flaw." She watched as the dealer swept his arm high over the table, announcing *no more bets*, waiting for the ball to settle into a new slot.

"Seventeen. Lucky seventeen," the dealer said. He winked at Natalie, "Should have listened to him."

"Guess so," she replied, sliding her stack of chips toward him. "Cash out." She pushed back her chair and stood, waiting for the dealer to count out her winnings.

"How'd you do?" Johnny asked, his breath slipping across her bare shoulders as he bent to talk to her. Natalie's pulse quickened at his closeness, at the heat of his body and the faint scent of suntan lotion that had seeped into his skin from long hours on the beach.

"I'm always a winner," Natalie quipped, sidestepping to put space between them. Her voice was deliberately cool, as she struggled to understand her attraction to this man. He was almost irritating. Almost. She looked up at him and he looked right back, steady and unflinching. His eyes. Bronze and olive eyes laced with gold flecks. She felt an overwhelming urge to take his face in her hands and stare at them until she could figure out for sure if they were more gold than bronze or more olive than either. Instead she turned away, found Annie winning at the tables, and told her she was quitting for the night, she'd see her upstairs.

"No problem'o," Annie said, grinning and eyeing the man standing next to Natalie. "Alone?" she mouthed the word.

Natalie's only response was furrowed eyebrows and a dirty look. "See you later," she said to Annie and took off toward the exit.

"I'll bet you are," Johnny laughed, following right on her heels.

"Are what?"

"A winner." He pushed against the casino door, holding it open with his body as she passed by him into the hotel lobby. "Let me buy you a drink."

"I don't drink."

"Okay, how about a Coke?"

"I'm not thirsty."

Johnny laughed. "Okay, how about a walk on the beach and some conversation. You do walk and talk, don't you?"

Natalie laughed back, but held firm in her rejection. "Not at the same time. Not with strangers. And not after midnight."

Johnny picked up Natalie's right hand and placed it in his. He stroked it for a moment and, as she began to pull away, turned the caress into an official handshake. "Let's fix the stranger part: I'm Johnny Conway. Lieutenant John J. Conway, at your service." He bent gallantly at the waist, returning Natalie's hand to her side. "How about breakfast?"

"Johnny J? Like John John? Your mother had a hard time coming up with two names?" Natalie laughed. This man made her laugh. Not at all like Chad, she thought, and then wondered where the thought had come from. Chad was her future. *Don't mess up, Natalie, remember what Chad said about women who cheat and lie. Don't fall for this guy's line, no matter how cute or funny he is.*

"Sorry. I don't consort with servicemen," Natalie said, deliberately avoiding eye contact. "Look me up when you're a private citizen." She pressed the button for the elevator.

"You've got me for the next three weeks. Otherwise, you'll have to wait two years. Don't break a Marine's heart. We're destined. Can't you feel it?"

"I'm sure your heart will survive just fine. Besides, I don't believe in destiny. And I'm not here for three weeks, so you're on your own." Natalie stepped into the elevator, laughing out loud at his over-dramatized look of distress.

"What's your name angel? What room are you in?" She heard his voice call out as the doors closed and the elevator hummed, carrying her up to the third floor.

179

That night, with the sound of the ocean below and a cooling breeze from the trade winds coming in off the open balcony, Natalie tossed and turned, her sleep restless with a collection of voices and images, moving in and out of a hazy, layered dream. There was her mother, stroking her hair, reminding her to be a good girl; there was Aunt Willie's strong, sturdy face, telling her to follow her heart; there was Pearl, with those same pigtails and wide smile, shaking her head in disapproval, questioning Natalie's loyalty and failed friendship; and way off in the background, there was a dark, angry man, shouting at her, wielding something long and shiny. Through it all, there were brilliant, searing eyes penetrating each layer of her dream, asking only to be recognized.

TWENTY-TWO

"You're late." **Johnny** grinned as Annie and Natalie stepped off the elevator.

"For what?" Natalie asked.

"Breakfast. Don't you remember. Last night? You promised?"

"You took a chance, waiting here. What if we'd gone down the outside stairs? Or right to the beach?"

"But you didn't. Deep down you knew I'd be right here. Waiting. And you promised."

"I did not. You persisted, I resisted." Natalie flushed, looking anywhere but directly at Johnny.

"I persisted. And you promised."

"I did not!"

"But you —"

"Oh brother," Annie interrupted. "Guess I'll do my own intro, seeing you two are busy pretending not to be incredibly attracted to each other. I'm Annie Roth. And you're —?"

"Johnny. Johnny Conway. We...she and I..." he pointed to Natalie and then back to himself "...we met last night, well you saw that, but I still don't know her name. She disappeared and I thought maybe she was a figment of my imagination. So, here I am, to prove otherwise."

Annie jabbed Natalie in the ribs. "At least tell him your name."

Natalie laughed. She couldn't help herself. This man was outrageous. And awfully cute. "I'm Natalie."

"The angel has a name, and it's Natalie. I'd have waited here all night just to see that smile of yours again. I'd walk a million miles for one of your smiles, Nat-A- Leeee." He danced a few steps and swung out his arms in a bad rendition of the twenties singer, Al Jolson. "Come on, let me buy you girls breakfast. Then we can plan out the rest of our life together."

"Absoluteamundo," Annie answered. "I'm starving." She grabbed Natalie by the hand and led the way to the coffee shop.

Natalie shrugged, knowing she had no vote in the matter and secretly glad Annie had taken over. *Remember Chad. . .Remember Chad. . .*she chanted to herself. Johnny walked beside her, and it was hard to remember Chad.

All through breakfast, while they made small talk, Natalie kept sneaking looks at Johnny, trying to understand what it was about him that she found so appealing. He was in the Marines for God's sake. The Marines. He might as well be a mailman. Probably poor as a church mouse. Wouldn't Marilyn just die seeing them here together. Except that it was a free meal, and Marilyn put great stock in things like that. Dating for Dinner, that's what Marilyn used to call it. Natalie noticed Johnny's hands, strong, tanned hands, hands that knew how to work and probably how to love.

Where did that come from?

"So, are we on?" Johnny asked, as they stood to go.

"On for what?" Natalie could feel the heat of a rising blush stain her face.

"What orbit were you just in?" Annie asked. "You okay? You look flushed all of a sudden."

"I'm fine." Natalie's voice was a little too sharp as she spoke only to Annie. "So are we going swimming now, or what?"

"It's more of an Or What," Annie said. "Weren't you listening? Johnny has his friend's jeep. We're going to go pick him up and joy ride around the island."

"Oh. I don't know. Is that what you really want to do, instead of the beach?" Natalie wasn't at all comfortable with the idea, as though agreeing to joy riding implied more than just an afternoon together.

"Are you kidding? Aren't you tired of being fried every day? Let's live a little."

"So, it's a yes?" Johnny asked, looking from Natalie to Annie and back to Natalie.

"I guess. Sure, why not?" Natalie shrugged to suggest it was no big deal, but, inside, she felt out of control, as though an invisible hand was at her back, pushing her into uncharted territory. "Where's this friend?"

Johnny and Annie looked at each other, rolled their eyes and laughed simultaneously. "Not like we didn't just go through this or anything," Annie said.

"With his grandmother," Johnny explained as they walked outside. "Up in the hills. I met Rick in boot camp. We've stayed in touch, on and off. His mother was born here. Left when she was about twenty and moved to Florida, then New Mexico, I think. Married some guy who was half Cherokee, had Rick and a passel of kids. He's out of the corps, staying here until he decides where to go next. I think we caught her up to date, don't you?" Johnny winked at Annie. "Hope you were daydreaming about me," he said, helping Natalie into the front seat of the open, army-style jeep.

"Fat chance," Natalie answered.

Annie climbed in back, sprawling her legs across the seat, and they were off, hair blowing in the wind, the sky blue and clear, the hot Caribbean sun beating down on them. Natalie began to relax, and when Johnny brushed against her hand as he shifted gears, trying to maneuver a steep, dirt road, she didn't pull back.

Iris Hodges lived in the hills of Saint Martin, on the Dutch side of the island. Each curved road that climbed upward was steeper and narrower than the road before and several times Johnny had to pull off to the side, wedging his jeep into the brush, to make way for an approaching car. Although the island was dominated by sky and ocean, it's true power was hidden in the hills, with its rural neighborhoods and magnificent vistas. Tucked in among trees, and along a road barely visible to the tourist's eye, was the four-room home of Iris Hodges, who had raised and buried three daughters, and, just last year, lost her husband to what the doctors called liver problems. The house was white with a red tin roof and shutters the same shade of pink as the corolita that grew along the stone walls marking the property's corners. Iris sat in a rocking chair on the porch of her home watching as her grandson, Rick, gave her house a fresh coat of white paint.

"Hey man, I found her," Johnny hollered to Rick even before he had parked the Jeep and turned off the ignition. He pointed to Natalie, "My angel. I found her. As a matter of fact, I found two angels."

Annie and Natalie followed Johnny up the worn path toward the small front porch.

"Hello, Mrs. Hodges, how are you? What a beautiful day." He bent down and kissed the woman on her cheek. "I want you to meet Natalie and Annie."

Iris Hodges smiled, a small, shy smile that grew wider, until it seemed to completely fill her round, brown face. "Sure is beautiful," she said fanning herself and popping a peanut into her mouth. "Hello girls. Make yourself at home." She held out a handful of newly shelled peanuts and urged them to take a few.

Rick put down his paintbrush, wiped his hands on his t-shirt, and sauntered over. "Found her, huh?" he said to Johnny and then turned to Natalie. "I don't know what you did to him, but he wasn't worth shit, excuse my French, when he got back here last night. Haven't seen a babe do that to him since —"

"Since nothing," Johnny interrupted. "Hey, man, forget the painting for today. Come explore the island with us."

"Can't. I promised my grandmother. Should have done this days ago. You guys go, have a good time. I'll drive the Chevy in later." He nodded in the direction of a car that was once blue, but now sported a variety of colors, the primary one being that of rust. "I'll pick up Bullface and Lance and we'll meet you at Little Bay around eight."

"Bullface?" Annie raised her eyebrows "Is that for real?"

"Realer than you would believe. It's an attitude AND a description!" Rick said.

"Why don't we help?" Natalie suggested.

"Help what?" Johnny asked.

"Paint. What else?"

"I could go for that," Annie said. "Like something out of Tom Sawyer. Cool."

"Yeah? You serious?" Johnny asked. "Not exactly an ideal vacation day, painting under the hot sun."

Out of the corner of her eye, Natalie noticed Iris Hodges listening to their conversation, rocking back and forth in her cane rocker, nodding her head in agreement. She had a quiet dignity that Natalie responded to immediately. Stern, warm, protective. A lot like Aunt Willie, she thought.

"You'd be surprised by my definition of an ideal day," Natalie said. "I'd really like to do this."

Rick immediately ran into the shed for three more brushes as though afraid they'd change their mind.

"Do you always get your way?" Rick asked Natalie, handing her a brush. "Not that I'm complaining."

"Most always," Natalie laughed, sticking out her tongue in teenage playfulness. *What was with her anyway?* She never acted like this. It was as though her new clothes and all this sunshine had unleashed some untamed side of her. She knew it was a non-Marilyn approved side of her personality and she'd have to keep it in check. But not today. Free and Fun. That was the order of the day. Natalie kicked off her shoes and wriggled her toes in the cool grass. She would work in her bare feet.

All afternoon, the four of them painted Iris Hodges' house, stopping now and then for a drink of chilled guava berry rum, which Iris served in short, wide-rimmed glasses. The air was thick and warm, cooled only slightly by an occasional breeze, and so they sprayed themselves with water from the garden hose until they were soaked through and their clothes nearly transparent. As twilight settled in over the hills, and the hot sun no longer baked the ground, neighbors began to gather outside, filling the emerging darkness with their chatter, as chicken and ribs sizzled on open fires.

It was an unspoken, essentially unplanned, ritual in the hills — the nearly-nightly merging of households as neighbors shared food and gossip, wandering from one house to the other, perching on a fence or picnic table as they ate and talked.

After dinner, the men played dominos by the yellow cast of flickering lanterns, while youngsters curled up in their mother's laps. Natalie and Johnny found an old blanket and wandered away from the others, spreading it across a patch of grass, settling down to watch the night sky.

"This is my idea of perfect," Johnny said, laying on his back, arms behind his head. "Nothing fancy, just real."

"We really do complicate life, don't we?" Natalie said, sitting with her knees pressed up to her chest, looking out over the hills. "Up here, everything good seems possible. It's different back home. Don't you think?"

In response, Johnny reached one arm up and pulled Natalie down to him. She didn't resist, didn't pull away from the sudden closeness of his lips or the intensity of his eyes. A soft mountain breeze wrapped itself around them, whispering ancient secrets, caressing the surface of their skin, still warm from the sun.

It felt as though he was kissing her, even though he wasn't. She could feel his breath on her face. Warm. Inviting. Patient. Johnny held her gaze tenderly, exploring, not so much her face as her soul, it seemed, stroking Natalie's hair, running his fingers across her cheeks, skimming across the skin of one arm and then the other with a touch so light she thought she might be imagining it. She could barely breath.

Natalie's heart beat faster as she pressed her body against his. She could feel him move beneath her, more like a slight shifting, nearly imperceptible, involuntary, as though he were controlling the intensity of his movements. Feeling the pulse of his body beneath her, she moved her face closer to his, their lips brushing one another's, softly, gently, flirting with their passion. Johnny pressed his hand against the back of Natalie's head, bringing her lips down on his in a kiss that seemed to be filled with fireworks and music. And, in fact, it was.

At the very moment of their first kiss, the night exploded with the sounds of a steel band — local boys playing their special brand of island music on oil drums and tambourines. Stunned by the sudden blast, Johnny pushed Natalie away, as though he'd been caught kissing on the battlefield. He jumped up and she fell backward. Both were embarrassed and disoriented. When he finally regained his balance, Johnny held out his hand, helping Natalie to her feet. They stood, breathing deeply, both trying to compose themselves. Natalie grinned; Johnny laughed out loud, taking her in his arms.

Feeling the lush mountain grass between their toes, they danced barefoot to the strains of a haunting, primitive beat. Johnny whirled Natalie around Iris Hodges' yard as a toothless brown-skinned man grinned approvingly.

For the first time in her life, Natalie felt filled up, rather than empty; satisfied, rather than searching; safe rather than vulnerable. A deep sense of knowing slipped across her body and into her consciousness; carried on the wing of a breeze, a soft whisper pumped through her veins: *listen to your heart, Natalie; listen to your heart.*

TWENTY-THREE

"**M**arry me."

"What?"

"Marry me," Johnny repeated.

Still wet from their swim, Natalie was nestled against Johnny's bare chest. Since that first evening, they'd spent nearly every minute together. So much for her promise to Annie about the two of them and no-one else on this vacation, but, remarkably, Annie was patient and forgiving, encouraging Natalie to find herself and, hopefully, true love in the process.

"It feels right," Annie told her, "you and Johnny. Go for it, Natie. And I think I'm going to go for staying here, at least for a while."

Natalie took Annie at her word and explored the island with Johnny. They found a private stretch of beach along the French side, protected by a grove of palm trees. That's where they were now when Johnny proposed.

She sat up straight, pushing damp strands of hair away from her cheeks, and studied his face for any hint of joking. "You're serious, aren't you?"

"I am," Johnny said, kissing her neck and shoulders. "I require very little. A good burger, an action flick now and then, and my woman loving me at the end of the day. I'm a low maintenance kind of guy who will love you forever." He continued kissing her. "And ever."

Natalie bent her head forward, like she'd done that very first day, feeling the breeze tickle her skin, making her feel like a palm tree growing in rhythm with nature. Now it was Johnny tickling her skin, sending small beats of desire from her head to her toes. She ran her hand across Johnny's thighs, strong and muscular, and then up to his chest where she twirled golden strands of short curly hair around her index finger. When she didn't answer, he tried again.

"I'm serious, Nat, marry me. There'll never be another woman for me. Only you."

"But how? When? You mean, when you get back from Nam, don't you?"

"No, before then."

Natalie bolted upright and looked at him squarely, almost angry, at the absurdity of his suggestion. "Right. Now there's a plan! I'm leaving in five days and you're not far behind. Except it's Boston for me and Vietnam for you. And we're going to get married? I don't think so."

"Why not?" He grinned.

"There are a thousand reasons why not. Don't joke about this. You're making me cry." She swiped at the tears threatening to fall.

"Natalie, Natalie, don't cry. I love you. I know it's fast. But I feel like we've been together forever. It's right. I know it is. Marry me. We can make it work."

"No we can't. You're a dreamer John Conway. It's not realistic, and you know it."

"Screw realistic. We'll make it work." He cupped her chin in his hands and talked so softly his words were nearly lost to the sounds of the ocean. "Listen, I'm insanely in love with you. I don't know how it happened, but it did. The moment I saw you looking at me in the restaurant, that first afternoon. And then you smiled. I was a goner, right then and there."

"I know. For me, too." She signed deeply and stroked his face. "But, still, we need a plan. We can't just get married."

"We'll figure it out. Just say yes, first."

Natalie looked out at the ocean, shading her eyes from the sun with her hand. Johnny allowed her the silence. He didn't touch her; he didn't talk; he didn't move a muscle. He simply waited.

"Yes first." Natalie looked up at him and smiled, the truest, widest, deepest smile she could ever remember giving someone.

"Yes!" Johnny shouted. "Yes! We'll figure it out." He kissed her eyes and her nose and then, deeply, her lips. "Yes." He whispered. "We'll figure it out."

Natalie held him close, inhaling his scent of sun and sea and Coppertone lotion, imprinting it onto her soul, as though she knew this couldn't possibly last and she'd have to remember this single moment of joy for years to come. Tears spilled down her cheeks, sadness falling like a shadow across her body.

"Natalie?" Johnny asked.

"I called my mother this morning, told her I'd met someone. I wanted her to be happy for me."

"And?"

"She had a fit."

"A big fit or a little fit?" Johnny drew hearts on Natalie's back with the tip of his index finger.

"Annie called it a shit-fit."

Johnny laughed. "That qualifies as big!" He laughed again, trying hard to lighten the mood. When it didn't work, he tried directness. "Natalie, sweetie, put it in perspective. From what you tell me, this is a woman who's so afraid of life she won't even acknowledge she has a daughter."

"I know."

"And here you are challenging her status quo, going against everything she brought you up to want."

"That's just about what she said." Natalie began picking at the hot grains of sand, examining them as if they might hold some answer.

"What else?"

Natalie shook her head and continued playing with the sand.

"What else did she say?"

"That I was betraying her. That I have no loyalty. That I'm an ungrateful and bad — she actually said bad — daughter. That falling for a serviceman is about the lowest, most awful thing I could possibly do to her."

"But did you tell her I'm a Marine? A Marine, for God's sake. You can't get any better than that."

"In Marilyn's book you can get a whole lot better. I didn't tell you before, because it didn't matter, but back in Boston I've been dating this guy, an attorney. He's pretty rich and Marilyn started having her heart set on him as a son-in-law, or should I say a brother-in-law. It's all so upside down."

Johnny stiffened. "You're seeing someone?"

"Not serious. I thought I liked him. Thought maybe he would solve all my problems. But then I met you. It's nothing serious, honest. A few kisses. I'm sure you've kissed a few girls in your day. Like that babe Rick mentioned —" She stopped and looked at Johnny, suddenly aware of how little they really knew about one another. All kinds of private memories and experiences they hadn't revealed. Not secrets, exactly. Just things. Untold and unexamined. It felt like they were on the brink of a fight, but she couldn't figure out exactly why.

"Point taken," he said, taking her hand. "Forget the past. From this point on, no more babes and no more men in Boston. Let's plan our future. I know how much you like to plan."

"I didn't have the nerve to tell Marilyn that you're headed for another tour of duty," Natalie said, her voice louder, angrier, than she'd intended. "I can't believe you're going back to Vietnam. Why would you do that? Why? You must be crazy. I'm in love with a crazy man." Natalie stood up and walked away from Johnny.

He followed her down to the water's edge. "Do you think I want to go? Do you really think that? How'd I know I was going to meet you, fall in love? Tell me, how could I know that?"

"Quiet. You don't have to yell."

"Why, who's going to hear me? There's nobody around for miles. Oh, I see, it's not the nice thing to do. Yelling isn't controlled enough for you. Well, I'm yelling. Do you hear me? I'm yelling."

"You're an ass." Natalie turned, kicking the water in front of her as she began walking the long stretch of beach away from Johnny.

"So are you," Johnny yelled back. "Do you think I want to go? Do you think I planned it this way? Right!" He shouted into the ocean wind, the words hitting her back, as Natalie continued walking away from him and he continued following, punching the air with his fists, casting out the darts containing the condensed story of his sorry life.

"Let's see, how's this for a plan: first I get so trashed one night that I call my brother to come pick me up so I don't have to drive home drunk on a crappy rainy night, but his shit-can of a sports car has no traction so it does a one-eighty on the wet pavement. He ends up under a truck. Cut in half. Him and the car. Now that's a plan. Right? Great Plan. Oh, and then, after the funeral, my dad never speaks to me again, after all, I killed my brother, *his favorite son*, so I quit college, give up my dream of becoming a journalist, and join the Marines, kind of like a penance, but instead of atonement, I get to watch my entire squad get blown to smithereens 'cause I'm a shitty leader. Then, here's the kicker, I figure, I'll try it again. Instead of sectioning out, I re-up for another tour of duty. See if I can make things right this time. Yup, there's John J. Conway, always seeking redemption."

Catching up to Natalie, he pulled her to a stop, their feet sinking into the wet sand. "So there I am," he said softly, "a fucking mess. So before my next tour, I come to a quiet island to see if I can restore my sanity, in thirty days or less, 'cause that's all they give you. And guess what? I meet the woman of my dreams. And then I deliberately head back to Nam. Maybe get my own head blown off in the process. Now, there's a fucking good plan if you ask me."

"But it's your plan, isn't it? You did come here. You did meet me. And you are going back!" Natalie could feel her face harden. When she couldn't bear to look at him anymore, she pulled away.

"Go ahead, say the rest. Say it: say because *you're responsible* for a decision that killed your brother and then nine Marines. Go ahead, say it."

"Why should I? You don't need me to punish you. You doing a great job all by yourself! She pounded on his chest with her fist. "And you are going back." Tears streamed down her face. "Damn you."

"Don't. Don't ever say that." Johnny grabbed hold of Natalie's fist. "Damn you — those were the last words my father ever said to me."

Tears and lost words burned in Natalie's throat. There was nothing more to say.

Johnny took her hand and pressed it against his chest. "Feel my heart, how it's pounding. That's what you do to me. Being with you is the best thing that's ever happened to me. Leaving you will be the worst."

"Then don't."

"I don't have a choice."

"We all have choices."

"Do we? Not always. Not once you've re-upped and they need more bodies to fight a war nobody believes in."

"Maybe you could explain it to someone, explain it was all a mistake, that you really don't want to go back to Nam. That you were distressed over what happened, not thinking clearly."

Johnny stroked Natalie's hair. "Everybody over there is distressed."

Natalie swallowed hard, tired of fighting, tired, even, of talking. They stood for a long time, holding onto one another, the water lapping at their ankles.

"Just explain it," she whispered into Johnny's chest. "It's bad enough you joined up when your brother died, as though destroying your plans would bring him back. But now, again? It's too much Johnny. Talk about self destructive."

"I know," he agreed. "It's a flaw."

"A big one."

"I'm working on it."

They headed back to their blanket and sat quietly. Natalie dug in the sand with her bare hands, digging deeper and deeper, pushing aside the hot grains as though an answer could be found if she just looked hard and deep enough.

She unearthed shells and cigarette butts and dried bits of driftwood, tossing them aside as she continued digging. When she came across a worn nickel, she wiped off the sand and looked for the date. 1947. The year she was born. *Find a coin, give it away for luck.* That was Marilyn's motto. One of them anyway. She turned to give the coin to Johnny, but he was lying down, his eyes closed, his arm shading his face from the late-day sun. Or from her. She changed her mind and reached over for her shorts, tucking the nickel into one of the pockets. If anyone needs luck, she thought, it's me.

After what seemed a lifetime, Johnny rolled over and touched her arm. "Let's not do this to each other. We have so little time left. Say you'll marry me. We'll figure the rest out."

"I already said I would. But between Marilyn and the Marines, I don't see how."

"I could have had a stateside tour." Johnny sat up, thinking out loud, trying to sort out the pieces of their future. "I'm the one who chose to go back to Nam."

"Oh Johnny, you think —"

"What if . . ." he said slowly. "What if. . ."

"What? What if what?"

"Well, it wouldn't exactly be the high life, but if they haven't drawn up my papers yet, there's a chance, just a chance, they might change my tour. Assign me stateside. I have to stay in, there's no changing that. But if I could change the tour, not go back to Nam — would you marry me, now, live as a Marine's wife, whatever that means, for a couple of years?"

"And then what?"

"Whatever life brings," Johnny said, taking her hand. "We'll move to the Cape. I've always wanted to live there, by the ocean. I'll finish college. You can have that shop you talked about. Or kids. We can have kids. Anything's possible. We'll figure it out."

"Oh, Johnny. Do you really think, is it possible?"

"I don't know, and I don't want to get your. . .our. . .hopes up. I'll make some calls. Fly to Guantanamo Bay. It's the nearest base. See who can do what for me. It could take a few days."

"Meanwhile," Natalie said, filled with the energy of anticipation, "I'll cancel my plans for going home until we know exactly what you're doing. I'm sure Uncle Jay won't mind if I say a few days longer, especially since Annie's staying on. Oh, and I'd absolutely love to be the wife of a Marine. As long as you're the Marine." She gave him a hard, playful kiss. "And I'll keep my mother under control. I'll tell her I'm marrying a hot-shot journalist-to-be."

"Not a lot of money in that. Lots of by-lines, a little glory. But not a lot of money. Can you live with that?"

"I can," Natalie answered.

"But can Marilyn?!" They said in unison.

They watched the sun drop, filling the sky with a burnt orange afterglow as it hit the cool ocean water and slid beneath the horizon. All they while, they talked out their ideas. First thing tomorrow, they would begin putting them into action.

As the sky darkened, Johnny lit a small fire; they sipped vodka tonics and ate the picnic lunch they'd forgotten about. One by one, the stars appeared. Johnny held Natalie in his arms, pointing out the constellations he'd learned as a young boy.

"That's the Archer," he said, tracing out the ninth sign of the Zodiac. "It's the centaur, half horse and half man. "It represents the conflict between the philosophical mind and the carnal instinct."

"And which wins out?"

"The carnal, I hope," Johnny answered, running his hands across her back, kissing her shoulders. He pointed upward, drawing a large curve in the air, with his index finger. "Can you see the curve of the horse's buttocks? Right there, do you see where I mean?"

"Sort of. It's kind of a stretch, like a dot-to-dot without enough dots."

"Only in the beginning. Squint your eyes and you'll see it all come together. That bright star, just where the buttocks curves the highest, below the centaur's wing, that's called Nunki."

Nunki.

The name resonated deep within Natalie, tugging at something hidden, something long forgotten. She wriggled in discomfort.

"You okay?" Johnny asked.

She nodded and then shrugged. Yes, no, maybe. Was an answer ever simple?

"Do you ever feel, I don't know. . ." she stopped and then started again, "you know how when you look through an old family album and you don't even know some of the people, they died way before you were even born, but yet there's something familiar in their faces, in the way they smile or hold their body? You feel connected, like you know them, know things about them, even when you don't?"

"Yeah, I do." Johnny stroked her bare arm. "I know what you're saying. Almost like there's this cosmic connection."

"Exactly. Sometimes that's how I feel. But not necessarily about people. Like when you just identified that star." She whispered the name — *Nunki* — and fell silent before continuing, absorbing the way it felt on her lips, the way it struck at her heart. "Sometimes I feel that deep down I know things that I don't even know I know. It's hard to explain. I feel like there's this door hidden inside of me and if I could just push against it hard enough, it would open and behind it would be all kinds of wonderful knowledge, answers about me, about the universe, about my place in the universe." She fanned her face as though trying to swat away the thoughts. "Anyway, forget it. I have a tendency to think too much."

Johnny looked up at the sky. "So, old Nunki stirred a few memories for you, huh? Kind of a cute name, don't you think? As a matter of fact, from now on that's exactly what I'm going to call you. "Nunki. You're my little Nunki."

"Don't you dare."

"Oh, my little Nunki. My sweet Nunki." He teased Natalie, running one hand across her hips and down her legs while he tickled under her arms.

"Stop right now. My name's Natalie," she giggled. "Stop, stop tickling."

"Make me."

"You asked for it."

Natalie pushed Johnny down on the blanket and smothered him with kisses that quickly went from playful to passionate. Under the stars, some scattered, some clustered into constellations, they surrendered to one another with a sense of knowing uncommon to new lovers. A light breeze ruffled Natalie's hair and from somewhere deep inside she heard a sound that reminded her of wind rustling through the trees.

"I found him," she whispered into the wind, her voice muffled by the sound of the ocean kissing the sand and the insistent pressure of Johnny's lips on hers. His hands glided across her hips, stroking her thighs, finding the sweet spot of warmth and wetness; he caressed that spot until the pleasure pounded in Natalie's head and she moved beneath him with urgency and abandon.

"I love you. I'll always love you," Johnny said, as he entered Natalie, giving her the fullness of his love and a promise of forever.

TWENTY-FOUR

Natalie was curled up on the bed when Annie walked into their room late the next afternoon and playfully punched her in the arm. "Hey, Natie, true love is supposed to be groovy, not gruesome. Cheer up, girl, he's only been gone what? seven or so hours, off to see the wizard at Guantanamo Bay, to try and get his orders changed. He'll be back in a few days. No sweat."

Natalie pressed both hands against her stomach and the hot searing pain that had hit like a fireball, all the while clutching the two-page telegram that must have cost Marilyn a fortune to send. Stress. Doctors always told her the stomach pain was from stress. The stress of not being a good enough daughter. They never said that, of course, but she knew that was the reason. If she could ever finally succeed in pleasing Marilyn, the pain was sure to go away.

Here she was, once again, being given the chance to show her loyalty, to prove her true worth and she was failing. That's what the telegram said: "A good, loyal, caring daughter would hightail it out of that God-forsaken land and work on marrying that boy Chad with the breeding and the money." And that was just one sentence of Marilyn's missive.

Annie wrenched the telegram from her friend's hand.

"Oh, God, Natie, I'm so sorry. How does she even know about you and Johnny?"

"Because I'm stupid. I called her. Somehow, stupid, silly me, I actually thought she'd be happy I'd found someone."

"Yeah, well. . ." Annie left the sentence unfinished. There was nothing to say that Natalie didn't already know.

"I really love him, Annie. I know it's been a short time, but it feels like we're meant to be. But, she's my mother. I know she wants what's best for me. Maybe she's right —"

"Listen," Annie said, "she may be your mother, but let's face it, in name only. A cash register is the only thing that rings her bell. Not your best interests. Definitely not your happiness."

"Don't say that. Please. She loves me, I know she does." Fresh tears tumbled across Natalie's face as she pushed against the pain, laying on her side, curling her knees up closer to her chest.

Annie leaned over and wiped her friend's cheek. "Think about Aunt Willie. She'd have a whole different take on this. You know she would. She'd say go for it, girl. And fast!"

"Except Willie's getting senile and Marilyn's the only one I really have. She's my only real family."

"Some family," Annie mumbled and was immediately sorry. "I'm sorry. I know she's important to you, and I know you need to please her, but not at this price, Natie. You're a grown woman. You can leave home. It's acceptable. My God, Natalie, it's 1970. Women have the vote. They even go braless!"

Natalie rolled over on her back and stared up at the ceiling. She didn't want to talk. She just wanted everything to be fixed. She wanted it to be okay to want Johnny.

"I don't know what you mean," Natalie said. "I've left home. You know that."

"It's a metaphor. And you exactly what I mean." Annie stood and paced the floor. "You haven't left anything or anybody. All

201

you did was change venues. How's that for a fifty cent word?" Annie turned and stood directly in front of Natalie. "She still runs your life. Her opinions still count too much. You are not Henny Penny. The world will not come crashing down on you if you're not mama's good little girl every single minute of your life."

"I know."

"Do you?"

"I don't know. I don't know anything."

"Listen," Annie said, lighting a cigarette, "Johnny will be back in a few days. Just hang in there until then. Can you do that?"

Natalie nodded and closed her eyes. Maybe if she rested for awhile. Maybe everything would work itself out.

"That's it. You take a nap. I promised Uncle Jay I'd run some errands for him. He needs the stuff for tonight. I might be gone a couple hours. Will you be okay?"

Natalie nodded as she swallowed back more tears. She watched Annie tiptoe out of the room and listened as the door clicked shut behind her. It seemed as though the world had gone completely neutral; with the windows closed, there was no air moving through the room, and it seemed to her that all the sounds had disappeared. As she lay on the small hotel bed, in this newly-created vacuum, the only reality was the sound of her mother's voice, pounding against the inside walls of her head, compelling Natalie to listen, and to obey. Natalie moaned and rolled over on her side, praying for sleep. She would hold on, just like Annie said. Before she knew it, Johnny would be back; he and Annie would help to exorcise Marilyn's voice from inside her brain. They would take away the horrible sick feeling that came from letting her mother down.

Natalie was in a half-sleep, her body racked with sweat, when the phone rang. Natalie jumped to answer it.

"Johnny?" she said, still drugged with sleep.

"No, Natalie. It's not Johnny." Marilyn's voice jumped out at her, filling the noiseless vacuum with its force, pounding at Natalie, not just from inside now, but from the outside as well. "Did you get my telegram?"

"Yes, mother."

"Quiet" Marilyn lowered her voice to a loud whisper. "What's wrong with you? What if Harry picked up the phone just as you said that? Are you deliberately trying to ruin my marriage? After all I've done for you?"

"No, I'm sorry, I just forgot."

"Well, next time think. That's your whole problem, you don't think. Now, let's get down to brass tacks."

Natalie rearranged her body, standing up as straight as possible, assembling fragments of strength, trying to access breaths that wouldn't come. Her chest was in a vice and Marilyn's voice was doing the squeezing: word by word, syllable by syllable, clamping down tighter and tighter.

"Hang on," Natalie said weakly and then, gathering courage, a little stronger, "Just hang on." She put down the phone and stretched her arms toward the ceiling, standing tall, trying to fill her lungs with air. Walking toward the door in order to turn on the switch for the overhead fan, she spotted the Polaroid picture Annie had taken of her and Johnny after dinner one night. Natalie picked up the picture, holding it tightly as she returned to the phone, standing, rather than sitting, as she prepared for battle. Standing gave her a greater sense of power; the image in her hand gave her strength and purpose.

Marilyn was shouting Natalie's name into the phone, over and over again. Natalie had to shout back in order to be heard.

"I'm here, I'm back. You can stop yelling."

"Well, I never! Here I spend all this money and my good time calling you in that God-forsaken place, and you just slap the phone down without a howdy-do to me. I knew you were a selfish kid, but that just takes the cake."

"I felt dizzy. I needed to turn the fan on. It's hot here you know."

"Yeah, well, by the looks of it you're more than a little dizzy. I think the sun has gone and fried your brain." Natalie stroked the image of Johnny's face as Marilyn continued talking. "My horoscope's been reading doom and gloom for nearly a week now, but these last couple of days, it's been giving me advice about takin' charge and fixin' matters. And that's exactly what I'm doing."

"I love him," Natalie said. "I love him and I want to marry him."

"Nonsense. It's probably the first good feeling of lust you've had in your twenty-odd years."

"Twenty-two, I'm twenty-two Marilyn, old enough —"

"Old enough for what? Don't get sassy with me, young lady. Old enough to ruin your life, maybe. Believe you me, I know. I just hope you've had the good sense to protect yourself, so you don't go endin' up like me, havin' to settle cause you didn't plan better. Not that Harry's so bad mind you, but I was meant for more, you know that. My destiny didn't work out. So now it's up to you, for the both of us. How many times have I told you that, huh, how many times?"

If they were in the same room together, this would be the exact moment when Marilyn would take Natalie's chin in her hands and squeeze, leaving behind blazing red marks that would last for hours.

"I know, I really do." Natalie voice was soft and pleading. "You've done your best for me, and now you want only the best. But, the thing is, Johnny is the best. If only you could meet him."

"If I met him, I'd see right through that fancy uniform of his. I'd see a Marine lookin' to take advantage of my kid sister." She exaggerated the words kid sister and Natalie knew that Harry must now be within listening distance.

"But. . ."

"No buts, no maybes, no nothing," Marilyn said. "This is the way it is, kid, and it's for your own good. You marry this guy, and what you've got is some husband you hardly know, off in the service — for how long? — you never told me for how long. Is he going back to Vietnam?"

When Natalie didn't answer, Marilyn continued. "He is, isn't he? Great. He'll probably get hooked on drugs, maybe mangled for life, and countin' on you to take care of him. You do that and it's all over little girl. You won't have any family to turn to. Aunt Willie is getting loony, and I'll have Harry help me sit Shiva for you — that's Jewish, you know, for when you disown someone and pretend they're dead — so, you have two choices: I sit Shiva or you forget this nonsense and get back where you belong, doing what you're supposed to be doing."

"Please, please don't do this." Natalie's hand went weak and the photograph in her hand slipped to the floor. "Please." She was crying audibly now.

"This is nothin' to cry over. It's puppy love, that's all. In a few months, you'll thank me for not lettin' you ruin your life. Now, here's the plan. I've reserved the seven o'clock flight for you back to Logan. You can use the return ticket you already have, just check in early so they can fix the paper work. As a matter of fact, it's four there now, you should probably leave right away, in case there's any glitches. Now, when you get to Logan — here's the surprise — take a cab right to the Ritz."

"I have a room. At the Y."

"Not any more," Marilyn said. "I was there just this morning, bright and early. Packed you right up."

"They let you into my room? They're not allowed."

"Well, actually, they didn't. But those flimsy locks respond real well to a bobby pin and a little persistence." Marilyn sounded proud of herself. "I booked you into the Ritz. You'll stay there for as long as it takes. You've got to live right to land the right man. That Chad fellow will be impressed. You've been doing it slipshod until now, that's why you got misled. Now you're back on the right track."

"I can't afford the Ritz."

"You can now. I paid three months up front, courtesy of Aunt Willie. If you need more time, we'll figure it out."

Natalie went numb. She was being sucked into a vortex and there seemed no way to battle the force. "Aunt Willie? But she's in no condition —"

"She loves you, although some days, like now, I can't for the life of me figure out why. Anyway, she's still pretty together, if you get my drift, and she agreed to help. Besides, what's she gonna' do with her cash now? She took that trip last summer. That's it for her. She can barely find her way to the bathroom. She'll be in a nursing home before you know it, ripping through every red cent."

"Can't we talk about this? Find a compromise? I really don't want to —"

"Don't whine," Marilyn interrupted. "Here are your choices, plain and simple: me, your mama," she whispered the word, "the Ritz, Boston, and the chance to be a really good girl who makes me proud, or that Marine, a few days of lust, and then sorrow for the rest of your life. The choice is yours, but you better make it good."

"Don't make me choose."

"I gotta' go," Marilyn said. "We're going out for buffet with some customers of Harry's and he's wavin' at me like crazy. I gotta go doll myself up. Call me from the Ritz. I understand they put a chocolate on your pillow every night. Now, that's class."

"Marilyn, wait, please, can't we figure something out?"

"It's already figured out. As I see it, there's no contest between the two choices. All I can say is call me from Boston, or don't call at all."

TWENTY-FIVE

Natalie left two notes, one for Annie, another for Johnny, hugged Uncle Jay goodbye and grabbed a cab to the airport. By midnight, she was settled in at the Ritz Carlton, which was everything Marilyn had promised it would be: Classy. Elegant. Old Boston in every sense of the word. A place of means and good manners. And Natalie hated it.

It took less than a week for Natalie to realize that the price of loyalty to Marilyn was too high, no matter how much she craved her mother's approval. Annie was right. It all came down to choices. And leaving Johnny had been a bad one. But fixable, Natalie decided. With love, anything was fixable. She called Aunt Willie.

Natalie had to explain the situation three times, in three different ways, before Aunt Willie was able to grasp what Natalie was saying and why she was asking for money.

"For a plane ticket and expenses," Natalie explained patiently, thinking maybe she should have visited instead of calling. "To go back to Saint Martin, to Johnny. I'll pay you back, someday. I promise."

Willie chuckled once she realized Natalie was in love and going after her man. "No need. You can have anything I have," she said, her voice weak but steady. "Vickie will wire the money as soon as we hang up." Vickie Barstow was a middle-aged divorced woman who earned extra money by helping Willie — running errands, making meals, doing whatever it would take to keep her from going into a nursing home. "We like happy endings, don't we Vickie," Willie said and Natalie could hear the smile in her voice. "Call and let us know it's a happy one."

The next call was to Annie. "I'm coming back. Tell Johnny, I'm sorry. Tell him I love him." She was so excited she could barely get the words out. "I just bought my ticket. I'll be there tomorrow night. Let him know. Or should I surprise him? What do you think, Annie? Should I surprise him?"

"He's gone," Annie said.

"What do you mean gone? His leave isn't up yet."

"He was pissed, Natie. Really pissed. He got back here two days after you left. Had his orders changed. You two were going to live stateside. Everything was cool. He was so excited, couldn't wait to tell you the news. I could get a word in edge-wise. I finally just handed him your note."

"Oh, Annie," Natalie sank to the floor, barely able to hold onto the phone. "What did he say?"

"Nothing, at first. Then he got wasted, big time, and ranted on and on about getting his orders changed back, going to Nam after all. *They need all the bodies they can get.* That's a direct quote. Didn't care if he lived or died."

"Oh, God, Annie. . .where is he now? I'll find him, explain, make things right."

"You can't. 'Cause I don't know. They all left. Johnny, Bullface, Rick. Island hopping they said. Looking for bad women and good booze. Another direct quote. Said I should tell you exactly that if we ever talked."

"There's got to be a way."

209

"If you have his ID number, you could trace him through the Marines."

"I don't. We never even thought about that. We were going to be together, forever."

"Natie, I'm sorry. He's gone. Aside from the photos I took, it's almost like he never existed. Like we made him up."

"What am I going to do?" Natalie choked out the words. "Annie, what am I going to do?" It was hitting her, the enormous price she was paying for her rash action. It felt like Pearl all over again. She was always making wrong choices. And for the wrong reasons.

"I don't know," Annie answered. "Find a way to move on, I guess. See where the path leads. I'm really, really sorry, Natie."

"Yeah, me too."

Ever since she returned from Saint Martin, Chad started taking Natalie out on weekends, introducing her to his friends, weaving her into the fabric of his life. There was an air of protectiveness in his attitude that some women might have found a little over protective, if not controlling, but Natalie found it comforting. She didn't have to think. She just had to be. She sat back and allowed Chad to decide where they'd go, what she'd eat when they dined with others, sometimes even what she should wear. Being with Chad was like being with a classy male version of Marilyn. He always knew what was best for her, always tried to improve her in some small way. But Natalie simply didn't care. Nothing mattered much since she'd lost Johnny.

She explained away her sudden move to the Ritz as a falling out with her roommates; come spring, she'd look for her own place. Meanwhile, her new residence was a plus for their relationship. They'd sit in the lobby after a date, sipping an after dinner drink, talking about the evening, gossiping about his friends, and planning out their trip to New Orleans. Chad was visibly excited. Time for "just them" as he put it.

Natalie was less than enthusiastic about the trip — and about Chad — although she tried not to show it. She smiled a lot and did her best to respond to his kisses, appreciating the fact that he was respectful of the boundaries she'd set for their relationship. Adding to her lack of enthusiasm, was an unbearable fatigue; no matter how much sleep she got, Natalie was tired nearly all of the time.

"I feel like I'm eighty and need an afternoon nap," she complained to Annie, calling her one evening and charging it to Marilyn. "And I got so dizzy yesterday, standing on my feet all day. We're never allowed to sit, not even between customers."

"See a doctor," Annie said.

"If it keeps up, I will. I think I'm just depressed and no matter how much I think I'm sleeping, I'm really not. My mind is always in turmoil and I wake up tired."

"I hope that's all it is. Listen, I asked Iris Hodges if I could write to Rick. Maybe we can find out where Johnny is that way, but he's heading to Vegas, wants to be a blackjack dealer, of all things. Or at least that's what he said when he left. But he's taking his time getting there. Apparently he's a free spirit."

"So another dead end?"

"It looks that way. At least until he has an address. But don't hold your breath."

"I love you Annie. You and Pearl were the best friends a girl could ever have. I messed up with her and I messed up with Johnny. Don't let me do that with you. Are you coming back?"

"Not for a while. I'm getting into this sun and sea bit and kind of like the hotel business. But no matter where I am, trust me, you're stuck with me."

"Thanks pal. Listen, I have to hang up. This is costing a fortune."

"And your point is?"

"Marilyn will kill me when she gets the bill. Really, I have to go. I'll call when I get back from New Orleans. Wish me luck."

"Luck. Whatever that means. I'd rather wish you good choices."

Twenty-Six

"They only have one room for us," Chad told Natalie, holding up a single key. He'd just checked them into the Royal Orleans on St. Louis Street, reputed to be the most beautiful of all the luxury hotels in the French Quarter.

"What do you mean, only one room?"

"Apparently they overbooked."

"Are you trying to pull a fast one?" Natalie's voice was low but urgent. The lobby was swarming with guests and she didn't want to embarrass herself. Or Chad. "You promised me separate rooms."

"I know what I promised. But it's out of my control. You may be cute, but I don't want you so badly that I'd lie for a little action." He cocked his head to one side, a strand of black hair falling across his forehead, and gave her one of his smug, rakish smiles. "Do you have that bad an impression of me — thinking I'd stoop that low — or is that your impression of all lawyers in general?"

Natalie's face filled with heat. Her jaw tensed and knots began forming in the pit of her stomach. "It's just that you promised."

"I didn't do this on purpose, no matter what you might think." He held up the room key and dangled it. "Yes? No? You call the shots. I'm warning you, though, they said the city's full. All kinds of conventions. Apparently, it's this or nothing." He stroked Natalie's hair. "I'm sure there's a sofa. You can sleep on that."

It seemed to Natalie that life was made up of impossible choices. She looked at Chad for a long, hard moment assessing her options. She didn't want to make too many waves. But she didn't want to appear easy either. And she wasn't ready to take their relationship to the next level. Would sharing a room give him the wrong impression? Make a decision, Natalie, and don't blow it, she told herself. She couldn't even ask herself, what would mom do? like some girls might, because she knew what her mother would do.

"Okay," she relented. "But no funny stuff. You promise me that, or I'm on the next plane home."

"Cross my heart. Nothing will happen that you don't want to happen."

"I'm going to hold you to that. Oh, and by the way," she grinned, "you get the couch, not me."

<hr />

It didn't take any time at all for Natalie to fall under the spell of New Orleans, especially the French Quarter, with its narrow streets, deep passageways and buildings with wrought iron balconies. Right out of an old Parisian magazine, she thought.

By the time they unpacked and headed out, it was late afternoon. Cool and drizzly. Raincoat weather. Natalie and Chad walked hand in hand, sipping tall sweet drinks, peering behind doors and examining the antiques in shops along Charles Street as they made their way toward Jackson Square. Block after block, she soaked in the sounds and aromas unique to New Orleans —

the spices and heat of Creole and Cajun coking wafting through open windows and half closed doors. . .the notes of deeply sensuous music, played out on nearly every street corner, sweet sorrowful notes that echoed her own lost and longing soul. All of Natalie's senses were aroused, her stomach swirling with both anticipation and a low-lying unexplained feeling of nervousness.

After exploring Jackson Square, checking out the artists and mimes, they rushed back to the hotel for the conference kick-off dinner, not because they wanted to, but because Chad believed it was a necessary evil: mingling, making connections, promising favors that would one day be returned, that's what it was all about in the end. Not what you knew, but who you knew. They joked and talked with the eight other people at their table, clapped for the key-note speaker, ate decent-enough food, and then snuck out before coffee and desert, both itching to experience the rhythm of the streets when the night turned dark and Bourbon Street burst into full color.

There was New Orleans by day, Natalie discovered. And then there was New Orleans by night. As they wended their way through the evening crowds, nothing could have prepared her for Bourbon Street's raw sexuality, dancers and drag queens in doorways, beckoning them inside, and adult toys on full display in nearly every shop window. She was embarrassed, yet fascinated, drawn in and, at the same time, repelled, not knowing where to look or how to act. *How do nice girls respond?* Suddenly she didn't feel so nice. Down toward the end of Bourbon Street, they wandered into Marie LaVeau's House of VooDoo.

"Oh, wow," Natalie said, stripping off her raincoat as they stepped into the small dimly lit shop, wrapping her arms across her stomach in an effort to ward off a sudden wave of heat and nausea.

"Incense. It's pretty strong," Chad said, keeping his hand on her elbow. "Be careful."

"Why, you think Madam LaVeau will put a spell on me?"

"She might. Except it would be the ghost of Madam LaVeau. The Queen of Voodoo is long dead. I was more worried about this step, right here. And your color. You look pale. Are you okay?"

"I'm fine." Her body cooled down as quickly as it had heated up. Natalie looked up at him and grinned. "Really."

Chad bent down and kissed her on the cheek. "A guy could fall into that smile of yours and never want to get up again. I think the guys at dinner tonight were right. I'd be a fool to let you go."

Natalie smiled up at him again and then wandered deeper into the small shop, picking up candles and objects, fascinated by their intended purposes. "I love this. There's history and meaning in everything. Look at this," she said to Chad, holding up a white candle, reading from a card tied to it with hemp. "Candles are a medium for transferring your desires into the spiritual realm for physical manifestation. Before using, cleanse and consecrate the candle by poking a hole into the top and filling with the herbs and oils appropriate to your desire. Light the candle and pray for what you wish."

"And I thought candles were just for romance and dinner parties," Chad laughed.

"I absolutely love it. We should have a dinner party and give one to each couple. We could have a cleansing ritual and then light them. Wouldn't that be fun?"

"Loads. If you want to scare away half our friends."

We. She had said *we* so casually, as though they were a couple with a future. And Chad had responded in like fashion with *our friends*. So far, they'd only felt like his friends. This was definitely something to report back to Marilyn. She would find all kinds of meaning in his comment.

"You're right," Natalie said, putting down the candle. "Definitely not Bostonian enough. How about this?" She held up a Voodoo doll. "It says here that the real meaning of voodoo is God the creator or great spirit and the dolls are not meant to be used for black magic. On the other hand, they can definitely hex someone!"

"Got someone in mind?"

"Yeah, I do." Under her breath she whispered *Mother-dear.*

"Who?" Chad asked, leaning in closer, whispering the question into Natalie's ear, brushing back her hair so that she could feel his breath on her skin. When she didn't answer, he said, "Come on. I'm thirsty. Let's get out of here."

They started toward the door when Natalie spotted something one aisle over. "Wait a minute," she said, maneuvering her way down one aisle and up the other. She picked up a small wooden box, its cover inlaid with mother-of-pearl. She ran her fingers over the design, feeling as though some lost memory was finding its way to the surface. By this time, Chad had joined her. "I'm going to get this," she told him.

"Why in the world would you want that? It's a piece of junk."

"I just do."

"Well then, I'll buy it for you," Chad said, reaching out to take the box from Natalie.

"No. Thank you. Really. I'd like to buy it. From me to me." Natalie walked over to the woman behind the counter and handed her the box. She was a short, slender woman with Siamese shaped eyes and skin the color of toffee.

"I am Marie LaVeau. Not the original Queen, you understand, her great granddaughter. We carry the name from generation to generation. Welcome to my shop. You wish to purchase this?"

"Yes. Thank you."

"Ahh. . .the lily of the valley." She ran her index finger over the mother-of-pearl design. "The only one we have. It called to you, no?"

"Yes, it did." Natalie glanced over at Chad, who was rolling his eyes in amusement, casting him a look that said you'd better behave.

"It is yours. Spiritually, I mean. Before this moment, it was simply a box. I watched you choose it. Carefully. Specifically. Now it is yours. Remember your quantum physics: the observer changes what is being observed. It now has your energy. And your intentions."

"It's just —"

"Nothing is *just*. $21.76 please."

Natalie handed the woman twenty-two dollars.

"It's to hold something special, no?"

"Yes."

"This flower, the lily of the valley? It symbolizes grief and remembrance. But you know that?" Marie LaVeau locked eyes with Natalie as she placed the change in Natalie's hand and handed her the small package. "You are being given a message: to remember what was; the guides ask me to tell you . . ." She stopped as though listening intently to someone and then nodded, as though confirming her understanding of the message, and continued. "The past is confronting the present. It is happening now. Be aware. Make good choices."

"What guides? What are you talking about?" Natalie asked.

The intense little shop seemed to close in on Natalie, settling over her like a blanket of fog, blurring all noise and activity beyond the commanding voice of Marie LaVeau. "Your spirit guides. Guardians, so to speak, from the other side. They want you to know this: keep the coin in the box. Someday, you will give it away."

"Natalie, let's go. Do you have everything?" Chad interrupted. He took hold of her arm and attempted to steer her toward the door.

"Yes. Wait a minute." Natalie started to follow Chad but then shrugged off his touch. "What are you saying? What do you mean, what about the coin?"

"Keep it until you give it away. For luck. That's all I know," Marie said. "The guides want you to be aware of how past and present are about to collide. That's all I can tell you. Next." She turned to the customer behind Natalie.

"Thank you," Natalie said as she headed toward the door with Chad.

"Oh," Marie LaVeau called out after her just as they stepped through the doorway and out into the rain. "The guides are impressing upon me: you are not an impartial observer in this life. You are a participant. You have choices."

"What a loon," Chad said as he let the door slam behind them. They walked back up Bourbon Street. "Let's hit the Absinthe House."

"What do you think she meant? About guides and all?" Natalie shivered. It had started to drizzle harder, the rain hitting her face like thin shards of ice. She pulled up the hood of her coat and tucked in closer to Chad.

"I'm sure if you paid her five bucks, she'd have told you. It's New Orleans, darlin. All part of the atmosphere."

"Maybe," Natalie agreed as they slid onto stools at the bar of the Old Absinthe House. "I feel like every time I turn around I'm getting the same message in different ways. From everyone. All about having choices. But do I? Really? Do any of us? Or are we just victims of everybody else's choices?"

"I think we make our own choices and our own happiness. Like right now, I'm going to choose drinks for us, which will warm us up, which will, in turn, loosen us up, which will, in turn, make us both very happy." Chad kissed Natalie's forehead and then helped her out of her wet coat. He then removed his own, shaking droplets of rain off both. "This is not the place to get serious. Take everything you see and hear with a grain of salt."

"Okay, nothing serious for the rest of the night," Natalie agreed. "So, on another note, help me understand. There are two Absinthe Bars, a block away from each other?"

"You're observant, I'll say that," Chad said signaling for the bartender's attention and then turning back to Natalie. "Do you mind sitting here, at the bar?"

"Not at all. It's beautiful, isn't it?" She ran her hands over the marble-topped bar, enjoying the smooth coolness beneath her fingertips.

"Here's how it goes: the other Absinthe Bar, down the street, was the first — and only — Absinthe Bar in New Orleans. That's where this bar top was. Then came prohibition and the good people of New Orleans worked to shut the place down. So, in the dead of the night, a bunch of guys dismantled the joint, hid all the fixtures in a warehouse, until, one day, they miraculously appeared here, when this place was built a few years later. So you have the original Absinthe Bar without any of the original fixtures and this newer one, a block away, with all of the original stuff. It's considered New Orleans' biggest practical joke on the powers that be."

"So you either drink at the original site or with the original fixtures!" Natalie summed up the story.

"That's it exactly. This place usually wins out; it holds drama for the tourists. That water dripper, it's an original piece as well." Chad nodded toward a fountain with brass fixtures, its marble basin pitted from decades of dripping water.

"Am I hallucinating or is it shaped in the image of Napoleon?" Natalie asked peering across the room at the fountain.

"You're good. Absinthe is originally a French drink. So they shaped the fountain in his likeness."

"Hi folks," the bartender interrupted, placing cocktail napkins down in front of them. "What'll you have?"

"An Absinthe Frappe for the lady. Absinthe Original for me," Chad answered. "Make sure you use Herbsaint."

"Is there any other kind?" The bartender said gruffly, slapping down a bowl of mixed nuts in front of them.

Natalie looked from the bartender to Chad. "What was that all about?"

"Herbsaint is the best Absinthe imitation, made right here in New Orleans. But some folks still order Pernod or some other anise flavored liquor. They don't take kindly to it. Not here. Back home, nobody knows, nobody cares."

"I did some reading after the Butler wedding," Natalie said. "I was curious. Absinthe is illegal. So I don't understand —"

"You bet it is. Except in the Czech Republic, places like that. Apparently it causes hallucinations, sometimes insanity. It's the wormwood, some kind of lethal herb. Instead of the buzz you get with regular alcohol, you actually see things differently. Read that —" Chad pointed to an engraved sign over the bar, a quote by Oscar Wilde: *After the first glass, you see things as you wish they were. After the second, you see things as they are not. Finally you see things as they really are, and that is the most horrible thing in the world.*

"I'd stop at the first glass," Natalie said with a laugh that felt too high and phony.

"You'd think," Chad agreed. "Apparently, seeing things as they really are led to some gruesome murders in France. They called them the Absinthe Murders. Lots of stabbings, I understand. They finally banned Absinthe in 1905."

Natalie shivered and wrapped her arms around her chest. There it was again, that sense of a memory floating by and a soft breeze, out of nowhere, making her aware and uneasy. But of what?

"Here you are, folks. An Absinthe Frappe," the bartender put the tall glass of Herbsaint and soda in front of Natalie. "And yours," he said to Chad, placing an antique short-stemmed glass in front of him.

"I love this ritual," Chad said, his eyes glassy with anticipation. "When Absinthe was legal and the fountains were active, that's where everyone would sit, using the cold water that dripped from the brass faucets. I would have loved to have lived back then."

Natalie was mesmerized as much by Chad's obsession with the drink as she was by the pouring ritual itself. She watched as the bartender poured pale green liquor into the glass, its sweet licorice scent soft, unassuming. Across the mouth of the glass, he laid a flat silver spoon, pierced with holes. An Absinthe spoon, he explained.

On top of the spoon, the bartender placed a single cube of sugar. Then, from a glass carafe he began dripping ice water. . . carefully. . . slowly. . .drop by drop. . .drop by drop; the green liquid turned milky, opalescent . . . drop by drop. . .the antique glass exploding with the smell of licorice and alcohol.

Natalie watched, and as she watched, pools of bile collected at the back of her mouth.

"I have to leave. Sorry." She grabbed her coat from the empty stool next to her, dropping Chad's on the floor as she reached for hers. "Sorry." She held her hand to her mouth as she stumbled out the door. Gathering her strength, Natalie rushed into the streets and alleys of New Orleans, the rain coating her skin and coat with a thin icy film.

"Natalie. Natalie. Come back." Chad's insistent voice followed her as she blindly found her way back to their hotel.

She shook off his touch when he caught up with her in the hotel lobby.

"I don't have a key," she accused him. "You didn't give me a key."

"Here. Right here. I have it. They only gave me one." Chad put his arm around Natalie, leading her into the elevator and up to their room. They didn't speak until the door was latched and he helped her strip off her wet raincoat and shoes. He sat her down on the bed and went into the bathroom, coming back with a handful of thick white towels.

"I can do it," Natalie said as he started drying her hair.

"I know. But I want to." Chad took small strands of her chestnut hair and patted them dry. "You need to get out of these," he said feeling the dampness of her blouse and slacks. "Me, too." He felt his own clothes.

"I'm sorry. I ruined things. I'm really sorry."

"What happened? The bar-keep said he never saw anyone respond to the Absinthe ritual quite that way!" Chad laughed just enough to try and get a smile out of her.

"I don't know. I kept watching the water drip onto the sugar cube and how it dissolved into that green liquor. It just hit me, the smell, the dripping. I can't explain it. I got so sick. My stomach . . ."

"Ahh, the green fairy."

"What?"

"That's what they call Absinthe. The green fairy. Sometimes, just seeing it and smelling it can affect people, those more sensitive —"

"I'm better now," Natalie interrupted. "I don't want to talk about it. I've had enough Absinthe — or whatever version of it you drink — to last a lifetime." She took a deep breath. "Let me go, get out of these and we'll figure out who gets the couch."

"I get it, remember?" But Chad didn't move. He reached up and began to unbutton her blouse, slowing, deliberately, one button after the other.

Natalie reached up and put her hand over his, to stop him. "Chad, don't."

"You need to get out of these clothes." He kept her hand on his as he moved to the next button. "You're beautiful," he told her, his eyes searching her face for an answer to his unasked question. He traced the outline of her neck with his index finger and then reached up to kiss her.

"You're so tense," Chad whispered. He pressed lightly against her spine, pulling her toward him, kissing her again. "That's better." He kissed her again and Natalie let him pull her in even closer. "And that's even better."

With each button, with each kiss, with each discarded piece of clothing, Natalie called to Johnny, a silent, unheard mantra seeking forgiveness as she surrendered herself to Chad. She felt oddly disconnected from the moment, watching herself from the outside, breathing life into some dusty, half-forgotten dream. As Chad ran his hands across her body, exploring and claiming her, his lovemaking became more and more possessive, as though driven by some private, unnamed demon. They were not tender with one another. There was lust and excitement and an undeniable current of electricity between them, but not the connective tissue of love and trust and unconditional belonging — all of the things she'd felt with Johnny. But, then, Johnny was lost to her, she reminded herself. And Chad was here. That would have to be enough.

Once Chad fell asleep, Natalie slipped out of bed and went into the bathroom. She turned on the faucet, mingling hot and cold water until it felt warm, nearly neutral. She then rummaged through Chad's shaving kit until she found what she was looking for: a new, clean, sharp, double-edged razor blade. This was a night of rituals. Rituals and new beginnings.

She held the blade in her right hand, keeping her left hand under the running water until she was certain she was ready. With a sharp intake of breath, she sliced into her index finger, the same finger she had used when she and Pearl had become blood sisters all those years ago. Squeezing her finger to keep the blood flowing, Natalie turned off the water, threw the blade into the toilet and flushed. She then tiptoed back to bed, smearing streaks of red blood across the spot still wet from their lovemaking.

———◆———

"Natalie." Chad looked at her accusingly the next morning as she emerged from the bathroom after a shower, wrapped in one of the terry cloth robes with the hotel's logo.

"What?" she looked over at him, her hazel eyes wide with questioning. "What?"

"Do you have your period?"

She blushed at such a direct question and was unable to maintain eye contact. "How could you. . .why would you ask that?"

"We're both adults, here. We just made wild, passionate love. It's a simple question. Do you have your period?" He pointed to the streaks of blood on the sheet.

"No." She actually was embarrassed. It was such a personal question. She didn't know what to expect after last night. But doing something and talking about it were very different things.

"Then what? Where did the blood come from?"

She shrugged and began fiddling with her damp hair.

"This was your first time," Chad said, watching her face for a response. "It was, wasn't it? I should have asked. You should have told me." He walked over and kissed her tenderly. "I would have been more gentle."

Natalie nodded, unable to trust her voice. "I have to get dressed." She pulled the robe tighter around her body. "Do you need the bathroom? Or should I get ready out here?" Suddenly she really was shy and uncomfortable. Getting dressed in front of him, in daylight, seemed too intimate.

"Yeah, let me go in. You can get ready out here." He raked his hand through his hair and then across the stubble on his chin. "Did I hurt you?"

"No. Really. I'm fine."

Chad went into the bathroom and she dressed quickly, pulling her still damp hair back into a low ponytail. When he came out, shaved and dressed, she was just putting on some lipstick. Looking across the room at Chad, she was struck by how handsome he was. And how well he wore his expensive, expertly tailored clothes. She felt like a department store reject in her off-the-rack outfit. Had she really slept with this man? What did he even see in her?

"Listen," Chad said, taking Natalie's hand and leading her over to the couch. "I've been thinking. . ."

"Chad, it's okay, really. I'm fine."

"Don't interrupt me." Chad pointed a finger at Natalie as thought addressing an adversarial party in a legal negotiation. "Listen, I'm blowing off this convention. I don't need a bunch of meetings telling me about the law. Instead, we're getting married. This afternoon."

"Chad —"

"Let me make an honest woman out of you." He looked over at the rumpled bed sheets. "I feel like you're mine now. Let me do right by you."

Another time, another place, Natalie would have argued with him. She wasn't anybody's possession. But Chad was about to solve all of her problems and she wasn't going to ruin it by challenging him.

"Even if I said yes, how can we do it?" Natalie asked. "It's Saturday. Town Halls are closed. And there must be a waiting period, blood work. . ."

"Honey, this is New Orleans," Chad stood up and grinned widely, "where anything can happen. There are approximately three hundred attorneys downstairs right now having breakfast. Guaranteed, somebody's in tight with a local judge. Some cash in the right hips and it's a done deal. You'll be my bride by sunset."

"You sound like a cowboy claiming his woman."

"I am," Chad said, flicking her ponytail. "If there's any blood work required, we'll have it done in Boston and dated last month. I can make that happen. No problem. We'll fill out a few forms, show our driver's license and we'll be married. That easy." He snapped his fingers.

"Chad, listen, before we do this. I need to tell you —"

Was she really about to confess that she'd laid a trap for him? Or that Marilyn was her mother and not her sister? Or that she actually worked for a living and there was no family fortune to be had? What exactly did she need to tell him? That she was in love with a man named Johnny, but didn't know where he was or if he stilled wanted her?

"Save the talk for later." He walked over and kissed her on the forehead. "We don't have all day."

"Chad, I can't do this."

"Of course you can." He stroked her cheek. "Here." He pulled out a wad of money from his pocket and peeled off five one hundred dollar bills. "Go get your hair done. Have them add some blonde highlights. Blonde is always better, don't you think? Buy a dress, something simple and elegant, and be back here no later than four. I'll do the rest."

She obeyed and by five o'clock, Natalie Marie Davenport was Mrs. Chadwick Hamilton, with enough blonde highlights to suit her discriminating husband and a diamond wedding ring that took her breath away.

"You're beautiful," Chad said, as they were finishing their candlelit dinner in the hotel's private dining room. Natalie was about to take her last bite of strawberries and whipped cream when Chad leaned over and took the spoon from her, running its cool, smooth silver bowl across her lips, teasing her with the fruit and cream. Just as the strawberry touched her lips he moved closer and kissed her deeply. "I can't get enough of you. You're mine, all mine," Chad said, kissing her neck, inhaling the intoxicating scent of her perfume, her signature scent, courtesy of him. "You're all mine," he repeated.

Natalie embraced Chad tightly, encouraging his passion despite the uneasiness stirring deep inside, despite the small knot taking form, calling attention to itself. She stroked his thick dark hair and imagined it was short, light brown, streaked by the Caribbean sun, and that his dark, probing eyes were really an amazing combination of olive and bronze. She held her husband and imagined the man she loved.

TWENTY-SEVEN

"It's all set," Chad said, hanging up the phone. It was after nine on Sunday night and they'd just gotten in from New Orleans, to what would now be Natalie's new home. Chad's Federal-style townhouse was located in Louisburg Square, the heart of Boston's exclusive Beacon Hill neighborhood, just north of Boston Common and the Public Garden. Everything here was refined, tasteful, elegant — old world, old money, preserved under glass — small, impeccably manicured lawns surrounded by ornate wrought iron, traditional New England brick walkways, and narrow streets lit by gas lamplights.

It was impossible for her to believe she would be living in such luxury. Not only living in it, but that it would be considered hers. One minute the Y, and now this. While Natalie was busy pinching herself, Chad had dropped their bags in the foyer and called his mother. He hung up after only a few minutes.

"She's coming to dinner tomorrow. I told her I have a surprise for her." He kissed Natalie on the forehead. "And you're it."

"I don't want to be anybody's surprise."

"Well you are. Get used to it."

"I don't know. What if . . ." Natalie covered her face with her hands. There were a thousand what if's rolling around in her head. And very few that she could actually share with her new husband. "Chad, I'm not a very good cook. My stomach. I can't handle this." A wave of nausea washed across her body. "Let's just go, get in the car and drive over there. Tell her tonight and be done with it."

Chad ruffled her hair. "Honey, I have . . .*we have*. . .help. Not live-in, but close enough. Every day except Sundays and Wednesdays. Sophie will help you figure everything out, and she'll do the cooking. She's a great cook. And my mother will love you. She'll be pissed as hell that I didn't give her the chance for a big wedding, but she'll get over it. She'll be happy for us. Trust me."

"Trust me. Famous last words."

"How about a tour of your new home?" Chad asked.

Natalie had been there only twice during the time they dated, and she'd been too nervous to notice much of anything. She still felt that way. She'd explore it on her own tomorrow, while Chad was at work. Right now, she felt shell-shocked, as though she'd just returned from some war, unable to understand, or even feel, the nuances of her life, as though some part of her had been left behind. At the same time, it seemed as though she felt everything — every nerve ending was raw, every action, every step magnified, aware that at any moment, her carefully constructed world could collapse.

"Natalie? Hey? I asked you a question. A tour of the house?"

"Sorry. I blitzed out. I'm so tired." She wanted to add, and nauseous, and reeling from the reality of this new life, such a huge step taken so quickly. Yet, what choice did she have?

"Well then, let me show you the master bedroom." Chad took Natalie's hand and led her up the stairs. "The most important room in the house," he said, sweeping Natalie into his arms and carrying her into the room. "Don't you agree, Mrs. Hamilton?"

"Absolutely," she said, shifting her eyes away from him so he wouldn't guess how badly she wanted to be left alone, to take a long hot bath, have a good cry. Maybe call Annie. And sleep. She was unbearably tired. But she was Chad's wife, his new bride, and if all he wanted was to make love to her, then it was her job to let him.

She didn't protest when he tossed her playfully on the bed and began stripping away her clothes. As Chad's hands wandered over her body, probing and stroking, working to excite her, Natalie closed her eyes and clung to the memory of a Caribbean beach and the seductive smell of sea and suntan lotion; when he entered her, she gasped, startled, as though being woken from a dream. Shaking off the memory of Johnny, she clung to her husband, accepting the rhythm of his thrusts, trying to accept that this was the beginning of the life she'd always dreamed of.

"Are you okay?" Chad asked when they were finished. He helped her off the rumpled spread and began turning down the covers. "You seemed different. Distant."

"It's just been a really long day."

Chad nuzzled her neck, running his hands across her naked body. "God, I love that perfume on you," he said, inhaling the scent of Jicky. "Don't ever change on me, Natalie. I want you just like you are tonight. Innocent. Flushed from making love. That incredible scent deep in your pores. It's like a memory. A dream. But then I look at you and it's real. You're mine. All mine."

———◆———

Thank God Josef's was closed on Mondays. It bought her a day of no questions asked. She slept late, then lingered in bed, trying to figure out ways to shift her former life into this new one. Should she just quit her job? She could tell Chad she wanted to be a wife first and foremost. He might even like that. If she continued working, pretending she was a niece-on-the-rise, preparing to own the store one day, how long could she

231

keep up the masquerade? More and more, she resented the lies and secrets, started by Marilyn all those years ago, and kept alive by her own desire to please her mother, to win her love. To make her proud. Well this should finally do it. She'd married the prince. And tonight she had to meet the prince's mother.

After calling Marilyn and listening to her squeals and I-told-you-so's, Natalie spent the afternoon preparing to meet her mother-in-law, changing clothes three times, finally settling on a long paisley skirt and cobalt cotton sweater. She knew the outfit shouted middleclass department store quality, but she had no choice. It was the best of what she had here from her trip to New Orleans. Her really good pieces, mostly work suits she'd found on sale, were still in her room at the Ritz; besides, they weren't really right for tonight, for a family dinner at home. But not any kind of family dinner. Not the Aunt Willie kind. This was new territory for her. She should go shopping, but she didn't have the time or energy. *It is what it is*, she finally told herself, praying she'd pass inspection, knowing somehow, some day, her house of cards would fall and she'd be exposed as an imposter. She just hoped it wouldn't be tonight.

Just as Chad promised, Sophie was a pleasant woman and a wonderful cook. She made beef Wellington and agreed to stay late and serve. The table was set; flowers arranged; wine uncorked. There was nothing for Natalie to do except wait. When the bell rang, she made Chad answer the door, letting mother and son greet each other privately. Once they'd gone into the living room, with its heavy drapes and dark cherry furniture, she made her appearance.

"Hi. Sorry. I was in the kitchen, checking on things," Natalie said, knowing they both knew there was nothing for her to check on. She looked over at the blonde-haired woman standing next to her son and froze. She took in the woman's blue eyes and soft porcelain looks, her beautifully cut bob and her expensive pant suit. *This was Chad's mother?* How could that be?

"Mom," Chad said, putting his arm around Louise Hamilton's waist, "this is Natalie. Natalie Marie Davenport Hamilton." He took hold of Natalie's left hand and held it out so that his mother could see the diamond and gold band on her ring finger. "My wife."

"Your what?"

Louise Hamilton didn't seem like the kind of woman who ever shouted, but the two words came out loud and high pitched.

"My wife," Chad said, flashing his mother a mischievous half smile. "Why don't I pop open some champagne and we can drink to it."

"But when? Where? New Orleans?" She gave her son a look that was both puzzled and disapproving. "You're joking?"

Natalie blanched. Was her new mother-in-law simply surprised, angry at being left out of such an important event? Or was she upset that her son had married the modern-day equivalent of a dime store clerk?

Chad uncorked the champagne he had chilled earlier and handed each of them a Waterford crystal flute filled with Dom Perignon. "It's no joke, mother. We'll tell you all about it over dinner. For now, let's toast to the newest member of our family."

Louise accepted the glass from Chad, her eyes never leaving Natalie's face; it was as though she was working through some puzzle in her head, trying to place Natalie, and, at the same time, trying to understand the place this stranger would hold in their lives. "I feel like I know you."

"She has that effect on people," Chad said. "That's exactly how I felt the first time we met. That's why we're married. I simply couldn't resist her." He raised his glass for a toast. "To my two favorite women."

"To your happiness, always," Louise said, her eyes never leaving Natalie. "I'm happy for both of you. Truly." She took a sip of her champagne, kissed her son on the cheek and gave her new daughter-in-law a warm, welcoming hug. "I really am happy," she said softly. "I've always wanted a daughter."

"Thank you, Mrs. Hamilton."

"Louise, please. Or Mom. I would love it if you called me mom."

"I'll try," Natalie said. Imagine being invited to call someone Mom. It would feel odd on her tongue. But nice. She would definitely give it a try.

Chad wrapped his arms around both women and led them toward the dining room. "Now that that's over with, let's eat. I'm starved."

During dinner, Chad entertained his mother with stories of New Orleans and how they'd decided to get married after a night — as he put it — "of unbridled passion." He grinned, knowing his brashness embarrassed both of them. At least he hadn't mentioned the blood on the sheets. Louise kept it light, giving Natalie woman-to-woman looks of conspiracy whenever Chad went too far in his descriptions. They settled into a comfortable banter, designed and executed by the man of the house. It was going better than Natalie could have imagined; by the time dinner was over, she was no longer on alert, waiting for the past to come crashing in on her.

While Louise and Chad caught up on family news, Natalie let her mind wander, filled now with the possibilities of her new life. She already adored Louise Hamilton, who apparently didn't remember her from that one encounter at Josef's; any other time she'd come into the store, she'd worked directly with Claudette, doing little more than politely nodding to Natalie from across the room. Natalie would go in on Tuesday and quit. Nobody would be any the wiser and she could breathe again, officially begin her life as the wife of Chad Hamilton, the woman who lived on Beacon Hill and had everything she had ever planned for.

Everything she had ever planned for. That seemed true enough, Natalie thought, remembering The Plan she'd come up with after Marilyn and Harry got married and left her behind. This really was everything she'd ever planned for. And yet it felt like she'd taken a wrong turn.

While Louise and Chad talked on and on about old friends, Natalie's mind began playing tricks on her. She saw herself as a carefree woman, sitting behind the wheel of a car, driving down a road that seemed to stretch out in front of her. She was in full control of where she was going and how she was getting there. The scene played out in her mind's eye, as though on stage, happening at that very moment. . .

She's driving down a long road, windows open, her hair blowing, her heart open and free, as though she's headed toward a place destined to make her happy. But suddenly, in the middle of this wide open road, there's a crossroads and a four-way stop sign. She stops, knowing it's time to make a choice. She feels certain that her happiness lies straight ahead, but she's being pulled to the left, toward whatever place that road would lead. She can't decide. A car comes up behind her and toots. She has to decide. It's time. She looks straight ahead. And then she turns her wheel and makes a left turn. She drives a while, and makes another turn, all the while her heart pumping, her hands clammy. Now the wind feels cold. By the time she acknowledges she's on the wrong road, it's too late. She's gone too far, doesn't know how to get back. She rolls up her windows and keeps going . . .

"Natalie? Natalie, dear, are you all right?" It was Louise's voice, bringing her back to the room and to the moment. "Your face just drained of all color."

"She's not much of a drinker," Chad answered for her. "I can vouch for that. Must be the combination of wine and champagne. You okay?" He stood. "Let's move into the study."

"I'm okay," Natalie assured Louise. "Really."

How could she tell her new mother-in-law that she'd married the wrong man, that she was sitting there at the dinner table suddenly and deeply aware that she'd taken the wrong road? Johnny was gone. For the rest of her life, there'd only be his memory to fill the empty spaces. She pictured the small inlaid box she'd bought in New Orleans and the coin she'd slipped into it last night after her bath, once Chad had made love to her and then fallen asleep. She should have given the coin to Johnny. For luck. She should have done that. *Please, God, keep him safe.* She stood and put her hands to her stomach in response to a sudden wave of nausea.

"I'm okay," she said again. "Too much excitement these last few days."

"Well, I can certainly understand that," Louise said as they both left the dining room.

Chad remained behind for a moment, thanking Sophie for staying and serving, for her wonderful meal.

"Isn't she a treasure?" Louise asked, linking arms with Natalie as they made their way through the living room and into the study. "And she speaks English so well. She's only been here, from Poland, for five years. Ask her to make perogies some time. And make sure to invite me when you do."

"I love this room," Natalie said, sinking into an oversized chair.

"But to be a true study, shouldn't it have more books than things?" Louise commented. They both looked around, taking in the floor to ceiling shelves filled with art and collectibles and the various artifacts Clayton continued to send Chad from whatever country he was assigned to in the Peace Corps.

"You're right." Natalie winked at Chad who'd come in behind them and was fixing himself a drink.

"I'll have a sherry, dear," Louise said. "Natalie?"

"Nothing. Maybe some club soda."

"Coming right up," Chad said. He was happy and agreeable and Natalie decided she could settle into this life after all.

"What do you think of that collection?" Louise nodded toward a long, low table displaying Chad's prized collection of original Absinthe spoons and crystal glasses, along with a bottle of Herbsaint and a small Lalique jar filled with sugar cubes. "Every now and then he comes home with a new piece from some antique shop."

Natalie rolled her eyes. "Apparently it's his passion. Personally, I can't imagine anybody caring that much about a drink that's no longer made."

"Ahh. But it is made. Once again. In Europe. And very underground. I have my sources trying to get a bottle for me." Chad handed Louise her sherry and Natalie a tall glass of club soda. "Are you sure you don't want anything stronger?" he asked taking a sip of his own scotch. I could make you one of those." He nodded toward the Herbsaint. "When I get the real thing, we'll all have to try it."

"No thanks. I had enough of anything Absinthe in New Orleans to last a lifetime."

"Maybe now that you're married, you'll give up this obsession," Louise said. "The smell is horrible and quite frankly, Chad, more than one drink of Herbsaint changes your personality. I can't imagine what the real Absinthe would do. I've told you that a million times — "

"Okay mother, that's enough."

"Changes him how?" Natalie asked. A slight breeze seemed to stir above her head.

"His mood darkens. He gets contrary, ready for a fight."

237

"For crissake, stop with your shadows and graves already." Chad took a swig of his drink and turned toward Natalie. "She has this idea that I was born with some kind of burden — that's what she calls my shadow — and that my interest in Absinthe fuels my 'shadow side.' It's a bunch of horseshit."

"Chad!" This was the second time tonight that Louise Hamilton had raised her voice.

Natalie sat up straighter, feeling suddenly as though a shadow was crossing over her own grave. "Do you really believe that?"

"Don't we have anything else to talk about?" Chad commanded.

"Okay, dear," Louise smiled, allowing the conversation to take another turn. "Let's talk about the reception I'm going to host, since you deprived me of a wedding."

"Oh Lord. I'd rather talk about my shadow."

"Well, I've been thinking about it all through dinner —"

"How is that possible?" Chad asked. "You talked all through dinner."

"You know I'm very good at doing two things at once." Louise smiled patiently at her son. "Here's how it's going to go: you'll arrange for the Somerset so that we have the reception within the month. Any later and it will feel like an afterthought. I'll take care of everything else."

Natalie knew about the Somerset, a very private, very elite club, where the members are voted in. It was a name she heard often from brides registering at Josef's. She tried to imagine Harry and Marilyn in that refined atmosphere and grimaced.

"Don't worry. It'll be a wonderful party," Louise said, catching Natalie's unspoken response.

"I'm sure, but —"

"No buts," Louise interrupted. "I insist on doing this. Chad, I just can't believe you got married like this." She looked at her son, clearly puzzled. "You never act this rashly. I don't understand it. No offense, Natalie. It's just so out of character for him. He's usually so controlled. Everything planned out." She paused and sighed. "Oh well, there's no use dwelling on what's done. We'll have a reception and be happy for that. I'll start working on the guest list. Natalie, you'll let me know who from your side should be included."

Natalie could feel the crushing weight of her past closing in on her. A wedding reception? With Marilyn and Harry? Who else? Certainly not Annie. Aunt Willie? She struggled to catch her breath.

"Natalie, you'll give me a list, right?" Louise repeated her request.

"I don't have a lot of people," Natalie said. "My parents died. I was raised by my sister."

"That's okay, dear. Whoever you have, is who will come. Don't worry about a thing."

That was easy for Louise to say. Natalie had everything to worry about.

"Now, Chad," Louise said, "as soon as you get the date from the Somerset, call me. I'll book a flight for Darrelle and let her know the details."

"Why would you do that, mother? You know I can't stand that old bitty."

"Because she's my good friend. And contrary to what you may believe, she thinks the world of you. I always promised her she'd dance at your wedding. Well, this is as close as it gets, thanks to your. . .spontaneity. . .shall we say? I was thinking about going to see her in the next couple of months. She'll come here, instead."

"Go where? Who's Darrelle?" Natalie asked. The name seemed to tug at the corners of her mind, asking to be set free from behind veils and cobwebs.

"She's some broad we met in France after my father died," Chad answered.

239

Natalie looked to Louise for clarification.

"It's hard to explain Darrelle," Louise said, ignoring her son and talking directly to Natalie. "She lives in France, just outside of Paris. We met there, when I took Chad and Clayton abroad, right after Everett died. I needed a change of scenery. We happened upon this sweet boutique on our second day. It's her place. We had this immediate connection, Darrelle and I, even though there's a twenty-three year difference in our ages. We ended up seeing her nearly every day. She showed us around. It was wonderful."

"Yeah, terrific. Hanging out with an old lady the whole time." Chad finished off his drink and poured another. "What a trip that was."

"Darrelle never married, never had children of her own," Louise explained. "I think that's why she took to my boys so quickly. Especially Chad. But he resisted her affection. She tried too hard with him, as though his approval of her mattered too much."

"Okay, let's change the subject," Chad insisted, "to something more pleasant."

Louise ignored Chad. "Come to think of it, Natalie, I remember, now, how I know you."

Natalie stiffened. She looked at Louise, silently begging her stop.

"You called me Linette, that first day we met. Darrelle did the same thing. Isn't that odd? She said I reminded her of her aunt, the one who raised her after her mother died, something about my presence, *my spirit*, she called it."

"You two have met before?" Chad asked.

"Yes," Louise said. "I just remembered. It was bothering me all night. I've been trying to place you, but didn't want to come right out and ask. It was at Josef's, that first day. . .that's when you called me Linette. You were tying to convince Avery to hire you."

240

"Why would she have to convince him? Her uncle owns the place. Avery works for him."

"No, you've got it wrong, Chad. Natalie was looking for a job and I intervened on her behalf." Louise looked from Chad to Natalie and back again. "What? Why do you both look so shocked? Natalie, you've lost all your color again. Chad, what is going on?" Louise stood to confront her son. "Tell me."

Chad ignored his mother and loomed over Natalie. "You lied to me?" She shifted in her chair, trying to back away from his rising anger. "You lied to me about working at Josef's? Why would you do that?"

Natalie met his eyes for a brief moment. Louise was silent, watching the drama unfold.

"Let's talk about this later," Natalie finally said. "When we're alone."

"No. Now."

"Chad, maybe I should go," Louise said, "and give you two some privacy to work this out."

"No, Mother, stay. If I'm married to a thief or a liar we should both know. Do I need to lock up the silver?"

"Chad!" Louise shouted.

"Oh my God," Natalie cried. "How can you say such a thing? It was such a small lie. So that you wouldn't stop seeing me." It was all falling apart. She'd been married for how many days? Three? And it was coming to an end. That had to be some kind of record.

"I don't get it." Chad picked up his drink and then put it down again. He raked his hand through his hair. "Why would you lie about being the heir-apparent to Josef's when you're just a clerk. That's what you are, right? A sale's clerk?"

"Precisely because of what you just said. *Just a clerk.* You wouldn't have given me the time of day if you'd known that."

"How do you know? You never tried."

"I did try. That night at dinner. You wanted to know all about me. Remember? I told you I was a working girl and this horrible expression crossed your face so I changed my mind about telling you. I didn't want to risk our relationship, it was too new. So I told you the truth about working at Josef's but then made up the part about my uncle owning the place. It just kind of came out. I didn't plan it. Honest." Her words tumbled out in a rush. Tears stung her eyes, and she fought the urge to cry. "And then I was going to tell you in New Orleans, but you stopped me with all the talk of marrying me by sundown. I just let it go. I'm sorry."

Chad stared at Natalie for what seemed an interminable amount of time. He glanced over at Louise and they both burst into gales of laughter.

"What?" Tears streamed down Natalie's face. "What?"

Louise was the first to gain her composure. She walked over to Natalie and put her arms around her. "My dear, a *working girl*? That's what you told Chad you were?"

"Well, yes. That's what I am. I'm not rich. I work for a living." She stood and began pacing the room.

"You do know what that implies?" Louise asked.

"That I work . . .ohmygod. . .that I. . ."

Chad and Louise both started laughing again.

"Walk the streets?" Natalie finished her sentence.

"Something like that," Chad said. "That's probably why "a look," as you say, crossed my face. This is definitely one for the books."

"Speaking of books, I have a good novel waiting for me at home. It's time to go. I'm glad we straightened everything out. Chad, take care of the Somerset. Natalie, get some sleep. And relax, child. You're much too tense."

After Louise left, Chad walked over to his wife and kissed her on the cheek. "Don't ever lie to me again, Natalie. I don't like being surprised. And I don't like being embarrassed. You did that to me tonight." As he talked, Chad squeezed the back of Natalie's neck, as though training a new puppy. He squeezed hard, and she winced. Still he didn't let go.

"I'm sorry." Natalie tried to wriggle out of his hold, but he only squeezed tighter. "I just didn't think."

"Well, from now on, you think. You hear me?" His tone was calm, his words delivered with the kind of deliberate precision that felt more threatening than if he had shouted. "You're my wife. You're Mrs. Chad Hamilton. That means you have responsibilities to me. No more lies. No secrets or half-truths. That's not too much to ask, is it Natalie?" He loosened his grip and stroked her cheek with one hand.

"Of course it's not." She met his eyes now. They seemed clouded, unreadable, except for some flash of. . .what?. . .anger? Not exactly. More like ownership. Natalie shuddered.

"Are you cold?" Chad asked.

"No, just sorry."

"I hope so." Chad took hold of both her hands. "Is there anything else I should know? Anything else you need to confess before we go to bed?"

Natalie thought about Marilyn and Harry and Aunt Willie. In her mind, she saw the streaks of blood on her bed sheets in New Orleans. She felt the warmth of a kiss brush her lips and the penetrating honesty of eyes that were somewhere between olive and bronze. She remembered that last night on the beach in Saint Martin, before she fled like a coward; her thoughts settled in on the fatigue and nausea she'd felt ever since, and the child she was certain she was carrying. Johnny's child.

She thought about it all in the flash of an instant and then answered her husband, never once allowing her eyes to leave his direct and unwavering gaze. "No. There's nothing else."

TWENTY-EIGHT

Forty-two Beacon Street: Old World. Old Money. Old Boys. That was the only way to describe the very private, very elegant Somerset Club, founded in 1851. A stately granite mansion overlooking Boston Common, it had been originally designed by Alexander Parris as a home for developer David Sears, Harvard class of 1807. Now it was home to Boston's most elite. By invitation only. Although Chad had been a member for only the past two years, the desire had burned in his veins nearly all of his life. Being invited to join this inner circle, following in his father's footsteps, meant he had finally arrived.

As they dressed for their marriage reception, Chad regaled Natalie with stories about the club and its exclusivity. In particular, he told the story that made all the newspapers back in January 1945 when the club had caught fire. Responding to the blaze, firemen burst through the front entrance, but they weren't allowed in. They were ordered to go around back and come in through the servant's entrance, so that club members wouldn't be disturbed. Many of them were still dining.

"Don't you love it?" Chad asked, knotting his tie. "Even the firemen, rushing in to save their lives and their historic building, weren't allowed through the front door." He chucked at the idea.

"Pedigrees only," Natalie responded. "No blacks. No Jews. No middle-class. Wonder how they'll take to me." She smoothed down the skirt of her dress and then lifted it again to refasten one of her garters, making sure her nylon stocking didn't bag at the knee. "It's probably a good thing Annie couldn't make it here. She'd end up wanting to picket the place."

Natalie had wanted the Blackwells to come as well, but thought better of it in the end. Maybe if Aunt Willie had been able to make the trip. In the end, she'd invited only Marilyn and Harry and a few of the girls she'd gone to Katie Gibbs with and still saw occasionally. The rest of the hundred and thirty people belonged to Louise and Chad. And Boston's upper crust.

"Forget about Annie. I don't know what you see in that hippie anyway." Chad wrapped his arms around Natalie's waist. "It's a great dress. Worth every cent. Very Audrey Hepburn. But it seems tighter around the waist than when we bought it. Have you put on a few pounds?"

"I don't know. Maybe. It's the good married life."

"Don't fall into that trap. I'll get you a spa membership, so you can work on it." He fingered her hair and the newly added highlights. "Glad you added more," he said. "As far as I'm concerned you can never be too blonde or too thin."

"Even if blonde and thin are against your true nature?"

"Don't spoil it, Natalie. None of that bra-burning talk. Not today."

She swallowed her retort and kissed him on the cheek, turning back to the mirror to finish getting ready. He was right. Not today. They'd had too many confrontations over the past few weeks. To Chad, she was a woman with potential: he would guide her and teach her and expect full cooperation. But to Natalie, it felt like she was a lump of raw material. Someday he'd make something out of her. Until then, he would mold and fiddle and redesign. And it was her job to be both pliant and

245

compliant. Already, she was fighting this expectation, speaking out when he felt she should be silent, asserting her sense of design and independence when he clearly wanted her to follow his lead. But today she would do just that. She would follow Chad's lead, let him guide her through the maze of friends and social proprieties, all the while praying that Marilyn would tone down her brashness and keep her silly superstitions to herself.

"You know," Natalie said, putting on the diamond earrings Chad had given her that morning, "My sister Marilyn, she can be —"

"Brash? Loud? Not very classy? You've warned me at least a dozen times."

"I know. I'm just worried."

"Well, don't be. We have a few friends like that. We'll put them together."

"Maybe she'll behave herself."

"And maybe not." Chad smiled his rakish half-smile while helping her on with her coat. "Who cares? Today it's all about us."

———◆———

You're absolutely glowing," Gracie told Natalie as the two of them stood off to one side. She was one of Natalie's Katie Gibbs friends, a warm, generous person who never seemed to have a hidden agenda. Nice was the best way to describe her. Feeling very much out of her element, with Chad off circulating, "working the room" as he called it, Natalie was more than a little grateful that Gracie had accepted the invitation.

"This is my boyfriend, Ray," Gracie said, indicating the tall thin man next to her, in his mid-twenties with dark-rimmed glasses.

"Great shindig," Ray said, rubbing his fingers together in mock appreciation of the dollars he knew this party had cost.

"Ignore him," Gracie said, wrapping her ample arms around Natalie in a bear hug. "He's an accountant, sees dollar signs everywhere. Thanks for including us. I knew you'd get your dream. I'm happy for you."

"Thanks. I really appreciate — "

"It's a sign. I know it's a sign," Marilyn interrupted, racing up to them in a flurry of distress. "Hey Gracie," she said. "Hi," she offered Ray, who she'd never met. "Natalie, baby, I just ran my stocking and I don't have a spare pair. I mean, who carries a spare pair? It's a sign for sure."

"Marilyn," Gracie said before Natalie could respond, "How could running your stocking be a sign of anything?" Gracie had always been amused by Marilyn's antics whenever she visited Natalie at school. "Everyone snags their stocking."

"You're right, Gracie, absolutely right. Every gal gets a run. And then what? Something bad always happens. A stocking in ruins portends something," Marilyn hissed. "My baby sister finally marries her prince, just like I planned for her all these years, and then I go and get a run. It means something. I just know —"

Before she could finish her thought, Louise came up and slipped into their small circle, inserting herself between Natalie and Marilyn. "Natalie, I can't get over how radiant you look today."

"That's exactly what I just told her," Gracie agreed, taking a sip of her wine.

"Mom," Natalie said, holding the word, letting it hit the air and stay in the room for as long as possible. "Mom," she repeated, watching as the blood drained from Marilyn's face and the only color left on her cheeks was a garish stain of coral rouge. Natalie took pleasure in this long-awaited moment of power, reveling in the how-dare-you-betray-me look seething in Marilyn's eyes. She hadn't planned to do this, to use her relationship with Louise to shock and scare Marilyn, but once it came out, she didn't regret it either. Natalie turned toward Louise and addressed her directly. "Mom, I'd like you to meet my friend, Gracie. Her boyfriend, Ray. You met my sister, Marilyn, earlier."

"Yes, of course," Louise said. "Gracie, Ray, I'm so glad you could join us. "Marilyn, I hope you and Harry are enjoying yourself. Natalie tells me that you two love to dance. After dinner, we'll be rolling up the carpet. The band is going to move from this classical music to some real dance numbers, big band, rock and roll."

"Mom?" Marilyn studied Louise. "She called you mom?"

"Well, yes. I asked her to. I'm so glad to finally have a daughter. What do you call your mother-in-law?"

"Crazy. Or at least I did until she died a couple of years ago." Marilyn's laugh was harsh. "Mrs. Golden, mostly."

"Well, Natalie and I have gotten off to a much better start, I'm glad to say."

"It's nice to have a mother after all these years." Natalie looked at Louise and felt honest love for this woman.

"Aunt Willie was like a mother. To both of us. Have you forgotten about her?" Marilyn flashed her a fake smile and Natalie instinctively took a step backward, expecting to feel Marilyn's hands pressing into the flesh of her face, leaving behind the imprint of her fingers.

"No, I could never forget everything Aunt Willie has done for us. Still, after all these years, it's nice to have someone you can actually call mother."

"Well, don't go forgettin' your real mother, just cause she can't be here, so to speak." Marilyn turned to scan the room. "Where's Harry? I need to go find Harry." But she didn't make a move to leave.

Louise placed her hand on Marilyn's arm while Gracie and Ray wandered off toward the bar with a look toward Natalie that said good luck, we'll catch you later.

"Marilyn," Louise said gently, "I feel like I've upset you in some way, and I certainly didn't mean to. Natalie has said wonderful things about you and everything you did for her after your parents died."

Marilyn shrugged and Natalie could see that she was swallowing hard. Suddenly, her comments about being able to call someone mother seemed spiteful and unnecessary and Natalie wished she could take it all back. Now that she was married to Chad, she understood a little more about hiding truths for the bigger picture. Natalie was about to try and smooth things over when Louise spoke again, breaking the tension.

"Natalie, I came over to tell you that my driver just called. Darrelle is on her way. Poor thing, she was so tired from the flight, she stayed back at the house rather than come in early with me. She'll be here shortly. I can't wait for you to meet her."

"Neither can I," Natalie said, struggling for an even breath. An unexpected wave of nervousness made her hands tremble; she clasped the sides of her dress to keep them steady. Why would the promise of seeing Darrelle, a woman she'd never met and would probably never see again, have such an impact on her? Maybe it was just nerves in general. It had been a hard month, getting her bearings as Chad's wife, trying to meet his expectations, while maintaining her sense of self and trying to keep her secrets. She worried every day about how it would all work out in the end.

Saliva and bile gathered at the back of Natalie's mouth while a flash of heat filled her face. She thrust her drink at Louise and ran towards the ladies room. Louise, in turn, handed off her own drink, as well as Natalie's, to Marilyn, who was left open-mouthed juggling three glasses, going on about bad omens and the run in her stocking.

Louise followed her daughter-in-law right into the stall of the ladies room. Bending over Natalie's crouched body, Louise encouraged her to let it all out as she wiped beads of sweat from Natalie's face. It was only dry heaves, but they wracked Natalie's body. A feeling of both dread and anticipation coursed through her veins.

"Are you pregnant?" Louise asked, as they left the stall and moved toward the sinks and mirrors, but not without first looking around the well-appointed bathroom to make sure they were alone.

"I don't know. I might be. That first night, we didn't use anything." She pressed a wet cloth to her face, glad to have something to hide behind. "But it's too soon for symptoms, isn't it?" Natalie knew that — at nearly two months along — it wasn't too soon at all. But as far as everyone else was concerned, she couldn't be more than a month pregnant.

"You can have symptoms within a week of being pregnant. Did you know that? Probably not." Louise had a habit of asking and then answering small questions that didn't require the other person to respond. "But you could actually be a month along," she continued, "if it happened in New Orleans. The body's a funny thing."

"I guess."

"Does Chad know?"

Natalie shook her head. "I wanted to make sure before I told him."

"Tell him tonight, dear. Let him in. He doesn't like secrets. Don't tell him I suspect. That would upset him, not being the first to know. And then get yourself to a doctor. Promise?"

"I promise."

"Which?" Louise eyed her in the mirror as Natalie reached into her purse for her lipstick. "To tell Chad or go to the doctor?"

"Both."

Natalie had seen her old family physician on her trip to Hartford last week when she'd visited Aunt Willie and he confirmed her suspicions. Now she'd have to find a doctor in Boston — one who would keep her timing a secret. Natalie kissed her mother-in-law on the cheek and then wiped away the crimson mark of fresh lipstick she'd left behind. "Thanks. Now let's go enjoy this wonderful party you've thrown us."

Regan Ainsworth came in just as they were leaving the ladies room. She was wearing the same amethyst necklace she had on at the Butler wedding. And the same condescending smile.

"Louise," Regan said. "You look beautiful, as always." She took in Natalie, her Christian Dior black dress and two-carat diamond earrings. "And you're certainly looking better," she told her.

"Marriage does that," Natalie quipped, linking an arm through Louise's.

"Nice comeback," Louise whispered as they walked away. "Poor thing. She's not a happy camper. She always thought she'd be the one to land Chad. I'm glad it was you instead."

"Me too." Natalie squeezed Louise's hand.

"There's Darrelle." Louise nodded toward the entrance. "Come on. Let's go meet her.

As they headed across the room, skirting around clusters of people talking and drinking, Natalie found herself mesmerized by the image of the tall, slender woman with high cheek bones and steel gray hair pulled back and tightly knotted at the nape of her neck. Darrelle wore a burgundy dress with a long, sweeping skirt and a deep neckline. She held herself with an air of precision and dignity that might make her seem unapproachable except for the tender smile on her face and the tapping of one foot to the music wafting through the ballroom. Natalie felt a pull toward this woman that she couldn't possibly explain as she struggled to keep pace with Louise and not rush out ahead of her.

"You feel it, too, don't you?" Louise asked as they approached Darrelle.

"Feel what?"

"Don't be coy with me, Natalie Hamilton. "I can sense it in you. It's the same way I felt when I first met Darrelle, drawn toward her in an inexplicable way. A lot like you and me. Connected. As though we're meant to know each other."

"Mystical. Annie would call it mystical."

"She's right, I think." As they reached Darrelle, Louise opened her arms widely and embraced her friend. "We were just saying how there is an attraction between us — Natalie feels it too — she described it with the word mystical."

"Ah, yes, that it a good word. So right for those things that cannot be explained." Darrelle smiled. Her English was remarkably good, laced with her French accent and the seductive velvety tone of her voice. Natalie tried returning her smile, but all she could do was stare at the necklace resting against Darrelle's skin. She moved to touch it and then pulled back, as though it might burn her; Natalie clasped her hands tightly behind her back in an effort to physically restrain herself from reaching out toward the small gold charm of white and green enamel fashioned to represent a lily-of –the-valley.

"It was my mother's," Darrelle said, her blue-gray eyes never leaving Natalie's face. "I will share her story with you. But not today. Today we celebrate your marriage to Chad. I will give you a welcoming hug, if I may, and then go find him. Although I am quite certain he is not enthusiastic about my being here. I've always tried too hard to please him. It makes him uncomfortable. But that is the nature of our personalities," Darrelle confided with a wink that accentuated the deep wrinkles around her eyes.

"May I?" She held her arms out to Natalie, awaiting permission to hug her.

About two inches taller than Natalie, Darrelle pulled Natalie to her, holding her in an embrace that was hesitant at first and then sure of itself, like an age-old hug between mother and daughter, ancient, comforting, without guile. They rested against one another in a moment when the rest of the world seemed to fade away, captured in a deep and distant moment when there was only the two of them: Natalie and Darrelle. Noelle and Darrelle. Nunki and Denebola. Natalie was the first to release her grip, as both women flushed and laughed self-consciously, brushing at their clothes and hair to cover up their discomfort.

Before she pulled away completely, Darrelle leaned in toward Natalie and whispered into her ear. "You are wearing Jicky. It is the same perfume as my mother wore."

TWENTY-NINE

"**Did you tell** him?" Louise greeted Natalie at the front door, urging her inside with a quick hug. It was Monday around noon and the three of them — Natalie, Louise and Darrelle — were spending the afternoon together at Louise's. Darrelle had a return flight to Paris early the next day.

"You didn't, did you? I can tell you didn't," Louise accused her daughter-in-law.

"I couldn't. We were both exhausted Saturday night after the reception. And he was in such a good mood yesterday, I didn't want to spoil it." She eyed Louise and told her honestly. "I don't know how he'll take it. He has such specific ideas about how I should look and be."

Louise hugged Natalie hard. "But it's his baby. How can he be anything but ecstatic? Don't keep it a secret. He hates secrets."

"I have a doctor's appointment on Friday. I'll tell him after that. If there's anything to tell." Natalie really did have an appointment; it was with a local doctor that Annie had heard about, one with a reputation for being kind and discreet when it came to girls in trouble. Since she was only two degrees away from being "in trouble" she figured he was the one to see.

"You promised me," Louise chided, leading Natalie toward the back of the house.

"And I'll keep my promise. Honest. I just want to be sure first. Where's Darrelle?"

"She's in the sunroom. I thought we should have lunch in there. It's the best room in the house this time of year."

It definitely was the best place in Louise's rambling old Tudor home, made of stone and brickwork that seemed to hold in the cold. Added on after the house was built, the sunroom was a true solarium, an open space with skylights and plants and even a small fountain. There were overstuffed chairs, a sofa, and a couple of rocking chairs, all in light wood. The upholstered pieces were covered in polished cotton and chintz, in a complimentary combination of solids, stripes and florals. Louise called it her quiet place. It's where she sat and listened to classical music, wrote letters to friends, looked at photo albums, or simply closed her eyes and allowed herself to be flooded with the memories of her life — memories of her husband, her children, things that worked out, and things that didn't. Like the baby girl she'd tried to adopt. She'd mentioned it only once to Natalie, never going into detail, the pain of that loss, of a promise unfulfilled, still raw even after all these years.

"Chère," Darrelle exclaimed as soon as Natalie entered the room. "I have been waiting for this moment." She rose from the sofa, stretched out her back, and walked across the room to embrace Natalie. Together they walked back to the sofa and sat side by side.

Natalie took hold of Darrelle's hand, stroking the woman's slender fingers, bony and wrinkled with age. She listened as Darrelle and Louise fell into a comfortable banter, talking about age and limitations and, on the other hand, the boundless possibilities of life. All the while, Natalie watched as Louise poured freshly brewed tea into Irish Belleek cups, so ivory and delicate that the tea's bronze color actually shimmered in the translucent china.

Focusing on the details of Louise's movements and the way her own hand continued to stroke Darrelle's, feeling every tendon, every ligament, every bone, Natalie's sense of connection to these two women became more and more palatable. She squeezed Darrelle's hand so tightly at one point, the older woman actually winced. It was as though Natalie was trying to hold onto something she was afraid would leave and never return. Darrelle gave her a long, knowing smile, removed her hand from Natalie's grip, and accepted the tea from Louise.

Natalie accepted her cup of tea as well, the cup chattering against its saucer as she struggled to keep her body from trembling. She shivered as the warm liquid slid down her throat.

"Are you cold, dear?" Louise asked. "You are, aren't you? Let me get you an afghan. I'll turn up the heat."

"No. Don't bother," Natalie said. "It's not that kind of cold." She took another sip of tea, followed by a deep breath.

"You were feeling it, chère, the feeling that has no name. Some call it a memory, as old as the stars. Others, like your friend, call it mystical."

Natalie felt something strange on her tongue, like tobacco. With as much delicacy as she could manage, she used her thumb and index finger to remove the foreign object.

"I should have warned you," Louise said. "I brewed loose tea today." She eyed Darrelle. "If the mood strikes, she may read your leaves later."

"Perhaps. We shall see," Darrelle said.

"What?" Natalie looked toward Louise for an explanation.

"She has the gift," Louise started, and then looked across the room at her housekeeper setting down bowls of hot onion soup. "Thank you, Rosa," Louise said and then to Natalie and Darrelle, "Let's eat. We can decide later about reading leaves."

"What gift?" Natalie insisted as they sat down at the round glass top table across the large sunny room.

"Of knowing," Louise explained. "Some call it second sight. She uses tea leaves — but they're just a tool, she doesn't really need them — to see into the future, or the past, whatever her guardian angel wants her to know. Or share."

"Oh, come on," Natalie laughed and then quickly apologized. "I'm sorry. I don't believe in that stuff. My friend, Annie, on the other hand —"

"Annie is a wise soul. She's here to help you." Darrelle spread her napkin across her lap and refused to say more. "For now, we will eat this delicious food. Later, perhaps we will see what messages the tea leaves hold."

Over lunch they talked about the differences between the United States and France, from clothes to politics to women's attitudes. They touched on events, such as the recent avalanche in the French Alps that killed thirty-five young people on vacation. One had been a twenty-year old girl who worked for Darrelle in her boutique. When the conversation turned to President Nixon and the escalating war in Vietnam, Natalie knew they could see the tears burning in her eyes.

"I have a friend over there," she said, tilting her head back and fanning her face in an effort to contain her emotions. "Sorry. It just gets to me."

"As it should," Darrelle said, patting her hand. "As it should."

As Rosa cleared the dishes, Louise suggested they have dessert and a new pot of tea back across the room, "in the comfortable chairs," acknowledging that the wrought iron set was pretty but not made for endurance sitting.

"We have chocolate cake for the soul and warm tea for the body," Louise tempted them.

"Or the other way around," Natalie laughed, wiping away the remnants of her tears. "Chocolate puts the pounds on, tea doesn't." She patted her hips. "Chad keeps reminding me not to get that married look, that's what he calls it, when women put on weight after the wedding."

Louise shook her head, dismissing her son's missives, and took a large bite of cake. Natalie and Darrelle followed suit, exchanging grins like wayward school girls. So much for Chad. They each arranged and rearranged their bodies, squirming until they were comfortable in the overstuffed chairs. Natalie took off her shoes, sitting sloppy and sideways, tucking her feet in under her thighs. For the first time since she'd been married, she didn't worry about being chastised or corrected. She let herself just be.

"Darrelle," Natalie said, "I'm sorry to keep staring. Your necklace. I noticed it at the reception. I can't seem to take my eyes off of it."

"The lily-of-the-valley. It means both grief and remembrance. I sense you already know that, oui?"

"Yes, yes I do." Natalie shifted in her chair, remembering the box with the coin, remembering Johnny.

"It was my mother's." Darrelle stroked the charm and its thin gold chain with her index finger. "She died when I was three. Stabbed to death by my father. She was gripping this necklace when they found her. The clasp had broken. She held it so tightly, they discovered the imprint was burned into the palm of her hand when they were able to pry it open."

"Oh my God," Natalie hugged herself against the sudden pain that sliced through her stomach. "My God," Natalie repeated. "How? What happened?"

As Darrelle told the story, her voice assumed more of her native French than her practiced English. She talked slowly, precisely, her eyes small and squinted, as though viewing those last moments with her parents from some distant stage and recounting them as they unfolded. Her control was in direct contrast to the emotions lying just below the surface, emotions that gave themselves away only by the way her hand trembled when she reached for her tea to help clear the words from her throat.

"It was my father," she said. "We were there, in our home, it was a modest house, much like what you call a cottage. It was a cold December afternoon, as it began to rain and turn dark. A cold icy rain. My sisters and I, we sat in front of the fire, holding hands, humming softly, trying so very hard to block out their angry words. I was too young to understand the argument. We knew, soon, there would be trouble. Papa had been drinking Absinthe all day, a drink that is illegal now. There was a string of murders. They were called the Absinthe murders. I learned this all later, when I was older and —"

"Chad told me about that," Natalie interrupted, "in New Orleans. He's fascinated by Absinthe, collects the spoon and glasses . . ." her voice trailed off as though she was trying to piece something together. She shivered, an automatic response to the shadow that seemed to walk across her body. The pain in her stomach had dulled to a deep consistent throb. She decided it was part of being pregnant. Sudden swift pain. Nausea. And then nothing.

Darrelle didn't speak for a few minutes; she seemed to be studying Natalie, confirming some private assumption about her. All three women remained silent until Darrelle was ready to continue. Rosa slipped in to remove the remaining dishes. From the front room, the grandfather clock bellowed the time — four o'clock — a sound that echoed through the eerily quiet room. Even their breathing seemed unnaturally loud. Finally, Darrelle continued her story.

"Mère was saying things, spiteful things, I can see her face even now, telling Papa something, something quite awful, but to this day I do not know what. It made no sense. I was only three. My sisters knew, but they never confessed. We did not see him take the knife and stab her, but we saw the blood and the look in her eyes. Such surprise. Such pain. She staggered out the door into the rain and died in an alleyway. When they found her, this necklace was clutched in her hand." Once again, Darrelle stroked the small gold charm that lay against her black sweater.

Natalie never saw Louise move from her chair, but suddenly, there she was, kneeling by her side. "I cried the first time I heard this story, too," Louise said, "but, my dear, you're sobbing." Louise handed her a linen napkin. "Here. Use this."

"That is enough," Darrelle said. "No more sad stories from what is a lifetime ago."

"Please," Natalie said, straightening her body and reaching across to Darrelle, not quite touching her hand. "Please finish."

"I am the only one still alive from that tragedy. An old lady now. It is my story to tell or to not tell."

"But what happened to everyone? To you? To your sisters? What happened to Charles?"

There was an audible intake of breath. First from Darrelle, then Louise. They both seemed to stop mid-motion and stare at her. Natalie stared back at them. "What, what's wrong?"

"How do you know his name? I have not said it. I never say it. Not even in a whisper."

"I don't know," Natalie stammered. "It just came out. Was that your father's name? How would I know that?"

The room fell quiet, filled with shadows and unclaimed thoughts. Unspoken memories. Throughout the silence, Natalie picked compulsively at a small nub of fabric on the arm of her chair. Louise was still beside her, but her attention was focused solely on Darrelle, as though they were speaking a private language fueled by energy rather than sound. Finally, Darrelle relaxed her body and spoke.

"Chère, I believe you. I believe you did not know my father's name until you just spoke it. This *knowing*, it comes from deep within." Darrelle swept her hand out in front of her, encompassing the three woman who seemed connected in a way that defied understanding. "There is something here. Between us. Between the names we call one another. There is some unseen link. I, too, called Louise by the name of Linette at our first meeting. Just as you did." Darrelle smiled at Natalie. "Yes, she told me. And, your name. Natalie. Is it simply coincidence that it is the English version of Noelle? My mother's name."

Natalie leaned across the coffee table that stood between them and clasped Darrelle's hands, nearly knocking over the teapot. "Please, tell me the rest. What happened to everyone?"

"Papa died in prison. I never saw him again. Never spoke his given name."

Darrelle went on to describe how she and her sisters, Simmone and Brigitte, were taken in by Linette and raised along with her children. "Linette died the year I turned eighteen. It was she who gave me Mère's necklace. To grieve. To remember. She said it should be mine."

"And your sisters?" Natalie whispered the question.

"Simmone became very fragile," Darrelle explained. "She had been so much fun. The talkative one is the way I knew her in those early years. She lost her will after the tragedy, poor child, she was always so sad, and so sick much of the time. She died of a pulmonary infection in 1924." Darrelle smiled at some memory. "Brigitte and I, we — how do you say it? — ahh, yes, the word, I believe is pooled . . .we pooled our money and treated Simmone to the Olympics held in Paris that year. It was her dream to go. So we took her. She died a week later."

"And Brigitte?" Natalie continued to hold Darrelle's hands, squeezing hard as she posed her question, as though letting go might mean stopping the conversation.

"That is too sad. She was all I had left and I disappointed her. How do you say it?" She thought a moment. "Yes. I let her down. But I did not see it that way at the time. I believed I was upholding conviction. Brigitte was a willful girl. She first married young and badly. Eventually she left her husband, he beat her, and fell in love with another. With a German soldier. Such a disgrace at the time. I could not hold my head in public. She left France with him. Went to Germany. They married. I saw her only once after that. We wrote. But not often enough. I was intolerant. Unforgiving. I am sorry for that. I will take it to my grave."

"Is she —?"

"She died only last year." Darrelle answered Natalie's unfinished question.

The grandfather clocked chimed again and this time Natalie reacted. She dropped Darrelle's hands and stood quickly. Chad would be expecting her home, to greet him at the end of his work day, to have a drink with him as he unwound. Even though they had Sophie to clean the house and start dinner, he liked his wife to serve it. Natalie didn't generally mind. It was a reasonable trade for the comfortable life he provided, as long as she didn't make him angry. She was terrified of being late. "I have to go."

"You must let me read for you first," Darrelle said, signaling for Natalie to sit back down.

"I can't. Chad —"

"Chad will be just fine," Louise chimed in. "I'll call him at the office and tell him you aren't feeling well. That you'll be home as soon as you can drive safely. He won't be mad, I promise. This gives you the perfect opportunity to tell him your news. Even if it's not confirmed. Tell him tonight, dear."

Louise made her call and returned to the conversation. "I left a message with his secretary. Don't look so frightened, Natalie, he's not that bad, is he?"

Natalie shrugged. "No, he isn't," she assured her mother-in-law. And he wasn't. Not yet anyway. But she sensed that he could be. And that's what scared her.

Darrelle picked up Natalie's tea cup and examined its contents.

"Excellent. There is just enough liquid left." Darrelle handed the cup to Natalie. "Hold it in your left hand, chère, and slowly swirl three times clockwise. Like so." Darrelle picked up her own tea cup and demonstrated the precise motion. "You will then invert the cup on the saucer, count seven seconds, allowing the liquid to drain out. You will then turn the cup right side up. Place it here, on the coffee table. Be sure the handle is facing you."

Natalie swirled and inverted and watched as the bronze liquid seeped out onto the saucer. After counting off exactly seven seconds, she turned the cup back over and placed it on the coffee table. Leaves from the freshly brewed loose tea had clumped together, forming patterns on the bottom and sides of the cup. In order to gain a better perspective, Darrelle slid off the sofa and onto the floor, kneeling over the cup as she examined it.

"The handle is facing you, chère, because you are the inquirer. Images to the left of the handle represent your past; to the right, they show me your future. I see these images," Darrelle said, looking directly into Natalie's eyes and holding her gaze, "but I see more than them. These tea leaves are only a gateway to knowledge. A starting point, if you will. Your guardian will show me what it is you need to know. And I will interpret, as best as I can. I have not been blessed with the gift to see past lives, but often I am able to glimpse the. . . *desafío*. . .how do you say it?" She grasped for the right word. "Oui. The challenge. The *desafío*," she repeated. We come into this world with certain karma, our need to atone for past wrongs. It becomes our earthly challenge."

263

Natalie looked from Darrelle to the tea leaves, scattered and lumped into various designs on the inside of the white bone china, and then over at Louise, sending her a puzzled look. Louise nodded, affirming what Darrelle had explained. "She's read me. Several times. Quite accurately, I might add. Although it is not a perfect science."

"How can it be?" Darrelle asked, "when life is so far from perfect. Always changing. Always at the whim of our will. Sometimes we take our life where it is not meant to go. Other times, despite all odds, we end up precisely where we are meant to be." She peered into the cup, falling silent now as she examined the designs made by the tea leaves.

"See here, the shape of a moon, a circle, not quite full? It suggests an incomplete love affair. I see both past and future. It has happened and the chance for it will occur again."

Johnny. That's all Natalie could think. *Johnny.* "But they're just some tea leaves clumped into a circle," she argued.

"You are correct. The gift is in the reading, in the knowing," Darrelle explained. "I tell you only what I know from deep inside. The leaves are only symbols, to be sure."

"What is said here, will stay here, in this room," Louise offered. "It's all sacred, Natalie. And very private."

She was being told she might complete an unfinished love affair and her mother-in-law was okay with this? If only Annie was here.

"This shape, here," Darrelle continued, "a knife, broken nearly in half, it is speaking of a broken friendship. Misplaced loyalty, false desires, you hurt someone you loved. The guides say to forgive yourself."

The guides? Just like in New Orleans. The Voodoo Shop of Madame LaVeau. Natalie's hand trembled as she spoke. "Pearl. You're talking about Pearl."

"Ahh, yes, her spirit says thank you for remembering."

"Chère, so much is being revealed to me. More than the leaves alone could ever say. For you, this is a lifetime of competing desires. Heart versus head. But there are no solid lines. No easy answers. Roads were chosen at your birth, roads different from what was planned. Despite unplanned choices, you were led to this house. To fulfill promises. To be where you were intended. But. . ."

"But what?" Panic swept over Natalie. Her stomach pulsated with pain and confusion. "But what?" she demanded when Darrelle remained silent.

"You must be careful," Darrelle met Natalie's eyes and continued slowly. "I see opportunity for great love. And great tragedy. Choosing right will be your greatest challenge. Your path is uncertain. As is the outcome. You must make good choices at every bend." Her index finger pointed to wavy lines and what looked like a forked road. "My dear, this message is from me and not the tea leaves or your spirit guides: when choosing look deep inside. Be true, always, to the person you know yourself to be."

Natalie wanted more. More reading. More comfort. More time. She wanted to crawl into the arms of both these women and fill up on their love and acceptance. Instead, the real-world Natalie looked at her watch and saw just how late it had become. No matter what Louise had said in the message she left for Chad, he would be angry when Natalie got home. There would be some kind of hell to pay. Maybe stone-cold silence, maybe a verbal lashing. She had to leave now.

Both women walked with Natalie to the front door. As Natalie gave them each one last hug, Darrelle reached back and unclasped the delicate gold chain holding her lily-of-the-valley charm. She placed the necklace in Natalie's hand, closing her palm over it.

"You must have it. You must remember me always and this will be the way. I have not said anything, but I am not well.

There is not much to be done and I am resigned. We will not see one another again in this life."

Natalie clutched the necklace, its thin chain slipping through her fingers and cascading across the side of her hand.

"It belonged to my mother. Then me," Darrelle whispered. "It now belongs to you. Someday, you will pass it on to your daughter."

As my daughter passes it on to me.

Natalie shivered, startled by that unbeckoned thought. Where had it come from? And what did it mean?

THIRTY

"**I'm pregnant.**" **Natalie** blurted out the news as soon as she returned home, even before taking off her coat, seeing the dark look on her husband's face when he greeted her at the door. She noted the half-empty glass of Herbsaint in Chad's hand and knew Sophie's dinner was probably warming in the oven and most likely overdone by now.

"I stopped at the doctors on my way back from your mother's house, to confirm the news," she lied. "That's why I'm so late."

Reading tea leaves with Darrelle would not have been reason enough to miss their nightly cocktail hour. It was a ritual Chad held sacred, unless, of course, he had a late meeting or dinner with a client.

"Is it mine?" Chad polished off his drink.

Natalie's face burnt with the accusation. She yanked off her coat and threw it, along with her purse, on the nearest chair.

"How dare you say that?" Her voice was righteously angry. Indignant. And hurt. The only way she'd been able to pull this off was to convince herself the baby was Chad's. Once she'd admitted her pregnancy to Louise, she'd actually begun to believe that it did belong to her husband, conceived that first night in New Orleans. How easy it had seemed, to rearrange dates in her mind and reinvent the truth. And now she was caught. Natalie couldn't breathe. She leaned against the credenza, taking huge gulps of air in an effort to steady her nerves.

"You have no sense of humor," Chad laughed as he walked across the room and wrapped his arms around Natalie. "I was just joking."

"It's not funny. How could you say such a thing?" She could hear the desperation in her voice as she looked up at Chad. "That wasn't funny," she repeated.

"Okay. Not funny. But how, when?"

"In New Orleans." She wriggled out of his grasp. It was hard to maintain eye contact. She sat down and fiddled with her coat. "We didn't use anything. And they say it happens a lot when, you know, the first time."

"You're embarrassed," Chad knelt down beside her. "That's so cute." He stroked her hair. "I hope it's a boy. Wouldn't that be perfect? A son to carry on the family name. The next one can be a girl."

"I just want it to be healthy."

"Of course, darling, so do I. When are you due?"

This was the hard part. Natalie knew her real due date was November fifth. With luck, she'd be late. Even two weeks late would help. Then she could pretend she was delivering early.

"Well," Natalie answered, "the doctor figures around December fifth. But he said first babies are unpredictable. They come early a lot, so don't be surprised if it happens some time in November."

"As long as it's not Halloween. Can you imagine being born on the Day of the Dead? What a way to go through life."

"Chad! What is wrong with you?"

"What? Can't a guy make a joke? You're so touchy."

"Well, you're not funny." Natalie stood up and headed toward the kitchen. "I'm hungry. Let's see what Sophie left for us."

"I know you're eating for two," Chad walked behind his wife and reached around to pat her stomach, "but don't overdo it. The more weight you put on now, the harder it'll be to take off later."

———◆———

The closer Natalie got to her actual due date of November 5, the edgier and more short-tempered she became. How would she explain a full-term baby delivered a month early? She could barely sleep with worry, praying for some miracle that would help her move forward in this chosen life. When November fifth, and then the twelfth passed without event, she knew her prayers had been answered.

"It's like a mini-miracle," she called Annie and told her. "Apparently, first babies are known for taking their time. And I told Chad they're known for being early."

"The universe provides," Annie said. "The timing won't be an issue now, you lucky shit."

Annie was right. She was lucky. Natalie relaxed into her chair and tried to forget her troubles. "I miss you, Annie. It's not the same here without you."

"Right. I'm sure Mr. Wonderful thinks that too."

"Who cares? Fill me in on stuff. What's happening? How's the tourist biz going?

"It's great. Uncle Jay is really busy. And, umm, well, there is one thing."

"Spill . . ."

"I met someone. Oh, Natie, it feels really right."

"Annie! When? How? Tell me everything. Why didn't you tell me before?"

"I don't know. You've been so sad and worried."

"And you figured your good news would make me feel worse? You're my friend Annie. Tell me everything."

"Well, his name is Andre. He works here at Little Bay. . ." For the next ten minutes Annie told her everything. Andre was an Islander, dark brown, beautiful eyes, soft voice, patient, and ten years Annie's senior. Uncle Jay was totally supportive, but her parents were going berserk, threatening to cut her off completely if she hooked up with this guy permanently. "They'll come around, I'm sure of it," Annie said. "I'm crazy in love and when they meet him, they will be too."

"True love is a gift, Annie, don't let go of it, no matter who says what. That's my hard-earned lesson."

When they hung up, Natalie felt a pang of guilt at having been so self-absorbed that Annie had been reluctant to share her news, the good and bad of it. She realized Annie was probably afraid Natalie would be envious. Or sad. Or both. And she was. But, mostly, she was happy for her friend; Annie's news felt like a bright spot, a small gift in the midst of her own chaos and loneliness, in the reality of being married to one man and pregnant by another.

⸻◆⸻

Janice Darrelle Hamilton was born on November 19, 1970 at 2:12 a.m. She was short and chubby, with brown spiky hair and skin so soft and pink Natalie couldn't stop stroking her cheek.

It had been a long, hard delivery. At one point, Natalie felt as though she'd left her body, entered a stream of healing white light and held a conversation with an angel named Enif. The doctors told Natalie that she'd lost consciousness for a moment, but there'd been nothing significant, certainly nothing to worry about. Maybe it was nothing to worry about. But it was definitely something significant.

With Janice cradled in one arm, Natalie leaned against her pillows and closed her eyes, recalling every nuance of that experience.

"I messed up," she confessed to a figure of light that seemed to represent love and protection. "There must be something really wrong with me, Enif. I keep doing the same thing over and over again."

"Some lessons are harder to learn than others. And Marilyn's capricious use of free will interfered with your intended destiny. But you have had choices, as well, Nunki. Jabbah was put directly in your path, just as you requested, but you turned him down. To whom were you being loyal? And for what reasons? Misplaced loyalty will pit you against deeper needs and values very time. Remember, Nunki, you have chosen difficult karmic challenges this time around. Already, you are repeating old, destructive patterns. Once again, you have married Cheleb. And deceived him. This child is not his. You have choices. You always have choices. What will you do? How will you break the cycle?"

"Enif. Enif." Natalie reached out to this friend of light, calling a name strikingly familiar to her old doll Edith, but she could feel herself being drawn back into the delivery room, into full consciousness, just the nurse laid her new daughter in her arms.

What will you do? The question with no answer and no earthly source burned in Natalie's mind now as she held Janice and marveled at the miracle of her birth. It made Natalie wonder about the thin line between this world and the next that Annie talked about. Had she crossed over that line while giving birth? Had she been to the other side and back?

"Well, well, well," Marilyn's high pitched voice cut into Natalie's thoughts, hitting the air even before she entered the room. "You went and had your kid without me even bein' here. Just like I don't count." She placed an enormous teddy bear on the side of the bed and a vase of pink roses on the window sill. "I had to hear about it from — oh, Louise!" She turned to see Louise coming into the room, carrying a thermos of coffee, and quickly modified her tone

271

"How good to see you," Marilyn went on. "Like I was sayin, it was so nice of you to call me just as soon as you got back home to shower. Looks like you were here with my little sister all night long. Now, where's that husband of hers?"

"He'll be back. He needed to shower himself. And make a few calls."

"Just like a man. Business first."

"He was here all night, Marilyn," Louise chided. "The two of us. We tried calling you, but there was no answer."

"Oh? Oh!" Marilyn giggled behind her hand like a school girl caught making out during recess. "We unplug the phone sometimes when, well you know, when we don't want to be bothered, if you get my drift. Goodness me, we must have forgotten to plug it back in. Guess Harry took care of that this morning. I tend to sleep in afterwards. Well, well, well," she said, playing with the ribbon around the bear's neck, "imagine, Natalie, you're a mother. Looking at you there, it reminds me of — oh nothing." She flung her arms in the air. "Nothing. Just some old movie I was recallin'. You named her Janice? What kind of name is that?"

Louise settled into the rocking chair by Natalie's bed and held her arms out for her new granddaughter. "That's just what Chad wanted to know," Louise answered for Natalie. "I explained how it was the feminine of John. That was my husband's middle name. I have to admit, Chad's not crazy about the name, but he finally agreed when Natalie told him the only other option was Jane."

"Plain Jane? I doubt he'd go for that." Marilyn smoothed her skirt and sat on the bed. "And Darrelle for a middle name? Why that must be drivin' him crazy."

"I wanted her to have names that mean something," Natalie said. "Darrelle means little dear one, or darling."

272

"You could have chosen Darlene. More modern, and close enough," Marilyn said. "Or Marilyn. That would've been nice. Besides that woman Darrelle died months ago. You won't even get credit for naming your daughter after her."

Natalie cast a glance at Louise. As expected, she blanched at the coarse reference to Darrelle's passing.

Marilyn gave Natalie's legs a playful slap through the hospital blanket. "Well, she's your kid, so I guess you get to choose."

"Right. And we both know how important a name can be." Natalie gave Marilyn a piercing look that said the conversation was closed.

The room went unnaturally silent. To break the tension, Louise held Janice out to Marilyn. "She's so beautiful. Would you like to hold her?"

"She'll be a real looker," Marilyn agreed, taking the baby into her arms, "as long as she doesn't hold onto that baby fat." Marilyn tweaked Janice's plump cheeks and laughed at her own joke. "Another princess in the family."

"Don't."

"Don't what? That was a compliment. She's going to be a princess, just like you. Just like we planned. Really, Natalie, what more could you want? Look at this gorgeous room, private and all. Not anything like the one run by the Sisters of No Compassion —"

Marilyn stopped mid-sentence, realizing she'd said too much. She bowed her head and focused all of her attention on the baby in her arms, a look of longing crossing her face that Natalie never recalled seeing before. It was as though Marilyn wanted to claim the role of mother she'd discarded all those years ago, realizing suddenly she'd also given up her rights as a grandmother. But it had gone on far too long and they'd all woven a tale too complex to set it straight now. Marilyn would forever be Natalie's sister and Janice's aunt, and part of Natalie would never forgive her for that.

"Here, go back your grandmother," Marilyn said, kissing Janice's forehead and handing her over to Louise.

"The Sisters of No Compassion," Louise said. It was a statement, not a question, nearly a whisper, as she rocked back and forth, stroking the head of her new granddaughter. "There was a home, in Fall River. St. Agnes. It was run by the Little Sisters of Compassion. We nearly adopted a baby girl from there."

"Pray tell," Marilyn said, fanning her face. "It's so hot in here. Isn't it hot in here?" She stood and walked toward the door, leaning against the woodwork.

"Yes, the Sisters had a baby girl all set for us; we drove all the way there and it seems the mother changed her mind. Something about naming her. It all boiled down to that. I was heartbroken. Inconsolable really, for years." Louise's voice cracked and she waited a minute before continuing. "We learned later, that the mother took $20 from one of the other girls and left in the middle of the night. Not that I blame her really. Who could part with something as beautiful as this?" She stroked Janice's head. "I've always wondered what happened to them, always prayed they were okay, that they made their way in the world."

"I'm sure they did." Marilyn's voice had risen to an unnatural shrillness, penetrating the room with her desire to assure Louise and change the subject. "Life has a way of working itself out. I believe that. I do. And look at this," she swept her hand across the room in a grand gesture, "you got yourself a daughter now. Just like you always wanted. And a granddaughter. Two for the price of one, you might say. Now, let's talk about happy things."

Natalie took a tissue from the bedside stand and wiped beads of sweat from her forehead, all the while looking from Marilyn to Louise and back to Marilyn. She inhaled deeply, once and then twice, feeling faint. Could it be?

She recalled Darrelle's reading: *Roads were chosen at your birth, roads different from what was planned. Despite unplanned choices, you were led to this house. To fulfill promises. To be where you were intended.*

Could Louise be the woman who was supposed to adopt her? She would have been her mother all along? And Chad would have been her brother? What did it all mean? If life had gone that way, would she still have met Johnny and had his child? Maybe they would be married right now, having this child together.

Natalie cradled her head in her hands, pressing her fingers against her temples, against the thoughts that flooded in, each one tripping over the other. This was all too crazy, too hard to comprehend and sort out. What did it all mean? Was there some kind of destiny at play? Do we end up with the same people no matter where life takes us? Or was this some kind of weird coincidence?

Annie would say there are no coincidences, that everything is related to something greater. Natalie's heart pounded heavy against her thin nightgown. Should she say something? Should she tell Louise who she was?

"Are you okay, dear?" It was Louise's gentle voice penetrating the maze of confusion filling Natalie's brain. "You don't look well. Marilyn, go get a nurse."

"No don't," Natalie all but cried. "Don't. I don't need a nurse. Let's just change the conversation. All this talk about giving up babies. It got to me, that's all."

"Well, do you need water then?" Marilyn asked. She poured a glass and handed it to Natalie. "What else? What can I do for you?"

More than any other time before, Natalie felt she understood Marilyn, understood how a person might weave lies and keep

275

secrets and how a need for something more in life might make you do certain things. She patted her mother's hand and then reached across toward the rocking chair and held Louise's hand, forming an unlikely circle of three.

"Relax," Natalie told Marilyn. "Sit down and hold baby Janice for a while. We're all in this together. You're going to make a wonderful aunt. And Louise, you'll be the world's best grandmother. Let's just enjoy the moment and not worry about anything else."

It was good advice and Natalie tried to follow her own wisdom, but she couldn't let go of the question that seemed to come from an invisible source of power and light — a question that nagged at her then and in all the years to follow: *what will you do? . . . what will you do?*

In the dark of the night, when she had trouble sleeping, when she still yearned for Johnny and prayed for a way to reconcile the life she had with the life she desired, she hoped "nothing" was a good enough answer.

THIRTY-ONE

July 1985

"**C**ome on Janice.** Stop dallying. It's nearly two o'clock. We're going to be late. Everything's in the car, except for you."

Natalie called toward her daughter's bedroom, knowing Janice was probably absorbed in some detail of her own life and oblivious to the time or their schedule. It's the age, Natalie reminded herself — almost fifteen, half-girl, half-woman — remembering her own teenage angst. At least Janice didn't have a mother telling her the only way to be loveable was to become a princess and then abandoning her for the first man who came along. Correction, the first man with money who came along.

Natalie pushed her hair away from her face with both hands, as though pushing away the memories and the nagging guilt that she'd done the same thing, run off with the first rich guy who came along. But at least she'd given her daughter a home with a father and a mother and unconditional love. Oh well, she decided for the millionth time in her marriage, what's done is done and we've all made the best of it. She scanned her bedroom one last time to make sure she hadn't missed anything. Satisfied she'd packed everything she'd need for a month at the Cape, she headed down the stairs and toward the front door.

"Time to leave?" Chad asked, eying his wife up and down the way he always did, not so much in appreciation — although, in his own way, he did appreciate her — but, more, to make sure she passed inspection.

"Yeah. Annie's plane gets into Logan at three. I'll pick her up and we'll head right off. Thanks for renting me that van. I'm excited about having all the kids with us this time."

Chad kissed Natalie on the cheek. "You're welcome. Those new slacks look good on you." He fingered the striped linen fabric. "But try not to say yeah. It's unbecoming."

"Yeah, all right," Natalie countered, watching as Chad pulled his lips across his teeth into a tight line of disapproval. She waited a moment and then smiled. "You're sure you don't want to come?"

Natalie knew Chad would never want to join them. She asked only out of politeness, part of the civil, unspoken dance of their marriage. Chad's time alone was sacred to him. He cherished the freedom her going away gave him — freedom from the unnatural constraints of marriage. . .freedom from Natalie's silent, stricken looks when he came home late, the faint smell of perfume lingering beneath his skin, perfume other than Jicky. . .freedom from that dark shadowy underbelly of rage and desire that surfaced more easily when she was near and seemed to subside when she was away.

Natalie was certain that, on and off, throughout their marriage, Chad continued to have "women on the side." It was a phrase she'd heard recently and found deliciously descriptive. *Salad on the side. Fries on the side. Women on the side.* As long as it didn't interfere with the main course, what was the harm? Apparently this was how cheating husbands justified their inner and outer lives, reconciling their married status with their extra-martial activities. Chad was one of those husbands. And because, in the dark of the night, deep in her soul, Natalie felt unworthy of her title as Mrs. Chadwick Hamilton, knowing her own secrets were just as vile and destructive, she never raised her suspicions or challenged her husband's affairs.

As Marilyn would say, *why rock the boat when you don't have a better one to jump into?* Despite everything, Chad was a remarkably good father. He adored Janice, and if Natalie didn't hold him back, he would spoil her totally. By most measures, Chad was not a bad husband, either. Natalie lived in a beautiful home, wore designer clothes and exquisite jewelry from the shop where she once was a sales clerk. She had the time and means to support philanthropic causes. It was a marriage worth hanging on to, even with his moods, his cheating. Even after what happened this past year. Even after that.

"Maybe later in the month. After she's gone. When it's just you and Janice," Chad responded after a long minute to Natalie's question about coming down. "Or maybe not. I may just stay here and work. It's a busy time for me."

Work. That's what he was calling it these days.

"Whatever's good for you," Natalie agreed and exhaled deeply, not realizing she'd been holding her breath, waiting for Chad's response.

Having him down at the Cape with Annie and the kids, even for a day or two, would have been unpleasant, if not disastrous. Chad had developed a disdain for Annie — *and her hippie, lack-of-respect, anti-establishment ways* — the first time they'd met, before Saint Martin and Johnny, when they were all still single. His distaste for her seemed to increase over the years, despite the fact they never saw each other again, but based on Chad's assessment of anyone who would remain on an island to help run "some second-rate resort." He was smart enough, however, not to try and stop Natalie from this annual get-together, which he saw as tiresome but essentially harmless.

Wait until he finds out that Annie's husband is an islander and their children are as brown as gingerbread. And he's going to find out, if things go my way.

Natalie shook away the unbeckoned thoughts and called out for her daughter.

"Janice! Now! We're leaving right now."

"I'm right here. You don't have to yell." Janice walked into the room and grinned up at her mother, a new camera hanging from a strap across her neck. At fourteen — *and three-quarters* — she was quick to remind her parents — Janice had grown into a quiet beauty, with long legs, sandy-colored hair, her mother's dimpled smile, and eyes the most incredible combination of gold, olive and bronze. She was stubborn, smart, and accustomed to getting her way, especially with Chad.

Slipping a hundred dollar bill into his daughter's hand, Chad ruffled Janice's hair and kissed her on the cheek. "Have a good time, honey. I may not get down to see you, but I'll call. Have a great time."

"Okay Daddy," she threw her arms around his neck. "Thanks again for the camera. I'll miss you." She opened the front door, skipped down the stairs, and settled into the rented van.

———◆———

Instead of returning to Boston after tourist season all those years ago, Annie discovered she really had fallen in love, not only with the island of Saint Martin, but with Andre, ten years her senior, who worked at Divi Little Bay as groundskeeper and general handyman. They married the following year and had two boys in succession, Rene, now twelve and Lincoln, who was nearly eleven. Except for Uncle Jay, who welcomed the additions to his family with open arms and good humor, Annie's family had all but disowned her.

"So much for that unconditional love we both thought my folks had for me," Annie told Natalie after she and Andre and been married for several years and her parents were still encouraging her *not* to come home for a visit. What would they tell the neighbors? They'd try to come see her, once they'd gotten used to the situation. They just needed time, they told her. But time had not changed their mind, or their hearts, and Annie hadn't seen her parents in thirteen years.

But Annie and Natalie? That was a different story. Despite time and distance and family obligations, they'd remained the best of friends. They talked on the phone twice a month and saw each other every July when Natalie gave herself the best birthday present she could imagine. She gave herself Annie. She would pay for her friend's flight to Boston, pick her up at Logan airport, and then the two of them would head out to Louise's summer home in Chatham on Cape Cod, a rambling two-story house with grayed cedar shingles and a wraparound porch overlooking the water. For seven days, they would simply *be* with one another, allowing their time together to develop its own rhythm, sinking into a comfortable combination of silence and conversation that ebbed and flowed like the New England tide.

This year, however, they were giving up their coveted private visit. They decided it was time for their children to meet, time to weave the next generation into the tapestry of their friendship. They approached the week with crossed fingers and hopeful hearts, fully aware that it could go either way, given two pre-adolescent boys and one headstrong teenage girl.

As much as Natalie wanted everyone together for all of the inter-generational friendship and bonding reasons she and Annie had expressed when planning the trip, Natalie had another motive for bringing them together. She would reveal it when the time was right.

The ride from Logan to Chatham was filled with non-stop talking and laughing. As soon as they pulled into the driveway of their Cape Cod home-away-from-home, all three kids jumped out of the van and ran down to the water, casting off socks and sneaks as they made their way through the grainy sand, just beginning to cool down from the day's heat. Natalie and Annie settled themselves on the deck, deciding to unpack after a late dinner.

"It's going to be a different kind of week, with these three," Annie said, taking a deep drag of her Virginia Slim cigarette, blowing rings into the air.

Natalie studied Annie for a long minute before responding, soaking in the presence of her friend. Annie's hair was still long and unruly, but now permanently streaked with blonde from so many years in the sun; her skin was so evenly and deeply tanned, she now seemed to be a native island girl.

"Not different enough," Natalie finally said, waving the smoke away from her face. "You promised you'd quit."

"I know. I will. Just not today."

"I know that feeling. Just not today."

"You still think about him?"

"I try not to. I wake up and say, today is the day I won't think about Johnny. Today, it's me and Chad and Janice. And then I look into those eyes of hers and how can I not think about him?"

"No kidding. She looks so much like him." Annie held out her cigarette to Natalie. "Want a drag? It might help."

"So would arsenic," Natalie laughed. "It was a moment in time, Johnny and me. No more. No less. I have to accept that. A wonderful, beautiful, fabulous moment that I should have made last a lifetime. But I didn't." She hesitated and then continued. "I never told you . . ."

"Told me what?"

"I went to The Wall. The Vietnam Wall." Natalie bit her lower lip and swallowed hard. She waited a moment, taking a slow slip of the sweet Guava wine Annie had brought with her. She closed her eyes, listening to the sound of the surf. "I went looking for him."

"When?"

"Last July. Right after you left. I got up the courage one day and went. Made up some story for Chad about having to go to D.C. for one of my volunteer boards."

"And?"

When Natalie didn't answer, Annie tried again. "His name was there?"

Natalie nodded, staring straight ahead, afraid if she looked at Annie, she would cry. And she didn't want to cry. She'd sobbed enough tears for a lifetime, for two lifetimes, when she saw Johnny's name engraved in the smooth cold black granite. She must have stood there for an hour, running her fingers across his name, wondering how she could have let it all go, wondering how it was that Johnny could be dead and she hadn't even known it. She'd always believed she would feel it, deep inside, if something had happened to him.

"Are you sure it was him?" Annie leaned over and touched Natalie's hand. "There has to be more than one John Conway? Are you sure?"

"John James Conway, Marine Corps, PFC."

"Oh, Natie." Both women fell silent watching their children run barefoot, along the sand, playing tag with the surf. "Wait a minute," Annie said, waving her cigarette in the air, "wasn't Johnny a lieutenant? I swear he was a lieutenant."

"He was. What's that got to do with anything?"

"You just said PFC."

283

"Did I? I don't know where that came from," Natalie shrugged. "It was him. John James Conway? Marine Corps? Vietnam? It was him, Annie. Johnny's gone and I have to accept it."

Annie stood and stretched, pulling her hair into a pony tail and then letting it fall back against her face. "I'm really truly sorry," she said, crushing out her cigarette into an ashtray made of seashells and wiping away her own tears. "I'm so glad you have Janice."

"Me too," Natalie said, clinging to Annie's hand. "Me too."

———◆———

Whenever people are apart for a while, it takes time to get back into the rhythm of being together. This year, it wasn't just Natalie and Annie finding their way back together, they had their children's eccentricities to consider as well. Rene was shy and easily bullied by his brother, who could suck the air right out of a room with all of his energy and talkativeness, but was sensitive to any kind of criticism. And then there was Janice.

She began taking photographs as soon as they arrived and never seemed to stop. Unless, of course, she was writing in her diary, both activities, she explained to whoever would listen, "essential disciples to her goal of becoming either a photographer or a journalist, or both." As the teenager of the group, older than the two boys and smarter and cooler than the two mothers, Janice immediately assumed the role of tour director, telling everyone exactly how they should spend their time to get the most from their week together.

"Enforced joy," Annie called it, laughing off Janice's bossiness while Natalie took her daughter into the other room to privately quell her queenly attitude.

By the end of their third day together, despite quirks and differences and personalities that waxed and waned, they were functioning as one large and happy family and the week began to fly by far too quickly. Come Thursday night, the kids decided to go into Hyannis with neighbors for shopping and ice cream and general hanging out, giving Annie and Natalie some private time to enjoy their tradition of watching the movie *Same Time Next Year*. After seeing it at the movies when it first came out in 1979, Natalie hunted around until she found it on videotape, surprising Annie with it the following summer.

"We're just like them, you know, George and Doris, except that we're female friends," Annie shouted into the living room from the kitchen, where she was popping corn. Natalie was setting up the video and pouring wine.

"You say that every year. I swear we are like them. Changing, but not. Wanting more, but still finding ways to be present to the life we have."

Annie walked in with a huge bowl of buttered popcorn and picked up a glass of wine, holding it in a toast. "Here's to *this* time, *this* year. I love you Natie."

"And I love you, Annie. I don't know where I would have been all these years without you in my life."

Natalie and Annie drank and ate and cried, feeling the pain and joy of the characters — played by Alan Alda and Ellen Burstyn — as they maneuvered through the challenges of their annual tryst, aging and changing and loving one another beyond all reason and still, somehow, remaining loyal and connected to their spouses. By the time the credits rolled, Natalie and Annie were surrounded by wads of used tissues.

"I wonder where we'll be in twenty years," Annie said as she ejected the video.

"Twenty? Where will we be in two?" Natalie countered. "Do you ever wonder about destiny? I mean, are we really, truly living the life we're meant to live? Or do we makes choices that lead us down another path. Or, do we end up in the same place with the same people, no matter what road we take? Like me and Louise. I look at her sometimes, even after all these years, and can't believe she's the mother who should have raised me. I've never told her. It feels like I'd be tempting something. Fate, maybe?"

"Yikes. What's gotten into you?" Annie tucked her feet under her legs and sat Indian style on the sofa, facing her friend. "This is SO not a Natalie-type conversation. Destiny? Fate? Free Will? I love it."

"Don't get carried away. You know I only believe what I can touch and feel. Still. . ."

"Still what?"

"I don't know. Sometimes it feels like there are unseen forces, things beyond us, things we don't know about, or maybe we do, but the knowledge is buried, not easily accessible." She shrugged her shoulders, at a loss to explain the unexplainable. "I don't know. Are you happy, Annie?"

"Happy enough. I love my husband and kids, but I'm really sad about my folks. I feel like an orphan, no parents, no cousins, and we have a shitload of cousins —"

"I was pregnant last fall," Natalie interrupted.

"Natie?"

"I know. It was probably foolish. In fact, I know it was foolish."

"You never said a word. What happened?"

"After I went to The Wall, saw Johnny's name, I had this, I don't know, call it an epiphany. You know, some momentary flash of enlightenment. Or something like that. I suddenly had this realization that I'd been living in this in-between place, kind of like between worlds, mooning over a lost life with Johnny and living with Chad but never really being with him, if you know what I mean. I was always someplace else. Here," Natalie pointed to her head. "And here," she covered her heart with the palm of her hand.

"Anyway," Natalie sighed deeply and continued. "I decided it was time to really give Chad a chance. After all, he married me, and he didn't have to. He's essentially a good man. And he's been such a good father to Janice. I decided, no more holding back. No more being only half-there. And it worked. We were feeling like a real family. Happy in our own way. I gave a little, he gave a little. We both decided it was time to have another child."

"And?" Annie took a large gulp of wine, wiping her mouth with the back of her hand as it dribbled across her bottom lip.

"And nothing. Or everything, depending on how you look at it. I got pregnant. We were thrilled, all three of us."

"And? Just spit it out. I hate it when you make me pull things out of you."

"I'm sorry. This is hard. You know Chad, how controlling he can be, calling me all the time to see where I am, what I'm doing, always trying to improve me?"

"Yup, you married the male version of Marilyn. We've had that conversation before. They say we marry what we know."

"Thanks Dr. Freud." Natalie swung a pillow at Annie, and then held it to her stomach. Despite the warm air, she suddenly felt cold. She grabbed the afghan and wrapped it around her legs. "Janice was out this one night and Chad started drinking, for no apparent reason that I could tell. He'd stopped for a while. Things are always better when he's not drinking. It was in early December; I was about two months pregnant at the time. It was Sophie's night off so I cooked. But I got distracted and burned the roast. He got really upset, called me stupid, inattentive. Then he told me I was getting fat, I reminded him that I was pregnant and then, can you believe this, he accused me of having an affair and maybe this baby wasn't his."

"There's some irony for you."

"No kidding. Anyway," Natalie continued, "we fought. Really bad. I almost told him about Janice, but caught myself

287

in time. But he kept accusing me of having an affair because I'm out so much. I do a lot of volunteer work and, I don't know, I see friends, spend time with Louise, especially now that she's getting older. I take her to her doctor appointments. Janice and I make a point of seeing Marilyn twice a month." Natalie felt like she was pleading for Annie to understand that she'd become a good and faithful wife, that Chad's accusations were totally unfounded.

"Natie, you don't have to prove anything to me. I know you and I believe you." Annie opened another bottle of wine and poured them each a glass. "Here, drink."

"He hit me."

"Oh, God," Annie said.

"It was more like a shove. On my shoulder. But hard. I backed away, tried to remain calm, but that just infuriated him. It was awful, Annie. He kept coming at me, kind of like play-hitting, swinging and missing and then laughing. I turned around, my back was to him at that point, and tried to get away. That's when he started pushing, really pushing. Harder and harder, his hand on my back. I couldn't get away; every step I took, he was right there, pushing and taunting, saying such awful things. He shoved me right into the corner of the long sofa table in the foyer."

Even now Natalie could feel the pain. Nausea swirled deep in her stomach; bile rose, mixing with the wine and popcorn. "The edge of the table. It's so sharp. It felt like a knife going through me."

Annie put her hands to her mouth as though she was going to be sick.

"I lost the baby. I told the doctors I slipped and fell against the table. It was the truth."

"Sort of," Annie said.

"Yeah, well. I didn't mention anything about Chad. What good would that have done? They said if something as simple as that caused a miscarriage, I would have probably had one anyway. It was nobody's fault, they said. Just nature doing its thing."

Annie shook her head, unable to say anything. Just as she seemed about to respond, Natalie continued, angry this time.

"You know what else those doctors told me?" She sat up straight and shook her index finger at Annie. "You know what else? They said I was too old to be having a baby. That I had some nerve mucking — they actually said *mucking* — around with mother nature. Can you *mucking* believe it?"

"Stupid ass chauvinist pigs," Annie said, grabbing a tissue and handing the box over to Natalie. They both blew hard, crying and laughing at the same time and then falling silent, listening to the sounds of the night beyond the open windows.

"You're still with him," Annie said after a while.

"I am."

Again they listened to the night.

After a while, Natalie turned to Annie and admitted her deepest fear. "You know, the thing is, when Chad accuses me of stuff, like having an affair, part of me just assumes he knows, he knows all about Janice, and he's been toying with me all these years. That I deserve whatever he dishes out."

"That's a crock. First, he doesn't know. Second, even if he did, nobody deserves to be pushed around. That's called abuse. He made you lose the baby, for God's sake."

Natalie took a deep breath and blew it out slowly. "Leaving doesn't seem worth the effort. There's nothing else to go to."

"Sometimes you just need to go from."

"Maybe. Maybe not. It's not all bad. He's not all bad. And there's something to be said for sticking things out. Being loyal to him, it makes me feel like a better person. Is that crazy? Am I crazy?"

"No," Annie said. "We have to choose what works for us, even when it doesn't work perfectly. It's all about balance. I've mellowed, Natie. I don't push so hard anymore."

"I've noticed. You've always been a good friend. But it makes you a better one. Easier to talk to."

———◆———

"Ta-da," Natalie said, a wide grin spilling across her face as she did a little jig and presented Annie with the book she'd been keeping tucked behind her back. It was early the next morning and they'd been sitting on the deck in pajamas and bare feet, drinking coffee, watching the beach come alive.

"What's this?" Annie asked trying to puzzle out what Natalie was handing her. Then she looked at the cover and started jumping up and down with excitement.

"Ohmygod, ohmygod. Already? You have it already?"

"It's a printer's proof."

"But it looks so real, like a real honest-to-goodness book."

"Well, it is," Natalie beamed. "It's on press as we speak."

"*Giving with Meaning*," Annie read the title, and then the subtitle, "*Learn how to make every gift special using folklore, legends and traditions*. "I love it! I love the concept, the name, the cover. I love it all. And I love you more!" Annie gave Natalie a bear hug and then opened the book to one of the entries.

"This is so fabulous," Annie gushed, "the way you take an ordinary thing, like a turtle, and then give the legend or meaning behind it. And then, you actually tell us non-creative types how to make it work for all kinds of occasions." She thumbed through the pages. "This is so cool."

"And, look," Natalie said, turning back to the turtle entry as an example, "then I give all kinds of ideas for turtle-type gifts, including "turtle candy" and even ideas for notes that someone can write, connecting the gift to the legend and the occasion."

"I can see that," Annie laughed, pushing Natalie's finger away from the page. "I, too, can read. It's great. Absolutely, positively great. I had no idea a turtle could help a pregnant woman have an easier labor. I could have used that one. Both times! And look at this," she said turning the pages and stopping on a listing for lettuce. "Sexxxyyy. I'll never look at iceberg the same way again." She waved her hand in front of her face in feigned embarrassment. "Great ideas for a shower gift."

Natalie was so excited she kept bouncing around on her bare feet. "See all the things you can learn with my book!"

"I can see," Annie grinned. "I thought it took at least a year to get a book into the marketplace?"

"It normally does. But this is a small, independent house, so they can pretty much create their own timeline. They decided they want it out in September. In time for the holiday season. So it's on press. Now. As we speak!" Natalie laughed. "I said that all ready."

"Say it again. ON PRESS. AS WE SPEAK." Annie cupped her hands and shouted out toward the beach and then turned and hugged her friend. "I am so, so happy for you. See, there's always a balance between happy and not happy."

"There's more," Natalie said, casting a mysterious side glance Annie's way, wanting to drag out the news for a bit. This was why she'd wanted the kids with them this week. If they all got along, then Annie would be more receptive to her idea. Annie and Andre might agree to move to Boson.

"Tell all. Don't keep me in suspense," Annie said.

"Maybe later."

"Later, my eye. It's now or never, my dear."

As though on cue, they linked arms and stood facing the water, breaking into a bad rendition of the song *Now or Never*, serenading the near-empty beach. They doubled over in gales of laughter as the folks next door waved from their deck and then joined in for a second round.

"Okay, that's all the fun I can handle. Now tell me the rest of your news," Annie demanded taking a swig of coffee, wrinkling her nose because it had gone from hot to luke warm.

"Okay, here it is. Listen with an open mind. Okay?"

"Me? I'm as open as they get. Shoot."

"All right," Natalie finally said. "Here's the deal. I pitched this book to my publisher based on the idea that everyone who gives gifts would want this book. And that's just about everyone!"

"And I concur," Annie smiled.

"Well, imagine a boutique where all the gift items come from this book, at least to start with. The idea is that everything in the store will have some kind of meaning behind it, some kind of legend or folklore or tradition and everything will come with a small card explaining the meaning. I'll keep adding items as I do research. And then, of course, my book will be there, autographed, making it a great gift in and of itself."

"It's a great idea. Fabulous, actually. Having a shop by the same name and with the same philosophy as the book—"

"It's more than an idea," Natalie interrupted, practically whispering the words, as though saying them too loudly would prick her balloon, maybe even make it deflate and disappear. "It's real. My store is going to open around October, just after the book comes out."

"Get out of here! How? Why didn't you tell me this was happening?"

"I didn't want to do it on the phone. I needed to see your face, tell you in person. Please, please don't think I'm a sell-out or anything." Natalie sucked in her breath because part of her did feel like a sell-out. "Chad's funding this, until I can make it work. He never believed in it, still doesn't, but after what happened with the baby, he's trying to make up for it in the only way he knows how."

"With money. You know he's buying you off? Instead of jewelry this time, he's giving you a store."

"I know." Natalie lowered her head, unable to make eye contact with Annie.

"So f'n take it!" Annie shouted. "Take it and live your dream, Natie, you deserve it."

"Oh, Annie, Annie, thank you." Tears fell across Natalie's cheeks. She knew Annie's approval was important to her, but never quite realized just how important until now. "Thank you," she whispered.

"Details. I want details," Annie called out as she padded into the kitchen to refill their coffee mugs. "Wait, don't say a word until I can give you my undivided attention."

They settled back into their chairs, sipping hot coffee and talking about Natalie's plans. The shop would be right on Newberry Street. Small, cute. Very inviting. Not pretentious. Renovations would begin as soon as she got back to Boston and it would be ready for a grand opening by mid-October.

"Yes. Yes," Annie shouted, punching the air. "I'm so happy for you."

"Want to make me happier? Say yes to what I'm about to propose. Come back, Annie. You and Andre and the boys. Help me run *Giving with Meaning*. You can be the manager. There won't be a huge salary the first couple of years, because everything has to come out of the business. Chad bought the building and he's giving me a ten-year lease at a very fair rate." Natalie was talking fast, wanting to get it all out before Annie could say no, "I have enough money from when Aunt Willie died to buy merchandise, and —"

"Whoa." Annie held up her hand. "Slow down. You're making me dizzy."

"Let me finish: you can see how well the kids get along, that's why I wanted us all here, together, this week. Kind of like a trial run," Natalie continued selling her idea. "We'd be one big happy family. Just imagine it. I'll get Chad to use his contacts for a low down payment, low interest mortgage so you can buy a home right away. I'm thinking Brookline, they have a lot of nice subdivisions going up, good schools, not too far out, and I'll use any connections I have to get Andre jobs building houses until he figures out what else he might want to do. You said he's a great carpenter."

"He is," Annie said, "and I'm sincerely, deeply overwhelmed."

Annie got up and hugged Natalie and then pulled away to look her friend directly in the eyes. "But there's a chink in this one big happy family idea." She let the words sink in and then continued. "The men have not yet met. Andre is no problem, you know that. But what about Chad? I don't see a warm welcome there. He has no idea that my husband is an islander, does he? Or that my boys are brown as berries, summer and winter?"

"Screw Chad," Natalie said without flinching, holding their eye contact. "You'll all grow on him. And if you don't so what? The key is to move this along before he knows those particular details. Move back. I'll put you up in a hotel until you close on a house. Once everything's in place, it'll be too late for him to make waves. You and Andre may even grow on him."

"Right. You're a dreamer, girl. Chad will be beyond pissed. You know how he feels about you keeping secrets from him. This will feel like a whopper."

"Probably. But I don't care. I want you to do this with me, Annie. What do you think?"

"Truth?"

"Truth."

"I think it's fabulous."

"Seriously?" Natalie grinned so widely her face hurt. She did another little barefoot jig and then stopped to assess Annie. "Really, truly, seriously?"

"Really. Truly. Seriously." Annie wiped away tears from the corners of her eyes. "We've been talking about coming to the States, but couldn't imagine how to make it happen. We don't have a lot of money saved. This is perfect. Thank you thank you thank you."

Annie pulled her hair back from her face and wrapped it into a ponytail and stood by the railing of the deck, staring out at the ocean. After a minute or two, she turned to Natalie, her voice shaky. "Are you sure? Is it true? Am I awake or dreaming? Pinch me."

Natalie came up behind Annie and pinched her friend's behind. "You're awake. And it's very, very true."

THIRTY-TWO

By mid-September, Natalie's book had come out and by early October, her shop with the same name, *Giving with Meaning*, was ready to open. Remarkably, Annie and her family had managed to move back, find a house and settle in, with the boys missing only the first few weeks of their new school. Natalie was finally feeling as though all the pieces of her life had clicked into place; she enjoyed a sense of contentment equivalent to a deep, satisfied sigh: she was tackling something new, something she'd always wanted to do. Her best friend was back; she had a healthy, happy teenage daughter and a marriage that basically seemed on par with most other marriages, certainly no better and probably no worse. Life was good.

While he hadn't helped out with any of the labor, Chad stopped by often during the renovations, and was supportive in his own way, offering suggestions, buying pizza for the workers and encouraging Natalie to "enjoy her little shop."

In designing the space, her priority was to create an open, inviting store that capitalized on the natural light pouring in from the front windows. At Annie's suggestion, she used colors like sand and sage green, punctuated by terra cotta and even a touch of periwinkle. The result was a soft, stress-free environment that invited browsing, very different from all the formal New England styling in the area.

Every item in the shop had the potential for "added" meaning because of the history and folklore attached to it. Her book was prominently displayed in the window, along with a sign promising that ten percent of all sales — books and merchandise — would be donated to a volunteer organization she'd helped establish a few years ago, *Keep Boston Warm*, which supplied blankets, hats, mittens, and coats every winter directly to street people, as well as to the city's emergency shelters. Her inspiration for the project had been Henry, who'd died years ago, but was never far from her heart.

Near the store's cash register was a crystal jar filled with strawberry Twizzlers and a sign that read, *Be Sweet To Yourself. Have a Twizzler!* Silly as it might seem to others, it was Natalie's way of keeping Pearl by her side. Beneath the counter, tucked way back on a shelf, was a small wooden box, its cover inlaid with a lily-of-the-valley mosaic; inside was the coin she'd found in the sand, the coin she should have given away, for luck, and had kept for herself instead. Surrounded by her own important symbols, Natalie was ready to open her shop and see her dream succeed.

On the afternoon before the grand opening, Annie was in the back room organizing a shipment that had just arrived. Janice had stopped by after school, meeting up with Rene and Lincoln, all three of them hanging out by the front counter, joking and eating Twizzlers. Meanwhile, Natalie was in a world of her own, obsessively arranging and rearranging small items and wiping away newly discovered specks of dust from glass top tables.

"The dust will be back in the morning. It's a losing battle, Natalie. And you shouldn't be doing that anyway. Isn't that what Annie is for?"

Natalie jumped at the voice in her ear. She hadn't heard Chad come in. "What are you doing here?" she asked.

"Checking up. Checking in," he grinned. "It looks okay. Actually, it looks more than okay. I'm proud of you." He stroked her hair and patted her head in approval. "I told all my friends to come in tomorrow, give you a boost. Meanwhile," Chad rubbed his hands together, "I thought I'd take my two best girls to dinner." He looked over at Janice and gave his daughter a mock salute and then turned back to Natalie.

"Who are those colored kids?" He asked. "They're standing right by the cash register. You're too trusting, you had your back to them —"

Natalie laughed out loud. She couldn't help herself, but even while she was amused, she felt nervous heat rise to face. "That's right," she said, keeping her voice deliberately casual, as though responding to something as ordinary as the day's weather. "You don't know them."

"And you do?" He grabbed her right hand, the one toying with the necklace she wore nearly all the time, the one Darrelle had given her. "Stop fiddling Natalie. It's unbecoming. I don't know why you always wear that piece of tin anyway. I've given you some nice pieces —"

"It means something to me," she whispered. "Let's not fight about it." She pulled her hand away from his and then tucked both hands into the pockets of her skirt. She nodded toward Janice and the boys. "Come on, I'll introduce you."

"Rene, Lincoln, I'd like you to meet my husband."

"Hey, Mr. Hamilton," Lincoln said.

"Hey," Rene echoed.

"Hi Dad." Janice gave Chad a quick hug. "We're going across the street for Coke and fries, wanna' come?"

"No. No, I don't."

"You okay? Something wrong?" Janice's eyes narrowed as she studied her father. Chad's voice had turned sharp enough to capture her attention.

Before he could answer, Annie came in from the back room, wiping her hands on her jeans. "All organized," she announced, "now all we have to do is —" Annie stopped talking and scanned the room. "Well hi everyone. Everything okay?" She cocked her head to one side, "Hey Chad, I see you've met my boys."

"Yours? These are your kids?"

"Last time I checked."

"Well, well, well," Chad said, moving his gaze from Annie back to her boys and then to Natalie. "Janice, no to the deli, I'm taking you and your mom out to dinner. You wait right here. Your mom and I need a private minute." He turned toward Natalie. "Let's go outside."

Natalie shrugged her shoulders and followed Chad, throwing everyone a look that said "uh oh," trying to normalize the mounting tension. She could feel four sets of eyes watching them as she and Chad stood just outside the store.

"Those are Annie's kids?" Chad hissed.

"They are." Natalie reached up, ready to fiddle with the charm on her necklace, but stopped mid-air. It was a nervous habit she definitely needed to break.

"Why didn't you tell me? This changes everything."

"First," Natalie spoke between clenched teeth, "I did tell you. I told you when Annie married and I told you each time she gave birth and we sent presents."

"You told me *what*? That she was married, that she had kids? Look what you *didn't* tell me. They're colored, for God's sake. Did that just happen to slip that pretty little mind of yours?" He tapped the side of her head with his index finger. "And now our daughter is hanging around with them?"

"And your point is?" Natalie kept her voice calm but strong, cool and direct. Even as Chad glared at her, even as a bead of fear slid down her spinal cord.

"Your hippie, gypsy Annie is bad enough with her mangy hair and stupid clothes. I've allowed you a lot of leeway with her, coming back here, helping with the mortgage. But colored kids," Chad sneered, "obviously a colored husband." He took hold of Natalie's upper arm and squeezed hard. "I won't be embarrassed like this."

"Allowed me? You *allowed* me?" Her voice pitched higher and louder.

"Yes. Allowed you. Have you forgotten who's funding this little endeavor?"

"In case you didn't know," she jutted out her chin, "nobody can embarrass you, you can only embarrass yourself. And you're doing a great job of it. You would have known sooner if you'd agreed to meet Andre, go out to dinner or a movie like I suggested." She nodded toward the store and the four people inside watching them. "What do you think Janice thinks right now? Oh, and by the way, the word is black these days, not colored, just in case you're looking to be properly prejudiced."

"Don't sass me Natalie. And don't play with me. Dinner? A movie? You expected me to go and then what? We'd meet in some public place and you'd spring him on me? Figure I wouldn't make a scene. Well, figure again, missy. As far as Janice goes, she'll think whatever I want her to think. I forbid her to hang out with those —"

"Those what?" Natalie cut in. "Those nice mannered young men who are the children of my best friend? You *forbid* it? Think again, Chad."

"She's my daughter. She'll do whatever I tell her to do. She is not going to hang out with those boys. Not now. Not ever. Do you understand?"

Natalie watched the color rise in Chad's face as the veins in his neck pumped with anger. He was standing so close now, his fingers digging into her arm, his words striking her face like darts thrown against a board. She wrenched from his grasp and backed away. She could feel it coming, years of holding back giving way, the words rising like bile, begging for release — *she's not yours, she's not yours. Look into those gorgeous eyes of hers and tell me you can believe, for one second, you actually fathered her.*

The words burned in Natalie. They begged for release.

A gust of wind blew at her skirt and across her neck. Natalie wrapped her arms around her body and backed away from Chad.

"That's what you think? You think because she's *your daughter*, she'll do your bidding like some witless puppy? Well, I've got news for you. Janice is not your —"

The wind kicked up again. Natalie ignored the warning she sensed in the burst of air whipping around her body. "Janice is not —" she repeated, "she's not —" Pain sliced through her stomach; she doubled over, unable to speak.

"She's not what?" Chad yelled, closing the distance between them, ignoring Natalie's distress. "She's not what?" he demanded.

Natalie pressed her hands into the heat of her pain, as she staggered toward the store's window and leaned against it for support. She closed her eyes and breathed deeply, the way she'd taught herself to do over the years, whenever one of these attacks occurred.

As the pain abated, Natalie regained her balance, swallowing down the spite that had risen so suddenly and unexpectedly.

"Janice is not —"

What will you do? The question from the light nearly fifteen years ago rose unbidden as the wind whirled around her body. *What will you do to break the cycle?*

"She's not your property," Natalie said, nodding, feeling the convergence of spirit and words in that simple statement. The wind began to die down. "She's not your property. Or mine. She's nobody's property." Natalie eyed Chad and refused to look away. "Janice is her own person and old enough to make decisions about her friends. As I am. Don't ever ask me to betray Annie or her family, because I won't. Don't make us choose, Chad. You'll lose, I promise."

"Don't threaten me, Natalie. I have friends in high places."

"I know. That's how we got married, isn't it? You looked under a rock and found a few friends of friends, all in high places."

"Has it really been that bad, Natalie?" Chad looked tired all of a sudden. She noticed a few gray hairs at his temple and wondered when that had happened.

"Look," Chad pointed to the store, "your dream come true. Don't spoil it."

"Don't you spoil it." Natalie stiffened as Chad wrapped his arms around her waist and pulled her toward him.

"Let's agree to disagree about Annie and her family," Natalie finally offered. "But quietly. And privately. No more confrontations. If not for us, let's do it for Janice."

"I'll work on it. But you have to do your part. Don't flaunt them. And don't expect me to socialize. They are not — nor will they ever be — part of our family or circle of friends. Remember that Natalie. And remember this: if I see Janice in any danger, socially or otherwise, all bets are off." He shook his head as though unable to believe this compromise. "I can't even imagine what my mother will say."

"Your mother?" Natalie laughed. "We've already been to her house for lunch. The whole lot of us. Twice in fact. And Andre is rebuilding her back porch."

"My dear mother, Boston's number one do-gooder. Okay Natalie, I'll let you have your fun."

He pulled her close, kissed her dramatically for the audience he knew was still watching, and then waved to Janice, Rene, Lincoln and Annie. He smiled down at her, a rakish half smile. "Just don't push too far. We all have limits, Natalie. I hope you know yours. And mine."

THIRTY-THREE

As fall turned to winter and winter to spring, Natalie and Chad seemed to have reached a workable truce, their marriage running along on what Natalie called "good enough." She suspected that Chad continued to see other women now and then, but he was discrete and she appreciated that. She, in turn, maintained a separate and fairly guarded relationship with Annie and her family. Life was moving along smoothly and at an even pace. What more could anyone want?

And then Louise was diagnosed with breast cancer.

By the end of May, Natalie was spending more and more time with her mother-in-law, nursing her through the side effects of chemotherapy. She never viewed it as a burden and never chastised Chad for not being more involved; surprisingly, it brought great peace to Natalie, as though lifting a burden she never knew she'd been carrying. "It feels almost sacred," she tried explaining to Annie one morning. "Aside from giving birth, being with Louise, helping her through this, it actually feels spiritual."

"Then it probably is," Annie offered, "the divine at work. Don't worry about the store. I'll take of things here, you take care of Louise."

And so she did. The worst times were the two days immediately following chemotherapy, when Louise could barely move and food was impossible to keep down. Natalie would relieve Rosa or one of the many nurses they'd hired, bathing Louise's parched skin and feeding her spoonfuls of broth. Sitting in the darkened bedroom beside Louise, watching her doze on and off, Natalie would remember how she and Darrelle seemed to have a cosmic memory of this woman, both of them calling her Linette, both being drawn to her on some mystical level. And then she'd try to imagine what those days at St. Agnes' Home must have been like, Marilyn deciding to keep her baby, Louise heartbroken over losing the child she'd wanted so desperately.

Should she tell Louise? Should she break her promise to Marilyn and tell Louise she's that daughter from long ago?

The question tugged at Natalie's heart more and more often these days. As did a lot of things. After Janice was born, Natalie began to see how life must have been for Marilyn; she stopped expecting from her mother what she could never give, and began to see what she had done for her. Although she never said the words out loud, Natalie slowly came to forgive her mother for the secrets and lies, much like Janice might have to forgive her someday.

Thinking about that place called *someday*, Natalie's mind often wandered to the bigger questions of life. Watching Louise struggle to live even as death became more of a certainty, Natalie thought about the choices we all make versus the choices that are made for us — like Marilyn keeping her when she shouldn't have — and how life seemed to be an experience in opposites — shadow and sunshine, sorrow and joy, loss and opportunity. Old dreams replaced by new ones. And every action, she realized now, had a consequence. She'd begun re-reading *The Prophet*, the same book she'd given Pearl the day she died; it had been found at the edge of the quarry and returned to Natalie. She kept returning to one passage in particular: *If this is my day of harvest, in what field have I sowed the seed, and in what unremembered seasons?*

Natalie suspected she had a lot of unremembered seasons, but dealing with the ones she remembered were enough for her at the moment.

One afternoon in early June, just after Louise finished a particularly bad bout of vomiting, Natalie and Rosa were working together to make Louise comfortable, changing her sheets and nightgown, wiping down the bathroom, when Janice burst into the house, accompanied by her girlfriend Allison.

"Mom, mom , where are you?" Janice shouted into the too-quiet house. "Are you here?"

Natalie came to the top of the stairs. "We're up here, putting Nana to bed. I'll be down in a few minutes."

When she got downstairs, Janice and Allison were in the kitchen, pouring tall glasses of Coke and munching on potato chips.

"She's bad, huh?" Janice asked.

"Yeah, she is. Hi Allison. How are you?"

"Great Mrs. Hamilton." She nudged Janice. "Show her."

"Later."

"No, now. Show her."

"Okay girls, what's up? Show me what?" Natalie ran her hands through her hair, trying to keep her voice even, free from the agitation streaming through her body. It wasn't her daughter's fault that she was so tired. "What do you want show me?"

Natalie reached into the newly opened bag of chips and pulled out a few. She noticed how excited Janice was despite her attempt at a cool, casual demeanor. It showed in her eyes, eyes that reflected all of her emotions even when she tried to hide them, eyes more olive than bronze today, with the same gold flecks as her father's.

Janice opened her notebook, took out several papers from the inside pocket, and slid them across the table to Natalie. "Permission papers. And a brochure," she explained. "Everything's here. Mr. C thinks I have talent. Natural talent, mind you." Janice blew on her fingers and rubbed them across her shoulder in mock self-appreciation. "Really, truly, Mom, he does, he thinks I'm talented."

"And?"

"He wants me to attend his creative workshop this summer. In July. It's a two-week residential thing in Provincetown."

"Mr. C? Mr. C? Who is this guy anyway? You talk about him like he's the next best thing to sliced bread —"

"What does that mean anyway?" Janice interrupted, impatient with her mother. "Best thing since sliced bread, like bread hasn't always been sliced. Really!"

"Well, actually, it hasn't," Allison offered, adjusting her tortoise framed glasses on her face. "Well it hasn't," she repeated when Janice gave her a dirty look, "at least not by machinery."

"Okay girls, stop the cat fighting," Natalie said. "I'm too tired for this." She closed her eyes and rubbed them for a minute. "I just want to know who this man is. Every time you talk about school, you talk about this Mr. C."

"He's a God, Mrs. Hamilton," Allison giggled. "All the girls think so. A tragic Greek God." She lowered her voice as though passing on knowledge of some government conspiracy. "He's kind of gruff, but in a really sexy way. Word has it he was wounded in Vietnam and that his heart was broken by a woman and he never got over it. Some of the guys were playing basketball with him and they saw all these scars on his left leg, deep blue, kind of purple, they said. Billie says it's from shrapnel, apparently his uncle was wounded the same way. Anyway, Mr. C, he has these fabulous eyes, but they seem so sad."

"Word has it? Whose word? Who, exactly, has all this inside knowledge?" Natalie smiled in spite of herself. Such romantic souls, these two were.

"Everyone. All the girls. Guys, too," Janice said. "But that's *so* not why I want to go. He's a true artist, mom. A writer, mostly. A journalist. AND a photographer. All the things I want to be. He's working on a book about Vietnam. Do you remember that war, or conflict, or whatever they called it?"

"Of course I do! I was in my early twenties at the time. The guys, *and gals*, I might add, who fought got a really bum rap. Annie always wore protest buttons: *Draft Beer, Not Boys* or *Make Love, Not War.*"

"Cool," Allison smiled. "You think she still has them?" She poked Janice, "I bet Mr. C would like to see them, that should earn us a few points."

"If he's doing a book on Vietnam, I'm sure he's unearthed things like that. I never told you, Janice, I went to The Wall. It turns out I lost someone very close to me —"

"Cripes, mom," Janice interrupted, "and you never told me? Does Dad know? I could have gone with you, taken pictures. Mr. C would have loved that. He's always telling us to capture moments of raw truth."

"Well, not my raw truth. I didn't need an audience, thank you very much. Anyway, what's this got to do with anything?" Natalie grabbed a few more chips from the bag and took a sip of Janice's Coke.

"Well Mr. C is only here, at our school, a couple of days a week this semester as a Visiting Writer. How cool is that? He goes to other schools, too. Every spring, he offers two kids from each school a scholarship to his Artists' Colony. It's called the Center for Creative Arts. It's in Provincetown, did I mention that? Anyway, all summer, he has these two-week workshops for all kinds of writers and artists, and then this integrated one —

307

that's what he calls it — for adults and young adults. We live there, study for two weeks, really immerse — don't you just love that word, *immerse?* — ourselves in our art form — for me that would be writing and photography — so that we can see if we have what it takes."

"Takes? To do what?"

"To follow our dream. To decide what we want to study in college, or if we even want to go to college, or if we want to go off somewhere and vagabond, explore life, figure out who we are and who we're meant to be. So can I?"

"Whoa. Wait a minute," she sat up, straightening her tired body up to its full height. "This doesn't feel right to me. I don't like the idea of this guy influencing you to make any choice that doesn't include college."

"Get real, Mom. I could make that choice anyway."

"Not while I'm alive and breathing. What else can you tell me about this so-called arts center, or whatever it is?"

"See?" Janice turned to Allison. "I told you she'd be skeptical. *This guy? So-called?* Why do you do that? Why do you say so-called when it's a real artists colony with real workshops? Read about it, you'll see." She reached across the table and pushed at the papers. "Besides, I'm practically sixteen, I should be able to call my own shots."

"You're fifteen and a half."

"Three quarters."

"Whatever. You'll call your own shots when I say you're old enough and not a minute sooner." Natalie's voice was edged with impatience. She knew Janice would beg and cajole until she wore either her or Chad down.

"You're right. I'm sorry." Janice came around the table and wrapped her arms around her mother. "Please, please let me go. We're down the Cape anyway in July so what's the harm? Just, instead of our place for two weeks, I'll be at Mr. C's center in Provincetown."

"We'll *only* be at the Cape if your grandmother stabilizes. Otherwise, I'm not so sure." Natalie unwrapped Janice's arms from around her shoulders. "I have to go check on Nana. And then I need to head home." As she turned to go, the look of devastation on her daughter's face was more than Natalie could bear.

"All right. I'll look these over," Natalie said, grabbing her oversized purse from the far side of the counter and stuffing the papers into it. "You two clean up after yourselves when you're done here. "I'll see you at home, later." Natalie hugged both girls and started out of the room.

"I'll tell you what," Natalie said, turning back toward Janice. "Call me silly. Call me overprotective or suspicious, whatever you want, but I can't just let you go to some residential workshop for two whole weeks without knowing more. If your Mr. C is all you say he is, then he'll be happy to tell me all about his program in person. Set up a time for the three of us to meet for lunch. On me. And we'll go from there."

"Yes!" Janice cried out. "Yes." She and Allison hugged. "You're gonna' love him, Mom. You'll beg me to go to his school so I can be just as good as he is."

"She's right, Mrs. Hamilton," Allison echoed. "You're absolutely gonna' love him."

THIRTY-FOUR

"He'll be here," Janice said, fidgeting with the straw in her Coke. She and Natalie were at a table toward the back of the deli across the street from *Giving with Meaning*. "He's late a lot. Well maybe not a lot, but sometimes. Like one of those absent-minded professors."

"Janice, relax. Traffic's bad out there today. You know how Fridays are. And it's the beginning of Memorial Day weekend. We should have done this another time." Natalie took a sip of coffee and checked her watch. They'd been waiting nearly fifteen minutes for Janice's incomparable Mr. C.

"There he is. He's here," Janice stood without taking the time to push back her wooden chair. Natalie caught it just as it was about to fall.

A girl with a crush on her teacher.

Natalie hoped this was a man who knew how to be gentle with the hearts of impressionable students. She smiled, watching her daughter half-run, half walk toward the front door where a man stood scanning the restaurant. The mid-day sun cast shadows across the shaded room, creating a silhouette of Janice's Mr. C as he followed her to their table. He seemed to be around six feet tall, give or take an inch, and had a gait strangely familiar to her. As he got closer, Natalie noticed that he had sandy brown hair, slightly wavy, slightly overgrown, especially around the collar, and skin that would turn pink in the sun before it ever tanned. By the time he reached their table, all she could focus on were his eyes, the most remarkable combination of olive and bronze, with gold specks.

Using her best manners, Janice began the introductions.

"Mr. C, this is my mother, Natalie Hamilton. Mom, I want you to meet —"

Natalie looked from Mr. C to Janice and back again, from one pair of remarkable eyes to the other.

"Johnny." Natalie whispered his name, covered her mouth with her hand, and ran from the table. Nearly kicking over her purse in the process, she swept it up in her hands and held it tightly to her body, maneuvering her way through the small, crowded restaurant toward the ladies room. Natalie heard Janice's startled voice calling to her. While she couldn't be sure, it seemed that an equally startled voice suggested they sit and order, that she'd be back when she was ready.

Natalie locked herself in one of the two stalls and bent over the toilet until her dry heaves passed. She then closed the lid and sat down behind the locked door trying to imagine what twist of fate had brought Johnny back to her.

Johnny. Mentor to her — their — daughter.

Johnny. John J. Conway, Marine, killed in Vietnam.

Johnny. The only man she'd ever loved.

It couldn't be. Something in this Mr. C just reminded her of Johnny. What a fool she'd made of herself, running from the table like a scared rabbit. Janice would never forgive her.

Natalie dug through her purse, looking for her compact, determined to fix her face and go out there and apologize, make them laugh at her foolishness. Where was that compact? She either needed a smaller purse or less stuff, or the energy to clean this one out. Between Louise and the shop, not to mention

Chad's demands, there never seemed to be time for the details of her life. She kept rummaging.

She pulled out a small stack of papers, holding them in one hand as she finally spied her compact. About to stuff them back into her purse, she took a quick look. Maybe they could be tossed. It was the information Janice had given her on the writing program — a one page overview, a permission form, a formal application, and a full color brochure. Flipping through the brochure, she was looking for one thing and one thing only: information about the man who ran it. There it was, on the back panel, a photo and short biography.

Natalie's limbs seemed to freeze in place, sitting there on the toilet, as her heart slammed against her chest and the only thing she could do was stare at the picture of Johnny. Her Johnny.

"Mom? Mom? Are you in there? Are you okay?"

Natalie hadn't heard the door to the ladies room open, but the voice of her daughter penetrated through the metal door of the stall and bounced off the tile walls.

"You've been in here forever mom. What's wrong? Mr. C said to let you be, but you looked so sick. I mean, what if you died in here or something?"

"Give me a minute honey. Nothing's wrong." She wanted to say *honest*, but she couldn't. How nuts is that? Natalie thought. I can make her whole life a lie, but I can't fib and say the word honest when I don't mean it. Natalie stuffed the brochure back into her purse and opened the door, avoiding eye contact with her daughter as she went over to the sink and pulled a paper towel from the dispenser. She dampened it and touched her cheeks lightly.

"What's wrong? What aren't you telling me?" Janice demanded, studying her mother's every move. "Is it Nana? Did something happen and you're afraid to tell me?"

"God, no, Janice. Honest." She picked up her purse, not sure even now if she was going to face Johnny or just walk out of the restaurant and hope he wouldn't follow. But that wouldn't be the end of it, she knew that much for sure. It would never be the end.

"Did you order?" she asked Janice.

"Yes, Mr. C thought we should. He said that by the time the food came, you'd be back out."

"Okay, listen, honey," Natalie put her hands on her daughter's shoulders, "I want you to do me a favor. Have them package yours up as take-out, go across the street and watch the shop, relieve Annie. I need to talk with John. . .with Mr. C. . .privately. Can you do that for me?"

Janice just stared at her mother, unflinching, unmoving, willing her to explain.

"Let's go," Natalie said. "We'll talk later."

"This isn't fair mom. Just because you don't want me to go to the Artists' Workshop, you can't go behind my back and say no without a reason, without my being there."

"Oh Janice," Natalie took her daughter's hand. "It's nothing like that. I just need —" she stopped and shook her head and then started again. "Okay, listen, remember I told you I went to the Vietnam Wall, saw the name of a friend of mine?"

Janice nodded.

"It was Johnny. Mr. C. His name is John Conway."

"No way. You're kidding. Were you two a *thing*? How could his name be on the wall if he's not dead?"

"That's what I need to find out. And we didn't have a *thing*, as you put it. We were friends. Seeing him just now, it shook me, I couldn't breathe."

"You recognized him. Right off? Do you think he knows who you are?"

"Did he say anything to you?"

"Nothing about who you were or anything. Just about ordering — he said I should order you a tuna on rye — and we should wait patiently."

He knows. Oh God, he knows. Now what?

"Why can't I stay? What's the big deal anyway? You found someone you thought was gone. How cool is that? And it's Mr. C. Wait'll I tell Allison."

"You can't stay. Take your lunch, go over and relieve Annie. And you tell no one. Not Annie. Not Allison. Not Daddy. No one. I need some time to talk with Johnny and I need you to promise to give me my privacy." She squeezed her daughter's hand. "Promise me, Janice."

"Alright, all ready. I promise." As they left the ladies room and headed for the table, Janice whispered. "I don't know what the big deal is, but he is cute, isn't he?"

———◆———

Cute was not the way Natalie would describe the older, wiser and more guarded John J. Conway. Intense. Compelling. Handsome in an artsy way. These are the words that first came to mind as she returned to the table. His hair, no longer Marine Corps short, fell across his forehead and curled slightly over the collar of his shirt. His body was as long and lean as she remembered, comfortable in his casual, slightly rumpled clothes. There was a small scar on his chin that hadn't been there before and fine lines around his eyes.

As Johnny stood to greet her, Natalie took a few steps forward, closing the space between them, driven by an overpowering desire to feel his arms around her. As soon as she was close enough to touch him, however, Johnny stepped backward and extended his arm, gesturing toward her chair and waiting lunch. Natalie reddened at Johnny's rejection but then tried to pretend it hadn't happened; maybe she'd just imagined the slight.

Sitting down at the square wooden table, Natalie immediately picked up her paper napkin, something to play with so he wouldn't notice how badly her hands trembled. She looked over at Johnny. There was a time when she could read his every thought simply by looking into his eyes. Now they seemed distant, sad, unreadable.

"Janice is having her lunch wrapped for take-out," Natalie explained as the waiter came and removed her daughter's plate. She nodded toward the front of the restaurant where Janice waited for her food. "She said to tell you she'll see you at school."

Johnny turned around and waved to Janice. "She a good kid," he said. "And talented."

"Yes she is," Natalie agreed.

"You look good," Johnny said.

"You too."

They fell silent. Small talk seemed almost silly and anything else seemed impossible. Johnny took a bite of his cheeseburger,

"It's good. I love a good juicy burger." He took another bite.

"I remember." Natalie toyed with her sandwich and took a sip of her iced tea.

More silence.

Natalie watched him chew and wipe the corners of his lips with his napkin. She watched him take a sip of coffee and then glance around the room. She watched the wall between them build until she couldn't stand it any longer. Any minute Johnny was going to finish his lunch and then just get up and leave. She stared at him until, finally, he looked back and held her gaze.

"It's really you," Natalie said, a whispered declaration." I don't understand."

"What's not to understand? I always figured we'd meet again. Didn't you? It never felt finished. Loose ends. I hate them."

"I went to The Wall last summer. I saw your name." Natalie reached across the table and put her hand lightly on top of his. "I thought you were dead."

After a few polite seconds, Johnny slid his hand out from beneath her touch. Tears collected in her throat at the sudden loss of his skin against hers.

An absence of feeling.

That's what it felt like: an absence of feeling. Johnny's entire demeanor suggested he had no feelings for her. It was as though she'd been excised from his heart. Natalie would have preferred anger to indifference. As least then, she would know, on some level, he still cared.

"I thought you were dead," Natalie repeated.

"You shouldn't take everything at face value, Natalie. If you'd looked harder, you would have realized it was the same name, different guy." His tone was mocking, not at all like the Johnny she remembered. "The devil is in the details," he said. "Those pesky little details, like the next tour of duty or where a newly married couple might live."

"Don't. Please."

"Don't what?"

"Never mind." She lowered her head, shook it ever so slightly in disbelief, and then looked back over at him. "It felt like I stood there forever, running my hand across your name. I always felt I'd know if something happened to you. But then I saw your name engraved in that black granite. I can't believe you're here, you're alive." Tears slid across her cheeks. She wiped them away with the deli's cheap paper napkins.

"Oh, things happened, all right, just not the big call home. No death card for me. But I damn well tried. Went back to Nam, figured I might as well get my head blown off for the cause. But I couldn't even manage that."

"Oh Johnny. . .Janice said something about shrapnel?"

"Yeah, those damn land mines, they'll get you every time."

He studied Natalie from across the table, as though considering what, if anything, to say next. She waited, knowing she had her own land mines to navigate.

"You ran," Johnny said after a while. "While I was off getting my orders changed, you packed your bags and left. I came back to a note, a goddamn note."

"I know. I'm sorry." *Sorry.* Such a lame word for something so huge. She tried again. "If it makes any difference, the minute I got back here, I knew I'd made the biggest mistake of my life. I called Annie, told her I was coming back. But you'd already left the island. I didn't know how to find you."

"You marry that rich guy, the one your mother was so hot on?"

She nodded her answer, unable to speak the words.

"Was that the plan the whole time? Get your jollies off on vacation and then come back to the rich guy?"

"Oh God, never. How could you even think that? I loved you —"

"Apparently not enough. You didn't trust me. You didn't trust us. Not even enough to stay and talk it out."

"I know. I was young. Young and stupid. I'm so sorry." She laid her hand on top of his, risking rejection once again. He didn't pull back this time. But there was no warmth in his staying.

"I can't do this," Johnny said. "I always imagined what I'd say to you if or when we met again. But it's irrelevant, isn't it?" He withdrew his hand from beneath hers, pulled some bills out of his wallet and tossed them on the table. "Lunch is on me."

He walked across the deli and out the door without looking back.

Natalie watched Johnny leave, willing him to turn around, just look at her, throw a smile her way, anything. It would be a sign. But there was nothing. He kept walking. Out the door and across the street, disappearing from into the crowd of Friday afternoon shoppers.

THIRTY-FIVE

He hated her. Johnny was alive and he hated her.

The reality of it haunted Natalie. It was easier, all those years, when she didn't know where he was, to imagine he still cared for her and that, if they ever did meet again, they'd fall madly into one another's arms, as though nothing had ever happened. Then, when she thought he was dead, she could soothe herself by pretending he'd died loving her. But this? The coldness. It kept Natalie up at night and unfocused during the day. She kept playing out their lunch — if you could call it that — reliving how she'd reached out to hug him or touched his hand, and how he'd pulled away from her. Not even a polite kiss on the cheek. Nothing. Natalie's emotions would swing from embarrassed to angry and settle in somewhere around sad and resigned. And short tempered.

Johnny was alive. And he hated her.

Thankfully, Janice showed very little interest in her mother's old friendship with Mr. C. In true teenage fashion, the only thing she cared about was how things affected her. She wanted to go to his workshop and she badgered Natalie every day until she finally gave in and signed the papers. Natalie had no real reason for saying no to her daughter. And she was too tired to try and come up with an excuse. Who knows, she reasoned, maybe it would be good for everyone. It would give Janice and Johnny a chance to know one another without the knowledge of how they were connected. Maybe it would make Johnny less angry with her, although why that would be the case she wasn't exactly sure. If she was really honest with herself, she'd admit it was a perfect way to keep him in her life, if only in the background. Beyond that, she refused to examine her decision and any ripple effect it could have.

She also refused to tell Annie what was bothering her. For reasons she couldn't quite define, Natalie needed to keep Johnny's reappearance private; she needed to hold it close to her heart without advice or interference or concern from anybody. And that included her best friend. But Annie was relentless.

"You look like hell," she told Natalie one morning before the store opened. "Look at those dark circles under your eyes." She pulled at Natalie's waistband. "And you've lost weight. What's going on?"

"Nothing. Let it alone."

"Is it Chad? Is he drinking again?"

"No, it's not Chad! We're actually doing okay. It's me. Okay? Just leave it —"

"Louise? Is she worse again."

"She's fine, Annie. Fine enough, anyway."

"Natie, tell me, you've been like a walking zombie for weeks now."

"Leave me alone. You're overbearing and nosey, just go away." Natalie took the paperweight she was about to place on the counter and flung it across the store, hitting a shelf and shattering a glass vase.

"Natalie!" Annie grabbed her friend and held tight, but Natalie shook her off.

"I said leave me alone. Go. Take the day off. I don't want you here. Come back tomorrow, but only if you can mind your own business."

Annie did as she was told. She came back the next day, the air between them shimmering with tension. They talked only about the store and only when absolutely necessary. Natalie could see the concern on her friend's face, but there was also anger and disappointment. Natalie wanted to reach out, tell her everything, but she was tired of being vulnerable. She didn't want to need anybody or anything ever again. At the same time, she was hurt that Annie could back off so easily and watch Natalie sink into her depression.

———◆———

It turned out that Annie was a better friend than Natalie gave her credit for. She didn't abandon Natalie, even as she gave her the space and quiet she seemed to want. She also went to Louise and vented her concerns. Together they came up with a plan and summoned Natalie to Louise's house for afternoon tea. Tea and intervention.

"Are you going to tell us what's wrong?" Louise asked.

"I'm just tired."

"I'm tired," Louise said. "I'm heading toward old age and I have cancer. This is what tired looks like." She pointed to her thinning face and the darkness around her eyes. "I'd say you're depressed."

"She's right, Natie," Annie said. "Whatever is going on, you're suddenly horribly unhappy. It's how you were right after Saint Martin."

"Saint Martin?" Louise asked.

"It was just a particular time in my life," Natalie answered, throwing a warning look toward Annie. "Let's not go there."

"All right," Louise agreed, her voice calm and soft. "Where shall we go then?"

"Nowhere." Natalie swiped at her eyes. Tears were always so close to the surface these days. And despite what they said or believed, she was deeply and unbearably tired. She had no inner resources to deal with any of this. "Look, I appreciate your concern. Please, just leave me alone. I need some rest, that's all."

"That's exactly what we think," Annie said. "Whatever's going on, you need to rest and heal and think."

"Great. Thanks." Natalie put down her tea cup and stood to leave. "I'll start now. Go home and take a nap."

Louise put out her hand and pressed it into the air, signaling Natalie to sit back down. "Don't get smart with me. We want to help. Now, tell me your plans for next week. Janice is going to this workshop in Provincetown, is that correct?"

"Yes, you know that. I'm going to drive her down on Saturday. Probably come right back, unless it gets too late. Then I'll stay over and come back on Sunday."

"Why don't you stay in Chatham for a few weeks?" Louise said. Annie nodded her head in agreement.

"I can't do that. It's tourist season. The shop will be busy. Besides, I want to be here for you."

"Nonsense. Annie and I have talked it over."

"Great. Now you two have become best friends, talking behind my back."

"Natalie!" Louise chastised her with a hard look, one she seldom used and then only on Chad.

"I'm sorry."

"Okay," Annie jumped right in, "here's the deal: I'll watch the store, get a couple of high school girls to help me. No problem. Rene and Lincoln can pitch it as well. So, no worries there."

"And I'm doing just fine," Louise said. "The treatments are over. I'm eating again. There's no reason on earth for you to stay in this hot city when you could be at the Cape."

"I can't."

"Yes, you can. And you must." Louise smiled at her daughter-in-law. "You need to get your balance back. Take this time to think and heal. And, when you're ready, come and talk to us. Whatever it is, my dear, it can't be that bad. And even if it is, we love you."

THIRTY-SIX

Natalie and Janice drove to Provincetown under a brilliant blue sky, each engrossed in her own thoughts, each nervous for reasons of her own. They rolled down the windows of Natalie's silver Mercedes, letting the warm air blow their hair as they cruised, listening to music, speaking very little.

In the end, Natalie had gratefully accepted the gift of time that Annie and Louise insisted she take. Once she dropped off Janice, Natalie would go to the house in Chatham and stay there for at least two weeks. With every mile, she actually felt a physical release from her pain and worries, as though her life in Boston was being lifted out of her body and cast into the summer wind. There was only her and Janice and the road ahead.

Before she knew it, however, they were in the outskirts of Provincetown.

"We're here, we're here," Janice shifted in her seat. "See, there are the dunes." She extended her arm out the window and pointed to the sand dunes on her right.

"Hold your water. We're getting close, but we're not there yet," Natalie laughed, her own nerve endings prickling with both fear and anticipation.

Once they'd driven through the rotary, they really were almost there.

"Okay," Natalie said, "you help me out with the street directions." She slipped the brochure out from beneath her visor and handed it to Janice, but not before glancing once more at Johnny's photo. She'd studied it and caressed it hundreds of times over the past month, willing him to call her, to stop by the shop, to get in touch with her in some way. But he hadn't. Maybe he didn't care. Maybe he figured it should be her move or nothing. And maybe it needed to be nothing. Maybe that was the right answer for all of them.

"Okay, Mom," Janice practically shouted, looking this way and that, "take a right onto Commercial Street, and then Howland, and then a left onto Willow Drive."

Natalie maneuvered the car along the narrow streets, breathing in the salty sea air, already feeling its healing power.

"There it is, there, right there, Willow Drive." Janice's voice was pitched octaves higher than its normal tone.

We're a piece of work, the two of us, Natalie laughed to herself, both nervous over the same man, but for totally different reasons.

"You'll do great Janice," Natalie said as she drove slowly, looking for the driveway. "He wouldn't have offered you the scholarship if he didn't see something special in you. Just be yourself. Make the most of this. It could influence everything you do from this point on; it could put you on a path you only now just imagine —"

"Mom!"

"What?"

"Geeze."

"Too philosophical?" Natalie grimaced.

"Kinda. Talk about pressure."

Natalie pulled into the parking lot and turned off the car. "Sorry, kiddo. Guess I got carried away. At my age, you tend to see deeper meaning in things."

"Yeah, well, it's an experience, not my whole entire life." Janice jumped out of the car surveying the place where she would be staying for the next two weeks. She looked over at Natalie, who was doing the same thing.

"Yikes, it's gorgeous," Janice said. "I excepted something kind of shabby, didn't you? You know like a starving artists' colony. This is —"

"Gorgeous," Natalie repeated, her eyes sweeping over the grounds: two buildings with a garden and walkway between them. "Absolutely beautiful," Natalie said under her breath. "Good for you Johnny."

She felt a sudden stab of . . . what? Jealously? Regret? Lost opportunity? That was it. *Lost opportunity.* Seeing where Johnny lived and worked made his life real. Would this have been our life, she wondered. Or would we have done something completely different if we'd stayed together? Natalie brushed strands of hair away from her face as though pushing away unsettling thoughts, questions with no answers.

She imagined a wife and five kids behind the scenes, helping to shape this life of his. Since that fated lunch, she keep obsessing about the details of his life — small things, like did he still like Raisin Bran cereal for breakfast, did he still use Coppertone, did he go out to dinner with friends every Friday night, was he single and alone? She couldn't trust the rumors at Janice's school about the sad, unmarried man with a heart broken by some woman years and years ago. She wanted to know everything and yet she didn't have the right to know anything. She'd given that up a long time ago.

She turned to Janice. "Let's get your bags out of the trunk and see where you sign in."

"Hi there." The soft husky voice sent shivers down her spine. Natalie straightened up from rummaging in the trunk to see Johnny standing beside the car. A lock of hair, streaked from the summer sun, spilled across his forehead.

"Welcome to my world," he smiled, handing a clipboard to Janice. "Go on in, join the others. Fill out the top sheet — contact info, emergency numbers," he pointed to the yellow page. "The rest is information for you. After orientation tonight you can decide which workshops you want." He turned toward Natalie. "I'll help you with these."

Johnny reached into the trunk and grabbed the largest of Janice's two bags. He eyed Natalie's new car but said nothing and, in that silence, it seemed to Natalie he was saying everything about her wealth and status.

"Johnny, this place is beautiful. I never expected —"

"That I'd do so well?"

She grabbed a grocery bag filled with Janice's favorite snack foods and slammed the trunk shut. "No," she looked him directly in the eyes, her voice matching his sharpness. "That's not what I meant."

"What did you mean?"

"Nothing. Forget it. Isn't there a parent's tour or something?" She walked ahead of Johnny, along the brick walk she'd seen Janice take toward the main building.

"There's no tour per-se," Johnny said, catching up with her. "I can have a staff member show you around. What's she got in here? Bricks?"

"Books. And camera stuff." Natalie laughed out loud. "She wants to be a writer. Or a photographer, remember? Be careful how you influence!"

"I'll remember that." Johnny smiled down at her and in that moment it felt like all the years had melted away.

"Excuse me, Mr. Conway?" I'm Phyllis Jansen, Craig's mother."

"Oh, yes, we need to talk," Johnny said. "Excuse me, Natalie. I'll bring Janice's bags in. You can go ahead and say good-bye to her, ask someone to show you around if you want." He smiled briefly and then turned to Phyllis Jansen. "Why don't you come with me."

Left on the sidewalk to fend for herself, Natalie felt like a kid dropped off at a new school, lost and invisible. Redundant even. The grounds were suddenly swarming with people, all looking for input and insight from the great Mr. Conway.

After a quick *be safe, call me if you need anything, I love you* to Janice, Natalie left. The last thing she needed was a behind-the-scenes look at the life and times of John J. Conway when it wasn't John Conway himself giving that guided tour.

Natalie sensed his presence even before she knew he was there, a long shadow blocking the sun, the scent of Coppertone carried on the summer breeze. She was sun bathing out on the back deck, floating in and out of an afternoon slumber, thoughts of Johnny drifting through her body, keeping rhythm with the surf rolling against the shore just beyond the house.

And then suddenly, as if she'd willed him to appear, there he was.

Natalie shot up into a sitting position, using one hand to hold the top of her two piece suit to her chest, acutely aware that it was unhooked and dangerously close to coming off. She shaded her eyes with her free hand and looked up at the figure standing over her.

"Johnny?"

"Natalie."

"What's wrong? Is Janice okay? Is everything all right?"

"She's fine. I rang the bell." He shrugged his shoulders, as if that explained everything.

Natalie grabbed the towel at the foot of the lounge chair and wrapped it around her body. Tucking it into place, she stood to meet his gaze.

"You're sure she's okay?"

"I told you, she's fine."

"She's just so young to be away."

He just shrugged and continued staring at her.

Stop shrugging, Say something. Anything.

"So then what are you doing here?" Natalie asked after what seemed like an eternity of awkward silence. She stopped and started again. "That came out wrong. I'm glad to see you. Just surprised."

She hugged the towel, keeping it locked against her body. and tried smoothing out her hair. She could just imagine how she looked, greasy from suntan lotion, her hair pressed against the back of her head, sticking out at the sides. "Give me a minute. Please." She walked toward the kitchen.

"I don't care how you look," he finally said. "I came to talk."

"I'll be right back," Natalie insisted, padding barefoot to her bedroom, careful not to slip on the tile floor. She sat on the bed and calmed herself with a few deep breaths. After a few minutes she quickly changed into shorts and a T-shirt, suddenly afraid Johnny might leave if she was gone too long. She took just enough time to run a comb through her hair and apply lip gloss. "It'll have to do," she muttered, heading back to the deck.

Natalie stood at the threshold between deck and kitchen silently observing the man she'd once loved. His back was to her now, as he leaned on the railing looking out at the beach.

Did she still love him or was it the memory of him?

She'd carried Johnny in her heart for so long now, it was impossible to tell the difference. All she knew is that she longed to tip-toe over to him, wrap her arms around his waist and press her face to his back, to feel the warmth and scent of him against her skin.

"Are you finished studying me, or do you need more time?" Johnny turned around and leaned his back against the railing. "Maybe a front view?"

Natalie reddened. "I didn't think you knew —"

"That you were there? You don't do two tours in Nam without developing a heightened sense of the enemy."

"The enemy?" Natalie moved toward him. "Oh, Johnny, I'm not —"

"Figure of speech."

She stopped, the coolness in Johnny's voice keeping her from moving closer, from reaching out and touching his bare, tanned arm. "How about a drink?"

"Nothing."

"Vodka tonic?" Natalie asked. *Would he remember they'd had vodka tonics that last night on the beach?*

"Nothing." Johnny repeated, his eyes dark and unreadable, just like they were that afternoon at the deli.

"Okay, then." Natalie walked over by the railing and stood next to Johnny, close, but not too close.

Without another word, he pulled a carefully folded piece of yellow paper from the back pocket of his shorts and extended it to her.

"What's this?" Natalie asked.

"You tell me."

Natalie unfolded the paper and immediately recognized Janice's handwriting. Puzzled, she lifted her shoulders as though asking a question. "It's Janice's registration form," she finally said.

"It's interesting what a simple form can tell you, don't you think?"

"I don't —"

"Understand?" Johnny finished Natalie's sentence for her. "You don't understand? Well that makes two of us."

The calm, collected way he was delivering his words sent shivers of warning down Natalie's spine.

"Johnny, what is it?"

"November 19, 1970?"

Natalie felt as though someone had taken a nail gun and pinned her feet and to the wooden deck. Unable to move, she whispered her reply. "November 19, 1970?"

"I did the math, Natalie. It's pretty unlikely she belongs to that husband of yours. Chad, isn't it?"

"She was early."

"Is that what he thinks?"

Natalie shifted her position a little, trying to get movement back into her body. She needed to run as fast and as quickly as her legs would take her. She needed to run back to Boston, away from Johnny, away from his questions and accusing eyes.

Just like last time, the voice inside her head chastised. *Things got tough and you ran.*

"I need that drink," Natalie said.

She went into the kitchen and fixed herself a vodka and tonic, feeling Johnny's eyes on her, tracking every movement. She felt like a character in one of those movies where the woman was taken in for questioning and the cop cut her a break by not handcuffing her but then watched every breath she took, knowing she might try to escape in any given moment.

"You sure you don't want one?" she called out to Johnny, swirling the ice cubes with her index finger and taking a sip." She threw him her most charming, most disarming smile. Maybe she could redirect the conversation.

"Nothing."

"You sure?"

"For Christ's sake, Natalie. I don't want a drink. I drank enough to sink three ships after you bailed on me. All through Nam. After Nam. I straightened up ten years ago and that cute, dimpled smile of yours is not going to sway me or keep me from finding out the truth about Janice."

Natalie just stared at him.

"So cut the crap. Are we clear?"

She nodded. She put her drink down on the kitchen counter and joined Johnny back out on the deck.

"Is Janice my daughter?"

"Johnny —"

"Is she?" Johnny took hold of her wrist and held tightly. "Is Janice my daughter?"

"Janice is *my* daughter. I'm the one who gave birth to her. And Chad is her father." Natalie sucked in her breath and jutted out her chin. "That's the truth you're looking for."

"Or one version of it."

"Look, you came for an answer. Now you have it." She wriggled out of his grasp and smiled up at him. "Tell me about your life. Married? Kids? I know about your work, a little, but tell me more."

"Short bad marriage — she was a good woman, I was a crappy husband, — divorced eleven years ago. No kids. Great work, now that I'm off the self-destructive kick. Both parents are dead. That's it, Natalie. Now let's get back to you."

"You have the answer you came looking for. It's clear you're still really angry with me, so we're not going to be friends. Let's call it a day." She turned to walk away from him. "I'll walk you to your car."

Johnny grabbed Natalie by the waist and pulled her toward him. He held her tightly, his breath warming her face. She pressed her lips together in an attempt to steady her own breath, to regulate the rhythm of her heart. How easy it would be to tilt her chin up, to stand slightly on her toes and kiss him. How easy.

And how wrong.

If nothing else over this past month, she'd done a fairly honest review of herself. So much of her life had been shaped by impulsive acts, from ratting out Pearl for fleeting popularity with the cool kids in high school, to leaving Johnny while he was trying to arrange their future, right down to marrying Chad. And then there were the lies — secrets and lies — an entire life built on them. It was as though she was always living in that undefined space between two worlds. Annie called it The Bardo — that place of transition between past and present — but Natalie saw it also as the place between truth and non-truth, between an authentic life and a fabricated one. Standing there with Johnny so close, with his arms still around her waist, his eyes locked onto hers, compelling her to be honest, Natalie was suddenly very tired of holding everything in, of keeping everyone's secrets.

"Please don't ruin things." The words were a mere whisper as she tried to look away, but couldn't. "Please." Fear collected in her throat.

"Why would I ruin things?" Johnny asked, his voice nearly as soft as hers.

"Because you could. Because Janice is your daughter."

THIRTY-SEVEN

There was no magical moment between Natalie and Johnny once she'd told him the truth about Janice. No, *we'll work this out together* sentiments. No, *don't worry, I'll keep your secret* assurances. Nothing. Johnny had simply nodded, as though giving external affirmation to his internal compass, to what he'd known all along to be true. He thanked her for doing the right thing — that's what he'd called it — the right thing — and then left.

Where do we go from here? Natalie tried calling out after him, but the words stuck in her throat.

Where do we go from here?

Everything in her life was about to change. She could feel it. As soon as Johnny drove away, she knew she'd made a mistake. Her stomach swirled with apprehension. And desire. That was the worst part. Equal parts of dread and desire had set up housekeeping inside her veins, each throbbing for attention.

All through the next week, Natalie longed to call Johnny, to beg him not to do anything foolish, to talk with her first. She wanted his understanding. And his forgiveness. But every time she picked up the phone, she put it back down again. What could she really do or say? The proverbial pebble had been cast into the lake long before this moment; now it was time to see exactly where the ripples would lead.

No longer at peace in Louise's beautiful Cape Cod home, Natalie shuffled from room to room, not knowing what to do with herself. She wanted to call Annie, but then again she didn't. She didn't want advice or chastising. Or even sympathy. She walked the beach every morning and night and even went to the library a couple of afternoons, trying to research interesting tales of superstition and folklore so that she could add new merchandise to *Giving with Meaning*. But even that failed; she couldn't concentrate on anything except the feeling that everything was about to change.

Sometimes, in her mind's eye, she rewrote the history of that afternoon. She watched herself fingering Johnny's hair as it curled at the nape of his neck; she could feel the sun beating down on them as she slipped into his arms and kissed him, softly at first and then with the intensity of reclaimed love. She could close her eyes and feel his body pressing against hers.

Other times, she replayed the afternoon exactly as it had happened, accusation and anger lying just below surface of his calm demeanor, eyes that turned from unreadable to cold as she finally told Johnny the truth; instead of taking her in his arms and forgiving her, he turned and walked away. Janice was his daughter.

What would he do with that knowledge?

Visions of Marilyn crept across Natalie's mind, all the secrets, all the lies, all of Natalie's misspent loyalty. She was no better than her mother, devising a reality to suit her own needs. The only difference is that she hadn't made her daughter a co-conspirator. Not yet, at least.

The week dragged on until, finally, blessedly, it was Friday afternoon. The next morning she would pick up Janice and, if the universe was good to them, Johnny would keep his distance.

They would spend one more week at the Cape and then head back to Boston.

If the universe was good? Is that really what she wanted? For Johnny to keep his distance? Not really. But what she wanted, she couldn't have.

She wanted to redo the past.

In her perfect world, she would be transported back to that afternoon in Saint Martin when she ran off; she'd get to make a different choice. She'd get to choose Johnny. But, as Marilyn had told her often enough, "you can't unring a bell and only misfortune can come from trying."

———◆———

Natalie was doing laundry when she heard the front door open and then slam shut. "What the. . .?" She dropped shirts and shorts on the floor and ran to the foyer.

There was Janice, all smiles. "Surprise! Your writer, photographer, very talented daughter is home. Did you miss me?"

"Janice? What are you —" Natalie stopped as the door opened once more and in walked Johnny with Janice's suitcases.

"Nice, young lady." He smiled at her. There was such affection in his voice. "You not only leave me with the baggage, but you close the door on me." He dropped her suitcases on the floor.

"Mr. C brought me home."

"I can see that." Natalie wrapped her arms around her daughter and hugged with all her might. "Boy did I miss you." She held Janice at arms length. "Let me have a look at you. Have you grown? You look different."

"Mom, pleezzee, it's only been two weeks. I'm heading to the beach, see who I can catch up with. You tell her all about it, Mr. C. It was awesome, Mom, really awesome — and don't forget the part about what a good writer I am."

Janice gave Natalie a quick kiss on the cheek and headed down the hallway, through the kitchen. Once Natalie heard the slider open and shut, she knew Janice had gone outside, working her way from the deck to the sand and down to the water.

"So?" Natalie said to Johnny.

"So?"

"What's wrong? I was going to pick her up tomorrow."

"Why does something always have to be wrong?"

"Well, then?"

"By Friday noon, the closing rituals are done. Most kids stay until Saturday because it's easier for their folks to pick them up."

"I could have picked up my daughter tomorrow with everyone else. Or even tonight, for that matter." Natalie pulled at her too short T-shirt and tried smoothing out the wrinkles in her shorts. "She should have warned me. I'm a mess."

"Why do you care so much how you look? I had errands down this way," Johnny said. "We thought it'd be fun to surprise you."

"Right. Errands." Natalie didn't believe that lame excuse for one instant. "We need to talk," she said. "You wanna' —"

"Sure."

"— come in," she finished her sentence and waved him into the living room.

"She's a good kid," Johnny said.

"The best."

Natalie sat on the sofa, on the edge of it actually, not trusting the moment, unwilling to sink into any semblance of comfort. Johnny stood by the fireplace responding to the silence that had fallen between them by looking at photos on the mantel, photos that captured the story of their times here at the Cape over the last fifteen years. Natalie watched as Johnny studied each one, seeing how Janice had grown from a brown-haired baby with her mother's dimple to an adolescent with sandy-colored hair and her father's eyes. Louise was in some of the earlier photos and there were lots of Annie and Natalie. Conspicuously absent were any of them with Chad. But then, he seldom joined them.

"You didn't have any errands, did you?" Natalie asked when Johnny finally turned to face her.

"I always have errands."

Once again silence filled the space between them.

Natalie played with the fringes of an afghan that Louise had crocheted years ago. Johnny simply watched her, as though trying to puzzle things out.

"Let's make a deal," Natalie finally said. "No more lies. Or half truths. Or evasions. Or games. I'm so tired of it all."

"None of that?" Johnny furrowed his eye brows and threw her a half-smile. "And here I thought that lies and half truths — and what else did you mention?" He paused a moment and looked at her hard. "Oh, right — evasions and games. I thought they were all part of your standard operating procedure. You give all of that up at once and where does it leave us?"

"For one thing," Natalie tossed her head back, "it leaves us without the sarcasm or stupid comments like *I always have errands*."

She stood and walked over to Johnny. "It leaves us with the truth." She extended her right hand as though closing a business transaction. "Deal?"

Johnny took her hand and held it. "The truth. Interesting concept. Like I said, where does that leave us?" He continued to hold her hand, stroking the tender skin of her palm with his thumb, a caress so delicate, and so intense, it made breathing nearly impossible.

"She's my daughter," he said. "There was no accusation in his voice, only a sense of wonder. "Our daughter." Johnny touched Natalie's cheek. "All those lost years."

337

"I know. I'm sorry. I've made so many mistakes." Natalie felt old and regretful as she reached up and played with a lock of hair straying across Johnny's forehead. "I thought you were dead." She swallowed hard. "I know it doesn't change what I did, but look at you, you're here. I can barely believe it."

"I am. I'm right here." He gently swiped at the tears falling across Natalie's face. With his touch, the years faded away.

She was twenty-two again, falling under the spell of the man she was destined to love, of the only man she would ever truly love. Once again she found herself lulled by the tender touch of his fingers caressing her cheek, by the scent of his skin — Coppertone and sunshine — and the warmth of his breath as he leaned in closer. She tilted her face up toward his, willing him to kiss her. If only she had trusted their future. If only.

As though from somewhere far away, Natalie heard Janice's laughter, making its way from the beach, across the still air and through the open windows. She and her friend were calling to one another now, their distant voices bringing Natalie back from the past and into the present where a married woman and her ex-lover were about to head down a path of no return.

"I have something for you." Natalie backed away from Johnny, her voice too loud for the room, for the silence they'd slipped into. She grabbed hold of both his hands, keeping them — and him — literally at arms length now.

The moment had passed. They both understood that. Johnny grinned and kept his distance.

"Okay. What do you have for me?"

Natalie reached up to the mantle and from behind a photo of her and Janice taken on the beach last year, she retrieved the small box inlaid with a lily-of-the-valley. "This is always with me. I generally keep it at the store, because that's where I spend most of my time. Something made me bring it here."

Johnny furrowed his eyebrows. Natalie laughed out loud. He looked like a cartoon character, huge question marks where his eyes should be. Without offering any explanation, she opened the box, took out the nickel and placed it in the palm of Johnny's hand.

"For luck," she told him.

"I don't understand."

"How could you?" Natalie said. "I've kept it all this time and I don't even understand why it's so important. I just know it is."

"Go on." Johnny fingered the coin, all the while watching Natalie as she spoke.

She reminded him about that last day on the beach in Saint Martin when they'd fought about their future and how he'd turned away from her when they'd gone back to the blanket.

"I was furious with you, with myself. I didn't know what to do with all that energy so I kept digging in the sand with my bare hands. I found this nickel. In my head, I heard Marilyn's voice, *find a coin give it away, for luck.* I turned to give it to you, but your eyes were closed and you seemed to be either sleeping or ignoring me, so I figured, screw it. I put it in the pocket of my shorts. When I got home, after I, you know. . ."

"Left?"

She nodded. "After I left," she whispered. "I got back to Boston and it was still there, in my pocket. I tried to come back to you, Johnny, but you'd already left. Annie didn't know where you were. I've kept it all these years. Just in case."

"In case of what?" Johnny was reaching into his pocket now. He pulled out his key ring.

"You're leaving?" Panic rose in Natalie. "Just like that, you're leaving?"

He didn't answer. Not at first. He seemed to be processing something. Johnny studied Natalie for a long moment, then the nickel, and then he pushed a few keys around on his key ring. "Look at this," he said.

On Johnny's key ring was a nickel. Natalie looked up at him. It was her turn to be puzzled.

"When I turned sixteen, my mother gave me two things: this key ring and the nickel. The key ring was a symbol, she said, of always finding my way home — which we know is a joke, given what happened with my brother, but she meant well — and this nickel — I had a hole drilled and put it on here so I'd never lose it."

"What was the nickel for?" Natalie broke away from Johnny. She walked over to the bank of windows hoping to catch a breeze. She felt dizzy, flushed with the afternoon heat and an overwhelming sense that all things in her life were converging and changing. Past and present tumbling over one another.

Johnny came up behind Natalie, picked up her hair and blew softly on her neck. "You okay?"

She nodded and then turned to face him. "What about the nickel?"

Johnny looked at the coin in his hand and then on his key ring." My mother told me that she'd had a dream — a *knowing*, she called it — that when the time was right, the woman I was meant to marry would hand me a coin, a *found* coin she said, and that I should keep this nickel to remind me to wait for that coin. And the woman who comes with it."

Chills traveled down Natalie's spine. "I don't believe in things like that."

"Like what?"

"Fate."

"Maybe it's more a question of faith. You didn't have enough faith in us." Johnny stroked her hair and then ran his thumb along her cheek. "Maybe I didn't have enough either. I could have come looking for you." He touched her lips with his fingers.

Natalie closed her eyes. "You must have been so angry with me."

She could barely focus as he moved even closer, so close now, there was no space between them. She could feel the heat of his skin against her bare legs.

"I was furious. For years."

"And now?" She pressed in closer.

"And now," Johnny whispered as he kissed her ear lobe, "we drill a hole in this nickel and put in on my key ring, right next to the one my mother gave me."

"And then what?" Natalie's voice turned husky, the words catching in her throat as Johnny lifted her hair and began kissing the nape of her neck, soft, wispy kisses that traveled the length of her body like bursts of electricity.

His hands slid down her back, pulling her tighter to him until she groaned at his heat and hardness. Natalie lifted her face toward Johnny, her lips parted and moist. He cupped one hand behind her head and pulled her into a deep, hungry kiss. It was impossible to know how long they stood in front of the window, wrapped in one another's arms, a light ocean breeze caressing their bodies.

A far-away sound called Natalie back to the present.

"The phone," Natalie said. She felt dazed, disoriented, as though she'd re-entered the world from some other planet. She looked toward the kitchen, as though trying to identify the harsh, unrelenting sound and where it was coming from.

"Leave it." Johnny nuzzled her neck, inhaling her scent. "You smell the same," he whispered, running his fingers through her hair, planting kisses along her neck and arms. "You feel the same," he said, moving one hand along her leg, upwards across her thigh.

Natalie bent into him like a willow giving in to the wind. She kissed him greedily, pulling him in tighter against the heat of her body.

Still, the phone kept ringing.

"I have to get it." She pulled away from Johnny.

"Don't." Johnny put his hands on the small of her back and drew her back toward him.

"I have to." She glanced toward the kitchen. *How long had it been ringing?* "I have to."

She broke from his embrace and readjusted her shirt and shorts, running her fingers through her hair, as though whoever was calling might see her, might see her and know. She tried to steady her heart rate as she ran for the phone.

"Hello." Her voice seemed breathless and unnatural.

"For Christ's sake, where were you? The phone's been ringing and —"

"Chad? I was outside. I ran as fast as I could, once I heard it."

"It's been hell around here. You should never have left Boston."

"What's wrong?"

"It's my mother. She's been bad all week. You should have been here."

"You should have called me."

"I'm calling you now. She's in the hospital."

"Janice just got back. We'll pack up and be there in a few hours."

Natalie hung up the phone and looked over at Johnny.

"You're leaving," he said. It was a simple statement, but Natalie heard the question beneath the words.

"For now. Not forever. My mother-in-law has cancer. She's taken a turn for the worse. I need to be with her."

He walked over to Natalie and took her in his arms. "I'm sorry. You do what you need to do."

342

"I'll call you. As often as I can. I promise. I'm going back to Boston, but I'm not running away from you. Not this time."

"I know." Johnny kissed her softly and then headed toward the door. Just before leaving, he turned and held up the nickel she'd given him. "I'll be waiting for you."

THIRTY-EIGHT

The cancer had metastasized to Louise's lungs. The doctors agreed there was little they could do now, except make her comfortable and honor her wishes to spend what time she had left at home rather than in the hospital.

"I know I don't have that long," she told Chad when he argued against her going home. "I could die tomorrow."

"Don't say that. With good medical care, right here, in the hospital —"

"Enough." Louise held up her hand, blue veins bulging against skin that had dried into a fine layer of parchment. "Enough, Chad, I want to go home. Whatever time I have left is precious to me. I don't want to waste it, not one blessed moment, in this place."

Chad finally agreed, coming up with a plan that would ensure his mother's comfort and safety. In addition to hiring full-time nurses, Natalie would spend most of her time, including nights, at Louise's, for companionship and to oversee her care. As usual, Rosa would handle the household chores. Chad would oversee the practical and financial matters, including flying Clayton and his family back to Boston. He'd set them up in an apartment so that his three children wouldn't disrupt Louise's peace. They would pitch in wherever they were needed, including helping Annie out at the shop so that Natalie could concentrate on Louise. Even Marilyn was included in the plan; she agreed to come in once a week to help out with general errands.

They all worked the plan, coming together as a team to give Louise the support and love she needed as she slipped further away from them. By the end of September, it seemed that every day might be her last. But she continued to hold on. By late November, it was clear she was reaching the end, and the only prayer any of them had was for Louise to be released from her suffering.

During those last few days, Natalie slept only when Louise slept, sitting with her mother-in-law in the darkest hours of the night when the pain medication did little to relieve her pain and nothing but the sound of Natalie's voice could soothe her.

"I'll sit with her." Natalie tiptoed into Louise's bedroom in the early morning hours of November 30th and whispered to the night nurse. "You get some rest." The room was dark, except for a dim light on the bureau.

"No need to whisper, dear." Louise's voice was raspy. "I try to sleep, but I can't." Her thin body shivered beneath the covers.

Natalie reached for a second blanket and placed in on top of her, wondering how Louise could be so cold. The heat had been turned up to eighty degrees and she was always covered up with extra blankets. She looked so lost and tiny under all the bedding.

"I'm not afraid, you know," Louise said, taking a sip of water from the glass Natalie held to her lips.

"I know you're not."

Natalie moved the nurse's chair closer to the bed and sat down, stroking the top of Louise's head. At the touch, tears slid from Louise's eyes and across her cheeks, settling into the lines of her face. Natalie blotted them gently with her index finger. She'd noticed that most of Louise's caretakers and visitors, including

Chad and other family members, had begun to maintain a certain physical distance from Louise, touching her only when medically necessary. In all fairness to them, it was probably because even the slightest contact seemed to hurt Louise's tender flesh. But Natalie sensed how deeply Louise craved the comfort of soft melodic strokes across her skin.

In the quiet of the room, Natalie continued to stroke Louise's hair as she began whispering in cadence with Louise's shallow breathing. She'd been reading several books on how to help loved ones let go and pass peacefully into death.

"It's okay to go Louise. Close your eyes. Find the light. We love you. We set you free. Let go. . .let go. . .our Father, thy will be done. . .let go. . ." Over and over, Natalie repeated the words in a low hypnotic pattern. "Find the light."

"Noelle." Louise opened her eyes and spoke with a voice so strong that Natalie actually jumped at the sound.

"Noelle, you are wearing mère's necklace."

Natalie's hand went to the lily-of-the-valley necklace Darrelle had given her. She touched the small gold and enamel charm.

"Louise, it's me, Natalie."

"Noelle. Thank you for taking care of me this time."

Natalie's throat burned with new tears. Louise didn't even know who she was anymore. She needed to tell her, now, before the chance was lost forever.

"Louise, it's me, Natalie. Can you hear me?"

Louise nodded her head but otherwise didn't respond.

"I want to tell you something." Natalie touched Louise's cheek and then reached for her hand beneath the covers. "I should have told you this a long time ago. I'm so sorry. I was trying to be loyal to Marilyn; it probably doesn't make any difference to you now, but I'm. . ." Natalie took a deep breath and blew it out. It was so unbearably hot in this room. "Louise, I was meant to be your daughter. I was the baby you were supposed to adopt."

"Today you are my daughter. Yesterday you were my sister." A small giggle escaped Louise's lips as though she was privy to some titillating secret. "Tomorrow. . ."

"Louise?" Natalie's stomach churned with confusion and uncertainty; her heart pumped hard against her chest. Louise was making no sense at all, yet somewhere, deep inside of Natalie, her mother-in-law was making perfect sense.

"Tomorrow," Louise repeated, looking straight ahead as though she could see down some future road, "there's a plan." She glanced over at Natalie and then looked straight ahead again, "For you and me. There's a plan."

Louise sat up against her pillows, using strength she no longer had, but showing no sign of exertion. Her eyes were bright, her skin luminous.

"Let me help you," Natalie said. "Please — "

"You have my dear." Louise's eyes were filled with love. "You have. One more thing. You and Chad must let go."

"Let go? Of what?"

"Of the past."

"I don't understand."

"It's time. It's so beautiful." Louise reached out for Natalie. "Darrelle's come for me."

Natalie's flesh turned cold as Louise's body slumped against the pillows, a wheeze signaling her last breath. Natalie climbed onto the bed and cradled Louise's head against her breast. She had been dying for so long now that Natalie had expected the final moments would last longer, would come with more warning. She expected that she would have more time to say goodbye.

———◆———

After a long while, Natalie kissed her mother-in-law goodbye and then summoned Rosa and the night nurse. She went into the kitchen, put on a pot of coffee, and picked up the phone. It was nearly dawn when she made her first call.

"She's gone."

"I'm so sorry. What can I do?"

"Nothing, Johnny, just love me."

"I do."

Since July, when Natalie had to leave the Cape to care for Louise, she and Johnny had slowly, carefully, been falling in love all over again. He'd called in a few favors so that he would be at Janice's school again this year, which kept him in Boston three days a week, close to his daughter, close to the woman he'd never stopped loving.

During Louise's illness, Natalie called Johnny nearly every night and they managed to have a quick dinner together every couple of weeks. In between, he would stop by the shop, on those days when he knew she would be there, if only for a few minutes.

Annie had been upset at first — not because Natalie was risking her marriage by renewing her relationship with Johnny — but because Natalie had kept Johnny's reappearance a secret for so long. At least she knew why Natalie had been so self-engrossed and short tempered last summer. And, in true Annie form, she forgave quickly and offered to help in any way possible.

"I know true love when I see it," she told them, "and you two are the real McCoy."

From the beginning, Johnny understood that caring for Louise was a priority to Natalie. Now Louise was gone, and Johnny was the first person she turned to.

"Just love me," Natalie repeated into the phone. "I hear Rosa. I have to go. I'll call when I can. Be patient with me, please."

"Always," Johnny said.

"There's so much to do. I don't know when I can see you."

"Natalie, honey, just take care of things. Do what you need for Janice. And for your husband. Get through the funeral and Thanksgiving. We'll figure the rest out. We have all the time in the world."

So she did just that. She spent the next few weeks staying close to her family, making arrangements, grieving Louise, helping Clayton and his family move into Louise's house until they went abroad again. Meanwhile, she moved back in with Chad and Janice. But it was just temporary, her returning home, making dinners, having drinks with friends, pretending to be content. She didn't want to live there anymore, and she didn't want to be Chad's wife. She wanted to take Janice and start over.

In the back of Natalie's mind, a plan was beginning to take shape, but it didn't yet have complete form and substance. For now, all she wanted was to spend some time with Johnny and give Janice a nice Christmas. Everything else would fall into place after that. The new year would be the perfect time for a fresh beginning.

THIRTY-NINE

All of Newberry Street was awash in white Christmas lights, glowing beneath a blanket of mist clinging, like angel hair, to the night air. Natalie shivered as she locked the front door to *Giving with Meaning*, glancing down one side of the sidewalk and then the other, before stepping into the street to hail a cab. It felt as though the eyes of the night were watching her, tracking her every movement. Guilt. Pure old-fashioned guilt, she decided as she opened the door to the cab and slid into the back seat.

It was six o'clock on a Thursday evening, the second week in December. She knew it wasn't smart closing up shop when all the other stores were open late for holiday shopping. Even less smart, was where she was going and what she knew she was about to do.

As the cab maneuvered through the city streets to Johnny's residential hotel across town, Natalie stared out the window, watching shoppers as they ducked in and out of stores, their arms burdened with shopping bags. She had the oddest sense of detachment, as though she'd just arrived from another planet and was examining the habits of these earthlings. Natalie knew it was because, once again, she was feeling as though she'd fallen on the floor between two chairs, stuck between the life she had and the one she wanted. She also knew her sense of detachment was a protective device. If she allowed herself to feel, she'd start to cry and probably never stop.

She'd cry for Louise. She'd cry for her lost relationship with Marilyn who, even after all these years, was still known as her sister. And she'd cry for all the ways she'd betrayed others, including Chad. She would be crying the tears of a woman destined to live with the ripples of choices she'd made long ago, and the choices she was about to make.

Natalie ran her fingers through her chestnut hair and closed her eyes. Maybe tonight, being with Johnny, would help her feel like she belonged, like she had a place in the world and that she truly mattered. They hadn't yet made love, both agreeing to go slow this time around, to get to know each other all over again, and to start their life together without feelings of guilt. Natalie didn't want to be the "cheating wife" and Johnny didn't want a woman who still belonged to someone else, if in name only. But tonight that was about to change. They hadn't decided it openly — that would have felt too deliberate, too clinical — but she knew it was going to happen. Tonight they would be together. Tonight she would betray Chad despite all her good intentions.

She walked into Johnny's suite and smiled, her eyes scanning the combination dining area and living room. She took it all in: champagne, strawberries, two kinds of cheese, crackers, shrimp cocktail; he'd set out an array of foods, lowered the lights, and lit a dozen or so candles. Soft, seductive jazz curled its way around the room.

Natalie let out a sigh of relief, suddenly aware of how desperately she wanted this and how disappointed she would have been if tonight had turned out to be just dinner and conversation, as they'd planned. She couldn't help the comparison that flashed across her mind. Once she and Chad were married, he'd never set the scene, never felt any need to seduce her. It was purely physical, sex without the lovemaking. Until this moment, she didn't realize how much she missed the tenderness.

"My lady." In a gallant gesture, Johnny bowed slightly and helped Natalie off with her coat. "It's wet," he said, noticing beads of mist glistening on the black wool.

"It's cold and drizzly out there, feels like it's going to turn into one of those horrid icy rains."

"Well, it's warm in here." Johnny pulled Natalie into his arms, pressing his body against hers. "Hot in fact." Natalie closed her eyes and responded to his embrace, hunger rising inside of her.

Johnny cupped Natalie's chin in his hands and tilted her face upward, drawing her into a long, deep kiss. And then another. And another. While he explored her mouth and the curve of her neck, she took his hand and guided it upwards, beneath her skirt and along her thigh until his thumb was stroking the silk of her panties along the swell of heat pressing against the fabric. Natalie inhaled sharply at the soft, fiery pleasure and arched toward the pressure of his hand.

"Are you sure?" Johnny whispered.

She nodded, pressing harder against him, unable to speak.

"You have to be sure."

"I am." She dug her fingers into his shoulders. "Honest. I am." Her voice was husky and urgent.

Johnny led Natalie into the bedroom, grabbing the bottle of champagne and two stemmed glasses from the coffee table. Natalie sat on the edge of the bed and watched as the cork flew across the room and Johnny worked to contain the overflow of liquid cascading across the neck of the bottle. He handed her a glass and then poured one for himself.

"You don't drink," she said.

"This isn't drinking, this is celebrating. I'm fine. Finer than I've ever been," he said, running his fingers across her lips, teasing her with the slightest of touches. Lifting her hair away from her neck, he kissed the tender spot just behind her ear. "I love you, Natalie."

"Oh Johnny. I love you so much it scares me." She put her half-full glass on the bedside table and pulled him down on top of her.

For one long moment, he held Natalie's face in his hands and stared deeply into her eyes, as though searching for the answer to some long-forgotten question. She responded by smiling, and Johnny laughed out loud.

"I was a goner the first time I saw you smile." He stroked her dimple. "And I'm still a goner."

Johnny's kisses were no longer soft, as he explored her mouth with his tongue. Natalie gasped at the intensity of his kisses, mingled with the sweet lingering taste of champagne, and the contrasting light touch of his hands exploring the wetness beneath her skirt. She ran her hand down the length of his back and curved her body up against his. Johnny moaned as he licked her ear lobe and then eased off Natalie and began to undress her. With deliberate slowness and intensifying need, they explored one another's bodies; Natalie could feel the summer sun on her skin and hear the gentle breaking of waves in the background, and when Johnny entered her, she could pretend they were young and in love and had their whole life ahead of them.

———◆———

Showered and dressed, Natalie and Johnny sat on the sofa, his arms wrapped around her as she tucked in against his body.

"I'm starved," she said, popping a shrimp into her mouth.

"You should be. You gave me quite a workout in there." Johnny kissed the top of her head.

She meant to keep up the banter, to turn and smile up at him and say something like *look who's talking* and tease him about his skill as a lover. Instead, tears fell across her face. She tried to hold them back, to keep Johnny from seeing what even she didn't understand. The last thing Natalie wanted to do was spoil this time between them.

"Natalie, what's wrong. Are you crying?" Johnny turned her face toward his and tried blotting the tears with his fingers. The more he wiped them away, the harder they fell, until she erupted in uncontrollable sobs and pushed herself from him.

"What's wrong? Did I hurt you?"

She shook her head, tucking into the far side of the sofa, just outside of his reach. No matter how hard she tried, no matter how much she sucked in her breath and held it, she couldn't stop crying.

All the feelings she'd kept carefully under control for so many years were suddenly at the surface, revealed and awakened. She buried her face in her hands and let it happen — waves of fear and loneliness, of guilt and pleasure, of happiness and renewed love — waves from a lifetime of secrets and restraint — crashing across her body, hitting shore and breaking into a thousand tears. Slowly, wave by wave, tear by tear, the torrent subsided and she was able to face Johnny. She swiped at the final tears with the back of her hands and looked over at him, breaking into a gale of laughter at the stunned look on his face. She must seem like a crazy lady, sobbing, laughing, mascara and eyeliner smudged across her cheeks.

"I'm okay. Really. A mess, but okay." She slid closer to Johnny and took his hands in hers.

"Is this going to happen every time we make love?" He was tucking her damp hair behind her ears, kissing her softly on the cheek. "What happened?"

"I don't know. It's as if I was feeling again, for the first time in years, but I felt everything, all at once."

Johnny sucked in his breath and let it out. "Wow. You scared me. We're okay, right, you and me?"

"We're more than okay." Natalie looked at her watch. "But I have to go."

"You're sure we're okay?"

She hugged him deeply, letting her head rest on his shoulder, breathing in his scent. "I love you. I think I'm scared of losing you again. Of hurting Chad and Janice."

"We'll work it out. I promise."

Natalie stood to go, but Johnny tugged at her hand, pulling her back down to the sofa. "Not yet. Not before I give you this." He reached behind a pillow and pulled out a small jeweler's box.

"Johnny?"

"Open it."

Nestled against black silk was a solitaire diamond ring, set in yellow gold, stunning in its simplicity. Natalie swallowed against a new wave of tears threatening to fall.

"It's beautiful. But I can't take it. You know that."

"I know. But it's here when you can. When you're ready. I just wanted you to know that. Call it an early Christmas present."

"Thank you. Really, truly, thank you. I love it. Even more, I love you. When the time is right, I want you to put it on my finger where it will stay forever and ever." She closed the box and handed it back to him.

Natalie looked at her watch again. Her stomach knotted at the lateness. She should go right now. But she didn't move to leave. Instead, she stayed seated, tucking her legs up under her as though she had all the time in the world. "I have a plan. Well, the beginnings of one anyway. Tell me what you think."

Johnny tipped his champagne glass to get the last few drops and then put it on the table. "Go ahead. I'm all ears."

"Okay, here it is. First, I absolutely need to wait until after Christmas, maybe even after New Year's to do anything. Chad just lost his mom, we're all still grieving. It's going to be a hard

Christmas, as it is. I don't want to make it worse, especially for Janice."

"Understood," Johnny said, reaching over and playing with strands of Natalie's hair. He let her take a deep breath and continue at her own pace.

"So, I'm thinking, I tell Chad in January that we need to take some time apart. I don't mention divorce, he'd go ballistic. I just say how we've been drifting for so long now, that maybe we need some distance to figure things out —"

"And he would buy this, why?"

"You sound like Annie." Natalie squeezed her eyes shut and blew out a long sigh. "I don't know. That's the first flaw in my plan."

Johnny laughed. "Okay, if he goes along with a trial separation, or whatever you want to call it, we're golden. And if not?"

"Well, I'm not sure we're golden, but it's a start. I mean, I could just leave. Take Janice and get my own place, without him agreeing to it, but I'd rather have it amicable, for her sake."

"All right, one way or another, you and Janice move out by, let's say, the end of January."

"I'll get a place close enough to where we are now."

"You're going to stay in Millionaire's Row?"

That's what Johnny called Louisburg Square. Natalie laughed. "Are you kidding? I couldn't afford a lamppost there. No, maybe something in Back Bay. There are some cute neighborhoods there and it's not too far away. I want to be close enough so that Janice can go back and forth between us. I don't want her to hate me. If she can still be near Chad, she might be okay."

"And what about me? Janice is my daughter."

"She loves Chad. As far she knows he's her father. We can't destroy that for her." Natalie took Johnny's hand and kissed it. "It'll work out. I promise. Here's the rest. Once Janice and I are settled into our own place, I'll take her out shopping and we'll "accidentally" bump into you. You'll offer to buy us dinner. She adores you, so there's no problem there. And then a few days later, I tell her you called and invited me to some art opening or something, something academic or cultural, so it doesn't sound like a date. And then we go from there!"

Natalie sat up straight and flashed Johnny a wide, dimpled smile. Hearing it out loud made it sound real, like a plan that could really work.

"It has possibilities," Johnny nodded in appreciation.

"We just have to be patient, keep our eye on what we want and not move too quickly." Natalie looked at her watch again and this time her stomach swirled with real panic. She had no excuse for getting home so late.

"I have to go."

They both walked to the door, knowing their time tonight had ended.

"Will you be okay?" Johnny asked as he helped Natalie on with her coat. He took her in his arms one last time and held tightly as though afraid she was about to disappear on him. "Try to call, let me know you're home safely."

"I promise. If I can't talk, I'll ring once and hang up."

"I don't want you to go."

"I don't want to go."

They stood for a long, slow motion kind of moment, where Johnny stroked her cheek. His fingers slid across her lips and landed on her dimple. "I'd still walk a million miles. . ." his voice trailed off.

"I know you would. That seems like a lifetime ago, doesn't it? You singing that silly song. "

"It caught your attention."

"You're right about that. But so much wasted time."

"So let's not waste any more. Right after Christmas, we'll start the new year concentrating on us. When everything's settled,

357

we'll go back to Saint Martin. Maybe even get married there, on the beach."

"Oh God, that's perfect. We'll do it." Natalie nodded and wriggled from his hold. "I have to go."

"I'll go down with you."

With his arm around her waist, they walked down the three flights of stairs rather than take the elevator. It was a way of easing into their separation, slowly, silently, step by step. But no matter how slowly they moved, eventually they were in the lobby and then out the front door.

The night air hung heavy with a wintery mist that seeped into their bones and wrapped itself around their hair and skin. Natalie shivered and pulled up the collar of her coat while Johnny hailed a cab. The sidewalks were nearly empty of pedestrians and there was very little traffic; in the stillness of the night, as Christmas lights glistened beneath the silent mist, a feeling of dread coursed through Natalie's veins. She had the sensation of stepping outside her body, watching the scene from afar: two people in love, hailing a cab, sending the woman home to her husband, courting the danger of the moment, feeling the anticipation of their future; a cab came to a quick stop beside them and the feeling passed.

As Johnny opened the door for her, Natalie reached up and fingered a lock of his hair, wet and cold from the night air. "I love you John Conway. It finally feels like all the pieces fit, like I've found my destiny."

Johnny put his hand to his heart and half-whispered, half-sang the line from a long-ago song "You are my destiny. . ."

Natalie kissed him quickly and slid into the back seat of the cab. Just as he was about to close the door, she laughed and sang back, "heaven and heaven alone can take your love from me."

Natalie blew Johnny a kiss as the cab pulled away and then settled back, eyes closed, trying to settle her nerves. If Chad was awake, there'd be hell to pay when she got home.

FORTY

It **was after** midnight when Natalie got home. She unlocked the door and tiptoed in, grimacing at the sound of her damp shoes on the hardwood floor. The house was dark except for a single soft light that had been left on in the foyer where she now stood; she glanced into the living room and saw the glow of logs burning themselves out from an earlier fire, their shadows dancing in the otherwise still and silent room, a room that seemed to be watching her.

A sensation — almost like an unseen presence — passed over Natalie. *Like someone walking across your grave*, that's how Marilyn would have described it. She shivered and pulled her coat tightly to her body. Not daring to put on a light, Natalie whispered into the blackness. "Hello? Chad? Are you there?"

There was no answer. No movement, no sound. Chad's study beyond the living room seemed to be as dark and vacant as every other room. It's just the fire, she told herself. *And your own guilt.* She stood still for another few seconds, trying to regulate her breathing. She then turned toward the phone on the table in the foyer and dialed Johnny's number.

"I'm home," she whispered. "Everyone's asleep."

"Are you okay? You sound funny."

"I'm all right. I just got creeped out for a minute."

"Natalie?"

"Dark house. Almost too quite. It's my guilt. I'm okay. I have to go."

"I love you," Johnny said.

"Me too," Natalie whispered and hung up the phone; she stood for a few moments, listening to the quiet, steadying her breathing, making absolutely sure the house was safe and silent. Finally, she slipped out of her coat, put in on a chair, along with her purse, and tiptoed over to the staircase, taking each step slowing, carefully. Hopefully, Chad was fully asleep and she could slip in next to him, no questions asked. She'd deal with any suspicions in the morning.

"Who's John Conway and why is my wife sneaking off to see him?"

Natalie froze and then slowly descended the few stairs she'd managed to take. The voice — Chad's voice — had come from the living room.

"Chad?"

She heard the clicking of ice cubes and saw the liquid in the glass, glowing in the light cast by the dying fire, but she still didn't see the form of the man sitting in the chair until he stood and began walking toward her.

"Chad! You nearly scared me to death."

"I asked you a question. Who is he?"

As he closed the gap between them, Chad began flipping on lights.

"Let me look at you," he said. "I want to see your face when you try and lie your way out."

With the living room in full light now, Natalie could see he'd been drinking Absinthe. On the coffee table was a slotted spoon, along with sugar cubes and a bottle of the "real stuff" as he called it, the Absinthe Chad had paid a small fortune for from an underground market.

For every step Chad took forward, Natalie took one backward, but in the confined space of the foyer, there was nowhere to go. Natalie found herself pressed against the wall by the front door with Chad pushing up against her, his breath hot on her face, thick with the sweet, sickly smell of Absinthe. Her stomach swirled with the scent of violence and unnamed memories.

"Chad. It's not what you think."

"How do you know what I think?"

Natalie took one hand from behind her back and stroked her husband's face. "Well," she tried laughing but failed, "I can imagine what you're thinking. But you've got it all wrong."

"So make it right." He blew the words across her face and then leaned back enough to finish off his drink. "Make it right!"

Natalie knew she couldn't make it right. She couldn't even come up with a plausible lie as Chad pinned her against the wall. The only recourse she had was to go on the offense. Maybe it would work.

"What did you do, follow me? How dare you?"

"How dare I? How dare I?" The words came out as a spray across her face. "How dare I? I come by to take my *lovely* wife out to dinner, to surprise her, well, well, the surprise was on me. I get to watch as she hops into a cab and goes to some crappy hotel."

"You had no right to follow me."

Chad pulled on her hair until her neck was bent to one side. "I have every right. You're my wife. I'll ask you once more. Who is John Conway?"

"Mom, Dad, what's happening?"

There was Janice, at the top of the stairs, in bare feet and flannel pajamas, her hair uncombed and hanging across her face. They both froze and looked up, startled at their daughter's appearance and what she might have witnessed. But her voice

361

registered concern only with her own needs. "Mom! Where have you been? I tried waiting up for you. I need you to take me shopping tomorrow, it can't wait."

Chad hollered up at his daughter, "Janice. Not now. Go to bed."

Natalie used the distraction to escape from his hold. She grabbed the front door handle, hoping her unspoken threat to leave would be enough to calm Chad. She didn't want things to go like this, especially not in front of Janice.

"What's wrong? Mommy, what's going on?" Panic rose in Janice's voice as she saw her mother was about to leave.

"Janice, honey, everything's okay here." Natalie kept her voice low and calm. "Daddy and I are just having a small disagreement. Nothing to worry about. Go to bed. I'll take you anywhere you need to go tomorrow. Just go to bed."

In that small space of time, Chad had gone into the living room to refill his drink. Natalie pressed her back against the front door still holding onto the handle, not knowing what to do next. Rather than leave, maybe she should try and make a run for the stairs, grab hold of Janice and sleep in her room tonight. Yes, that's exactly what she should do. Chad wouldn't bother her there. They'd lock the door. Together, they'd be safe. Tomorrow everything would be better.

Natalie let go of the door handle and ran toward her daughter. Her foot was on the third stair when Chad wrapped his hands around Natalie's waist and dragged her down.

"Mommy! Daddy! Stop, please stop." Janice collapsed into tears. "Please stop."

"You're not just a bad wife. You're a bad mother. Look what you're doing to my daughter." Chad twisted Natalie around and held her back against his body, yanking her hair so that she was looking up at Janice. "She's terrified. It's all your fault. You don't deserve her."

"*Your* daughter?" Rage and terror slammed through Natalie's body as she wrenched free of Chad and ran toward the front door, grabbing hold of the handle.

A breeze stirred overhead. It was nothing more than a slight movement of air, but Natalie shivered at its presence. *Had she opened the door without realizing it?* No, it was still closed. This breeze had come from somewhere else. And it seemed to come with a warning.

"Who is John Conway?" Chad spit out the words as he moved toward her once again.

"Daddy. Daddy," Janice's tear-filled voice was urgent, as though she held the answer to the riddle that would solve all their problems. "That's Mr. C, my writing teacher. You know, from the Cape last summer?"

Chad looked up at Janice, trying to understand what he'd just heard. "He's your teacher?"

Janice nodded and Chad turned back toward Natalie.

"You're having an affair with her teacher?" Chad's words came out hollow, void of any understanding.

Natalie pressed down on the handle. The door gave way and opened slightly. She could run now if she needed to.

"With her *teacher?*" Chad repeated, the truth sinking in, raising his hand as though to strike Natalie.

Seeing his raised hand, smelling the Absinthe on this breath, remembering past betrayals — *women on the side* — Natalie's anger bubbled to the surface, taking on a life of its own.

"I'm not having an affair with *her teacher*. I'm having an affair with *her father*." Natalie heard the words leave her mouth even before they hit the air.

What had she done? It wasn't supposed to happen this way. After Christmas. She was supposed to wait until after Christmas. She was going to leave Chad. But she wasn't ever going to tell him about Johnny. Or about Janice.

363

"What do you mean? What are you telling me?" Chad's voice was no more than a whisper now, slurred by anger, disbelief and Absinthe. His lips were tight across his teeth, his jaw rigid, as he struck Natalie, the palm of his hand burning her cheek.

The scent of blood hit the air. As her tongue found the cut on her bottom lip, the metallic taste pushed Natalie outside of her body into a scene that seemed strangely familiar.

Three girls were sitting in front of a fireplace. *Darrelle.* One was Darrelle. *How could that be?* They were holding hands, silent and terrified, watching every move of the man and woman in the scene. The woman was angry, shouting out spiteful words, and the man — he was picking up a knife. . .

Natalie doubled over in agony, feeling the knife slice through her stomach, smelling the release of blood into the room.

"What did you just say? What are you telling me?" Chad was shouting.

His angry words brought Natalie back to the moment, to the house on Louisburg Square; his hands dug deep into her shoulders as he shook her, harder and then still harder.

"Mommy, Daddy, stop," Janice sobbed, clutching at the railing as though afraid of being sucked into the drama exploding all around her. Her pleas were lost in the violence.

"Leave me alone," Natalie screamed, punching at her husband's chest, trying to free herself. She looked down at her stomach wondering if she could stop the bleeding. But there was no knife. No blood oozing through her clothes. Nothing. Just pain. Deep penetrating pain.

"I want the truth from you. And I want it now." Chad raised one hand, readying himself to strike her again, staggering backwards as he lost his balance. In that moment, Natalie was able to shove Chad away, adrenalin pumping through her veins.

"You want the truth?" Natalie spit out the words she'd been harboring forever. "Here it is: John Conway is Janice's father. He's her real father and the only man I've ever loved."

She grabbed hold of the door and flung it open. Slashes of icy rain hit her face as she stumbled down the stairs, gripping the wrought iron railing for support. Chad stood in the doorway, calling to her, his voice piercing the night. But it sounded like he was calling out for Noelle. Why would he call her Noelle?

Her stomach throbbed with pain — hot, liquid, searing pain — as though she was being stabbed over and over again by thin shards of glass. By a knife that didn't exist from a scene that never happened.

"Natalie, come back here. Now!"

She ran from the words, from the anger and spite that seemed to have a will of their own, from the breeze that stayed with her, crying for attention, whispering into her ear the name of her childhood doll.

I'm here, Natalie. It's me, Edith.

Why would her doll be whispering to her? Was she going crazy?

She reached the bottom stair and unlatched the front gate. Standing on the brick walk, she heard it clank shut behind her, like a prison door, metal against metal, separating her from the life she had known. She had no idea where she was going. She just knew she had to keep moving, away from Chad, away from his insistent voice and the memories that trailed along with it.

Natalie raked her wet hair back from her face and scanned the area, dark and eerie under the yellow glow of gas lamplights. Clutching her stomach, she maneuvered herself between parked cars and escaped into the narrow street. Stumbling mid-way, she put her hands out to keep herself from falling and then pushed herself back up, struggling to regain her balance.

That's when she saw the car, coming from the top of the hill, its headlights pressing forward in the darkness.

That's when she heard the screeching of tires on wet pavement and put up her hands to warn the driver that she was there.

But it was too late.

They made eye contact — she and the stunned driver — through the rain-drenched windshield, just as the car careened into Natalie, thrusting her into the air and slamming her onto the icy pavement.

FORTY-ONE

Natalie stepped into the light willingly. And then she took some time to feel its warm, radiant love while disentangling her spirit from her earthly body. It had been such a sudden and traumatic death that Enif allowed her to stay on the earth plane a few minutes longer than usual in order to work through the transition.

"Are you ready?" Enif asked after a while.

She studied her lifeless form for the last time, drawn to the image of her hand clasping the necklace she always wore, the gold and enamel lily-of-the-valley that Darrelle had given her. In the last seconds of her life, she had reached for it, as though it held some kind of bond between this world and the next.

Chad and Janice were kneeling by her side. Chad was stroking her hair. Janice was sobbing, begging her mother to wake up. They looked up now at the sight of the ambulance approaching them, lights whirling, sirens blaring, as though there was an emergency. But there was no emergency. Not any more.

"What will happen to them?" she asked Enif.

"They have their own destinies to fulfill, their own choices to make. It will work out however it works out."

"What have I done?"

"You exercised your free will. As did Marilyn, all those years ago. As they will. It is always a challenge, managing your chosen destiny with the freedom of so many choices."

"Like sending your child off to college? Or camp? She gets to do whatever she wants no matter what you've warned her about, no matter how much guidance you provide."

"Precisely. No matter how much you whisper into her ear. Now, it is time to go. You have many souls waiting to greet you."

"I'm ready." Natalie's spirit radiated her answer. She appreciated that Enif let her remain for a while, to grieve the unexpected loss of this lifetime. But she also knew it was time for her to move on and, eventually, to start over again.

She moved her light closer to her guardian and dear friend. "That was you, wasn't it? You're Edith?"

"That always tickled me," Enif told her. "Thinking my name was Edith and naming your doll after me. I have been with you always, as I promised long ago, in the whisper of the wind, in the silent voice of your heart."

As they ascended, she recognized the very moment when her silver cord snapped, freeing her soul from her broken earthly form and the weight of her most recent life, and she twinkled knowingly. With Enif by her side, she traveled the white light through all the stages of the Bardo, until she found herself in a place of light and love and hope, in a place that would provide insight and a new beginning.

"Welcome back, Nunki," Enif said. "Welcome to the Bardo of Becoming."

Know that from the greater silence I shall return... A little while, a moment of rest upon the wind, and another woman shall bear me. . . If in the twilight of memory we should meet once more, we shall speak again together and you shall sing to meet a deeper song.
— Kahil Gilbran

To My Readers:

In response to your overwhelming requests,
I have written a sequel to Field of Destiny.

to be released in 2011 —

A Thousand Whispers

FOLLOW JANICE'S STORY as she uncovers
family secrets and struggles to survive tragedy.

DISCOVER HOW NATALIE AND JOHNNY meet
again to live out their destiny as soul mates.

EXPLORE THE MEANING OF TRUTH and the
possibility of "getting it right" across lifetimes.

Here's the first chapter . . .

ONE

A Thousand Whispers:
September 13, 1987

John Conway was dead. And Chad Hamilton was on trial for his murder. It was that simple. And that complicated. Just before daybreak, on what he presumed would be his last day of freedom, Chad removed $50,000 from the wall safe in his study; he closed it shut, spun the dial, and then methodically replaced the oil painting used to hide its presence, straightening the frame until it was perfectly squared on the wall. There, in his Louisburg Square home, with only the light from a small desk lamp to guide his movements, one of Boston's most prominent attorneys hunched over his desk folding hundred dollar bills and then loading them into a leather money belt.

Once it was fully loaded, Chad zipped the belt closed and secured it around his waist. He then placed several hundred dollars beneath the inner sole of his loafers, a thousand dollars in his wallet, and the rest in the duffel bag resting on the sofa. He opened his navy blazer and patted the left side of his shirt, satisfying himself once more that his nylon shoulder wallet was in place and his passport was safely tucked inside. His new passport, with his new name.

Everything was set.

Or was it?

How could anyone be ready for something like this?

Chad picked up a framed photograph from a side table and studied the image, as though he were an impartial observer, an anthropologist seeking to understand how this family of three had gotten it so wrong in some long ago world.

They looked like a normal happy family, posing for their annual Christmas card photo. He was standing between his two women — a thorn between two roses, he had joked — an arm wrapped around the waist of each of them: his wife, Natalie and their sixteen-year-old daughter, Janice. *Their* daughter. What a laugh. He shook his head at the incomprehensible turn of events, even as he continued to study the photo. The printed Christmas cards were still sitting in the bottom drawer of his desk. Just days after they were delivered, Natalie had been killed, fleeing from him into the icy night after they'd argued.

After they'd argued. Such a nothing phase. Not at all telling. No hint of lovers or fear or violence. No hint of John Conway, his wife's long-ago lover, back on the scene to pick up where they'd left off sixteen years ago.

Chad raked his hands through his freshly cut hair — thick and black, sporting traces of gray at the temple — and tried once more to make sense of everything that had happened. But how could he? How could any man?

One minute you're breezing along, everything pretty much on track and, then, with no warning, someone opens a window and in crawls a shape-shifter, transforming your life into something dark, unrecognizable. The scene from that December night, just nine months ago — a lifetime ago — burns its way across your brain, playing itself out for the millionth time.

There's Natalie tiptoeing through the front door around midnight, not realizing you're in the next room, drinking

Absinthe, waiting to confront her. You'd followed her that night, knew she went to see some guy named Conway, apparently one of Janice's teachers. A common man, a teacher, for God's sake; she couldn't even find a blue blood to screw. Violence and rage fill the air as you accuse her of being a bad wife, of being an unfit mother to your daughter. That's when she lets you have it.

"*Your* daughter?" She spits the words in your face. "I'm not having an affair with her teacher. I'm having an affair with *her father*. John Conway is Janice's real father and he's the only man I've ever loved."

Janice is at the top of the stairs, witnessing everything. You reach up to strike Natalie for a second time, but she escapes. She runs out into the darkness, gas lamps creating false shadows on the icy street. Moments later, she's killed by an oncoming car.

As if that's not enough, on the night of her funeral, that same lover — John J. Conway — is found dead in Boston Common. Shot to death, it seems, by your gun.

Anyone could have taken the gun from your bedroom and then returned it, sight unseen. *Anyone.* The house was crawling with people after the funeral. You try explaining that to the police when they come to arrest you. But they don't buy it. You're arrested, arraigned, and released on two million dollars bail to await trial. The bail is offered as a professional courtesy: you're a wealthy, well-known attorney with ties to the community and a daughter who needs looking after. But courtesy only goes so far; you're also required to surrender your passport.

By the end of August, you're sitting there, on trial for murder, watching your future disappear, watching your fate be decided by a jury — not of your peers — but of ordinary, working folks not the least bit unhappy to see a man of means taken down. You watch, day in and day out, as these ordinary people hang onto the prosecutor's every word as he presents his case, an *airtight* case, he emphasizes, offering three irrefutable facts: there's the letter found in Conway's hotel room, addressed to Chad, ready to be mailed, admitting paternity of Janice and demanding custody of his teenage daughter; there's the fact that Chad knew about the paternity allegations and has no alibi for the time after his wife's funeral, except to say that he'd been home, in his study, drinking away his grief; and then there's the most damning evidence of all — the 38 caliber gun that Chad kept stashed in his bedroom; it matches ballistics, leaving no doubt that it's the murder weapon.

Motive. Means. Opportunity. That's what the prosecution presents. And that's what the jury is buying. It shows in their faces, in the tightness of their lips, in the hardness of their eyes, in the stone-cold set of their body.

That's why you decide to leave.

You see the word *guilty* etched on their faces long before closing arguments and you know what you have to do. You start planning it all out, creating a new identity, wiring money offshore, arranging finances to protect Janice. From the moment the trial started, you knew it could come to this. But you never quite believed it would. There was always a bit of hope. *Reasonable doubt*, it's called. So, even with everything in place, you wait until the very last moment, until there's no more time to wait. No more hope. No more doubt. It was leave tonight while the jury was still deliberating or risk life in prison. Once they returned with a verdict — and his lawyer sensed it would be tomorrow, the next day at the latest — there would be no chance to escape.

Chad shook off the memories, tucking the photograph into his bag, but then changed his mind. Where he was going, he didn't want reminders of the past, nor any proof of who he was. He replaced it on the table, angling it just right, and then glanced around his study, at the books and artifacts and his collection of Absinthe glasses and spoons. He would miss all of this. And Janice. He would miss Janice. He didn't care about the so-called truth, he was Janice's father and he'd do anything for her. She was the one person he could honestly say he loved purely, no agenda, no baggage, no expectations. Maybe that's because she seemed to love him the same way. Unconditionally.

Chad picked up his duffel bag and walked quietly toward the foyer and the front door where he'd left a single packed suitcase. His hand on the door handle, he stopped, looked around one last time and then, on impulse, released his grip and climbed the stairs to Janice's bedroom.

Standing in the doorway, he watched Janice toss fitfully in her sleep, sheet and comforter twisted around her lean body. She was never fully rested anymore. Her sleep was dominated by loss and by the feeling that, somehow, she was responsible for everything bad in their lives, as though she had the power to stop the waves of destruction crashing across their once happy family. Gone was his joyful, optimistic daughter, whose biggest problem was getting her driver's license and deciding whether to become a writer or photographer, or both. Here was an anxious young woman living in the shadowy mist of death, with a father on trial for murder — a father who wasn't even really her father — and haunted by memories she couldn't retrieve.

There were several hours from the day of Natalie's funeral, after they'd buried her, after everyone had come to the house in droves and then left in small groupings, that Janice simply couldn't remember.

She recalls standing with Chad, closing the door on the final stragglers, swallowing hard against tears as Chad brushed her aside, saying he was going into his study and she should go upstairs and rest. She remembers climbing the stairs and crawling onto her parent's bed, fully dressed, tucking into the warmth of her mother's comforter. She thinks she remembers hearing the door bell ring, but it could have been a dream. Probably was a dream, she suggests. And then nothing. Her memory was blank, picking up again with the next morning's breakfast.

Maybe she'd slept the whole time, so there was nothing to remember. But that seemed unlikely. There were traces of her having moved about the house. The doctors suspected psychogenic amnesia, a delayed response to the trauma of her mother's sudden death and the truth revealed that night about Janice's paternity. Lost memory in the wake of severe trauma was not unusual, they testified, and often not retrievable. She was not a reliable witness to Chad's whereabouts after the funeral.

Every day since then, she'd struggled against those lost hours, believing there was something there, some telling detail, some hidden truth that would fix everything, that would give Chad the alibi he needed, turning her life right side up again. *If only she could remember.*

Chad spotted Janice's journal, open on her desk. This is where she poured out her worries when she couldn't talk about them, where she tried pushing against the lost memories. He tiptoed across the room and studied her neat, fluid script, not reading the words, but simply committing her handwriting to memory. He turned to a fresh page and wrote quickly: *I have to go. Remember I love you. Someday you may understand just how much. Don't ever let your memories keep you from becoming the wonderful woman I know you're meant to be. Make me proud. — Dad.*

He then walked over to Janice and, sweeping her honey-colored hair from her face, whispered into her ear. "You'll be okay, kiddo. I love you. Try and love me back."

He left her bedroom without looking back, descended the stairs, picked up his bags, and drove his Mercedes toward New York's JFK airport.

As Chad traveled Interstate-95 from Boston to New York, the sun rose and the sky settled into the kind of misty fog that promised to burn off by noon. He unzipped his duffel bag, on the front seat beside him, and pulled out mints from an inside pocket, nodding at the stacks of money. His safety net. Just looking at it made him feel better. This would get him started, help him take a very long and winding road to where he was ultimately going, paying only cash, so that nobody could trace his tracks. No matter how safe he felt looking at the money, or how hard he worked at remaining calm, his lungs burned with anxiety; he needed real air to steady his nerves. He popped a mint into his mouth and turned off the air conditioning; he lowered his window and opened the moon roof, taking in deep breaths. That was better; now he could concentrate on his plan.

He knew exactly where he would be by noon. Once more, he went over the details in his head. He'd park his car at the Holiday Inn's indoor garage, on a high floor, off in a darkened corner and replace his license plate with one from Michigan that he'd bought from the sleazebag who'd sold him his new passport. With any luck, this would confuse the authorities enough so they wouldn't trace his Mercedes back to him for at least a month. By then, his trail would have gone cold. At least that was the hope.

After wrapping his license plate in an old towel and stuffing it into the middle of his suitcase, he'd walk through the hotel lobby and hop on the airport shuttle with all the other hotel guests, disappearing into the crowd before his late afternoon flight.

He regretted what his leaving would do to Janice. The bail bondsman, the press, the prosecutor, all hounding her, looking for him, each with their own axe to grind. It would be messy. And prolonged. But he had no choice. The two million dollar bond would be revoked and the collateral that secured it would be seized, including the house at the Cape. The assets that had been frozen would now be unfrozen and handed over to the bondsman. Still, Janice would be okay.

"She'll be okay," he said out loud, trying to convince himself. As though money itself would heal her wounds. She'd have the townhouse, some stocks, and the cash he'd left her in the safe. Annie, Natalie's long-time best friend, would help, he was sure about that. He'd deeded the store, *Giving with Meaning* to her, just the way Natalie would have wanted, with the stipulation that Janice receive a percentage of the profits throughout her life. Annie would take her in, watch over her.

"She'll be okay," he repeated, shaking his head, trying to wrangle the worries from his brain. What's done is done, he told himself. No looking back now. He needed to look ahead.

As he reached New Haven, Connecticut, along Long Island Sound, the low-lying fog crept in around him, thick and wet, heavier now, dangerously reducing visibility. He pushed ahead to catch up with the truck in front of him, and then backed off, using the truck's lights as a guide, setting cruise control to keep pace with the trucker's rate of speed.

"Brad Harrison." Chad said his new name out loud, trying to get used to its sound. The sleazebag had advised him to choose a name close to his real one.

"Less slip-up," he'd warned. "And when you do screw up, you can recover. You can stop mid-sentence and correct yourself. When someone calls out Brad, it's close enough that you'll turn around. Choose something like George and you're dead from the start."

As Chad continued trying out his new name in comparison to his real one — Brad Harrison . . . Chad Hamilton . . . Brad Harrison, noticing the subtle differences in the movements of his lips and tongue — he realized he was gaining on the truck. Apparently the fog had made the driver uneasy, slowed him down, while Chad had maintained the same speed. He cancelled cruise control and sat up straighter, giving his full attention to the road. They were passing through Stamford now, with visibility less than a hundred feet. Through the haze, he saw the trucker's red brake lights pumping on and off. He heard the blast of a horn and a thunderous sound, like waves crashing on rocks. And then nothing. No sound. No lights. Nothing.

He peered through the windshield into the nothingness, searching the road ahead for the truck. But it seemed to be gone. *How could that be?*

Chad took a deep steadying breath as he tried to reason things out. The truck was nowhere within his sight, as though it had been lifted into a black hole, leaving him alone on the Interstate. There was only the fog and him and a thick eerie silence. He punched the button for his flashers and changed lanes. It was the only thing he could think to do. That was just before the rumble. Just before his car was lifted into the air and sent spiraling downward into Connecticut's Mianius River.

———◆———

The tragedy captured the attention of the nation. As the press headlined the bridge collapse that swallowed up a truck and more than a dozen vehicles, search and rescue teams worked to recover victims from the frigid water. Remarkably a few people survived; most had not.

Newscasters at the scene detailed the discovery of personal effects — a single red high-heeled shoe . . . a wallet with ruined photos of loved ones . . . an infant seat — using them to personalize the disaster.

The most intriguing story — the one that led to media speculation and dinner-table discussions around the country — was the mystery surrounding the hundred dollar bills found floating on the water's surface. Where did they come from? Who did they belong to? And why?

Within days, as vehicles were lifted out of the water, identified and matched with victims, both dead and alive, it was apparent that several people would never be recovered: while their personal effects were found, it was evident their bodies had been carried out to sea along the river's tide and then swallowed up by the ocean.

Chad Hamilton was one of them.

Field of Destiny:
Reading Group Questions & Topics for Discussion

1. Discuss the relationship between free will and destiny. Do we come into this world with a certain destiny that is realized no matter what road we travel, or do our choices have the power to alter the course of our life?

2. Natalie comes into the world determined to learn the lessons of loyalty. How does she handle this challenge? Examine how she is both the betrayed and the betrayer.

3. According to the laws of karma, everything we put out into the world comes back to us, both good and bad. How does this idea of cause and effect play itself out in *Field of Destiny*? How do you see it operating in your own life?

4. As a child, Natalie is described as out of sorts, as though she knows Marilyn's free will has altered her destiny: "she was aware of the empty space inside of her that never seemed to fill up." Have you ever felt there was something else waiting out there for you, another road you might have taken?

5. Discuss this passage, just before Pearl learns that Natalie has betrayed her: "The winds of destiny were stirring and only later would Natalie begin to understand how every moment touches the next, how even one minute—sixty brief seconds— can alter the course of things."

6. Natalie continually makes choices based on the need for her mother's approval. Do you find this realistic? Do you believe children will do nearly anything to win their parents' love?

7. Discuss your feelings about Marilyn. Are you angry at her, or do you feel compassion for the young unwed mother who tries to build a life for herself and her daughter? Given the times, is she simply a misguided person living from a place of fear or do you experience her as mean and selfish?

8. As soul mates, Johnny and Natalie are instantly drawn to one another. Have you ever felt that kind of immediate connection to another person, as though you've known them before? Have you ever had a memory float to the surface that you couldn't place, but believe to be true?

9. Does the idea of many lifetimes help you understand why we experience certain challenges, sometimes over and over again? Are they lessons we need to learn for our spiritual growth?

10. Examine those moments when Natalie tries to do right by the people in her life — her relationship with Louise, for instance, standing up for Annie, or finally telling Johnny the truth. Do you believe she has grown in this lifetime despite repeating destructive patterns? Why or why not?

11. Have you ever felt the warmth and protection of a guardian angel? Have you experienced a warning in the stirring of a breeze, or a whisper in your heart? Do you listen to the voices in the wind or ignore them?

12. Discuss this line from The Prophet that haunts Natalie as she sits with Louise: *If this is my day of harvest, in what field have I sowed the seed, and in what unremembered season?* If we do, indeed, reap as we have sown, is it in a single lifetime or across many?

About the Author

Patricia Herchuk Sheehy is an award-winning author with a passion for exploring the connection between mind, body and spirit. In her novels, she seeks to understand how the past shapes our present experiences and the deep, often unexplained, connection people feel for one another.

Her articles and essays have appeared in local and national publications. She writes marketing and advertising copy for a wide range of businesses and organizations. In addition she offers individual and group mentoring to writers and holds workshops on writing and publishing.

A Connecticut native, Patricia holds a master's degree from Wesleyan University. Having grown up in the north end of Hartford, she called upon her childhood experiences of time and place as the setting for the early days of this novel; she and her husband now live in the historic town of Wethersfield, CT.

Patricia invites your comments and would love to hear from you. Write to her at: patriciasheehy@aol.com or visit her website: www.patsheehy.com